THE TREACHEROUS DEAD

Paula Harmon

COPYRIGHT

Copyright (c) 2022 Paula Harmon

The moral right of the author has been asserted.

Apart from any fair dealing for the purposes of research or private study, or criticism or review, as permitted under the Copyright, Designs and Patents Act 1988, this publication may only reproduced, stored or transmitted, in any form or by any means, with the prior permission in writing of the publishers, or in the case of reprographic reproduction in accordance with the terms of licences issued by the Copyright Licensing Agency. Enquiries concerning reproduction outside those terms should be sent to the publishers.

This is a work of fiction, some of which is based on real events. Names, characters, businesses, places, event and incidents are therefore either the products of the author's imagination or used in a fictitious manner. Any resemblance to actual persons, living or dead, or actual events is purely coincidental.

Book cover: https://100covers.com

DEDICATION

This book is dedicated to the memory of Emily Hobhouse (1860-1926), reformer, and to anyone who fights to make the truth told and action taken, in the face of ridicule and disbelief.

Monday 6th May 1912

One

'What did I do?' Mr Sullivan demanded of the heavens, straightening his waistcoat to relieve its straining buttons. 'It's Monday morning, there's orders coming outta my ears, I got idle machines, flat-foots all over, and the only tailor in the place is dead. How's a man supposed to eat?'

Ignoring him, Margaret Demeray crouched by the body.

'He was Abram Cohen,' said Inspector Green. 'Tailor.'

Apart from Mr Sullivan, two police constables and Inspector Green, the sweatshop in Ravel Street, Whitechapel, was crammed with twenty-five tables, each bearing a sewing machine and baskets of items to be sewn, facing the window by a larger cutting table.

Each seat, however, was empty. A strike starting with six thousand London garment workers the previous week had been joined by Mr Sullivan's staff when Sabbath started on Friday evening, which begged the question as to why Abram Cohen was wedged between two tables, a tape measure loose over his shoulders.

Nearby stood a female mannequin dressed in part of an impractical yachting costume: a white blouse with eyelet lace, a white skirt trimmed in a wavy line of navy blue. A cartwheel hat festooned in ostrich feathers, which wouldn't last five minutes on a yacht, had slipped sideways. A hatpin with an inch-long anchor-decorated cylinder for its head lay half-obscured by the mannequin's skirt. Somehow, her blank face conveyed deep disapproval of the whole sorry situation.

The floor was lint-covered. Whoever was responsible for sweeping, then sieving the findings for stray pins at the end of each day hadn't done much of a job.

Viewed from outside, the building appeared to lean forward. Inside, none of its corners were square. Plaster crumbled from moulded ceilings, faded panelling had split. It had probably been a fine old house once. This room might have held nothing but a loom where a silk weaver worked and grew wealthy, turning the colours of his lost French homeland into intricate designs. But it had long since lost its value, sold and sold again until it became a disintegrating container for East End sweatshops.

'Are there many of my people idling outside?' said Mr Sullivan, extracting a silver fob watch, contemplating it, then sighing.

'There's a picket line,' said Margaret, kneeling in the dust. 'Two men and two women. They thought I was a seamstress from elsewhere you'd induced to break the strike. I said I was better at sewing wounds than clothes, then someone recognised me as a doctor and they let me through.'

She didn't add that the whole exchange had taken place in Yiddish, which she barely knew and muddled with German. They'd laughed, but whether it was because of what she'd said or how she said it wasn't entirely clear. She also didn't add that, knowing nothing about Abram, they had debated whether to let a doctor in at all, until the unseen woman yelled, 'She's a doctor. What's the worst she can do? Find Sullivan's heart and make it work?' Margaret had half-recognised the voice, but couldn't make out who had called among the huddles of bystanders.

'So you can sew,' said Mr Sullivan. 'Could you *try* with the seams? If this strike goes on I'll be ruined. The paper says there's more than thirty thousand out now. Can that be right? Thirty thousand?'

'Don't you think this man's demise is more important than your orders, Mr Sullivan?' said Inspector Green. 'If not, I'll start wondering why.'

'Hey, I called you in! If I'd wanted to cover anything up, I'd have found someone to help dispose of him. They're two a penny round here and you know it.'

The inspector turned to Margaret. 'What do you reckon, doctor? We've photographed him every which way but it's all a bit odd, which is why I asked for Dr Jordan from St Julia's to look at him before we moved him, and—'

'You Dr Jordan, then?' said Mr Sullivan to Margaret, checking his watch again.

'Dr Demeray. Dr Jordan has laryngitis.'

'He can't pass anything on to Abram,' snorted Mr Sullivan. 'But Abram's not important enough, I guess, so he sends a woman.'

'Dr Jordan can barely talk,' said Margaret. 'He thought Mr Cohen important enough for the inspector to hear someone's conclusions.'

'Ignore him,' said Inspector Green. 'What do you think?'

Abram Cohen was almost face down but not quite. He had been in his middle twenties, small and thin. One arm was trapped under his body, the other near his face, the fingertips half-curled against his palm. It had been a warm night. Rigor mortis had set in hours before, then passed away. Margaret touched his head and face. There were no contusions, no lumps or hollows, no blood on the boards. His eyes were half open, a little bloodshot but otherwise normal. None of his bones appeared to be broken. It was as if he'd walked between the lines of tables and at the end, simply crumpled. Once her head was level with his, she could see where his thimble had skittered across the boards to hide under the mannequin's skirts, beyond the hatpin.

'At first sight there's nothing to suggest foul play,' she said. 'Maybe once you've moved him we'll see more. There might be something under the body, though if he was injured, it's odd that there's no blood. Nothing to suggest poison. His neck and throat seem intact.'

'That's what I thought too,' said the inspector, motioning to his constables to lift the body from the gap. 'Heart attack? Apoplexy?'

'Some sort of bleed on the brain, I suspect. It's hard to be certain without a post-mortem, but—'

'Post-mortem?' said Mr Sullivan. 'Is that where you —'

'Look inside,' said Margaret. 'Yes.'

He went a little green. 'You'll be lucky. His family's very orthodox. Very orthodox indeed.'

'What I want to know,' said the inspector, 'is what he was doing here. Any ideas, Mr Sullivan?'

Mr Sullivan rubbed his nose then resettled his bowler hat. 'Well…'

'Yes?'

'Abram was a bit of a perfectionist. He was working on that costume and there was extra bunce in it for him. With the picket line starting today, maybe he decided to come in as soon as Sabbath was over to finish it before he had to join the other slackers… Then perhaps someone came in looking for my safe – which ain't here – and did for him.'

The constables had placed the body on the narrow piece of floor by the mannequin. Over his left arm, Abram had been holding a white jacket with intricate twists of navy-blue trimming, now dusty and covered in lint. There wasn't a mark on him.

'Look at the state of that jacket!' cried Mr Sullivan. 'That's a special order, that is!' He waved his arms, knocking into the mannequin, whose hat slipped further askew. He cursed, looked down, picked the hatpin up and jammed it through the hat and into the mannequin's head.

'So he "decided" to work?' said the inspector. 'Do you mean he was "encouraged", in exchange for a last wage before the strike? Has he got a wife and kids?'

'Not my job to know anything about my workers,' said Mr Sullivan. 'It's not like we're chums.'

'But you know he's orthodox.'

Mr Sullivan shrugged. 'His family is. It pays to know that sort of thing. I don't follow any religion—'

'Apart from money,' muttered the inspector to Margaret.

If he'd heard, Mr Sullivan ignored him. 'I don't care what people think they *can't* do, as long as what they *can* do includes fulfilling my orders. He said he might finish this and I let him have a spare key, but he said he'd be gone by dawn.'

'By dawn?' said Margaret. 'So he might have been working for more than thirty hours without rest, or food, or—'

'I didn't make him. But if he had, that woulda been nearly eighteen shillings earned.'

'Had he been complaining about illness?'

'Bit of a headache maybe, a little nausea.'

Margaret turned to the inspector. 'Possibly a cerebral haemorrhage. Overwork can do that. As to who "did" for him…'

'I didn't make him do nothing,' said Mr Sullivan, folding his arms. 'I told him to go home for Sunday supper whether he'd finished or not. This strike won't last: they can't afford to live without wages. I bet half the girls are popping their husband's suits at the pawnbrokers as we speak.'

'Don't they have to do that most Mondays?' said Margaret. 'What wages do you pay?'

'The same as everyone. Sevenpence an hour for journeymen tailors like Abram. Eighteen shillings a week for the women.'

'Regardless of whether they work forty hours or a hundred?'

'I bet that's more than you pay your maid.'

'She doesn't have to pay for bed, board or uniform, or support a family,' snapped Margaret. 'And she gets at least a day and a half off per week and a week's paid holiday and she's employed all year, not laid off every summer—'

'Anyway,' said the inspector, 'I'll speak with Mr Cohen's family and see if…'

The main door opened and a man stepped inside, barely visible in the darkness of the landing, brushing the sleeves of his jacket as if afraid of catching something from the building. 'How is this strike going to affect our orders, Sullivan? We need—' He halted, taking in the scene. 'Wh-who's that?'

'One of the tailors,' said Mr Sullivan, stepping forward. 'An 'eart attack or something. Now then, sir, why don't we talk in my office?'

The man looked past the huddle on the floor to a door on the far side of the room. As things were, he'd either have to step across Abram Cohen, or walk between the machinists' tables and the cutting table, past a low cupboard with packing boxes on it and then squeeze past the policemen. 'You're evidently busy,' he said. 'I'll come back in an hour, but I expect some sort of answer then and I daresay the next chap will too.' He spun on his heel.

'Don't tell the lot outside about the, er, incident,' pleaded Mr Sullivan. 'I'd rather break it to them gently myself.'

The man waved a hand and left. Inspector Green signalled to one of the constables to follow him.

'Customer,' said Mr Sullivan gloomily, answering an unspoken question. 'He orders for the export trade: ready-made garments for the upwardly inclined colonial. He sends my stuff all over, with some other geezer's name on the boxes. Still, money's money.'

'Is the "next chap" the same?'

'I was only expecting Mr W today. The strike might have brought the others out. Oh – this bloke's a bluebottle. You can tell a mile off.'

A different man had walked in, followed by the scowling constable, and removed his hat to reveal greying hair. He appeared to be in his forties, taller than average and thin but solid, his shrewd eyes the colour of cool steel. He strode forward as if he'd bought the building and everything in it and intended to knock it down and start again. 'Inspector Green? I'm Inspector Silvermann of N division, Islington. Is that Abram Cohen?'

'Yes.' Inspector Green stood up and offered a hand. 'N Division? This is a W division job.'

'Maybe not,' said Inspector Silvermann. 'Damn. Dead, is he?'

'Very,' said Margaret.

Inspector Silvermann scanned her grey working outfit from the small, plain hat to her dusty hems and sensible shoes. 'Factory inspector? Wouldn't it make more sense to inspect the place when it's full?'

'I'm Dr Demeray from St Julia's,' she said, rising to shake hands. 'Inspector Green asked me to see the body in situ before it comes to us for post-mortem.'

Inspector Silvermann shook hands briefly with a firm, hard grasp then considered the body again. 'Damn,' he repeated.

'Why is N division interested?' said Inspector Green. He turned to his constable. 'And why didn't *you* go and ask that Mr W what he knows, if anything?'

'Cos *he* said it wasn't necessary.' The constable jerked a thumb at Inspector Silvermann.

'You report to me, not him. Now get back outside.' Inspector Green folded his arms. 'This is W division, Inspector Silvermann, and it's a natural death. Just one of those horrible things.'

'How do you know without a post-mortem?'

'You're not doing it in here!' exclaimed Mr Sullivan. 'Don't even think it. A man's got limits!'

'I don't know for certain,' said Margaret, 'but evidence so far suggests a cerebral haemorrhage. Maybe a stroke.'

Inspector Silvermann focussed on her again. 'Caused by?'

'Without an autopsy…'

'Use your imagination. A blow?'

'This is a matter for facts, not conjecture.' Margaret narrowed her eyes. 'There's no evidence of a blow so far. That doesn't mean there wasn't one, just that I haven't found one.' He wasn't going to trap her into saying something she couldn't support.

'Shaken? Threatened? Frightened? Shock? Stressed to boiling point?'

'The first will show in a post-mortem. The others—'

'Either way,' insisted Inspector Green, 'it's W division.'

'Is it?' said Inspector Silvermann. 'Very late on Saturday night, someone saw Abram Cohen in the Angel Inn, Islington – which is *my* division – arguing with a salesman called Joseph Kavanagh, whom I want to question. Then Cohen left. Kavanagh followed and hasn't been seen since.'

'Joseph Kavanagh?' said Mr Sullivan. 'Travelling salesman? Haberdashery?'

'That's the man,' said Inspector Silvermann. 'Know him?'

'He's all right,' Mr Sullivan replied. 'A bit nosy, perhaps. Always laying on the patter until you forget what you're saying. Didn't think he'd have the energy to row. He's not well. And what was Abram doing all the way over in Islington?'

'It's five miles,' said Inspector Silvermann. 'A man's allowed to travel once the Sabbath's over, and there were other journeymen tailors there talking about how they could earn money during the strike if it continued – co-operatives and so on. They knew Cohen. The witnesses aren't much use in saying what the argument was about, except that this' – he surveyed the room – 'delightful establishment was mentioned by most of them.'

'So what?' said Inspector Green. 'A haberdasher sells to sweatshops—'

'Garment factories, if you please,' snapped Mr Sullivan.

'Men argue in pubs,' continued Inspector Green. 'It's what happens after a few pints. Are you so short of work in N division that you've got to arrest people for a beery row?'

Inspector Silvermann's face remained unreadable. 'Like I said, Kavanagh's wanted for questioning but he's gone to ground. The last thing anyone saw him do is argue with Abram Cohen. And now Abram Cohen's dead.'

Two

The mortuary wing at St Julia's was quiet when Margaret returned at twelve.

Darnell, the clerk who'd taken over from Mr Holness after his retirement, looked up from his ledger in surprise. 'I thought maybe you couldn't come in today, Dr Demeray. I hadn't seen you.'

'You weren't on the desk when I came in. Then Dr Jordan asked me to help the police in Whitechapel while he went home. He's rather poorly.'

'Ah,' said Darnell. 'Yes, his laryngitis is worse. He can't speak without coughing. A suspicious death?'

'Possibly not very,' said Margaret. 'The body should be here some time early afternoon. Could you let the orderly in the cold room know?'

'"Should" be here?'

'The inspector in the case wasn't entirely sure where he'd send it.' Margaret removed her gloves. 'In case anyone wants me, I'm expecting Dr Jordan to telephone. I'll take my post to his office so you can put the call through there.'

'Very well, doctor.'

Dr Jordan telephoned when Margaret was halfway through the correspondence, and hoarsely declared he'd return to assist with the post-mortem at two o'clock.

After lunch, she waited for news of Abram Cohen's body and prepared the laboratory with her new assistant, Cyril Purefoy. A star pupil from the hospital's training school, he had taken the place of Algie Hardisty.

After qualification, Algie's father had insisted he take up general practice in Worcestershire, but Margaret suspected his days buried in a country town were numbered. If Algie's letters were anything to go by, he'd offered his pathology skills to the Worcester Royal

Infirmary and was already making a name for himself. Margaret missed him terribly.

Cyril was still an unknown quantity. She'd only known him a few weeks, since she'd recently returned to St Julia's after giving birth in late October. She found him intelligent, earnest, serious and utterly exhausting. Margaret suspected he read surgical manuals for light reading until he fell asleep with his Latin dictionary as a pillow.

The day had grown hot, and Margaret was just hoping Dr Jordan's return to work wasn't a waste of time when word came that Abram Cohen's body had arrived. Inspector Green entered the laboratory with it, hands nonchalantly in his pockets, but his face matching his name. 'I told the family you'd treat his body with utter respect and that you were only doing it to confirm there was no foul play,' he said. 'The mother felt his ghost wouldn't let her rest if it wasn't done, and she persuaded the rabbi. So there's reluctant agreement, provided they have it back today for the burial.'

'We can do that,' Dr Jordan wheezed. 'Do you want to stay?'

'I'll, er... I'll sit in the corner if that's all right.'

'What did his mother say about his general health?' asked Margaret.

'Recently he's had severe headaches, eyestrain, a struggle to focus and increasing nausea. Apart from the last, aren't those occupational hazards for a tailor?'

'Possibly.'

'She also said he'd got in with a dubious crowd. I took her to mean going to pubs with gentiles, but she could mean that he'd joined a strike committee – or given where he lived, anarchists. That seemed to be what that Inspector Silvermann was hinting at. But I dunno… His mother was mostly worried about things not being kosher.'

Margaret and Dr Jordan, with Cyril taking notes, worked as swiftly as they could. They could find no wounds on his body. No cuts or unusual bruises, no lumps or broken bones. Abram Cohen, they concluded, was in relatively good physical condition despite being undernourished, and showing slight evidence of cotton lung. What had killed him was a bleed on the brain which appeared to have been sudden and fatal.

'He'd have been dead before he hit the ground,' said Margaret.

'Did anything external cause that?' asked the inspector. 'A blow? Being shaken?'

'There's evidence of previous small bleeds,' wheezed Dr Jordan. 'If he was experiencing all the symptoms you describe, it was just waiting to happen. It's impossible to say whether anything specific triggered it.'

'So not deliberate.'

'There's no evidence of murder,' said Margaret. 'But this is exactly what has killed other people working consistent long hours under extreme stress.'

'Can't pin it on Sullivan. He'll argue, quite rightly, that Abram Cohen chose to work those hours and worked for more than one employer. Not that I care about Inspector Silvermann, but I presume you can't pin it on a row in the Angel?'

'You can't arrest a man for arguing,' said Dr Jordan.

'Good,' said Inspector Green. 'I'm glad to get N division's sticky fingers off my patch. And I'm glad I can tell Abram's mother no one murdered him. Just bad luck, poor chap. Sullivan will be pleased too. Well, a little.'

'Because you can't arrest him?'

'Because a ghost who dies of natural causes is less likely to haunt him. Right, I'll leave you to finish up. I'm going for a smoke.'

They were meticulous in stitching the wounds back together, smoothing Abram's hair over the incision line on his forehead. Margaret wondered if Abram's mother was a seamstress and might touch the wounds with professional knowledge as well as loving grief – check the neatness of the stitches, and judge them by it. Perhaps she'd wish she could have done that last service for him herself. Or perhaps she'd never look.

Margaret always tried to work as if the body belonged to someone she loved. She hoped she'd never have to check that someone had done the same for Fox because his luck had run out.

It hadn't so far. He was due home sometime after seven that evening. She glanced at the clock as she packed up and saw she was half an hour later than she'd intended. It wasn't so bad. She would still be home in time to play with the children before getting ready for him.

Saying goodbye to Darnell, Margaret ran down the steps of the building and stood in the busy street, letting the evening sunshine warm her face. Rushing commuters swerved round her while she debated whether to take the bus instead of the tube and have a better view, her heart light at the thought of seeing Fox after three weeks' absence.

She went to the front of the hospital where the flower-seller was, bought a small bunch of carnations, then made her way to the bus stop.

'Hallo, doctor.' The young woman's voice was both familiar and strange, and for a moment, Margaret couldn't work out where it came from.

Then by the wall of the nearest building, she saw a small, thin woman in her early twenties, wearing a simple but well-fitting suit with a white, collarless, pin-tucked blouse beneath. Sleek, thick, dark hair was bundled under a boater adorned with a plain blue ribbon, matching the trim on her suit. Her sapphire eyes watched Margaret with the expression of a wary cat. It was a warmer expression than she'd worn the first time they'd met, but only warmer in the sense that putting a matchstick on top of Big Ben made it taller.

Anna.

'Miss Balodis!' said Margaret, dodging commuters to join her. 'I thought you were in America! I hoped you'd write. I'm glad to see you looking so well.' The latter wasn't entirely true. Anna looked better fed, but that was about it.

'How's tricks?' said Anna.

'I've had twins. A boy and a girl. They're seven months old.'

'Why doesn't that surprise me?' Anna's face lightened with a smile. 'Got the impression you never do nothing by halves. What they called?'

'Alexander and Edith. Well, Alec and Edie.'

'Fancy. But you're working again.'

'Two days in St Julia's, two days' research at home, and I give health talks to women…' Margaret stopped before she mentioned the book she'd been asked to help write, or that she had two maids now and Dinah still came three days a week to help with the cleaning. 'I keep busy. What brought you back?'

Anna stepped away from the wall. 'Know what's different about New York?'

'I've only ever seen it in moving pictures,' said Margaret. 'What's it like?'

Anna surveyed the sooty walls and traffic. 'Taller. Organised. Whoever set out the roads there had a plan and a ruler. London's like someone put paint on a rabid dog's paws, fed it beer, smacked it on the arse to make it run, then built a road wherever the dog left its paw prints. New York roads are like a checkerboard – I mean a draughts board.' She crossed her hands at right angles to show what she meant. 'Avenues one way, streets the other. Organised.' It wasn't clear if she approved or not. 'Some teacher told us that a bit of London was a Roman town once and the Romans liked straight lines. Whereabouts? Do you know?'

'We're standing pretty much in the middle of it, I think,' said Margaret, 'or at least above it. I'm not certain.'

'Gawd. Goes to show how easy it is to bury things.'

'I don't think it was intentional,' said Margaret. 'It's better now than it was a hundred years ago.'

'If you say so. My English nan said they cleared out the rookeries without caring where the people would go, then complained when they shacked up in Whitechapel.'

Margaret watched Anna as she peered around her, trying to work out what had changed since the last time they'd met. She seemed a little pinker and better off. However, the tense mistrust and anger of the previous year was still there, overlaid with something else: a pain that was more than physical, a weariness that sat wrong on such a young person. Margaret wondered whether Anna's brother Andris had stayed in America.

She took a glance at her watch.

'Would you like some tea?' she said. 'I'm not sure anywhere's open, but—'

'I'd rather a glass of porter,' said Anna, raising her eyebrows. 'But I bet you won't go in a pub. Anyway, I don't want anything much, just to chat. Which way you going? West obviously, but tube or bus or cab?'

'Bus, but I have time. It really is nice to see you. I never thought you'd come back after going for a new life.'

'Yeah, well,' said Anna, moving forward. 'There's new and new. Andris got a job with *The Call* newspaper: his limp didn't matter. Me, I tried the fancy dressmakers, but it was no good. No references, see. But you know what's the same about New York? The sweatshops. Before I knew it, there I was working in a building higher than Nelson's Column waiting for it to burn down like the Triangle one did, wondering why I'd travelled all that way to be just as miserable as I was in Whitechapel. They said I could get on if I just put the effort in. But what does getting on mean? Running a sweatshop myself?'

Margaret frowned. 'You'd never do that. Couldn't Andris find you a job on the – *The Call,* was it?'

'Andris died.' Anna looked into the distance for a second, then back. 'Another cut got infected. They couldn't save him this time.'

'Oh Anna, I'm so sorry. And you returned so you could be with friends and relations here?' It seemed unlikely. With their parents dead, Andris and Anna had left for America the previous August, sending Margaret a short goodbye letter which read like a dismissal.

'Sorta.' Anna's mouth wobbled a little. 'Andris died January. I came back after and got a job. Although now…'

'I imagine you're striking.'

'Yeah, and I'm a sorta go-between. Anyway, none of that is why I'm here, but I thought it'd save time to tell you given how nosey you are.'

'Thanks.'

'My pleasure. What I want is for you to tell your bloke something.'

'Fox? What?' Margaret was puzzled. The bus was nearing the stop. She'd have to miss it. Anna had been involved with anarchists before, and it sounded unlikely that her views on sweatshops had changed. 'Go-between' presumably meant a liaison between her employer and striking employees, so perhaps she was on a strike committee? She'd never inform on anyone, so what could she mean?

'That copper called Silvermann, the one who went to Sullivan's this morning after you—'

'It was you who told them to let me through!'

'Yeah. He's barking up the wrong tree. Kavanagh never hurt Abram.'

'You know them? I'm so sorry about—'

Anna dismissed Margaret's pity with a wave of her hand. 'I grew up with Abram and we both know Kavanagh through work. Abram shoulda been resting. If he had, and he'd left rooting round at Sullivan's to someone else, maybe he'd be all right.'

'Maybe,' said Margaret. Anna's expression had barely changed, so it was hard to gauge how she felt on a personal level about Abram's death – and harder still to know how she knew an argument in Islington had been blamed for it. 'I doubt Fox would get involved. Abram's death was tragic but not suspicious.'

'Silvermann will make it sound suspicious.'

'You said you know Kavanagh. Is he—'

'He's all right. He's not done nothing against the law. Silvermann's a fool. Tell Fox what I said, will yer? Here's yer bus.' A tiny wry smile appeared. 'Just a bit of advice…'

'Yes?'

'If you ever want to sail the Atlantic, don't do it in February. I never been so sick in all my life.' Anna mimicked vomiting and grinned at a revolted person in the queue.

'After what happened to the *Titanic*, I'm not sure I want to sail the Atlantic at all,' said Margaret.

Anna's face closed again as the bus pulled up. 'Just tell your bloke, OK? Get him to rein Silvermann in. See yer round, doctor. Or maybe not.'

Three

Margaret arrived home to the sound of wailing. In the nursery, she found the children in their bassinets, bawling. Tucking them awkwardly onto each hip, their wails reduced to sobs, she went to seek their nursemaid.

Sixteen-year-old Nellie stood in the middle of Margaret and Fox's bedroom, where shoes and clothes were strewn across the floor, with tears in her eyes.

'What on earth happened?' exclaimed Margaret.

'I'm s-so sorry.' Nellie sniffed. 'Vera had her afternoon off and… and…'

'Oh Nellie, I didn't mean to be so late. But I didn't ask anyone to turn out my wardrobes.'

'We didn't. This was…'

Margaret's mind raced. Her flat had been searched before, but much more professionally. Had they been burgled? 'Nellie! Did someone—'

'It's not like that, ma'am.' Nellie found her handkerchief and took Edie into her arms. 'I don't want to tell tales, ma'am, but—'

'Go on, you're worrying me.'

Nellie forced a smile to cheer the twins up. 'Around the time you were due home, your friend Mrs Holbourne came round with her two little boys.'

'Oh,' said Margaret. Realisation dawned. 'Let me guess. You put them in the sitting room and went to make tea. Sam and Johnny escaped and ran amok while Mrs Holbourne chose a gramophone record to play.'

Nellie nodded. 'It wasn't for long. Mrs Holbourne yelled – I mean called for them and they came back saying they'd wanted to play hide and seek. I didn't realise they'd been in your bedroom till after Mrs Holbourne gave up waiting and took them home. I think they was chasing Juniper too. I'm so sorry, ma'am.'

Margaret peered under the dresser and saw her cat glare back. 'It's not your fault, Nellie. The boys are positive menaces.' She shifted Alec into a more comfortable position. He had his nose buried in her jacket, doubtless to the detriment of its cleanliness. 'I should have been home earlier. You look exhausted. Go and rest.'

'Oh, but ma'am, the children!'

'They're *my* children. I can manage.'

An hour later, the twins were settled in their bassinets, Vera had returned and Margaret was trying to distract herself from waiting for Fox by tidying up the remaining chaos in the bedroom.

'Hello, Mar—' Fox stepped into the bedroom, tripped over a shoe lying in the doorway, then saw the mess. 'What the— Have you called the pol—'

'Fox! You're early!' Margaret sprang to her feet and pulled him into an embrace.

He returned her kiss, then held her at arm's length. 'Don't distract me. What happened?'

'The burglars were four and six.'

'Ah,' said Fox, relaxing. 'Maude and Geoff's demons?'

Margaret chuckled. 'Can you help me?' She dropped to the floor again and peered under the dresser. Her cat's glare had mellowed and Margaret wondered what she was hiding behind the flicking tail.

Fox crouched at her side and looked round the room. 'How many shoes does a woman need?'

'I'll let you know when I've reached my limit.'

'I'll go and kiss the children in case they've forgotten who I am, *then* help,' said Fox.

'They'll be asleep.'

'I can soon stop that.'

'Don't interfere with Nellie's routine.'

'Pfft,' said Fox, and left the room.

By the time he returned, Margaret was stacking her scattered sketchbooks.

'Did you wear these when you were widowed?' Fox pulled a froth of black lace and a decorative Spanish comb with six-inch tines from underneath the wardrobe.

'Oh the little— No, of course not. Owen wasn't worth it. That's a mantilla and peineta Father brought me from Spain when I was ten. I'd forgotten about them by the time I had enough hair to fix them in place. They *were* safely stored in a box with old souvenirs.' Margaret groped under the bed. 'Here's the lid. Where's the rest?'

Fox reached down the side of the wardrobe and pulled out an old wooden box, its contents jumbled.

'That's it,' said Margaret. 'Is everything else present and correct?'

'How should I know?' Fox held up an exercise book and then a dance card. 'What's supposed to be in here?'

'I can't remember.'

A hollow clatter made Margaret look round. Juniper was batting a red and white glass ball towards the wall. She snatched it away and held it in her palm. 'Mother gave this to me to put on the Christmas tree. Katherine had a blue one. I'd forgotten. How lovely.'

Fox had fallen silent but Margaret wasn't paying attention. The bauble brought a sudden, sharp image of her mother: the face of a woman younger than Margaret was now, with much redder hair dressed in curls and ringlets. As the image faded, other memories took over: scents of lavender and cinnamon, pine and candles; the swish of a silk dress and the crackle of a winter fire; pine needles pricking as Margaret was lifted in warm arms to hang the glass ball in a Christmas tree's branches.

'Perhaps you should deal with the rest,' said Fox. His face was pale. A bundle of letters tied in pink ribbon had risen to the top. 'Who are these from? Or don't I want to know?'

Margaret took the letters. 'Honestly, Fox, look at their age and the address.' Pink dye stained the envelopes where it had touched them. The paper was yellowed, the address her sister Katherine's. 'These are twelve years old. They were from someone called Joel Gifford. He was a doctor.'

'Was?'

'He died in Kimberley aged twenty-six.'

'Oh,' said Fox. 'Kimberley, South Africa? Boer War?'

'Yes. He was an army medic and he died during the siege.' Margaret tried to picture Joel and failed. She had no photographs: just his letters and a memory of pleasant evenings in quiet restaurants. 'We were friends.'

'Just friends?'

Margaret touched the letters. 'Perhaps if he'd lived it might have become something more, but he didn't. These aren't love letters. They're descriptions of South Africa, his cases, his opinions and his responses to my ideas and attempts to get a good job. I haven't looked at them for years.' She put them on the floor. 'I should have burnt them when I married Owen, but I didn't. I suppose I should have done it when I fell in love with you, but I'd forgotten them. I'll do it now.'

'Why?' Fox reached for her hand. 'I still have Cynthia's letters. I haven't read those since 1896, but she's part of who I am. Do you want me to burn those?'

'Of course not, Fox! She was your wife.'

Fox returned Joel's letters to the box, tucking the mantilla over the top. 'Memories of people we loved are things we should keep. It's the bad memories we should burn.'

They sat in silence, staring at the box. A movement alerted Margaret to Juniper reaching for the bauble again. 'Good grief,' she said. 'This is rather maudlin. It's quite unlike us.'

'I've been away too long.' Fox pulled her into a hug and kissed her slowly. 'We need to stop tidying and get reacquainted. Then we'll be in a fit state to start arguing again.'

***

'Anna Balodis?' Fox said later, when they settled down to dinner. 'I ought to have known about her return. The benighted soul keeping track of known anarchists slipped up.'

'Does it matter that she's back?'

Fox poured wine. 'I doubt she's stopped being an anarchist, and the paper she said Andris was working for might be called anarchist by some. Why come back? Is she part of a dissident group trying to stir up trouble, under cover of all the recent strikes? Yes, I should have known.'

'Surely she's too insignificant to be important.' Margaret felt guilty about referring to Anna as insignificant. It was exactly what the young woman had been fighting all her life. 'When she got to New York, she couldn't find work other than what she'd tried to leave behind.'

'Couldn't she?' said Fox. 'Why not work with Andris? She's probably capable of writing better English than she speaks, and definitely passionate. And how did she pay for her passage back? Steerage isn't free. How did she look? Still poor?'

Margaret shook her head. 'Her clothes weren't expensive but they were well made, with little extra touches.'

'Secondhand?'

'The style was up to the minute and they fitted really well, so if they were, she'd remodelled them.'

'Interesting.'

'Can't the poor woman start again without being under suspicion? No wonder she's constantly on the defensive. Maybe she has a better-paid job now or saved money in America, or *The Call* gave her something after Andris died.'

'Maybe.'

Margaret speared a potato. 'Anyway, it seems unlikely Anna would come to us for help if she – or Kavanagh – was doing something treacherous. She knows you're connected with the police.'

'And what's Kavanagh supposed to have done again?'

'Argued with a young man called Abram Cohen about something unspecified till the young man went away and died from stress.'

'Unlikely.'

'Possible if you have the right underlying condition, but the person you're arguing with can't know that.'

'Yet this inspector wants to arrest Kavanagh.'

'He said he wanted to question him. Is that the same thing? He wasn't going to tell *me* anything and neither Inspector Green nor Sullivan were going to tell *him* anything.' Margaret frowned. Anna had been among the bystanders, unseen. Had she already known that Abram was dead?

Fox ate in silence, pushing the wine glass in circles on the tablecloth.

'It's hard to like Anna because she's so prickly,' said Margaret, 'but I respect and admire her. Growing up in Whitechapel with a foreign father, working in conditions one step up from slavery, yet ending up literate is impressive in itself. To have lost her whole family before the age of twenty-three and still be fighting for a decent standard of living, not just for herself but for others, is astonishing. Plenty of women would have tried an easier route to earn their income.'

'True.' Fox sat back. 'I'll make discreet enquiries at work tomorrow as to why I don't know about Anna's return, and see if Kavanagh is someone I need to know about too.'

'Thank you.' Margaret put her cutlery together and sighed. The day was catching up on her. She'd promised herself to be sparkling for Fox's return, but she simply hadn't the energy.

'You seem exhausted,' said Fox. 'Are you sure—'

'Yes, I can manage. Work is tiring but it'll get better, and I'd be so bored at home. I'm lucky St J's agreed I could come back, even if it's because they couldn't find anyone to replace me.'

'Cheer up,' said Fox, rising from the table and reaching for her hand. 'Your lord and master is home, your offspring asleep, the moon bright, the wine red. Let's dance.'

In the sitting room, he put a record on the gramophone and pulled her into his arms. She wondered if she'd ever get used to his absences or become indifferent to his return. 'How was … Germany?'

'Wales.'

'Wales?' Margaret blinked. For three weeks she'd been imagining Fox in pretty half-timbered German streets. Now she had to adjust the image. The previous year, she'd gone to a Welsh mining town with Fox's colleague Elinor. It had rained, and everything merged like a monochrome watercolour with too much wash applied, the streets grim, unappealing, and slick with rain. Since then, in her mind, Wales had been grey, dark and hiding secrets. She'd not had the chance to visit the parts Elinor had said were beautiful. 'Where do foreign agents lurk?'

'Shh.'

'Vera's in the kitchen and Nellie's two floors up. They can't hear anything.'

'All the same,' Fox kissed her head, his voice low. 'These walls aren't thick enough. I was in Pembrokeshire. Very lovely. We should go to Tenby as a family. I like you in a bathing suit.'

'We're going to Brighton for Whitsun at the end of the month. That'll have to do for now. Why does your work always sound like a holiday?'

'You can't call it a holiday when people wanted to kill me! But yes, I can think of worse places to die.'

'Don't ever say that.' Margaret leaned back. 'Pembrokeshire? Were you there to protect Denys Corbett-Wilson's attempt to fly to Ireland?'

'Corbett-Wilson was supposed to be flying from Holyhead. His presence in Pembrokeshire was a blasted nuisance.'

'Why?'

'We were looking for a photographer, and all of a sudden there were dozens of them. I swear they emerged from nowhere like mushrooms.'

'Did you find him?'

'Her, as it turned out. Arrested on Tuesday, charged on Wednesday. Bert and I spent the last few days before bringing her back here gathering evidence. Now the questioning has to start again. She's working for someone, but won't say who. I'm not convinced she knows who, to be honest, or even why, but I swear she's tempted to tell me something. She let slip that someone was coming in from somewhere else to take control. Otherwise, all we've established is that whoever they're taking over from is here in the Smoke.'

'Did they have her photographing potential targets for Germany?'

The dance tune ended. Fox selected an orchestral piece and sat down in a chair, pulling Margaret into his lap. 'The photography itself is irrelevant. It's more likely to be about the fight for Irish independence. We had wind of that much. "Photographers" carrying equipment cases with space for arms, letters and plans, to be swapped with other "photographers" travelling back and forth by ferries and private yachts and pottering round all those pretty little towns.'

'She had all those things?'

'No arms, but there were coded letters and lots of little innocent female odds and ends as cover: hatpins, brooches, hat-trimmings. She's a cool young woman, but we'll find out what she's hiding. It'll take time but we'll get there.'

'But Ireland… It'll be almost impossible to overturn the Home Rule Bill now.'

'You think it'll be that simple?' Fox sighed. 'Not all the Irish want it. Not all the English want the Irish to have it. The Unionist element is gathering strength. If I'm surer of anything than war with Germany, it's that Home Rule won't happen without bloodshed. And now it seems I should know about someone with an Irish name who knows Anna Balodis.'

'But you have Anna on a list of anarchists, not Fenians.'

Fox grunted. 'People's causes change. People don't.' He sighed. 'Some days I wish I'd run away to join the circus. Sticking my head in a lion's mouth every day would be a lot less dangerous and depressing.'

Four

'What are you up to today?' said Fox, over breakfast.

Margaret looked up from the envelope in her hand, wondering if he was really interested, given that he was frowning at the newspaper rather than her, or whether they'd already reached the stage of married life which consists of repeated litanies.

Then he looked up with an expression of genuine enquiry. 'Are you doing research, or writing that essay for Dr Naylor's book on "educating the working-class woman in basic scientific doodah", or whatever terrible title she's planning? Isn't that her awful writing? Is she chasing you?'

'It's her writing,' said Margaret, applying the paper knife. 'And the title won't be that bad, I hope. The essay isn't due till August, though, so this'll be about something else. As for today, I'll be in Fulham this afternoon, leading a Mothers' Union discussion about old wives' tales at Aunt Alice and Lucy's church. The results will form part of my research.'

'You started that essay two months ago. It must be the length of *War and Peace* by now.'

'I haven't actually started writing it yet,' confessed Margaret, extracting the letter and wishing for the hundredth time that Dr Naylor would employ a typist. 'I admit I'm beginning to wonder how I'll make sense of the information gathered so far. Women can be very contradictory.'

'I'd never noticed,' said Fox, with a grin. He tapped the newspaper. 'There's a second-hand Ford here which might do for us. Fifty pounds. Expensive as that is, I'm worried it's too cheap, so I'll ask Bert to come with me to look.'

'Good idea.' Margaret squinted at the letter. 'Oh.'

'"Oh" what? Good oh or bad oh?'

'She's asking if I want a job at the Dorcas Free. It's a new women's hospital opening in Marylebone in July.'

'A hospital for women, run by women?'

'Don't be ridiculous, Fox. For women, run by men. It seems the board wants to see if a hospital with a higher-than-average number of female medical personnel is able to "manage". Dr Naylor says she'll put me forward for a senior role in the pathology department if I'm interested.' She pondered. Before her marriage, the board at St Julia's had been considering whether she might take over Dr Jordan's lead pathologist role on his retirement. That opportunity had been lost. Could she start again elsewhere? Marylebone would be much easier to get to than the edges of the East End. But she liked geographical separation between home and work, and she loved St Julia's.

'That's a worrying experiment,' said Fox.

Margaret came out of her reverie. 'Why? Because you think it wouldn't work?'

'Of course I think it could work, even if most men – and most women, come to that – would argue that the only institutions safe to be run by women are girls' schools and nunneries. I'm worried because it sounds like someone's planning ahead.'

'In what situation could a hospital possibly be run solely by women? There are so many more male doctors than female.'

'Maybe they're planning for a situation where there won't be.'

'I'll be long retired if not dead by then,' said Margaret, putting the letter back in the envelope. 'Anyway, I'll think about it: there's no rush. Now I have to prepare for the discussion, and you need to tackle an Irish revolutionary.'

'If that's all she is,' said Fox, lowering his voice. 'She was trying to pass on information about Avro aeroplane factories, although she denies knowing that's what it was. Avro is one of the manufacturers developing planes for possible warfare. They'll be armed.'

'Oh God,' said Margaret. 'I thought things had settled down.'

'Only to a very slow simmer. It won't take much to bring them back to the boil.' The morning, already chilly and overcast, seemed darker and colder.

The telephone rang and Fox went to answer it. From his staccato answers, it sounded like bad news. His face when he returned to the dining room confirmed it.

'The only London lead we had turns out to be a dead end,' said Fox. 'But I'm sure the woman's on the verge of telling us something. It's possible that sabotage is planned, and if so, it's likely the Germans are behind it. But is she a traitor, or innocently conveying things for money to support her cause? If she's the latter, I've a feeling she'll tell us eventually. But I've got to get her to trust me first before someone gets to her and says she can't. Or worse.'

***

The discussion went as anticipated. While the younger mothers were willing to embrace new ideas, the older ones and grandmothers were wedded to traditional wisdom, including a local conviction that wearing bright-blue beads from babyhood could ward off pneumonia. One matriarch shook her head throughout Margaret's counter-argument, but as she left, offered to tell her where to buy the authentic article to protect the twins, whom Margaret had brought to make herself seem more human. It had worked, to some extent: the women were less inclined to outright contradiction when faced with small children.

Now that it was over, Alec remained propped up in the pram chewing on a rattle, his blue eyes closing, his little cap with the plain pleats and navy trim aslant. Edie had tipped sideways onto him and was dozing, fingers in mouth, the top half of her face hidden by the frills of her bonnet. They looked like a pair of overdressed drunks.

Margaret's eighteen-year-old cousin Lucy seemed agitated. Margaret wondered if it was embarrassment at the mothers' ignorance, the twins' presence, or frustration that she wasn't qualified to join in with any authority, since no decent hospital would train her till she was twenty-one.

There was only one way to find out. 'What's wrong?'

'I hoped Mrs Moore would be here.'

'She's not going to turn up now and we have to leave. Who is she, anyway?'

'The daughter-in-law of the old man I help with.'

Margaret hefted the pram through the parish-room door. It hit an uneven bit of paving, jerking the twins and jolting her wrist. 'I hope you're not worrying that you're no use. I'm sure she's really grateful for your help. And ultimately, any nursing experience you have will stand you in good stead when you apply for training.'

'It's not that,' said Lucy. 'It's whether he's said anything else since this morning.'

'About what?'

'I probably ought to explain about him,' said Lucy, locking the parish-room door. 'He's in his second childhood and generally rather sweet. He sometimes thinks I'm his sister Lily who died in 1860, and asks me where his wife is even though she's been dead for twenty years. Mrs Moore finds it very hard, and I think it's getting worse. The moments when he's childish are longer and more confused. The times when he's aware are rarer but more distressing.'

'That's so sad.'

'Mrs Moore won't send him to the workhouse, which is the only alternative. Her children are grown up, her husband's retired from the army and works in a shop. Mr Moore senior is her job, but it's wearing her out.'

'I don't know much about treating senility,' said Margaret, 'but I can find a doctor who does if you want advice. Would that help?'

'Ed says all the little countries are squabbling and the big countries are poking their noses in, and if someone doesn't stop it, there'll be a war.'

Margaret stared at Lucy's change of subject. 'I thought you thought your cousin was an idiot.'

Lucy shrugged. 'He turned seventeen in January,' she said, with all the maturity of someone fifteen months older. 'So he's improving. He says we'd win quickly, but men would still die, wouldn't they? I bet Fox thinks he's right.'

'I—' Margaret's voice felt unsteady. Fox was also sure that war was on the horizon. He wasn't so sure it would be over quickly. Would intelligence officers like him have to fight? He was approaching forty: surely he wouldn't. But his junior officers Bert and Pigeon were younger. Then there was Ed himself, hell-bent on going to Sandhurst instead of Oxford when he finished school. What if war came and Fox had been right about how long the conflict would last? Ed, her lovely, argumentative, funny, clever nephew and her sister's only child.

Margaret gripped the pram handle and concentrated on speaking normally. 'I don't know, Lucy. Let's hope war doesn't happen at all. I thought you wanted to talk about Mr Moore. I know he's an old soldier, but surely he's far too old to worry.'

'It's not that. He said something I think Fox would want to know about. Fox is in Special Branch, isn't he? I mean, I know he's probably busy with criminals, but he can tell the right people.'

'Er, yes.' None of Margaret's family or friends knew that Fox was an intelligence officer, even if her sister Katherine had probably guessed. Everyone else accepted the cover that he worked for Special Branch. 'What did Mr Moore say? And why should it mean anything? You said he's rarely lucid.'

Lucy shrugged. 'What he said seemed quite clear and normal. It might be nothing. But it might be something.'

Margaret raised her eyebrows. 'To do with war?'

'To do with Germany. Ed says Germany's the problem, even though everyone else says we have more in common with Germany than we do with France and it's silly to—'

'Keep to the point, Lucy. Tell me what it's about and I'll tell Fox.'

To Margaret's surprise, her cousin gave a sudden chuckle. 'Talking of foxes, they come into it.'

'Do I have to shake you until you explain?'

'I'm sorry,' said Lucy. 'It was like this. I borrowed a wheeled chair and took Mr Moore around Bishops Park this morning. He was pointing at people and making comments about their hats and parasols and so on, and I was pushing quite fast in the hope no one would hear him. Then he asked me to lean down so he could whisper and he said, "Your hat's very silly too, Lily. Those feathers are ridiculous." Before I knew it, he'd yanked out a couple of pins, pulled my hat off and flung it towards the river.' Lucy rubbed her head. 'It really hurt, and I didn't know what to do first. He was brandishing the pins as if they were rapiers and the breeze was blowing my hat towards the river. Go on, laugh if you want.'

'So what *did* you do?'

'I grabbed the pins before he hurt himself, parked the chair near a bench and ran for my hat. It was caught in mid-air by a terrier belonging to a runny-nosed little girl, who then tried to kill it. The dog tried to kill the hat, I mean. Anyway, I rushed back to Mr Moore. I was afraid he might have fallen out of the chair, but he was quite calm, if a little pensive. I said "Let's go home, shall we?" and he whispered, "Yes, home. Quick march. Where's the captain when we need him?" I pointed at one of the boats on the river, but he shook his head. "Not them. My old captain. Someone ought to know." I asked him what he meant but he kept shaking his head and saying "Quick march" so I started pushing. After a while, he looked back and pointed at the couple on the bench where I'd left him. and said "I heard them," he said. "They don't need to be afraid of knocks, because after all this time they know where the fox is and they can get the doings to the Germans. They can kill the vermin".'

Margaret sighed. Lucy must be more bored than she'd realised to think that what Mr Moore had said amounted to anything sinister. The chances were that the man on the bench had some sort of pest-control business and was expanding onto the continent. 'I'm not sure—'

'Honestly, Margaret, for those moments, Mr Moore knew what he was saying. He was afraid, trembling. I tried to jolly him along and said it was probably all to do with trade and nothing ominous, but he shook his head and said "I need to talk to the captain, Miss

Frampton. After what he did last time…" I asked him who had done what, but he fell silent.' Lucy's face clouded. 'It's so frightening, Margaret. It's as if he goes through a gateway out of the light into a world full of fog. Then he twisted round and said "Here, Lily, remember this one?' and started singing…' She paused. 'It's not very nice.'

'I'll survive.'

'"Ding dong bell, Gassell's in the well. Thanks to good Old Nick, he's sinking like a brick. Foxy's pulled him out, but he's drowned without a doubt." I told him he had the song all wrong and wheeled him away as fast as I could.'

'Good grief. Did the people hear?'

'We were too far away. Isn't Old Nick the devil?'

'Yes.'

'I thought so. Anyway, I told Mr and Mrs Moore. I thought they'd just shrug and look sad, but Mr Moore junior seemed worried. "What did this man look like? Did he take any notice of Pa?" But of course I didn't know. All I remember noticing was the woman's jacket when I parked the wheeled chair. It had lovely embroidery: wild-rose vines up the lapels. I memorised it to draw later, in case Mother can buy similar panels to sew on mine. I said we would have looked quite uninteresting and just what we were: a confused old man being pushed by a perspiring young woman. Mr Moore junior seemed mollified, but then said "If it *was* him, pound to a penny he'd sell secrets to the highest bidder just like he did before."'

'Lucy, I—'

'I know it's unlikely, Margaret, but it might mean something. Will you tell Fox, just in case?'

Margaret sighed. 'I'll tell him over dinner. If he wants any more information, I'll let you know.'

'Thank you,' said Lucy. 'Will you tell him about the nursery rhyme?'

'Of course,' said Margaret. 'Who wouldn't like to be immortalised in poetry as a sort of hero?'

Five

In a private alcove at their favourite restaurant, Fox and Margaret discussed how their respective days had been.

'Mine was inconclusive,' said Fox. 'Yours?'

'Full of obstinate women.'

'Has Anna been in touch again?'

'How could she? She knows I'm connected with St J's and that's all. I suppose you read the riot act to whoever should have informed you about her return.'

'She sailed back in March.'

'March? I had the impression she'd sailed in February.'

'Did she say so?'

Margaret thought. 'She said Andris died in January and she came back. I assumed one followed the other.'

'The art of misdirection.'

'Or my failure to ask the right question.'

'Perhaps. After disembarking, she stayed in a small family hotel in Southampton.'

'Southampton?'

'They couldn't say a lot about her.'

'I'm surprised,' said Margaret. 'She's quite memorable.'

'The owners exist in a fog of grief,' said Fox. 'Their fifteen-year-old son was a stoker on the *Titanic*.'

'Oh no.'

'Every time a ship returns from America, a little bit of them hopes it's bringing him home… then dies when it doesn't. Half the town is in a similar situation. Going back to Anna: after a week, she left for London. If she's in Whitechapel, she's gone to ground.'

There was a pause as ballotine of turkey was placed before them and their wine glasses refilled.

'I have a feeling she's somewhere else,' said Fox. 'Do you agree?'

Margaret nodded. 'What about Kavanagh?'

'Inspector Silvermann's investigation – which took some string-pulling by Special Branch to obtain – is based on information that a commercial traveller called Kavanagh might be a receiver of stolen goods, though it's unclear what the goods are, or possibly doing something more worrying. The evidence is largely based on hearsay, which is why Scotland Yard haven't taken over yet. They might, so the inspector's rather irritated. I can't see anything that you or I need worry about.'

'Good,' said Margaret. 'I can concentrate on teaching Cyril to express emotion for the patients.'

'They're dead.'

'That's not the point. Besides, he doesn't just train in pathology. He's on the wards too.'

Fox laughed. 'I assume your obstinate women were in the Mothers' Union.'

'Yes,' said Margaret. 'But also, surprisingly, Lucy. She insists I tell you a story which includes a silly poem.'

Fox raised his eyebrows and his expression became sceptical as she repeated what she could recall of Mr Moore's confused allegations. But when she quoted the rhyme his mouth dropped open. 'Can you repeat that?'

She obeyed. 'I think I've got it right. You're not offended, are you?'

'No more now than when I first heard it.'

'*First* heard it?'

'What's the name of this old man?'

'Moore.'

'Soldier?'

'Retired. His son was, too. How did— Oh, I always forget you joined the military police after Cynthia died. Did you know them? Surely there are lots of Moores in the services.'

'Technically, I've never left the military police,' said Fox. 'That aside, a quartermaster called Moore gave evidence in the last investigation I undertook before transferring to intelligence. The rhyme was something his fellow soldiers made up. If it's the same chap, I'm sorry to hear his mind is fading. I wonder why some things surface and others don't. Surely Lucy knows it's just a lot of confused nonsense, though.'

'It was the son's reaction that made Lucy want you to know. He took it seriously.'

'Really?'

'Where was the investigation?'

'Pretoria, in 1902.'

Now it was Margaret's turn to gawp. 'You never said you were in South Africa! Not even when I was talking about Joel.'

Fox pushed his plate away. 'I hated that stinking war. Boer women and children becoming living skeletons in British camps, our soldiers dying more from cholera than injury.'

'Joel felt the same.'

'Did he? Good. Nowadays they say it was mismanagement rather than malice, but when it's under your watch, what's the difference?'

'None.'

'All the victory parades and statues don't alter the fact that the rest of the world despises us for it. It was a bastard of an investigation, too.'

'Was it like that case – Lieutenants Morant and Handcock, wasn't it? The ones who were executed for murdering unarmed Boer civilians.'

'I didn't know you knew about that. The army tried to downplay it.'

'Well, I do,' said Margaret. 'Was it the same?'

'I was only a second lieutenant,' said Fox, 'but I was given free rein to investigate an officer for suspected treason. The war was all but over by then. Norris Gastrell – not Gassell – was allegedly cruel, though not in Morant's league. Although there was a suppressed suspicion that he might be guilty of crimes against enemy civilians. The main allegation was that he was a traitor and there was a possibility another officer was too. But ultimately, I couldn't get them to court-martial Gastrell and I couldn't identify the other man, if he existed. I failed. Moore provided evidence that should have damned him: a transaction overheard between Gastrell and a double agent. Partly through that, I uncovered the fact that Gastrell was selling the location of landmines to the Boers. Not, I believe, to save anyone's life, but so that they could be extracted and used against the British. He would receive the new placements in exchange for more information, so he could ensure he wasn't blown up.'

'He? Or his men?'

'I doubt he cared about them,' said Fox. 'Anyway, they wouldn't order a court-martial without more evidence. The double agent denied everything and Moore's evidence was treated as hearsay. The rumours about the other officer were exactly that. I couldn't find anyone who had concrete evidence. Every time I thought I would, I was somehow diverted. But I continued to investigate,. I was this close -' he put finger and thumb nearly together, 'to finding out if he really had an accomplice when Gastrell ended up in a river and drowned and I was told to stand down. They say the devil knows his own, but it didn't feel like justice to me.' Fox shuddered. 'Both Moores were there when I dragged his accursed body out of that river.'

'*You* dragged it out?'

'That's what the rhyme means. Norris Gastrell should never have drowned: he was a man born to hang. I thought I'd save him for that, but I couldn't.' Fox shook his head. 'What did Moore say he overheard?'

'It was something like, they knew where the fox was and whatever they had for the Germans could kill vermin.'

'What if the words Moore heard weren't in English but German? Not fox, but *flugzeug* – aircraft? Not vermin, but *abwehr, minen* – defence, mines?'

'That's too much of a stretch,' said Margaret. 'I can't remember exactly, but whatever he told Lucy was a sentence which made sense. His disquiet was less about what he overheard than who he saw.'

'Anyone from that time will be ten years older now,' said Fox, relaxing a little. 'If Moore's mind is as you say, he wouldn't recognise them.'

'Yes,' said Margaret. 'Seeing the river probably stirred a memory. But I can telephone Lucy and arrange for you to meet him.'

Fox nodded and indicated to the waiter that they were ready for dessert. 'It can wait till Thursday: I'm too caught up in the other thing at the moment. We'll go together. Just like we used to.'

***

On Thursday, Fox and Margaret went to meet Lucy and Mr Moore in Bishops Park.

'If we had a collapsible pram and you'd borrowed the car, we could have brought the children,' said Margaret, tucking her arm tighter into Fox's. Even as she spoke, she knew she didn't mean it. She was conscious of bubbling resentment, blaming it on meeting Mr Moore, which she thought was a waste of time, and longing to be alone with Fox on a day when neither of them was working.

'They're happier at home,' said Fox. 'And I'm enjoying being with you.' He squeezed her arm and looked behind them at the rows of houses sprawled beyond the park. 'You'll hate me for saying this, but I've been thinking—'

'We need a bigger house.' Margaret sighed. 'I know.'

'Not necessarily *much* bigger, but different. A garden. Good-sized rooms for the servants to sleep in, a proper nursery, a garden. Somewhere we – you and I – can feel private when we want to. I hadn't lived with servants for so long. It's very trying.'

'It is.' She tucked her arm more tightly in his, feeling a sense of betrayal to her pretty home. 'But we can't buy a house in Fulham. It's too far out and Father would visit constantly.'

Fox grimaced. 'I wish you'd seen my family's garden in Hertfordshire. I built a sort of tree-house. I wonder if it's still there.'

The only photograph Margaret had seen of Fox as a child showed him sitting on his mother's lap, but she could imagine him sitting like an emperor in a tree-house, surveying his countryside kingdom. She felt envious. Apart from holidays in the New Forest, the only trees she and Katherine had had at their disposal were in genteel parks. Boys weren't supposed to climb them: girls were positively forbidden. 'Take me to see it one day soon,' she said. 'Do you honestly think meeting Mr Moore is worthwhile?'

'Not really.'

'But Mr Moore mentioned Germany…'

'It doesn't necessarily mean anything. The rhyme Moore quoted was about a man who's dead. I suppose I just want to be sure there's nothing about this man who jogged Moore's memory that I need to know.'

'It all seems such tarradiddle.' Margaret scanned the park and saw her cousin rushing towards them. She'd sounded happy on the telephone the previous evening, but now appeared flustered and anxious.

'Mr Moore's had a stroke,' she said as soon as she was close enough. 'There's no point in Fox visiting. The doctor says—' She swallowed. 'He won't last till tomorrow. Poor Mrs Moore found him on the floor in the kitchen early this morning. I don't think she's had anything to eat since last night. Will *you* come anyway, Margaret? Maybe the doctor's wrong. He seemed so well yesterday.'

'Let's both go,' said Fox. 'We can talk to his son, if not him.'

Margaret shook her head. 'We can't intrude like that. Lucy, I'm sure if the doctor says—'

'We needn't make it an intrusion,' argued Fox. 'You help Lucy and I'll commiserate with Mr Moore junior. It seems odd that a relatively healthy man sees something strange, then has apoplexy. Just like that tailor of yours.'

'It's not the same, Fox. We can't.'

'We can,' said Fox. 'Put your professional face on, Margaret, and I shall put on mine. Besides, Lucy may need your help persuading Mrs Moore to rest.' He put his other arm out for Lucy. 'Which way? What can you tell me about this man who disturbed Mr Moore so much?'

Lucy pointed towards the houses. 'Not much.' She blushed. 'I'm observant, usually, but I was a little embarrassed by Mr Moore, and I could hardly turn and stare. I remember the man as just average. And the woman with him was just average too.'

Fox sighed. 'It's a never-ending nuisance how average so many people are.'

***

Mr Moore's unfocused gaze seemed to follow a butterfly dancing to a manic mazurka: settling on the people around him, then the curtains, then the clock, then the door, perhaps searching for something to make sense of. He focussed on Lucy and with an effort, down to her hand holding his.

'It's me,' she said. 'Miss Frampton. Sometimes you think I'm Lily.'

His blue eyes flickered over her face, her eyes, her ears, her hat. The right side of his mouth worked, stickiness gathering in the left corner, but no sound came. His eyes widened a little as they moved, then settled on Lucy once more. Maybe the movement in his right hand was trying to reach for a sister who'd been dead fifty years, or maybe it was nothing.

'He's not really there, Miss Frampton.' Mrs Moore's voice was a whispered sob. 'This isn't Pa any more.'

Lucy turned to Margaret, who shook her head just a little, 'Miss Frampton will keep your father-in-law company, Mrs Moore,' she said. 'I'll get you some tea. You need rest.'

'Let me stand you a beer, Moore,' said Fox. 'I went through this with my own father. I know how hard it is.'

'I don't like to leave him.'

Fox looked at Margaret, who nodded. 'Half an hour won't make any difference, Mr Moore. I'll come and get you myself if necessary.'

***

It wasn't until three hours later that Margaret could talk with Fox in private.

She thought back to that afternoon. Mrs Moore had argued with Margaret and Lucy: '*I don't need rest. Our doctor said we'll have him with us for a good few hours yet, so I want him to be as comfortable as can be.'* She'd gone on and on before she finally agreed to let Margaret make tea while she lay down.

Fox had returned from the pub with Mr Moore junior soon after, and he and Margaret had taken their leave.

'Poor old chap,' said Fox now. 'They were the Moores I knew. But now Moore can't talk, and all I have is an average man and a woman with an embroidered jacket – which sounds like the title of a bad novel – talking about vermin. Much as I hate to admit it, you were right all along.'

'For what it's worth, I think what he said he'd heard, especially the word *fox*, dragged up a memory you want to forget because you think of it as failure.'

Fox grunted. 'It *was* failure.'

'I doubt it,' said Margaret. 'If the authorities didn't want to admit to all the things wrong with that war, perhaps they didn't want to admit publicly that one of their officers was a traitor.'

'He's dead,' said Fox. 'That's all that matters.' He heaved a sigh. 'But I think you're right. After the last few weeks everything seems suspicious.'

'If you need to talk about Norris Gastrell to get him out of your head, I'm listening.'

'There's little more to say,' said Fox. 'Afterwards, Captain Selkirk recommended me to Hare, who was setting up a special intelligence unit. I sometimes wish he hadn't.'

'No, you don't,' said Margaret, kissing him. 'Because then you'd never have met me.'

Six

Lucy telephoned that evening to say that Mr Moore had died. She sounded drained.

'The funeral's on Saturday. They've asked me to help in the church hall afterwards, and they'd like you and Fox to attend if you can.'

'But—'

'They were so touched by your kindness. They'd really appreciate you being there.'

'Then of course we shall.'

The Moores were very traditional. Only the men attended the internment, while the women prepared for the reception.

Mrs Moore's face twisted in a kaleidoscope of emotions: grief for her loss, relief at her freedom, joy at her father-in-law's, grief, relief, joy, guilt, grief... Her eyes filled with confused tears which she viciously rubbed away. When she faltered, her daughter, awkward in late pregnancy, led her to a chair and they sat for a while, Mrs Moore's hand gentle on her daughter's bump. Her grey sorrow lifted for a moment as she felt her grandchild move. Margaret's thoughts rephrased those old words: *In the midst of death, we are in life.*

A crowd of women bustled. Parishioners of various ranks filled urns, straightened plates, laid tea cloths over sandwiches. Lucy was stationed near a huge brown teapot. The vicar's wife arranged chairs. Two well-heeled ladies waited to serve cake, taking their orders from Mrs Tranter, a bird-like market trader in a very out-of-date greenish-black outfit who said she'd run a stall since she could see over a barrow, around the time of Waterloo, however unlikely that was. Despite a lack of teeth and grammar and the use of long-obsolete slang, she mesmerised the ladies into doing what she wanted. It was a scene of egalitarian perfection.

Discouraged from helping much on the grounds that she was a guest, Margaret watched rain trickle down the windows. It was a perfect day for a funeral.

A little before twelve, the male mourners returned.

Mr Moore's son and grandsons, in army uniform, entered first. They were introduced to Lucy, and Margaret watched the youngest, a lad of about nineteen with eyes red from rubbing, straighten up a little as they shook hands. He smiled shyly as he accepted the tea Lucy offered with a shy smile of her own, their hands touching with almost visible electricity. Margaret felt a slight pang for the days of adolescence, but once again the thought returned: *in the midst of death, we are in life*. It was right and proper.

Then she looked for Fox.

He entered with a tall officer in his late fifties, and there was something about the way they stood that made Margaret think they must know each other. She couldn't read Fox's expression at all, even when, after greeting Mrs Moore, her daughter and daughter-in-law to offer condolences, he led the other man over.

'Margaret, may I introduce Major Sir Broderick Selkirk, whom I met in South Africa in '02 when he was a captain and I a second lieutenant. Sir Broderick, may I introduce my wife, Dr Margaret Demeray.'

They shook hands. 'Delighted to meet you, Dr Demeray.' Sir Broderick had a kindly, serious face, with the deep lines and dark marks of someone who has spent much of his life in hot countries. 'I don't suppose you know a Mr and Mrs Holbourne, do you?'

'Actually, yes,' said Margaret. 'They're close friends.'

'What a small world! I know them through fundraising at the Union Jack Club. There was a charity ball there a month ago, and your name came up when Mrs Holbourne was trying to convince my wife about women's suffrage. I had no idea the distinguished woman she was talking about was technically Mrs Foxcroft-Sionnach, and if I had, I'd have asked to be put in touch. Not that we ever called Foxcroft more than that, of course - far too much of a mouthful. It's unusual for a lady to keep her maiden name, as I'm sure you'll agree, but I can see why, in the circumstances you've kept it for professional purposes. Much easier than using your married one.'

'Er … yes.'

'It's delightful to make your acquaintance. I daresay you know Foxcroft investigated a crime in my regiment, although you won't know the details. I was delighted to recommend him for, er…' He took a sip of tea and frowned a little.

Margaret saw a flicker in Fox's expression and finished the sentence. 'You were delighted to recommend him for civilian police work.'

'Yes.' He relaxed and smiled. 'Yes indeed. I'm retired, you know, as Moore junior is. Both of us injured. A shame. I think both of us had hopes of furthering our careers. And with, er, things as they stand, I'd have been proud to serve my country again. Then again' – he nodded at Mr Moore's uniformed grandsons – 'there needs to be young blood.'

'Not spilt, I hope,' said Margaret.

Sir Broderick looked askance. 'It's what a soldier thinks his blood is for, you know.' His kind smile returned. 'Any man who isn't prepared to spill his blood to protect his country, his womenfolk, his family and his fellows isn't a man at all in my view, and ought to be put down. But there you are. Perhaps there won't be a war after all.'

'It sounds as if you think that's a pity.'

'Ha ha.' Sir Broderick chuckled. 'Don't try and trick a simple soldier into saying what he doesn't mean, doctor. Only a fool wants conflict, but one has to be prepared. It would be good to show anyone muscling in that they'd bitten off more than they could chew. Mark my words, if there *is* a war, we'll win it within three months. Don't you agree, Foxcroft?'

Fox didn't answer, but his neutral expression softened. 'How did you hear about the old quartermaster?'

Sir Broderick waggled his head. 'His son wrote to me through the regiment on Wednesday morning and they forwarded it on. He said his father wanted to talk to "the captain". He explained that the old chap was rather addled, but thought I might be able to calm him a little. I replied to say I'd be delighted to visit on Friday – but of course, by then it was too late. Poor feller. And Mrs Moore was distraught. I gather she's been caring for him as he got worse and worse. It's no pleasure to watch a man deteriorate like that, nor to see every drop of someone's love wrung from them as they cope. They say that women are the weaker sex, don't they?' He took a deep breath. 'Nonsense. Poor Mrs Moore deserves a campaign medal. I'd have a woman like that in the ranks any day.' He fell silent, staring across the room.

Margaret glanced at Fox. The burst of sentiment appeared to have surprised him as much as her. Around them were the subdued sounds of crockery clattering, chatter, the occasional wistful laugh, footsteps on the wooden floor, a tiny, quickly suppressed sob. The men were eyeing their teacups with mild disdain. At some point they'd make their way to the pub and see Mr Moore off in a different way.

Sir Broderick cleared his throat. 'I gather you saw him on Thursday because he'd asked for you, Foxcroft. What was it all about? I couldn't make much sense of things yesterday.'

Fox shrugged. 'He thought "the captain" – presumably you – ought to know what he'd overheard in Bishops Park. I think it reminded him of South Africa.'

'Harrumph,' said Sir Broderick. 'The brain is a peculiar thing, isn't it, doctor?'

'Yes,' said Margaret.

'You're probably right,' said Fox. He scanned the room, his face closed again. Margaret followed his gaze, sensing his frustration. She knew he'd never fail to wish that he'd spoken to old Mr Moore before his stroke and wondered if Sir Broderick, despite his words, felt the same.

'I'd love you both to meet my wife,' Sir Broderick was saying. 'We live out in the country. Only a short distance, though. The Holbournes are coming to visit on Saturday and staying overnight. Would you care to come too?'

'We'd be delighted,' said Fox, without pause. 'Wouldn't we, Margaret?'

Margaret opened her mouth and shut it again. What about the children? She'd have to ask Maude what the protocol was. Could she take them and Nellie? Could she leave them behind? How freeing … how terrifying. She hadn't been apart from them for more than nine hours since they'd been born. Fox, as a man, had clearly not given them a moment's thought. But it would be delightful, and somehow or other she had to make it work. 'Yes, we'd love to. Thank you, Sir Broderick.'

'Excellent, excellent.' Sir Broderick smiled. 'I think the chaps are leaving for the Crown and Sceptre, to send the old quartermaster off with something stronger than tea. Are you coming, Foxcroft?'

On the way home, Margaret asked Fox why he hadn't told Sir Broderick more of what Mr Moore had said.

'Too many people about,' he replied. 'But I can ask at the weekend. I'm looking forward to it, especially as Maude and Geoff will be there. It'll be nice to have some time away with you, having my doubts cleared *and* avoiding Vera's cooking.'

At home, the children were red-cheeked, grizzly and miserable. Margaret spent the afternoon helping Nellie try to calm them, then telephoned Maude to tell her about the visit to the Selkirks and ask her advice.

'That's wonderful,' Maude had assured her. 'You can leave the children at home with Nellie. If they're teething, they'll prefer a familiar environment.'

'Will they? We're all going to Brighton at Whitsun - what if they're still—'

'That's different and you'll have Nellie with you. Stop worrying. You'll love Archers Steading. It's beautiful.'

Dinner was interrupted by Fox's senior officer Hare telephoning. From Fox's staccato answers, it sounded like bad news. His face when he returned to the dining room confirmed it. 'The Irish photographer we arrested in Carmarthenshire has managed to escape custody. I need to go, and I'll probably be working tomorrow too.'

'Have they only just found out?'

'Someone was covering up her absence by saying she was sick enough to stay in her cell but not enough for the hospital wing. No one checked. She could have been gone hours.'

'Does she have a name?'

'We hadn't discovered her real one,' said Fox, kissing her goodbye. 'If I'm late home, I'll sleep in the spare room. Then I won't disturb you.' He hesitated, holding her tight. 'I love you.'

'I love you too. Don't worry about disturbing me.'

'You're exhausted, Margaret. Spend tomorrow at Katherine's. I'll see you in the evening.'

That night Margaret lay awake for hours waiting to hear Fox return and listening out for the twins above, even though there were two maids in the attics ready to care for them. In the end she fell asleep, and in the morning discovered that either Fox had not come home, or had left very early.

On Sunday, she took the children and Nellie to her sister's as Fox had suggested. After lunch, exhausted by Ed's enthusiastic conversation, which bounced from the Royal Flying Corps to British tennis triumphs at the Olympics to whether the *Titanic*'s sinking was the result of something sinister, she went to rest in what had once been her own bedroom, when Ed had been newborn and somehow less exhausting.

Fox returned home on Sunday evening, an hour or so after she and the children had come back from Katherine's. 'We've got the weasel who helped her escape. There's nothing more terrifying than the sort of martyr who doesn't care what the cause is, as long as he can convince himself his death will be glorious to make up for a life that's anything but. He'd quite like someone to torture him to tell us where she is, but I doubt he knows.'

'Have you any idea?'

'The world, my dear, is her oyster. And we only have so many people to watch so many ports and stations.'

'I bet she's still in London.'

'Me too. She can speak like a native Londoner as easily as she can speak like a native Dubliner. Either way, she could quite easily disappear in the East End until she thinks it's safe to leave. But finding one Irishwoman among thousands will be hard, especially when we're not sure of her real name. I wish I knew what she was doing, Margaret. It felt like she'd taken on something she wasn't sure about herself. Someone was controlling her. I'll have to leave early again tomorrow, but for now I'm going to bed.'

He fell asleep moments after lying down, but his eyes twitched under their lids. It was hard to feel enthusiastic about their stay at the Selkirks' if it meant another day or two when they'd barely spent any time alone together.

In the early hours, Margaret dreamed.

She was eight, sitting in the shadows of a window seat in a quiet holiday house which should be full of laughter and games, but was full of murmuring misery because Mother was not there and never would be again.

Soon, someone would ask her to stitch something ugly, read something dull or help with something boring.

She stared out at sunshine dappling the New Forest and couldn't bear it any longer. Despite the stiff, frilled, hateful mourning dress, she climbed through the window and ran out of the garden and across the heath. Then, suddenly, there was a perfect, climbable young oak. She stripped off her shoes and stockings and started to climb.

The bark scraped her bare legs and caught on the furbelows of the awful clothes. Her arms ached, her feet were scratched, her hair tangled in twigs. But she was free, hidden high in the branches with no one to tell her what to do, no one to tell her to look miserable or sit still. Mother was dead, but she hadn't gone. Mother was in her heart, the voice in her mind that said 'Don't be shy, don't weep, don't be afraid to try something new.' Mother could never be trapped under the cold earth.

Margaret stared up into the scudding clouds, then down on the anchored world. Running through the bracken and gorse came Aunt Alice and Katherine. They looked like copper-topped crows in their black clothes, their red hair coming loose as they ran in different directions, hunting for her. Their voices were anxious and strained. 'Meg! Meg! Where are you?'

But Margaret was free. She didn't call back.

A leaf stroked her cheek and...

'What were you dreaming?' asked Fox.

'I was climbing a tree to get away from things.'

Fox grunted. 'If only.'

Seven

'Isn't it nice?' said Maude, as the car emerged from the trees to reveal Archers Steading the following Saturday afternoon.

'Lovely,' said Margaret. 'It's not remotely what I expected.'

The week had passed swiftly. When she'd had time to think about it, she had imagined the Selkirks living in a large, cold-faced, Georgian building with perfect symmetry, or perhaps a large, draughty, early Victorian house with a veranda. But it was Tudor and not particularly big, with tall twisting brick chimneys, mullioned windows and a welcoming air that somehow promised that while it might be a little dark, there would be warm corners in winter, cool ones in summer, and a room full of old books in tooled leather. An arbour, glorious with wisteria, stood to the west of the house and a broad path to the east led to stables and outbuildings.

Two horses cropped the grass in an apple orchard, a tabby cat stretched out on the windowsill, soaking up warmth, and a black cat sitting primly on a fence post turned its languid attention from a sky full of unattainable swallows and chorusing skylarks to watch them, opening its mouth in a welcoming miaow.

Maude leaned closer. 'I bet this is the sort of place Fox has in mind. Would it suit you?'

In the front seats, the men had fallen silent and Margaret tried to work out Fox's reaction from his shoulders. The house and surroundings were beautiful. There were trees for climbing. There was also an awful lot of countryside between it and any sizeable town.

'No.'

'You'll have to use your womanly wiles to persuade him out of it, then.'

'I don't think he'd consider anywhere so far out of London.'

'Are you sure?' When Margaret didn't answer, Maude chuckled. 'I'm looking forward to this. The Selkirks are very nice, and we haven't done anything together without children for ages. Some fresh air and time away from London will do you and Fox the world of good. Both of you look as if the world is on your shoulders. Can you talk about it?'

'Fox is on a tricky case,' said Margaret. 'He keeps meeting dead ends and feels guilty about leaving others to carry on without him this weekend.'

'But what's wrong with *you*? I promise the children will be fine. I was in Holloway Prison for a month in March for window smashing, and I swear even Johnny barely noticed. Geoff and the nursery staff made sure they had too much fun. We'll enjoy being fed and watered by the Selkirks and dance till dawn like people without a care.'

'I doubt I can stay awake till dawn.'

'I was being figurative. The Selkirks keep country hours.'

The car jerked as it hit a stone. Geoff crunched the gears and swore. The horses lifted their heads and cantered to the opposite side of the orchard to watch from a safe distance. The black cat jumped down and disappeared, but the tabby continued to snooze in unconcerned wantonness, its legs splayed, its stomach exposed to the embrace of the evening sun.

'Dear God, I'll be glad to remove this accursed veil,' said Maude, coughing as Geoff brought the car to a halt outside the house.

'Me too. I swear they trap more dust than they keep out.'

A manservant opened the front door, Sir Broderick and Lady Selkirk emerged from the arbour to greet them, and a groom appeared from the other side of the house and strode up to the car.

There are exits and entrances everywhere, thought Margaret. *Stage left, stage right, centre stage. Are we the audience, or part of the troupe?* But their hosts' smiles were genuine and the servants displayed inscrutable perfection. She chided herself.

'Good evening, good evening!' boomed Sir Broderick. 'Welcome! Price will take the car to the garage and Starky will take your bags. Ladies, let me help you out!'

'Welcome, all,' said Lady Selkirk, shaking hands. 'Sarah's waiting to take your travelling things and show you to your rooms. Come down as soon as you're ready. The gong will be rung at seven, but do join us outside in the sun beforehand. And don't forget, we're very informal here. No starched shirt fronts or ties needed for dinner.'

'That's a relief,' said Maude. 'I left mine at home.'

Lady Selkirk gave her a maternal smile.

The inside of the house was brighter and more modern than Margaret had expected and the bedrooms more so, filled with modern light-oak furniture, the walls papered in cream. She and Fox had been divested of travelling coats, scarves and veils, revealing the clothes underneath as fairly clean of road dust, but they bathed and changed nonetheless. Margaret redressed her hair and put on a pale-blue silk gown before joining Fox at the window. From it, they could see the orchard and the horses and the hills beyond. Their hosts, sitting below them in the arbour, were still enough to be statues, comfortable enough in each other's company to sit in silence. Fox put his arm around her. 'Lovely, isn't it?'

'Yes,' said Margaret. 'Although it's also very, very quiet. I'll be unable to sleep without traffic and footsteps and distant police whistles and anticipation of imminent burglary.'

'It's noisy enough,' said Fox. 'Can't you hear sparrows squabbling in the eaves? And there'll be wood pigeons in the morning.'

'And foxes and strange dogs barking in the night. I've stayed in the country a good deal, remember.'

'You'll have me to protect you.'

'Mmm.' Margaret snuggled into him. 'Maybe I'll protect you.' She paused. 'Do you suppose they've had a telephone installed?'

'They're too far from the exchange,' said Fox. 'Don't worry, the children will be fine. And so will you.'

Margaret decided to cut to the chase. 'Is this the sort of place you had in mind for us?' Mentally, she crossed her fingers. 'Trees for climbing, room to ride, fresh air…'

Fox stared out at the scene and said nothing. His arm was warm around her waist. Then he turned her to face him and kissed her. 'Not yet,' he said. 'Being this far out would be no use: I'd hardly ever be home. And you couldn't do your job. Not the one at St J's, at any rate – or even one in Marylebone. I'm afraid we'll be suburban for a few years yet. Do you mind?'

'I'm relieved.'

He chuckled. 'Then why ask? One day, I'd like to be somewhere like this. Not here, though. Somewhere by the sea. Water, anyway. Or France. Or both. What do you think?'

'Maybe,' said Margaret, heaving an inward sigh of relief. 'When are you going to ask Sir Broderick about Gastrell?'

'When the moment feels right, if it ever does. Come on, let's go down.'

The evening was enjoyable, dinner deceptively simple and quite delicious, the conversation light and innocuous. Afterwards, Sir Broderick acceded with a laugh to Maude's suggestion and had the port brought into the garden where they watched the last sunlight dip towards the hills. As the temperature dipped, they retired to a room which opened onto the garden and took it in turns to entertain each other on the piano.

Margaret, whose piano skills had never warranted public exposure, persuaded Maude to do a duet in which Maude took the main part and Margaret accompanied as softly as possible. Fox performed 'The Spaniard Who Blighted My Life' with more confidence than strict accuracy, but it didn't matter since he, Maude and Margaret drowned any duff notes by singing along. Then he and the major took it in turns to play polkas while the others danced, until, saying it was still too hot for such liveliness, Lady Selkirk played a slow waltz and watched as the two younger couples spun indolently in the small space.

Finally, to Margaret's surprise, Geoff took over at the piano and launched into ragtime. 'I didn't know he could play anything so complicated,' she whispered to Maude.

'He has many talents,' Maude whispered back, then said loudly, 'Come along, Sir Broderick and Lady Selkirk, let Margaret and Fox teach you the Grizzly Bear!'

Laughing, they carried the dancing into the garden and jiggled and twisted under the dusky sky until Lady

Selkirk begged for a reprieve and staggered from Fox's arms to her husband's. 'Broderick, rescue me! My knees aren't young enough for this sort of thing, and nor are yours! Let's go inside and play cards. Mrs Holbourne, dear, will you ring? We need coffee and brandy.'

Fox caught Margaret and twirled for a few more steps, pulling her close.

'Time for a cigar, Foxcroft,' said Sir Broderick, returning through the doorway and handing one over. His face was genial in the light of the lamps hanging from the arbour. To the west, the glow of the setting sun was a rim of pink edging the hilltops. 'It's nothing like South Africa, is it? British sunsets are sort of soft, like a maiden aunt. Not fierce like a warrior queen.'

'I was only in South Africa for a month, Sir Broderick.'

'Long enough, surely, to know how astonishingly beautiful it is.'

'The scenery? When I was looking at it rather than at a soldier, and saw a bit that hadn't been blown up, very much so.'

'Now, now, Foxcroft, it wasn't that bad,' Sir Broderick chuckled, or perhaps he cleared his throat. 'Don't dally out here, Mrs Foxcroft … I mean Dr Demeray: come in before you get chilly. Perhaps you can help with the conversation. They're discussing suffragettes.'

'I hope Maude's not haranguing you in your own home, Lady Selkirk,' said Margaret as she entered. 'She's apt to argue till she runs out of breath if you give her free rein.'

'So are you,' retorted Maude. 'And you're even worse when you get on to housing and working conditions. Didn't St J's do the post-mortem on that poor tailor the other week?'

'We did. And I saw the sweatshop where he died.'

'The inquest said that overwork killed him,' said Maude.

'A ruptured aneurysm killed him. Overwork didn't help; however, there's no way of telling for certain. In terms of a working environment, the sweatshop was a fire risk. You could barely see your fingers at the back of the room, let alone a needle, and wherever you walked you stirred up lungfuls of fibres. I wouldn't leave a dog there.'

'Perhaps I should look into this strike and report on it for *Athene's Gazette*.'

'Perhaps you should. Oh, I'm sorry, Lady Selkirk … we do tend to get sidetracked.'

The older woman smiled broadly and winked as she patted the chair beside her. 'I enjoy your passion, my dears. I quite like being able to say I know someone prepared to go to prison for her beliefs, even if I'm not sure I approve of smashing windows to get the vote.'

Maude shrugged.

'Unrepentant,' said Lady Selkirk, with a grin. 'Honestly, you're both refreshing after all the stuffy army wives and worthies and all that relentless protocol: having to agree with the colonel's wife even if she was being a fool, and the junior wives having to agree with me when I was one. I know Broderick misses the army, but I have to say I don't. But I'm a little tired of debate. Let's enjoy our brandy, play some cards and change the subject. Tell me, what is your view on this season's hats?'

'I favour a fedora myself,' said Geoff, taking his seat on Lady Selkirk's other side and dealing cards. 'It can take being sat on without entirely losing its shape, which in our house – what with out-of-control children and worse-behaved suffragettes – is essential.'

Lady Selkirk chuckled. 'Flowers or feathers as a trimming?'

'I hadn't considered flowers.' Geoff put his head on one side and looked at Maude.

'Daisies,' she said. 'Or carnations. They'd go with your eyes.'

'As long as I don't have half a stuffed bird on my head, like some of your friends. Now then, Margaret, I hope your wits are as sharp as your politics. We need to beat Maude.'

Eight

Geoff was to be disappointed.

Margaret half-watched Fox and Sir Broderick as they shared brandy and cigars near the garden doors. She wondered what Fox was saying. Sir Broderick knew Fox was in intelligence, since he'd recommended him for it, but they had continued the pretence that Fox was a police superintendent throughout dinner.

'Come along, M,' said Geoff when they lost another hand. 'Stop woolgathering.'

Fox leaned forward and Sir Broderick frowned. 'Oh!' said Margaret. 'I've left my wrap in the garden. And the record has stopped. Why don't you put another on while I get it, Geoff?'

'Will you promise to concentrate if I do?' moaned Geoff. 'We're down sixpence.'

'Of course.'

Neither Fox nor Sir Broderick paid Margaret any attention as she slipped past. After finding her wrap in the gloom, she waited just outside the door. Fox was speaking, his voice low. 'Whatever he saw or heard reminded him of Norris Gastrell. Remember Gastrell?'

'How can I forget him? The two of you struggling in the river: one minute your head above water, then his. Thought you were both goners, to be honest, until one of the men got a rope to you. And then you insisted on trying to revive him, even though no one would have blamed you if you hadn't. But Gastrell's dead. I've rarely seen anyone deader who was still in one piece.' Sir Broderick's voice had risen and he lowered it again. 'As I said at the funeral, poor old Moore's brain probably had bits from now, bits from then and bits from God knows where, stirring about in a godawful mess.'

'I know,' said Fox.

The gramophone started, then stopped as Lady Selkirk's voice rang out: 'Not that tune, dear.'

Little country noises rustled in the garden behind Margaret. The cold evening air stroked her arms. She pulled the wrap tighter.

'We always thought he had an accomplice,' said Fox. 'Moore reported Gastrell talking to someone else that day, but wasn't sure who it was. What if he recognised the voice in Bishops Park, and this time recognised the man? Was there an officer in the battalion I should have paid more attention to?'

Sir Broderick puffed out his breath. 'There was that snivelling little chap who idolised Gastrell. And then there was that Irish feller. A bit insubordinate, republican tendencies – name's gone. Neither was any loss to the army when they resigned their commissions. In fact, the milksop was encouraged to go. He hadn't the brains to do anything on his own initiative. I daresay the Irishman is up to his ears in Home Rule nonsense by now. But the double-agent had links with German West Africa, not just Boers, and when the whole thing was blown open, they sidled back behind their borders. It was one of the West African Germans, I'm sure of it – said so at the time. Gastrell didn't care: he'd have sold his own grandmother if he could have got her out of Hades without burning his fingers. It's done and dusted, Foxcroft. Poor old Moore was about to die and his life was probably flashing before his eyes. I bet if you asked your missus she'd say the same. Pity you can't explain it to her. Top secret, and all that.'

'Top secret.'

'If it makes you happier I'll dig about in my diaries, but I won't find anything relevant. Gastrell's dirty work ended when he did. I can believe the Germans are busy making sneaky plans now, but linked to a long dead traitor? Not in a million years. He was far too unimportant. Do you want to play billiards while the others play cards?'

'Why not?'

Margaret waited till they moved away. Behind her, the country darkness rustled and closed in a little more and she shivered. She slipped back into the room.

***

She woke in the night, unsure whether it had been a noise or the lack of noise which had woken her. She rolled over to cuddle up to Fox and realised he was awake too.

'Shh.'

From outside there was a slight rustle, then close by, *Twit ... twoo.*

'It's just an owl,' whispered Margaret.

'It isn't.' Fox pushed the covers back. 'Only a townie thinks one owl makes that noise. It should be two: one calling, one answering. The female is the twit.'

'Is she, now? And what do you mean, should be?'

'I doubt whatever made that noise has feathers. It's either two educated people signalling to each other or one ignorant townie inadvertently flirting with himself. I'm going to check.'

They left the bed to look outside. The sky was dark with cloud, but low light from the room below spilled onto the arbour. As before, the Selkirks sat there, very still. Margaret, fresh from sleep, had the disquieting thought that they only came to life when visitors arrived, until Sir Broderick shifted a little closer to his wife and she leaned against his shoulder. Then both of them sat up.

Someone tall stepped into the arbour. While it was hard to be sure from silhouettes seen through foliage, there were no apparent greeting gestures. A cigarette glowed. It couldn't be a manservant: he wouldn't smoke in his employers' presence, and nothing about him suggested subservience. He stood for a while, then sat beside Sir Broderick and leaned close. Nothing could be heard. The visit took moments, then the man stood and slipped into the shadows.

'Keep watching,' whispered Fox, so quietly that she felt the words rather than heard them. He ducked behind the curtains.

The Selkirks remained still, then Sir Broderick pulled his wife into his arms. They rose and retired into the house. Margaret heard the lock turn on the door below as the first drops of rain fell.

She leaned out of the window, feeling cool drops patter on her warm skin. She peered into the darkness, trying to work out if she could see anything, but there were too many shadows. She returned to bed and after a minute or so, Fox joined her. 'I looked out of the landing windows, but it was too dark. Perhaps he left a horse or car at the end of the drive. It's half a mile to the nearest house and nearly four to Ruislip.'

'Perhaps he's still here,' said Margaret.

'Perhaps.'

***

When morning came, Margaret woke wondering where she was and why there was no sound of babies from above. She longed to rush home and lift the twins, hold them close and breathe in their milky sweetness.

'You look weary,' Maude said at breakfast, with a wink. They were on their own in the dining room, the maid having reported that Lady Selkirk was nursing a headache but would be down before Margaret and Fox left. 'Busy night without interruptions from teething infants?'

'Could be,' said Margaret, with as enigmatic a smile as she could muster.

'Fox still sleeping it off?'

'No, he's gone riding with Sir Broderick.'

'We should have done that.'

'You weren't up, and I didn't bring the right clothes.'

'I'm sure Lady Selkirk could lend you something,' said Maude. 'Why not stay? The Selkirks' horses are beautiful and the riding around here is excellent. You and I don't often get the chance to ride, and it's lovely and sunny. Beating you in a straight gallop would start off the day nicely.'

'You've never beaten me yet and you never will. I'm shorter and less top-heavy, so I have a lower centre of gravity.'

Maude compared Margaret's bust with her own. 'Not since you've become a mother.'

'Rubbish!' Margaret replied. 'You're still top-heavier.'

'Only by about a handful.'

'Huh. At least two.'

Maude shrugged. 'Geoff doesn't complain. Come on, Margaret, why not let Fox go back to town on his own? Geoff and I can bring you back this evening. When was the last time we had a day in the country?'

'We can arrange another one. Besides, I'm missing the children. Don't you miss yours?'

Maude's smile faded. 'Of course, but since I went to Holloway they've become clingy. Sometimes it's rather trying.' Her face darkened a little.

Margaret watched her friend butter a slice of toast she would only nibble at. Maude's appetite had changed since her prison sentence. For all Margaret's teasing, Maude had lost some of her curves. Her waist was almost as small as it had been at eighteen, in the days of tight lacing. But while the fire in her eyes burned, the shadow of what had happened in Holloway lurked like a bailiff.

She had only described it to Margaret and their friend Phoebe once: hearing the barricaded doors of other cells broken open one by one till they came to hers; arms wrenched as she was hauled out; wardresses restraining her as they strapped her into a chair; trying to concentrate on the pain of the bruises to take her mind off what happened next, but failing; gagging as the feeding tube was forced down her throat, tears of fury, pain and terror running down the sides of her face into her hair. Then afterwards pretending to the children that she had been away for a month having fun with friends, even though her ten-year-old daughter knew what had happened from taunts at school, and wasn't sure whether to be ashamed or proud.

It was no good asking Maude if she thought the cause was worth it. The fire in her eyes would never be extinguished till victory was won.

'I will do whatever is necessary for us to get the vote, Margaret.' Her cheerful mood returned as she chose which marmalade to put on the toast. 'But not today. Please stay.'

'I honestly can't. But if Fox and I are invited to come with you again, we'll go riding.'

'You will be: Lady S likes you. Maybe she'd let us bring the children if she could disconnect them from her own.'

'I didn't think they had any.'

Maude pointed at a watercolour of a happy little girl in a frilled blue dress clutching a doll, and next to it a simple sketch of a young army officer, at ease, smoking a cigarette and looking towards distant hills. 'A daughter lost to measles aged about two and a son who died in his early twenties. They don't like to talk about it.'

Margaret looked at the little girl, frozen in her moment of joy. The longing to be home made her ache. If Alec or Edie contracted diphtheria or tetanus, there would be little she could do but hope and pray. The fear of infection stalked her more as a mother than it ever had as a mere doctor. 'Poor woman.' She sighed and shook herself. 'Where's Geoff?'

'Still in bed, the lazy oaf. He woke up and was restless in the middle of the night. At one point he wandered downstairs to read. He often does it when we're away and I'm always worried he'll be mistaken for a burglar.'

Margaret forced a chuckle. It must have been Geoff with the Selkirks, and she and Fox had seen mysteries when there were none. Presumably Fox was now finding out the same as he chatted with Sir Broderick. Her cheeks burned as she realised they'd been spying on their hosts and a beloved friend, and she lifted her coffee cup to hide her face.

The dining-room door opened. Sir Broderick and Fox came in, chatting, closely followed by Geoff, and then a maid bringing fresh coffee, tea and toast.

'Morning, ladies!' boomed Sir Broderick as he went to the chafing dishes. 'You missed an excellent ride. As did you, Holbourne!'

'I was just telling Margaret that,' said Maude.

'Next time, I hope, Dr Demeray?'

'I'd be delighted.'

'Excellent. Excellent. Now then, what have we here? Sausages, black pudding, bacon, eggs…Aha, kidneys! Food for a king! Excellent!'

Maude took up her toast again. 'Is it really true that the tailor died of natural causes?' she asked softly.

'Yes.'

'But the conditions of his employment didn't help.'

'Maude, I can't say that for certain. Please don't make out that I did.'

'But their working conditions really are as bad as the strikers say?'

'Yes.'

'Then I want to report on it. My readers all order dresses and suits without thinking. *Athene's Gazette* is meant to support women's freedom and fair treatment, yet half the letters I've received recently have complained about the strike: women doing the Season who are terrified they'll have to wear last year's outfits. I don't feel I'm doing my job if I can't show them that there are plenty of things worse than that.'

'Good for you,' said Margaret. 'About time, too.'

***

Sir Broderick was affable as he drove them to Northolt Junction to catch their train, begging them to return for a longer visit as soon as possible.

In the train, Fox shook his head at Margaret's suggestion about Geoff. 'Someone who's got out of bed in the night to read doesn't get dressed first, let alone wander into the garden to scare his hosts. Even Geoff. In fact, especially Geoff. It might be a lot more mundane. We were talking about law and order while we were riding, and Sir Broderick complained that as a magistrate he's often required to sign warrants in the middle of the night. He didn't say that had happened recently, but perhaps he said it in case we'd been disturbed.'

'I realise you country people are odd,' said Margaret, 'but surely the local police don't announce their arrival by hooting like an owl?'

Fox chuckled. 'Maybe they do in Middlesex. But if anything is weighing on Sir Broderick then he's covering it up well. I wouldn't have credited him with that sort of imagination.'

'Maybe it was just a neighbour and we were being ridiculous.'

'You're probably right. I'm seeing miscreants in the countryside because I ought to be in London hunting one down before she does any damage.'

'What's her name?'

'She called herself Molly Malone, which was obviously nonsense, but we'll be asking for Dervla Mallowan, which we established is almost certainly her real name. We don't know whether she's going by that, Molly Malone, a combination or something else entirely. But we'll find her.'

Nine

Back at home, after playing with the children, Margaret and Fox contemplated lunch. According to Vera it was boiled beef and cabbage, but it appeared to consist of a disintegrating portion of an Egyptian mummy's buttock, accompanied by a mound of its bandages mixed with wallpaper paste. Even Juniper sniffed the air with disdain, disinclined to emerge and beg for leftovers.

When the telephone rang Fox answered it with relief, returning a few moments later to announce in apologetic tones (though not expression) that he was needed at the office an hour earlier than expected. 'I can't say I'm sorry about lunch.'

'You bloody traitor,' Margaret replied. Even the usual frisson of worry she still felt when Fox was on a mission was tempered by resentment.

'Language, dear,' he murmured, kissing her goodbye.

Vera appeared shortly after his departure to see how she was getting on. Margaret expected her face to cloud with disappointment at the uneaten food, but instead it broadened into a smile. 'Never mind, madam,' she said, clearing the plates away. 'I can turn it into cottage pie. Shall I bring some ginger biscuits and tea?'

'Yes, please.'

'Then you can go and have a nice lie down.' Vera winked.

It wasn't until Vera had gone that Margaret realised she thought another baby was on the way. She grimaced. As if two weren't enough. Her stomach rumbled.

Juniper slunk from under the sideboard and jumped on her lap, settling into a hard disgruntled crouch and glaring up with a clear message in her topaz eyes: 'Don't you dare go anywhere ever again.'

Margaret stroked Juniper's head, the sleek, soft fur as comforting as ever, but felt pinned down by the cat's hard little paws.

An image of herself and Maude galloping in the countryside came into her head – no hats, hair streaming, the thud of the hooves beating into her heart... In the image they were eighteen again. No husbands, no children, no servants to manage, no causes to die for, and adventure just waiting over the horizon.

Those days had gone, but she couldn't moulder at home all afternoon. She'd walk to Katherine's, meeting her sister around halfway at Speaker's Corner in Hyde Park: something they often did.

'It's the day of rest, ma'am,' said Vera when she came off the telephone to Katherine. 'You should be resting.'

Margaret ignored her. 'Ask Nellie to pack what I need for the children. You two have a lovely afternoon. Eat as much as you like of the beef. For supper, the master and I would like plain, simple cheese on toast. That would be absolutely perfect.'

'If you insist, ma'am,' said Vera, turning to go. Under her breath she could be heard muttering 'Waste of my skills' but Margaret didn't care.

***

It took no time to get to Speaker's Corner. Rocked in the perambulator by Margaret's brisk walking, the twins babbled under the veil which shielded them from the sun, Edie's head tucked into Alec's shoulder.

There were four speakers on upturned boxes, their voices and messages criss-crossing. Most of the milling observers were mellow, enjoying a little after-lunch entertainment. A few, fresh from some nearby public house, jeered at intervals. Journalists with cameras and notebooks were dotted about, some climbing onto fences and benches, waiting for something to happen. Turning towards the heavy clump of feet in the near distance, Margaret realised what. Hundreds of marchers were approaching with banners held high. They must be the striking garment workers.

Something about the back of a tall man standing nearby seemed familiar. He turned and as he did so spotted Margaret. It was the desk clerk, Darnell. He paused for the briefest of moments, then came forward to greet her, tipping his hat. 'Good afternoon, doctor. It's the wrong day for the WSPU.'

'I know. I'm just having a stroll.'

'Ah. I fancied listening to a bit of tub-thumping.'

Margaret smiled politely.

'You missed a busy time yesterday,' he said, lighting a cigarette and belatedly offering her one, which she refused. 'Dr Jordan had another police case to manage. Never mind.' He looked down at the perambulator. 'A mother can't be everywhere.'

'Tricky case?' Margaret chose to disregard his snideness.

Darnell shrugged. 'I'm just the clerk. Shall we see you tomorrow?'

'We shall,' said Margaret.

'I'm not waiting for the tailors. They should get on with their work: I have a bespoke suit on order. Good afternoon, doctor.' Darnell tipped his hat again and joined a straggle of people heading towards Marble Arch. If he wanted her to think he lived in Mayfair and bought his suits from Saville Row, he was more of a fool than Margaret had previously thought.

She realised the twins would be scared by the noise, and in the gathering crowd she and Katherine might miss each other. A group of inebriated men barged past, bumping the pram without apology and also, it seemed, two of journalists who had their backs to Margaret. One was a youth standing so as to slightly obscure a thicker-set companion, though she could tell from the older man's stance that he had been looking down the viewfinder of a camera towards the marchers. He lifted his head to curse as the camera nearly slipped from his hands.

'No knocks?' said the youth.

'Not yet.'

The younger man lit a cigarette. 'Oughta be in the country.'

'He wants me here.' The older man bent his head towards the marchers. 'Makes sense. Shouldn't you be flushing out a lair?'

'Don't know where it is yet.'

'The scent will get picked up. That's hunting for you.'

The younger man rolled his shoulders. 'I quite like foxes.'

'More fool you.'

'Is that him over there?'

Margaret instinctively looked where he pointed, her heart thudding, but apart from Darnell, pausing after all to watch the tailors advance and a man who briefly looked familiar and then after a moment's reflection didn't at all, she saw no one she recognised.

'There you are, Meg!' Katherine was at her side.

The crowd had started to bustle, nudging the pram. The marchers' rhythmic cries for justice were louder. The twins' happy burbling stopped and Margaret lifted the veil to reassure them. Scared little eyes stared up. If Margaret and Katherine didn't leave soon, the children would be screaming and they'd have to fight their way through a crowd to get anywhere.

'Let's go.' Margaret wheeled the pram forward. She was being absurd. The older photographer was tasked to report on the main story of the day, the younger man evidently lumbered with the perennial argument about fox hunting. Yet somehow her bones felt chilled. She turned to look for the men again, but the crowd had absorbed them.

***

Before eight the following morning Margaret was already running behind. Fox had come home despondent the previous evening, Dervla Mallowan's trail stone cold. It seemed pointless mentioning the journalists, but it was hard to stop her mind going in circles. She was so distracted when she arrived at St Julia's that she almost missed Anna, who was waiting nearby again.

'How's Fox?'

The question jolted Margaret's nerves. Not 'Did you tell Fox?' or 'What did Fox say?' but 'How's Fox?' The simple answer was: 'Fraught', but that was none of Anna's business.

'I told him about your concerns,' was all she could think of to say. 'If I'd had your address, I'd have written to say he's not interested in Mr Kavanagh.'

'Silvermann's still sniffing about.'

'I think he wants to ask Mr Kavanagh about supplies.'

'The stuff he sells to Sullivan's? Bits and bobs for ladies with spare money to match their outfits? He should be more worried about what happens next. And maybe Fox should. If Kavanagh was arguing with Abram about anything that night, he was telling him to stay home.'

Margaret's senses tingled. She waited to see if Anna would elaborate, but she didn't. 'I have to go,' she said. 'I'm late for work. I hope—'

'I gotta go back to Affpuddle Street,' said Anna.

'Still striking?'

'Of course, though today I'm negotiating.' Anna turned to leave, then paused. 'I work for a dressmaker in Islington and I was getting somewhere. Ellen's got me doing designs, even the embroidery trim. Every time anyone orders one, I get a fee. Only—'

'Hopefully you will again soon,' said Margaret, looking at her watch and wincing. 'Take care, Anna. Maybe tell Mr Kavanagh to explain to Inspector Silvermann.'

'Last time I saw Kavanagh, he said maybe Fox was the one who ought to look out.'

'Is that a threat?'

'Not from Kavanagh,' said Anna. 'See you round.'

Margaret entered the mortuary wing ten minutes late. It was impossible not to sense a hovering heavy mood.

Almost-tangible emotions often stalked the hospital when the staff had been unable to prevent something tragic. Shared shock, anger and grief formed an entity as dense as fog yet as invisible as oxygen. But the emotion Margaret sensed was neither grief, nor shock, nor misery, nor anger. It was pity. And it seemed directed at her. Every member of staff gave her a nervous smile before rushing by, but Darnell's expression was a twitching smirk.

'Inspector Silvermann's back,' he said, before she could ask anything. 'I put him in your room.'

'On what authority did you do that, Darnell?'

'Where would you have me put him? In the cold room with the corpses?' His stare was defiant, but she could outstare him.

'I think you mean "I'm sorry, Dr Demeray. I should have asked him to wait out here, or leave a message and come back when invited. I won't do it again."'

There was a cold silence. Darnell dropped his gaze, took a deep breath and looked up again. 'I apologise, doctor. I assumed you'd rather get his visit over with, especially given what's happened.'

'What *has* happened?' Margaret snapped.

Darnell handed her a London newspaper. 'I assumed you'd seen.'

'I haven't had time to buy a paper.' The headlines gave no clue. They were what she'd have expected: the strike, news from Berlin and Paris, the Olympics. 'What should I be looking at?'

'Page two.' Darnell shook his head. 'Most unfair, I'm sure. You'll have time to read it before you get to Inspector Silvermann. I'll send in fresh tea.' The smirk reappeared. 'I think you'll need it, doctor.'

Margaret waited till she was out of Darnell's sight before opening the paper.

Chest Hospital for the London Poor: Experiment a Failure

Readers may be unaware that for the last seven years, one of London's charity hospitals has been undertaking police post-mortems. However, two recent post-mortems have raised doubts as to whether correct conclusions have ever been reached.

The first was an enquiry earlier this month into the death of a tailor. It occurred as the strike commenced and the coroner inferred that overwork was a factor, thereby casting blame on the man's employer, even though that employer had not expected him to work that day. This post-mortem was undertaken in unseemly haste.

The second case was brought to the hospital yesterday and in this instance, an entirely different conclusion was reached. A girl was declared the victim of murder on the basis of the flimsiest of evidence. Might an innocent man subsequently be arrested?

Is the hospital making errors?

Readers may also be unaware that alone of all charity hospitals in London, this one employs a married female doctor in a senior position in the pathology department. This vociferous suffragette has undertaken the majority of the post-mortems since 1909.

Even in this modern age, can a married woman, weak from childbirth and burdened with family concerns, undertake such mentally taxing tasks? No wonder serious errors have been made.

Should all post-mortems undertaken at this hospital since 1909 be reviewed? Perhaps the doctor in question should be encouraged to embrace her natural role as wife and mother and abandon pretensions to the responsible role of physician.

The paper shook in her hands. Of all the utter nonsense! Margaret had never undertaken a police post-mortem alone. Dr Jordan had trained her, then they had worked together. As for the two cases mentioned, they had made no public statement that overwork had caused Abram Cohen's death, and she knew nothing about the post-mortem on the girl since she hadn't been involved. Who could have given such an inaccurate, inflammatory report to the newspaper?

Margaret wished she could go and speak with Dr Jordan, but he was visiting St Thomas's and wouldn't be back till eleven. And now she had to face Inspector Silvermann. She refolded the newspaper, took a few calming breaths and entered her office.

Inspector Silvermann sat in the spare chair like a monarch, writing in a notebook.

'Good morning, Inspector,' she said. 'If it's about a post-mortem undertaken yesterday, I'm afraid I wasn't here.'

'I know. I watched Dr Jordan do it myself. Very informative and mostly what we'd suspected. The poor kid's neck had been broken, but it was made to look like she fell downstairs. The body's here. The file's here. I'm surprised Dr Jordan hasn't told you about it.'

'I was delayed coming in.'

'Traffic gets worse every day.' Inspector Silvermann shook his head.

Margaret wished he'd come to the point, or better still, leave, but before she could say so, tea arrived. She laid the newspaper to one side. Inspector Silvermann gave it a cursory glance as she did so, his face unreadable. If he knew what was in it, or worse still, had instigated it, she wouldn't like to play cards with him.

'How may I help you?'

'I wondered why your husband's interested in Kavanagh.'

Margaret's skin prickled. 'My husband?'

'Come now, doctor. Special Branch deigns to speak with the lowly Met occasionally, especially when they want to poke their snouts into other people's investigations. I know what your husband does.'

'If you know what he does, you know he'll keep his own counsel,' said Margaret. 'If you want to know what he thinks, why not ask him directly? It has nothing whatsoever to do with me, although of course I will help with anything that I am qualified for.'

'You mean post-mortems.'

'Yes,' she said. *If anyone will ever let me do one again.*

'What's in that paper?' said Inspector Silvermann. 'You've been giving it the evil eye ever since you put it down.' He snatched it up before she could stop him. 'Is it a report on the girl we brought here yesterday? Ah, here it...'

Margaret felt her face burn as he read, his frown deepening, until he slammed the paper down. 'Good God Almighty! You shouldn't expect anything else from this rag.'

'I thought you might agree with them about me.'

The inspector scowled. 'There's a difference between objecting to your suffragette views, Dr Demeray, and thinking you're incompetent in your job. Don't let this pile of manure trouble you.'

'How would you feel?'

'I'd frame that article and stick it on the wall to show the world how little it bothered me. Then I'd get another copy, stick it to a dartboard inside my cupboard door, and do a bit of darts practice on the days when it did. Always remember: if today's newspaper isn't wrapping fish and chips by tomorrow, it'll be in squares in the privy.'

Margaret's mouth twitched into a half-smile. 'That's sound advice, Inspector Silvermann, but I'm still no clearer as to why you're here. You could have asked about my husband over the telephone.'

'That would be unsubtle.'

You mean you wanted to see my reaction, she thought. 'I'm glad you've arrested someone for the girl's murder.'

'I haven't, regardless of what this bum-wipe of a paper says. Yet.'

'When you say girl, how old was she? Fifteen? Twelve? Younger?' An image of Edie's bright smiling face came into Margaret's mind and she felt nauseous.

'Not a baby, surely? And can't you give her a name when you speak of her?'

'She was a maid aged twenty-two who went by the name of Olive Nolan. Neck snapped like a twig. What's interesting is that she left her job then came back to be murdered, which is odd. Even odder is that the agency who sent her don't recognise a sketch of her face. So far, so peculiar. But what's more interesting is that in her otherwise extremely anonymous things was a scribbled note saying *Moore's dead because he knew who really killed Gastrell. Watch your neck. There's no mercy in either an old soldier or a fox*. Mean anything to you, doctor? Do you know who Moore is, or what it means about the fox? Or should I ask your husband about that too?'

'Please do,' said Margaret. 'I'm sure he'd be delighted to help.' She kept her hand steady as she sipped her tea, so he wouldn't know how appalled she felt.

They had been wrong to ignore what Mr Moore had said. Totally wrong.

Ten

Margaret accompanied the inspector to the main door.

Darnell watched them pass with blatant curiosity, pen poised over the ledger, and only lost interest when she returned to enter the laboratory.

Cyril was at the end of the bench, looking at his notes. He blinked like someone coming out of a dream, then smiled.

'Can you set up, please,' said Margaret. 'We have two lungs to dissect and compare. I'll see if Dr Jordan has left any instructions in his room.'

Margaret couldn't telephone Fox's office from the desk without sending Darnell on some meaningless errand. Darnell wasn't like his predecessor Mr Holness, who'd buy cakes for everyone on the slimmest pretext as long as Margaret was paying. Darnell thought fetching and carrying was beneath him. And she couldn't, having arrived late, go out and send a telegram.

In Dr Jordan's office, she found the file on Olive Nolan, lifted the telephone receiver and gave the number for Fox's office. She waited for one of Fox's colleagues – Elinor Edwards, perhaps – to answer the call. Instead it was Fox himself.

'An item has come to light which might interest you,' she said. 'You, personally.'

'Is that so?' he answered.

'I wondered if we could —'

'Where is the item?'

'Here.'

'In what condition?'

Margaret looked down at the file, labelled *Property of St Julia's Hospital Mortuary Wing*. 'Rather cold.'

'No longer working?'

'No.'

'But recognisable?'

Margaret paused. 'Apparently an interested party didn't know it from a sketch.'

She heard a sharp intake of breath and her mind, until now focussed only on the inspector's potential threat, realised what she'd said.

Why hadn't the agency recognised Olive from the sketch? Even if Olive's murder had been covered up by pushing her downstairs, there would surely be little major damage to her face. 'I'm seeing if there's a photograph... No, just a sketch.' It showed the corpse from the shoulders up and was presumably a copy of what the agency had been shown, with a note of height and build. The bruising up to her chin, just visible along the edge of the sheet which had been pulled up to cover it, and the marks on her face were in stark contrast to the whiteness of the woman's skin. Her hair had been sketched to suggest fairness. Her face was narrow, her nose pointy, her cheekbones like blades, her upper teeth protruding through parted lips. Her staring eyes had been drawn open, but looked both dead and angry. She looked a little like a blonde rodent. 'It's sharp, small and ... golden.'

'Interesting.'

Margaret frowned, looking down at the dead face in the photograph and wondering what Fox meant. 'Will you send someone?'

'Later. Thank you. Goodbye.' The line went dead.

Margaret glanced at the door, closed the file, then wrote Dr Jordan a note and looked at her watch. Before she had to return to Cyril's tuition, there was just enough time to visit the area of the wing where they kept bodies awaiting collection by an undertaker.

It took moments to look at Olive's waxy face. It was barely scratched.

'Everything as it should be with the body?' said Darnell as she returned to the laboratory.

'Perfectly,' she replied.

'You're content with everything that's been done?'

'Of course I am.'

'Excellent,' said Darnell.

'If anyone arrives to see me or Dr Jordan, please let me know.'

'Of course. But I'll keep them firmly out of your offices till you say otherwise.'

'Good.'

It was hard to concentrate on teaching. She and Cyril, with a pair of lungs each, started work, but Cyril rushed and made so few observations that after ninety minutes Margaret snapped, 'It's not a race to the finish. What is the whole point of this exercise?'

'Marks.'

'If you persist in that attitude I shall stop giving you extra tuition,' said Margaret. 'It's to see what we can learn about what killed these two people, so that one day a similar death can be prevented. That's assuming I don't kill you first.'

'Yes, doctor.'

She sighed. 'I need to see if Dr Jordan has returned, but I don't trust you to work alone without slicing your fingers off. Go and have some tea and come back after thirty minutes in a more clinical frame of mind, please. Then we'll take it in turns to work and take notes for each other.'

'Yes, doctor,' said Cyril. He looked down for a while, then said, 'That article in the paper is so unfair, Dr Demeray. I'm proud to be here, and proud of you and Dr Jordan too.'

'Thank you,' said Margaret, managing a smile. 'I appreciate that.'

Dr Jordan was on the telephone when she arrived in his office, the newspaper open in front of him, his usually kindly face dark with an anger she'd never seen before. 'Of course there's no foundation in fact,' he snapped. 'Every single piece of work undertaken here has been completed with due process, proper record keeping and no complaints from anyone. On the rare occasion that second opinions have been requested, nothing has been found to contradict our findings... I have absolute faith in her, as I have said as often as possible, and—' He spotted Margaret and waved her to sit down. 'This is a piece of utter fiction. The only accurate fact is that we have a senior female doctor here. We undertake post-mortems in pairs. If either Dr Demeray or I are absent, another doctor assists... Whoever wrote this article could be prosecuted for libel if they'd named the hospital... Someone must investigate to see if this originated from within the staff, although I can't think of anyone who would do such a thing. Please pass that on to the rest of the board. Good day.'

He slammed the telephone receiver into its cradle, screwed the newspaper up into a ball and threw it in the general direction of a wastepaper bin, which it missed entirely. Before he could speak, Darnell put his head around the door. 'Dr Jordan, there—'

'Get us some tea.'

'But I—'

'If it's beneath you, Darnell, ask someone else to get it. We want tea.' Dr Jordan slammed his fist on the desk.

'Yes, sir.' Darnell withdrew.

Margaret had never seen Dr Jordan so angry nor so rude. She had no idea what to say.

'I'm very sorry, my dear,' he said, after an awkward pause. 'It's quite appalling. Not to mention pointless. What do they expect to gain?'

Margaret explained Inspector Silvermann's views on what it would be used for the next day. The flush in Dr Jordan's face receded a little and a smile flickered.

'The privy's the place. It's not fit to wrap good fried fish.' He ran his finger round his collar and sat back. 'Did you want to discuss it further?'

'No,' said Margaret. 'I'm interested in the post-mortem. Not because I wasn't here, but to see why they've raised a doubt about it. Inspector Silvermann seems content that it's murder.'

'It was,' said Dr Jordan. 'Very little effort had been made to make it appear otherwise. Her neck had been broken with great efficiency, possibly from behind. There is bruising on her jaw which looks like hand marks. They may have twisted her head.'

'No sign of a struggle? Even someone highly skilled in doing that sort of thing would meet with resistance. If someone grabbed you from behind, even unexpectedly, and grabbed your chin, the first thing you'd do is tense your neck muscles. The victim might have time to put up a fight.'

'She might have been rendered partially unconscious through a blow to the temple, but there are no defensive marks on her arms, nor tissue under her fingernails.'

'And the alternative if it wasn't murder?'

'She was found at the bottom of a steep back staircase with uneven treads and poor lighting, the kind they tell householders to replace because they're death traps.'

'But if she'd tripped or slipped and then fallen…'

'There would be injuries from her efforts to stop herself: a sprained or broken ankle, a wrenched wrist or grazed hand. Yet there are none.'

The door opened and an orderly came in with a tea tray and an envelope. His expression was thunderous. 'Here you go, doctors, as ordered by *Mr* Darnell. And here's a letter for you, Dr Jordan.'

'Thank you very much,' said Dr Jordan, mollifying the man with a kind smile, then turning to the envelope. 'Ah, excellent. The photographs have been developed.' He spread them on the desk for Margaret to see.

The first photograph showed Olive at the bottom of a staircase, lying as if she'd decided to have a little sleep. It was dark and hard to make everything out clearly, but no marks could be seen on the walls. There was another of her on the slab in the mortuary wing, fully dressed, then another naked – a short young woman, slender to the point of boniness – then various photographs of her face, neck and arms.

The orderly returned. 'Mr Darnell wants you to know you've a visitor called Superintendent, er … Foxy-McScone? Something Scotch, anyway.'

'Foxcroft-McSionnach?' said Margaret, surprised.

'That's the geezer.'

'Send him in,' said Dr Jordan. 'And we'd like another teacup.'

Margaret was perplexed. While they knew the Jordans socially, Fox had only ever come to the mortuary wing twice: the first time in disguise, the second only seen by the clerk who'd preceded Darnell. As much as they could, Fox and Margaret kept their work publicly detached.

Now he was ushered into the room and bowed to Margaret as if they were strangers.

'Er … good morning,' she said.

'Good morning,' said Fox. He turned to Dr Jordan. 'I'm here on police business, sir, therefore I'll address Margaret professionally.'

'Oh, I quite understand. Keep it all separate. How can we help you?'

'I believe you have a body of interest to me. May I see a depiction before I see her in the flesh? Perhaps I could compare it with this one.'

He handed Margaret a small picture frame. Inside was a photograph of a young woman, small, blonde and slender. Her face was broad, with a button nose and a wide mouth. Despite the formality of the pose, she looked as if she knew a saucy secret and was about to burst into laughter.

'Who is this?' said Margaret.

'It's a photograph of Olive Nolan on her twenty-first birthday. This woman,' Fox held up the file photograph, 'is someone else entirely.'

'Goodness me,' said Dr Jordan. 'But when the police brought her, they expressly said she was a maid called Olive Nolan.'

'Who identified her?'

Dr Jordan shrugged. 'I have no idea. Presumably someone from the household, but I didn't ask.' He compared the photographs. 'They're not dissimilar, but they're not so alike you can't distinguish them.'

'They're quite different,' said Fox. 'Olive's parents thought their daughter was in Halifax with a theatrical troupe. Hopefully she still is, because the woman you have here is someone my men have been looking for. A criminal. How did she die?'

Dr Jordan summarised as he had for Margaret and added 'It seemed like, if I might be fanciful, an assassination.'

'I believe Inspector Silvermann thinks so too,' said Margaret.

'Mmm,' said Fox. His expression was grim.

'Perhaps you ought to view the body so that you can see for yourself,' said Dr Jordan. 'They say the camera never lies, but that's nonsense. All the same, I'd put money on these being different women.'

'Yes,' said Fox. 'After you, doctors.'

'Certainly,' said Dr Jordan, opening the door for Margaret.

'After you, sir,' she said, once they were through. Before they turned into the main corridor she whispered quickly to Fox. 'Anna was here and says Kavanagh thinks you're in danger. Inspector Silvermann was here, too. The maid had a note in her pocket referring to Moore, Gastrell and maybe you. I've written down what he said. Here.' She slipped a piece of paper into his hand.

Fox's stride slowed and his scowl deepened. 'I see.'

'He hinted that he suspects you're connected.'

'Well, I am.' More loudly, he said. 'Thank you for doing this at such short notice, doctors. Which way now?'

They followed Dr Jordan along the corridor and entered the cold room. The orderly mopping the floor looked up in surprise. 'Is there another? It's like Clapham Junction in 'ere these days. One in, one out. We'll have to expand, that's all. Get tracks and junctions and signal boxes for the stretchers.' He gave a wheezy laugh.

'There's no one new,' said Dr Jordan. 'I just need to let this gentleman see Olive Nolan.' He looked around. The area was clear and pristine, the air a sickening mixture of carbolic, Jeyes fluid and lilies. 'Where is she?'

'Gorn.'

'Gorn? I mean, gone where?'

'She's been took.'

'Who by?'

'The undertaker, acourse.'

'Why?'

The orderly gripped the mop. 'I don't argue with people with paperwork. It said they 'ad aufority to take 'er.'

'Whose authority? Where's the paperwork?'

'Dunno. Ask Darnell, 'e's the quill-driver. He brung 'em in and took the paperwork away while they took 'er out through the undertaker's bay into a van.'

'What's happened?' growled Dr Jordan as they left. 'The police haven't said they're happy for the body to be released. Darnell's arrogant and officious, but he's competent. It's unlike him to make a mistake.'

They approached the desk and Darnell, busy paying the telegram boy, looked up in surprise. 'Is anything wrong, sir?'

'Why has Olive Nolan's body been released to the undertaker?'

'Because they came for it.'

'I realise that, but on whose authority was it released?'

Darnell looked nonplussed. 'Dr Demeray's.'

Eleven

Fox and Dr Jordan turned to stare at Margaret.

'I did no such thing!' she exclaimed.

'Inspector Silvermann telephoned to say he was content with the post-mortem,' said Darnell, picking up a piece of paper. 'And said that if you doctors were too, someone would be collecting the body. I asked if *you* were content, and you said yes.'

'I didn't say I was content about releasing the body!'

'How was I supposed to know?'

'By asking a direct question,' snapped Margaret. '"Are you happy for the body to be released, doctor?", not "Are you content with what's been done?" I thought you were talking about the post-mortem.'

'Here's the form.' Darnell handed over a typed letter with the Metropolitan Police crest at the top. A signature which could be made out as 'Inspector E Silvermann N Division' requested the release of Olive Nolan's body to the undertaker.

'Who was the undertaker?' said Fox. 'It's not on this letter. We need to get word to them urgently.'

Darnell glanced towards Dr Jordan.

'Answer the man.'

'I'm not sure, sir,' he said, opening a small drawer and flicking back and forth through a series of cards with agitated fingers. 'They looked like undertakers and they had the letter. They gave me a card, but all I recall is a black rose on the corner… Ah, here it is. "N. Bythesea and Sons, Paradise Road, Islington, N1".'

'Is there a telephone number?' said Fox.

Once again Darnell looked to Dr Jordan for instruction and seeing his exasperated expression handed the card to Fox. 'It's Islington, sir. How many clients will have a telephone to call them with?'

'Darnell!' snapped Dr Jordan. 'Please speak to the superintendent with a little more respect. You released a body without explicit permission from either me or Dr Demeray and you seem blissfully indifferent about it.'

'I'm sorry, sir. *Sirs.* I didn't realise I was doing anything wrong.'

'Damn,' said Fox, turning the card over to find its reverse blank. 'It's probably quicker for me to drive than send a telegram but I'll do both and have my sergeant visit Inspector Silvermann. Thank you, doctors. Thank you, Mr Darnell. I'll see myself out.' With a mere tip of his hat to Margaret, Fox strode away.

'What a nightmare,' said Dr Jordan. 'I'll telephone Inspector Silvermann too: I fear this could add fuel to that vile newspaper's fire. However, if this is reported, at least this time it'll be the clerical rather than the medical team who'll get the blame and we'll know who's responsible. Knowing the pride the *other* clerks have for their work, Darnell, I'd have a cold compress ready for the inevitable black eye.'

'But sir—'

'I see Cyril returning to the laboratory, Dr Demeray. I'll call the police station.' He turned his attention back to Darnell. 'Then I shall ask the hospital's chief clerk to remind his staff of their responsibilities if they wish to retain their positions.'

'B-but I—' sputtered Darnell.

'I have nothing further to add. We must all now get on with our work.'

***

At lunchtime, Margaret sat in her usual café, wondering if Fox would come and find her. He didn't. She thought back to what Anna had said and wondered how she would ever get her address to ask more about what Kavanagh had meant.

It seemed harder to concentrate these days. A few months ago she wouldn't have needed to dig around in her mind for clues. Was it motherhood? All the broken nights' sleep and the underlying worry? Maude seemed sharp as a tack. Maybe it wore off in time.

Pull yourself together, woman, she chided herself. *She said she works for an Islington dressmaker. Ellen Affpuddle? No: she referred to the business as Ellen's and later said Affpuddle Street. And the items have embroidered trim. That's not cheap. Maybe she could identify the design Lucy copied. Ellen must advertise in a local paper, which won't be hard to get.*

Margaret returned to the hospital wing fifteen minutes early and Darnell acknowledged her with a polite greeting, his face pale but still smug. If she had anything to do with it, the man would be made to work for Matron, who'd offer to wipe that expression off with a scourer.

As she was packing up after teaching a class of female first-year students, Darnell entered the room. 'There's a telegram at the desk for you, Dr Demeray. And Dr Jordan had a telephone call from the police station to say that the matter was in hand.' That explained it. He was no longer truculent because the situation was, to some extent, resolved.

'What a relief.'

'Yes. That superintendent seemed a tricky sort.'

Margaret glanced at him, but it appeared to be a simple statement of his view. 'He did, rather,' she said.

At the desk, Margaret took the telegram from the delivery boy.

It's been too long. No tea, bad wine, good beer, as soon after five as free. Cave ne canem neque anatem. F.

Margaret scrabbled in her memory for Latin that wasn't related to medicine. *Canem* ... *canis* meant dog. That was easy. *Cave Canem* – beware of the dog. *Cave ne canem* – don't beware the dog. *Anatem* must decline from *anatis* but she couldn't recall what it meant. Bad wine, good beer? A pub. The Dog and Duck. *Anatis* must mean duck.

'Any reply, madam?' said the boy.

Margaret looked at the clock. It was ten past five. 'No, thank you.' She folded the telegram, went to obtain Dr Jordan's permission to leave early, then collected her things from her own office.

'Goodbye, Darnell,' she said as she passed. 'I'll see you on Wednesday.'

'Doctor, I apologise for the way I've been today. I have things on my mind. It's hard to talk about, but perhaps if you knew...' His gaze lowered and he twisted the pen in his hands.

Margaret donned her gloves. 'You don't have to explain. I accept your apology.' She stopped herself from adding *this time*.

'No, really, you ought to know. I, er... I wasn't meant to be a clerk. My family had money. I didn't think I'd ever have to work for a living.'

'There's nothing to be ashamed of,' said Margaret, feeling irritated. 'It's more honourable than idling about.'

'My brother went abroad to set things up for us to start again. Only he ... the *Titanic*. Every day I look in the newspapers, just in case they've ... he's...'

'Oh my goodness, Darnell! I had no idea. I'm so sorry.' Margaret felt mortified. Why had no one mentioned this?

Darnell said nothing, his head still bowed.

'I really am sorry. That must be a terrible thing to bear.'

'When one cannot express them, grief and disappointed hope emerge in funny ways,' he muttered. 'In my case, apparently, rudeness. Once more, I apologise for not behaving like a gentleman and for my errors of judgment.'

'And I once more accept it. Let's shake hands and put today behind us, Darnell.'

She reached over the top of the desk, and he took her hand. His grip was stronger than she'd expected, her fingers squeezed hard enough for her knuckles to crunch against each other. The words *snapped like a twig* came unbidden into her mind. Darnell let go with an apologetic smile. It would be fruitless and unkind to say that she hoped he'd hear good news. There was no possibility that any more survivors would be found, even so soon after the ship had sunk. 'Well, goodbye,' she said, feeling inadequate. 'I'll see you on Wednesday.'

Sensing his gaze on her back, she left the building and flagged down a cab.

It was nearly two years since she'd last been inside the Dog and Duck, but it hadn't changed and nor had its clientele. It was still as dark and smoky, the walls half panelled and half papered in a dark green, the wallpaper stained by decades of tobacco and coal smoke. Light reflected from a long, sparkling mirror behind the bar through the bottles of spirits and onto the gleaming pump handles. The men in their well-tailored city outfits watched warily as she passed through, wondering if she was a wife or mistress about to disturb the peace of their sanctuary, or something even less desirable. The barman and barmaid also watched her progress.

She walked behind a pillar and spotted Fox in a booth with a dark leather bench. He was nursing a pint of beer and had a notebook open in front of him., the page blank. A glass of something pale and clear with slices of lemon in it waited nearby.

'Hello, Fox. Fancy meeting you here.'

He looked up. 'I wasn't sure if your Latin was up to it.'

'It isn't,' she said, taking her seat. 'But my deductive skills are.'

'Mmm.' He squeezed her hand gently but didn't kiss her. That probably marked her out as a wife if nothing else did, and since she didn't seem angry, the attention of the other clientele faded. 'I bought you a very weak gin sling and promised the landlord you'd behave. He decided it was worse for his reputation to serve a drink without alcohol than to serve a woman.' There was a shadow of a smile. It seemed longer than two years since she'd braved meeting him here and been faced with jaw-achingly acidic hock.

'What would you have done if I hadn't turned up?'

'Drunk it myself, probably.'

She took a sip of the gin sling. It was almost entirely lemonade, the gin a mere hint of juniper. 'If you want to drown sorrows, this won't help. I shan't be carousing.'

'Good. We don't need any attention.'

'Then why ask me to meet you in a pub?'

'Neutrality. And I wanted a beer and no fuss.'

'I told you what Anna said. It's occurred to me that she might be able to identify the dressmaker who sold that embroidered jacket. I've bought the *Islington Gazette* to wade through and find her.'

'Excellent.' Fox clinked glasses with her, but otherwise seemed downcast.

'At least you know Dervla Mallowan is no longer at large,' said Margaret. 'She must have been mistaken for this Olive Nolan and it's up to the police to solve that. We just need to find out—'

'I'm every bit as interested in finding Olive as the police are. Did she swap places with Dervla voluntarily, or was something else afoot? Was the note in the pocket of the maid's apron meant for Olive, Dervla, or put there to confuse? Now I have to find Dervla again, and she can't even tell me anything.'

'She's at the undertakers. Byther-whatever they're called.'

'There's no Paradise Road in Islington and no such undertaker either.'

'But—'

'Inspector Silvermann didn't sign that letter, nor would he have made a request for release of the body without speaking directly with Dr Jordan first and sending a man to oversee.'

Margaret sat back, aghast. 'I don't understand. Did her colleagues steal it so she wouldn't get a criminal's burial?'

'Only someone highly trained could have killed her so cleanly and efficiently. She'd barely have known what was happening. But it doesn't seem the sort of thing Fenians would do. If they'd found her, they'd be more likely to get her away. Unless they killed her because they thought she was a traitor, in which case why worry about her burial? It's something else.'

'To do with Norris Gastrell.'

'It seems that way.' Fox drank some beer and made little marks on the blank page with his pencil. They looked like tiny explosions. 'And that turns the attention on me.'

'Yes, but why? That's what I don't understand. He died ten years ago.'

'What if the treachery he started had continued? And Dervla was involved, and someone wants the police to think I'm responsible for her death too.'

'You wouldn't kill anyone like that!' Margaret put her hand on his. 'You wouldn't attack someone from behind.'

Fox pulled his hand away. 'You forget what my job is, Margaret. If I had to, I could. And I have men working for me who could do it too.'

'You wanted Dervla brought to trial and given the chance to defend herself. You wouldn't kill her, then leave her body like a discarded glove. That's not the kind of man you are.'

'Aren't I?' said Fox, downing the remainder of his beer. 'Inspector Silvermann thinks I am.'

'On what evidence?'

'I don't think he's got it yet, but he clearly believes it's within his grasp. And by God, I intend to find it first.'

She put her hand over his again, and this time didn't let it slip away. 'We,' she said. '*We* will.'

'You can't—'

'We've had this out before, Fox. I can't just carry on as if nothing's threatening us.'

'You have to carry on as you intended to.'

'But—'

'Listen to me.' Fox squeezed her hand gently. 'I said "carry on as you intended to", not "carry on as if nothing's wrong". The inspector's scrutiny needs to move away from you. But you can look at things from a different angle, and help that way. Olive worked for a household near Tufnell Park. Her employer's been away and says he knows nothing, but the tweeny was there and might. She won't talk to a policeman, but she might to a nice lady doctor. Do you fancy doing that? It worked before. And as you say, Anna might be able to identify the woman in the jacket.'

Margaret pondered, her eyes scanning the dark, masculine room, with its deep thrum of male voices, the smells of tobacco, smoke and beer, the sparkle on the bottles and mirror, the lawyers, clerks and businessmen sharing jokes and looking at papers as they discussed politics or sport. 'I'll talk to the tweeny. And if I can find out where Anna works, then maybe I can find the woman myself and not risk compromising her.'

Fox drew a house on the blank page, with four dots inside and a circle round it, then closed the notebook, picked up his newspaper and stood up. 'Come on,' he said, 'let's go home. No one's going to arrest me if I can help it, and certainly not tonight. We have better things to do.'

Twelve

Margaret dreamed. She was four, sitting with her family in a church pew with a little door on the end. Some Sundays she pretended they were in a toy box, being good toys. Today, she just wanted to get up and run around. To do something.

The vicar was speaking in his comforting, familiar, droning rhythm. Margaret knew from the lulls and pauses, from the high and lower pitched words, that he was nearly at the end. Soon she'd be on her feet singing, unable to see anything but the wooden ledge where she'd put her penny ready for the collection.

Kitty's penny didn't shine like hers. She didn't want Kitty to swap. Margaret reached for it. Kitty whispered 'Meg! Sit still!' and pinched her.

Margaret slipped, banging her head and knocking the penny to the floor. Then she was in Mother's lap, snuggled against a soft rabbit-fur collar. 'Shh, shh, don't cry. It'll be all right.' She buried herself in the fur and reached out to stroke the copper-coloured ringlets that lay on her mother's chest, hearing the steady thump, thump of her heart...

She woke from the dream, her head on Fox's warm chest, hearing the steady thump, thump of his heart. He was stroking her shoulder idly. Light filtered through her eyelids, and outside, sparrows squabbled like barrow boys.

'You're awake,' she murmured, cuddling closer to kiss him.

'You were dreaming. Was it a nice dream?'

'I was very little, in church. Mother was there. I had a shiny penny. Yes, it was nice.'

'A memory?'

Margaret mumbled through a yawn. 'Maybe. Kitty pinched me.'

'Naughty Katherine.' Fox kissed her head. 'Go back to sleep. It's barely five o'clock.'

She lay against him, eyes closed. He continued to stroke her shoulder. His heartbeat was a little fast. The tethers to her dream started to loosen, reality coming slowly into focus. She couldn't go back to sleep.

Her own heart started to race, and she held him closer. 'What do you need to do?'

'Trace Dervla's body,' said Fox. 'Find out what connection there is between her and Gastrell. Nothing springs to mind. When he died, he was around thirty-four and she'd have been thirteen. But he wasn't, as far as I can recall, either married or Irish. If he were Irish, I doubt he'd have felt strongly enough either way about Home Rule to put his life on the line for it. Someone else's, maybe. I was certain he was working with another British officer and maybe his colleague built on the connections they'd made after Gastrell's death. Dervla must have worked for him, and when he heard who had arrested her, he decided to have me discredited before I could work out the link.'

'By killing his own agent and putting the blame on you?'

'There was something about her. She was an experienced member of a revolutionary organisation, but you get a feeling for a double agent. Whatever she was prepared to tell us, it wouldn't have been to the detriment of her own cause. I'm sure this was nothing to do with a free Ireland. She was after something else.'

'What?'

'I don't know. But I think they suspected it too and they couldn't risk her telling.' Fox sighed. 'As for you, wouldn't you prefer to keep out of things?'

'No. Have you set things up at Tufnell Park?'

'Mr Webber is expecting you at twelve to explain things on behalf of St Julia's to the tweeny in a suitably girly way.'

'Does Inspector Silvermann know?'

'No.'

'Won't it annoy him if he finds out?'

'Do you care?'

'No.' Margaret looked up at him. 'How did Norris Gastrell end up in the river? Suicide?'

'Accident. He was trying to get away and slipped down the bank.'

'Why was he trying to get away, if it was unlikely there would be a trial?'

'I wasn't going to give up till there was.' Fox's hand had stopped caressing her shoulder. 'Sooner or later, the evidence would have caught up with him.'

'So no one murdered him. How can they implicate you?'

'Because appearing to save someone from drowning could very much be the opposite.' He pulled her closer into his embrace. 'Be careful, Margaret. I don't know if Dervla would have talked: before she could, someone helped her escape and she was murdered. And here am I, a man they deem responsible for Gastrell's death, now potentially responsible for hers. Don't let anyone connect you with me. Don't let anyone know that you know more than you should. Stay safe.'

***

Margaret's plan had been domestic, safe, simple and discreet. She would go to Islington alone first thing to visit Ellen's, then collect the children and spend the day with Katherine, leaving them with her for a short while in the afternoon to visit Mr Webber. But when she left the house at eight, she knew almost immediately that she was being followed.

Of all the men rushing to catch a train it was hard to know which to worry about, but after feigning to post a letter, Margaret returned to the house to think. Half an hour later, she was at the tube station with the baby carriage, determined to draw as much attention as possible.

Mr Edwards, the ticket clerk, was a shy man who took the collection in church most Sundays. He peered over the counter at the pram in surprise. 'I suppose someone's meeting you and taking them while you go on the train, doctor.'

'No, they're coming with me.'

'I'm not sure you can turn a perambulator into the carriage,' he said, the ticket poised on the wrong side of the glass.

'One can but try.'

'They could have stayed home with Vera – Mrs Fender – or Miss Pinter! I mean, you know what's best.' He handed over the ticket.

'One hopes so.'

At the top of the staircase to the platform a kind man, without prompting, lifted the front end of the pram as she bumped the back wheels down the steps, watching the children slide under the covers.

'Just as well you didn't have triplets,' he said at the bottom of the staircase, straightening up and rubbing his back. He strode down the platform without any further sign of being interested in her. None of the other men on the platform showed anything but disapproval of the baby carriage. Except one. A man in a bowler hat who had followed her from the house was consulting his watch and looking irritated. He was as aware of her as she was of him. And she was certain another, unseen follower was nearby.

When the train pulled in, there was the usual bad-tempered dance between the passengers alighting and those embarking. Both sets glared at Margaret. She waited till the flow had reduced and glanced at the man in the bowler. He had entered the train and found a seat. Margaret tipped the pram to get its front wheels onto the step.

In theory, there was plenty of space within the carriage if she could get inside, but the only way in was via a narrow platform attached to the end of the carriage. She could get the pram on the platform, but the angle to get it through the carriage door was too tight. The twins crowed in delight as they bounced and jiggled.

'You're holding up the train, madam!' The guard was alongside, eyeing the endeavour with frustration. 'And you're going to damage the paintwork.'

'You're right,' said Margaret, pulling the pram back onto the station platform. 'Never mind. It was worth a try.'

'There'll be a new design sometime soon, madam,' said the guard. 'You'll be able to get straight in through the side. Maybe wait till then.'

'When will that come in?'

'Not today. Stand clear.' The guard blew his whistle and the train departed. The man in the bowler half-stood, frowning, but made no effort to try to get out before the train entered the tunnel.

'Thought so,' muttered Margaret, as she tugged the pram back up the steps. 'Time for some brisk walking, children, till I find the right-sized cab.'

Katherine was typing in her study when Margaret finally arrived in Marylebone. 'You pinched me in my dream last night,' said Margaret, as they embraced.

'I daresay you deserved it. Were you being late?' Katherine followed her into the hall, then took Edie from the pram and kissed her.

'No,' said Margaret, lifting Alec out and letting the maid wheel the baby carriage off to the garden. 'I'm late because I couldn't take the tube.'

'With the pram? I'm not surprised.'

'I fancied an experiment.'

'And when it failed, why didn't you take a taxi or ask me to collect you?' Katherine led the way to the drawing room and they sat on the sofa.

'It's a nice day. I decided to meander a little,' said Margaret. 'Including visiting a shop full of baby stuff.'

Katherine raised her eyebrows. 'We could have done that together.'

'I was trying to lose the men who were following me.'

'Followed? Here? Who by? Call Fox – I mean the police!'

'No. I just want to behave normally.'

'I'm not sure trying to take a baby carriage on the tube is normal, but I assume you've managed to shake them off?'

'I lost one of them at the station,' said Margaret. 'The other is a stout little man with a thick brown moustache who was puffing like a steam train and sweating like a navvy last time I saw him. He makes me think of the Walrus in *Alice in Wonderland*, only redder and sweatier. I hoped to bore him with my maternal shopping, but though he seemed quite taken with this year's rattles, I think he followed me even after I caught a cab.'

'If you hadn't brought the children,' Katherine pointed out, 'you could have outpaced him ages ago. You should call the police.'

'I don't think he means me physical harm.'

'Then why—'

'And there's a reason I brought the children. It's part of being normal. Have you anything in particular to do today?'

'Yes. Spend it with you.' Katherine's frown deepened. 'What's going through your devious mind? You're not planning to hunt that man down and ju-jitsu him, are you?'

'No. Can you manage the children for me?'

'I thought we were—'

'Just till a little after lunch.'

'Not if you won't tell me what it's about. Why are you being followed? Is this to do with that awful piece in the paper? If I can help…'

Margaret bit her lip. In the twenty-one years that Katherine and her friend Connie had run the Caster and Fleet Detective Agency, Margaret had had nothing to do with it, except when inadvertently caught up in events. Margaret had never asked her sister for more than advice and support. She was reasonably sure the Walrus was one of Inspector Silvermann's men, but to say so to Katherine would bring a million other questions. 'He might be a reporter for that terrible paper, waiting for me to undertake disreputable suffragette activity, so I want to look like a good mother instead.'

'You *are* a good mother. How about being a good little sister?'

'I have to do something first.'

'If you want to put them off the scent, why don't you and I have a proper excursion?'

'We can this afternoon, but I need to speak with someone first. It can't wait, and I can't take the children: it's too far. But...' Margaret busied herself with the twins to avoid her sister's quizzical stare and lifted Alec onto the floor. 'I don't want the Walrus following me. I'm wearing my cycling skirt. If I borrow one of your coats and a boring hat and your bicycle, I can leave the back way.'

'So let me clarify: you want to leave me with the Walrus watching my house, thinking I'm entertaining you, when in fact I'm trapped dealing with your offspring while you gallivant on *my* bicycle,' said Katherine. 'Never mind pinching you in dreams, I'm tempted to do it now.'

Margaret squeezed her sister's hand. 'Please, Kitty. I know it's an imposition. But think of all the times I looked after Ed while you went out to dinner with James.'

'Pfft,' said Katherine. 'You only did it when there wasn't a young man available to take you gallivanting. Why don't you find a policeman and report the Walrus?'

Because he might be a policeman, thought Margaret. *But if he's trailing me, he's not trailing Fox. And the more disconnected I am with the whole situation, the better.* But she couldn't say that. 'I won't be long, I promise.'

'All right,' said Katherine. 'I'll look after your children and let you run footloose and fancy-free, even though you're not telling me the whole truth.' She lifted Edie and stood up. 'You don't have to try and do it all. You'll explode.'

'What are you talking about?'

'You have a nursemaid. The children would be better off with her than with you when you need to do something else. Don't feel you have to look after them and become frustrated.'

'I'm not.'

'You are.'

'You combined your job with caring for Ed when he was a baby.'

'I didn't combine them: they were two separate things. I was happy knowing he was having fun with Gwen or flirting with Ada for biscuits in the kitchen, or making mischief with you, while Connie and I got on with a case. And when I wasn't on a case, I spent as much time with him as I could. It was fun, because both of us were happy. He was surrounded by love, just like you and I were as children.'

'Mother didn't have a job.'

'She ran the house and looked after Father. That's a whole job in itself.'

'I suppose so.'

'If Fox needs your help, let Nellie care for the children, as she does when you're at the hospital. You're paying her to do a job, so let her do it. Then you'll look forward to playing with the children when you've finished.'

'Do you ever stop being right?'

'No. Take care, Meg. I love you.'

'Stop fussing, Kitty. I'm perfectly fine.'

Thirteen

Islington's busy high street was daunting. Margaret, who hadn't ridden a bicycle since early pregnancy, found herself weaving between cars, cabs, delivery boys and pedestrians, feeling vulnerable, forgotten muscles aching for the first time in a year. The Angel Inn stood, grand and imperious, on the corner where Margaret needed to turn. It was so splendid that it made the Dog and Duck look like the Puppy and Egg in comparison, but there was no time to admire it, nor find out where Kavanagh and Abram Cohen had had their argument.

Affpuddle Street was pleasant. After an hour poring through Islington's newspapers, Margaret had established that she wasn't looking for somewhere called Ellen's, as she'd thought, but Helene's: a business with ambition and a French name to suit.

Even if it was off the beaten track, it portrayed West End elegance. The external woodwork was painted cream, the floor of the display window was strewn with paper flowers and bunting hung round the inner frame. A notice said 'Outfits for every budget: bespoke and ready-to-wear'. The dresses on the mannequins were up to the minute and elegant. Those of cheaper fabric had no less style than the richer ones. A jacket on one figure had an embroidered pattern very similar to the one Lucy had drawn from memory. Margaret took it from her bag and compared it, then took a pencil and pretended to sketch in case anyone was watching.

'You won't go wrong with Helene,' said a passing woman. 'Only a few of her staff are striking. She hasn't missed an order so far. She's just carrying on steady.'

Margaret nodded her thanks and entered the shop. It was bright and appealing. A mannequin stood just inside, wearing a dove-grey evening dress and ostrich-feather stole dyed in silver and blue. A stand on the counter bore a matching feathered hat and another displayed a rose toque with a plume dyed in a complementary shade.

A tall woman in grey stood behind the counter. She appeared to be in her mid thirties, with smooth fair hair and a bright, welcoming smile.

'May I speak with Madame Helene?' said Margaret.

'I'm she,' said the woman. 'As you can hear, I'm as French as London Bridge, but people like a name that goes with the job!' She grinned. 'How may I help you?' Her eyes flickered over Margaret's clothes in expert appraisal. 'That's a well-made cycling skirt. I can see you're discerning. What are you interested in?'

'I'm wondering about this,' said Margaret, handing over the piece of paper. 'Someone in the know told me it might be from here, so I came and was delighted to see something almost identical in your window.'

Helene perused Lucy's drawing with a frown. 'It's certainly very like one we sell. Did the owner of the jacket tell you about me?' She looked up, curious.

'I've never met her,' admitted Margaret. 'A friend saw her in … dear me, I've forgotten where. Nowhere near where I live. Somewhere in the West End, I think.' Margaret wondered whether she'd made the right decision not to mention Fulham. She didn't want to drag Lucy into anything.

Helene was looking dubious: she had to press on. 'I said it sounded lovely and wondered how I'd ever find out where it was from, but then I saw your advertisement in the *Gazette* and the bespoke item looked so similar that I thought I'd come along.' Margaret smiled in what she hoped was a benign way and sent a mental apology to her own dressmaker. 'I gather you have good working conditions. Since finding out what's behind the strike, that's become very important to me.'

'Oh, I see.' Helene's face cleared. 'Yes, they're important to me too.'

'Wonderful! Then I'd love to order a summer dress with a similar pattern. Linen, perhaps. Blue on ivory. Would that be possible?

'If you're not in any great rush, it should be,' said Helene. 'In normal circumstances we turn simple outfits round in about a week, more complex ones in two. I won't rush my staff. But those with embroidery take a little longer and, as I'm sure you understand, cost more. And as long as the strike continues, the more delay there will be. I won't push the non-striking staff to do more than they should. An order like this could take a month, as things are.'

Margaret paused as if to consider. 'Yes, that would be all right. Aren't you concerned about how the strike is affecting business?'

Helene shook her head. 'Our orders are steadier than a West End business's. We make good-quality ready-made clothes too, which are becoming more and more popular. Hardly any of what we do is tied to the Season, so we don't lose out in summer. I've never had to lay off a single girl in eight years, and I only have a few striking. I'm in negotiations with one of them about her and her colleagues coming back to work. She's extremely talented: in fact she created this design.'

'What a shame she isn't here to discuss it,' said Margaret, cursing herself for not having shown Anna the design when they'd last met. On the other hand, it was as well they didn't have to pretend not to know each other today.

'I expect she's helping in an East End soup kitchen. She was here yesterday explaining what her colleagues want. Pay remains the main area of discussion.'

Margaret tried to imagine Anna's negotiation techniques and felt glad she wasn't Helene.

The other woman put her head on one side. 'A woman like her could be a good politician if she were allowed. Certainly an improvement on the ones we have.'

'That wouldn't be hard.'

'True. If the potential delay should this strike continue puts you off, I quite understand. I don't charge West End prices, but I'm not cheap. Otherwise, depending on what you want, a bespoke dress as you suggest would cost between five and eight guineas. Would that suit? Off the peg is rather cheaper. It could be altered to fit and ready-made embroidered panels added.'

'I'd like bespoke, please.'

'If you'd like to come into this side room, I'll have someone take measurements and discuss details. Would you like some tea?'

'No, thank you,' said Margaret as she took her seat in a bare, bright room. She didn't need another dress, desirable as it was, but it would seem very odd to leave without a fitting after all the preamble.

'May I take your name?'

Margaret hesitated for less than a second. If the woman who'd ordered the jacket ever heard of her question, it was wise to be cautious. 'Dr Perry,' she said, giving her mother's maiden name on the grounds that it was similar-sounding enough to Demeray that the postman, used to all sorts of variations, would deliver anything necessary.

'A doctor? How interesting. Someone will be with you shortly. It won't take long.'

***

There was a long queue in the street where the soup-kitchen was, mainly made up of little girls with string bags. As each one came out with a can of soup and a lump of unappetising-looking bread, a woman shouted 'Schnorrer!' from a window.

Most of the children ignored her, keeping their eyes downcast. Some made a rude gesture. One little girl burst into tears and ran, the bag banging against her thin legs.

Margaret was allowed through without difficulty and found Anna behind a counter with another woman, filling the children's bags and bestowing on each a smile that transformed her face. The smile changed to astonishment at the sight of Margaret, and she gestured to go outside.

In the street, hearing the woman in the window abuse the children, she rattled off a stream of Yiddish too fast for Margaret to follow. With a final, incomprehensible insult, the woman slammed the window shut.

'What was she shouting?' asked Margaret.

'"Beggar". I said "Who's the beggar? You had to cadge a pot to piss in when you came here from Russia".'

'Did she?'

'Dunno. That's not the point. Who'd you borrow that coat off of? It's so tight I'm scared them buttons are gonna pop off and take my eye out every time you breathe in.'

'My sister,' said Margaret.

'She needs feeding up. How'd you find me?'

'I worked out where your workplace was, even if I was looking for Ellen with an E instead of Helene with an H.'

Anna chuckled. 'You never asked. Why'd you go to Helene's?'

'I wanted to find you,' said Margaret. 'Mostly to ask what you meant about Kavanagh being worried about Fox, but also to see if you or your employer recognised a certain design. When I got there, I realised I should have asked you the other day.' She showed Anna Lucy's sketch. 'Is this one of yours? Helene said it was.'

Anna took it. 'I think so. What did you do then?'

'I ordered a dress. Helene said it was a shame I couldn't meet you but you'd be at a soup kitchen. She seems to understand about the strike.'

'She does. She's all right like that.'

'The picket line at Sullivan's sent me here. Can't you make fresh soup? Does it have to be tins?'

'It's what's donated. How's one of those little girls going to lug a family's worth of hot soup home? Anyway, what's this jacket got to do with the price of beer?' Anna traced the design with something approaching pride.

Margaret's heart started to pound. 'Do you know who you made it for?'

'I'm not responsible for the paperwork, and I don't remember talking to anyone about that design. Someone else must have. What's it got to do with anything?'

Margaret thought. Mr Moore hadn't said anything about the woman on the bench speaking. Was she, like Dervla, a courier? 'Have you heard about the maid who died near Tufnell Park?'

Anna nodded.

'This woman might know someone who's involved. There was a threatening note in the pocket of the girl's uniform.'

Anna wrinkled her nose, her eyes thoughtful. 'So the woman might be in danger. Was this girl murdered or was it an accident? The papers made it sound like the police weren't sure.'

'It was murder.'

'Right.' Anna pursed her lips.

'If I tell you something, will you keep it secret?'

'If there's one thing I'm good at, apart from sewing, it's that.'

'I think the young woman who died wasn't the maid but someone who looked like her,' said Margaret. 'She was Irish.'

'So's half the maids in London.' Anna frowned. 'I know they haven't given out her name, but didn't her boss know it was someone else? Don't tell me they were long-lost twins.'

'Her employer was away and the tweeny was out. She was found by one of the delivery boys and taken by the police before anyone who knew her was home.'

'Why's she dead? A bloke after something she didn't want to give?'

Margaret remembered the autopsy report. No injuries suggesting a moment of frustrated brutality had been mentioned. 'It didn't look like there had been a struggle, or she suffered for more than a few seconds.'

'Blimey. It was planned?' Anna absently patted one of the children as she passed.

'She may have known something the authorities want to know, perhaps about the fight for Irish independence, but possibly something else entirely.'

'I thought Home Rule was a sure thing.' Anna frowned. 'Hasn't the government said yes?'

'Parliament has. The Lords are still resisting.'

'The Lords,' spat Anna. 'The Crown. The Empire. How can a bunch of toffs know what's right or wrong for people? They just care about who owns land. The British government's never done nothing for Ireland that it should be proud of. Are you saying she was knocked off by a copper?'

'Or maybe someone on her own side, if she was about to share information.'

'Don't believe it.' Anna folded her arms, her expression closed.

'Anna, why did you come back from New York? Did you have wind of the strike and want to be involved? I'm not criticising. I can see why you would.'

Anna wouldn't meet her eyes. 'Did you really order a dress from Helene?'

'I'll never say no to a dress. Is Mr Kavanagh a Fenian? Do you think he might know about an Irish girl who might have got a maid's job?'

Anna shrugged. 'I'll ask him when I see him. What's her name? And what about the girl she swapped places with?'

Margaret was in a quandary. The police hadn't released Dervla's details. If she told Anna without confirming with Fox, she couldn't be sure what he'd say, or how much danger she'd put Anna in. 'I'm not sure of it.'

Anna stood, holding Margaret's gaze. It was all hopeless. If she knew anything at all, Margaret wasn't sure if Anna trusted her enough to say, any more than Margaret was sure she trusted Anna. She looked at her watch. Time was running short, but there was still time to do what she'd planned.

There was sad doubt in Anna's eyes. 'I'll see if I can look in the order books next time I'm at Helene's.' She cleared her throat with an irritated cough and a scowl. 'As long as you promise that no one innocent will get trapped by the police.'

'They won't. Thank you.'

Anna was staring down at the design. There was that bruised pride, and a future that she faced alone. If Margaret had started out the same, would she have survived as well? 'Call me Margaret.'

Anne transferred the stare to her. 'Me?'

'I call you Anna: why shouldn't you call me Margaret? You want a world where the rank you were born to is less important than the person you are. So do I, even if you don't believe me. Without your help last year, I might have died and so might Fox.'

'Gawd,' said Anna, handing back the sketch and turning to the soup kitchen. 'Cut out the slush. Without your help, Andris would have died, but I don't go on abaht it. Get on with you. Just let me know, and don't let anyone kill you too.'

Fourteen

The house where Dervla had died was in a forty-year-old row of tall, narrow red-brick buildings.

A stocky middle-aged maid opened the door, took Margaret's card and ushered her into the hall. She went to fetch a plump man in his mid thirties who shook hands then led Margaret into a small, dark sitting room. He was balding, the remaining hair light brown, his moustache, beard and sideburns almost blond. He had the kind of nondescript familiarity that reminded Margaret of Fox's irritation with everyone's averageness. Even if he hadn't had an alibi, it was hard to imagine Mr Webber threatening anyone, let alone an Irish gunrunner.

'Pleased to make your acquaintance, Dr De Merry,' he said. 'Sergeant Ainscough wired to say I should expect you.'

Margaret smiled blandly, wondering who Sergeant Ainscough was. 'How do you do, Mr Webber. I'm sorry to hear of the trouble you've had.'

'No more than I,' said Mr Webber, running his hands through his hair. 'I can't begin to say how thankful I am that you're here. I had to take leave from the office to visit my wife in the country, and now I've had to take more to sort out the immediate consequences of this terrible death. Little Sally is threatening to give notice, so I'm hoping you can reassure her. With my only other maid, er, gone, I was on my own, yet the domestic agency was reluctant to help. How do they expect a man to manage? At least they've sent Esmerelda. A mature woman, less likely to be approached for, er, abduction.'

'Could Esmerelda take me to the kitchen?'

'Goodness, I don't expect you to slum it,' said Mr Webber. 'Sally can come in here. I'll sit in the corner, quiet as a mouse.' He went into the hall.

Damn, thought Margaret. She looked round the room. It was feminine, with kingfisher-patterned wallpaper, gilt lamps and romantic novels in the bookshelves. This must be Mrs Webber's room.

Mr Webber returned and smiled inanely. 'Sally will be here shortly. I'll merge with the armchair.'

Silence fell.

'I hope your wife is well,' said Margaret.

'Just in need of some country air. London is rather stuffy at this time of year.'

'Of course.' Another silence.

'I hope you won't have to take too much more leave.'

'I'm just a Civil Service cog,' said Mr Webber. 'You may not know the Civil Service, Dr De Marry. It doesn't like the unexpected. I shall have to complete a million forms in triplicate when I go back. Ah, here she comes. I shall become mouse-like.' He put his finger to his mouth and settled into the armchair in the corner behind a newspaper.

Esmerelda brought a maid of around thirteen into the room, then withdrew.

'Do sit down, Sally,' said Margaret.

'Oh I couldn't, ma'am. Not on the missus's sofa.'

'Of course you can. I'm sure she's a nice mistress.'

'Very nice, ma'am.'

'Then I'm sure she wouldn't mind.'

Sally hesitated, then sat on the edge of the sofa. Her gaze flickered towards Mr Webber, then back to Margaret. 'Is it true you'll tell me what happened to Molly?'

'Was that her name?'

'Yes'm. Molly Malone, like the song. She didn't really just fall down them stairs, did she?'

'No. But she died very quickly and probably without much pain.'

'And she hadn't been – touched or anything? You know.' Sally squirmed, her face red.

'No.'

'Good. Only a maid nearby almost got took a few weeks ago and she said he tried to – you know – before she fought him off. It must be the same bloke.'

Margaret nodded, wishing she could ask about the maid who'd been assaulted. But judging by Sally's desperate glances towards the corner of the room, it would be impossible. 'I'm sorry to ask you this, Sally, but I gather you didn't see Molly's body.'

Sally shook her head. 'They'd took her away by the time I got back, ma'am, else I'd have told them it was Molly, not Olive. It was the butcher's boy what found her. He's new. Does the rounds in the wrong order. Comes an hour early and doesn't know who's who yet. He got Mr Rainer next door to come and help, and how would *he* know our names? He's been here less time than the boy.'

'Did you know Molly well?'

'Not really, ma'am. Olive always looked out for me, but she left without much notice. Molly was waiting the next day in the kitchen when I came down at five thirty. It was a relief, I can tell you.'

'She would watch out for you like Olive did.'

'Yes'm. She was nice. I didn't get the chance to get to know her proper, but I'm sorry that she—' Sally swallowed hard.

'What were you doing when she died?'

Sally looked a little truculent. 'Like I told the police, ma'am, I had to go and buy toiletries. I had quite the list from the master, for when the missus comes back to London. When I got in, there was a policeman here and he told me Olive was dead. I started to cry. I thought things mustn't have worked out for her. I asked the copper where Molly was. He said he didn't know who I was talking about. I said Molly was the other maid and he said there was no other maids. So then I thought maybe Olive came back and Molly pushed her down the stairs then legged it. I didn't half cry. Olive was a pal. It wasn't till yesterday that I found out it's Molly what's dead and Olive what's missing.'

'She might not be missing,' said Margaret. 'The police are looking for her.'

Sally wasn't convinced. 'Am *I* safe?'

Margaret hoped her face was neutral and friendly. 'Would the maid who was frightened by a man tell the police what happened? Maybe it'll help them find the murderer.'

Sally flushed even redder, looked at her hands and then the wall without moving her head, then back to Margaret. It was an odd gesture, but there was nothing else forthcoming.

'Mr Webber will make sure there's no more trouble here,' said Margaret, 'and Esmerelda looks like she'd fight off anyone who tried to hurt you.'

'Yes'm.'

Sally's misery hadn't decreased, but while her employer was listening, Margaret couldn't ask if she or Olive had overheard anything that might help. Now she was for ever complicit with Mr Webber's presence: the girl would never tell her anything of use. It would have to be a job for someone else.

***

Later, at home, Margaret gratefully handed the children to Nellie. She had returned to Katherine's house unnoticed, but when she, Katherine and the children left in Katherine's car, the Walrus had emerged from the park opposite Katherine's house, hailed a cab and followed them. He'd remained on their trail the whole afternoon until they arrived at Margaret's house at six.

She telephoned Fox's office and asked to speak with Elinor Edwards. 'Hallo, dear.'

'Margaret!' Elinor, normally a dour woman, sounded sickeningly girly. 'How delightful to hear from you!'

'Could you come round this evening? We could take a turn in the park.'

'Are you feeling lonely?'

'*Quite* the reverse, dear, though rather sick of men. It would be lovely to see you.'

'I'll see what I can do. If I'm not there by six thirty, assume I can't. Toodle-oo.'

'Cheerio!'

On that nauseating note, knowing Elinor would tell someone that a man was watching the house from the park, Margaret took her correspondence and the selection of newspapers she'd asked the newsagent to deliver to the upstairs sitting room. Juniper sat on the windowsill looking out, giving Margaret an excuse to pick her up and hug her while looking out too.

The Walrus had been replaced by the man with the bowler, who was seated on a bench, reading a book. One of Fox's colleagues would no doubt find a way of removing him.

Feeling a little reassured, Margaret settled down to read. The loathsome paper that had printed the story of her supposed incompetence had not followed it up, although there were the predictable letters in support of and in opposition to female doctors. The remaining papers were either so densely packed with dry articles that it would take a year to find anything interesting, or so scandalous or chatty, with their advertisements for Dr Williams's pink pills or Mother Siegel's Syrup, that she might disappear into a labyrinth of half-truths while chasing stories.

The loss of Dervla's body was mentioned nowhere, but then who would admit its loss? Margaret felt as if the day had been more or less a failure.

The letterbox rattled, then the door rattled and she heard it open. Heart thudding, Margaret went to the top of the stairs. She peered into the dark hallway and saw a man silhouetted against the open doorway, crouching to pick something up. For a moment she felt dizzy with apprehension, then realised it was Fox.

He looked up at the same instant, stood up and closed the door. 'Why are you lurking? You look like you're about to pour boiling oil on my head.'

'I wasn't sure who you were. I don't know that hat.' She descended the stairs and hugged him. 'Or this coat. They smell a bit … mothbally.'

Fox put the hat and coat on the rack and kissed her. 'Had to change. Where are Vera and Nellie?'

'Nellie's in the nursery with the twins and Vera's in the kitchen.'

'Let's go to the sitting room. Here's a letter for you.'

'What do you mean, you had to change?' Margaret took the letter and followed Fox into the sitting room where he pulled her onto his lap.

'Pigeon and I are pretty sure we were followed from the start,' he said. 'I didn't think it would be possible with the motorbike, but we had some plans in case someone managed it. And they did. So we stopped at Clapham Junction, which was in its usual morning chaos. There was a convoluted exchange of outer clothes and personnel. Pigeon went off to his favourite garage, carrying a different man wearing my things and followed by the other motorcyclist. I carried on alone in these. Or rather, when I say I carried on, I doubled back and got the train to Gastrell's regiment's headquarters.'

'Are you sure there wasn't another follower?'

'Fairly sure. Why?'

So he hadn't reported in or heard from his office. 'It's the sort of thing that happens,' said Margaret. 'What did you find out?'

'Gastrell's date and place of birth, and the record of his career up to my investigation. There were the briefest of notes about the allegations. A dishonourable discharge was planned if he didn't resign his commission without a fuss. Then a note as to his drowning. That's all.'

'You don't think Inspector Silvermann got there first and took something?'

Fox's face twisted in thought. 'I doubt it. Gastrell's date and place of birth might be useful for something.'

'Somerset House? Parish register?'

'Somerset House will repeat what I know, though it might turn up a marriage. However, there was nothing about any dependents in his file. The money from death in service went to his parents.' Fox sighed. 'Searching parish registers is something I hadn't thought of: a rector may know what a public servant won't. And it's in the country, so we can look together under cover of house-hunting on Friday.'

'How far into the country?' said Margaret, leaning back and scrutinising Fox's face with narrowed eyes.

He chuckled. 'Is my little town mouse scared by big expanses of green?'

'Not on holiday, only if she's made to live there. At least the Walrus's budget won't stretch that far.'

'The walrus's what?'

'I think Inspector Silvermann sent men to follow me. I had to evade them,' said Margaret. 'Only—'

'Are you sure they were police?'

'Pretty sure. Regulation boots. Anyway, I found out pretty much nothing, except that getting a baby carriage on a tube train is impossible and while a change of clothes worked for both you and me, I'm the only one who lost a button. And it wasn't even my button.'

Fox blinked at her. 'Starting at the beginning, why did you try to take the pram on the underground?'

'To look as boring and ordinary as possible.'

'And evade a ... walrus?'

'I also know where the embroidered jacket might be from, and the tweeny seemed to be dropping hints about the man next door. Perhaps he has something to do with Dervla's death other than identifying her as Olive, theoretically out of ignorance.'

'Then you found something out and we can look into it. Thank you. But you need to explain the walrus.'

Margaret studied the envelope in her hand, addressed in somewhat laboured handwriting. She extracted the letter.

Dear Margaret,

I found your address in the telephone book. I thought you might not get this for days if I sent it to the hospital. I met Kavanagh in New York. He's looking for someone who's been used by someone who's using Sullivan too. K wanted to get inside Sullivan's. Sullivan won't let me in after the machines got smashed last year, so I wrote to Abram to see if there was anything different there. He said he thought something was up in the export side, and would see what he could find out. K said to wait till he came back. I didn't want Abram to take it on alone so I came back too. When the strike started Abram said he'd snoop around while it was quiet. K said to wait till he knew more. Abram said it was the best time. That is what the row was about.

I don't know if Abram found anything out. It ain't Fenians and it ain't Anarchists, it's something else. I don't know what.

You said to use your name, so you must trust me. So now I'm trusting you. It's true I don't know where K is just now. But before he went off he said he knew Fox, and Fox was as straight as coppers get. He said to lie low till he's back because they'll stop at nothing if they get wind of us looking.

So watch your back and Fox too.

Anna

'She thinks I trust her,' said Margaret. 'But I wouldn't give her Dervla's name, nor Gastrell's. And now…'

'And now you're keeping her safe. I'm beginning to wish you weren't connected with any of it.'

'I'm connected with you, Fox,' said Margaret. 'There's no choice.'

Fifteen

'May I speak with you, doctor?' Cyril asked, after the morning's tutorial. The zeal of Monday put aside, he had compared observations in a clinical way and argued in a logical and polite manner. Margaret wondered if it had in fact been she rather than he who had been irrational.

'Yes, of course. Come through to my office.' It was a nuisance, but Margaret couldn't show how she felt.

The worst of only working two days a week at the hospital was that there was so much to fit in. She needed to prepare for laboratory work with Dr Jordan before lunch, and for a full class of male first-year students afterwards. She also had filing to do, and wanted to reread the post-mortem reports on Abram Cohen and Dervla Mallowan to see if anything had been missed. And she wanted to ask the cold-room orderly everything he recalled about the fake undertakers, even though he'd been asked so many times that she was likely to become a victim of murder herself. It was really Darnell whom she ought to interrogate, but now that he was contrite, he was more irritating than when he was officious.

More than anything, she wished Inspector Silvermann would visit so that she could tell him what she thought about being followed. No one had done so today, as far as she could tell. Somehow, that was more unsettling.

There were too many things swirling in her head to want to listen to Cyril nitpicking over forensic techniques, possibly in Latin. However, he seemed on edge, sitting on his hands on the very edge of the chair, chewing his lips and wrinkling his nose. It was unattractive and a little alarming.

'Is something wrong, Mr Purefoy?'

'I ... er... It's Papa.' Cyril's gaze dropped to the floor.

'Oh no!' Margaret reproved herself for her impatience. She knew Cyril was the youngest of six, the only son of a West London doctor, so presumably the father wasn't young. 'Is he ill? Is he... If you need to—'

Cyril looked up, his expression more pained than ever. 'No, Papa's quite well. In his body, that is. I mean, in his mind too. I don't mean he's insane. I mean he's rather, er, vexed.'

'Oh. I see.' She didn't. 'What about? Not you, surely. Your work is excellent and you are highly likely to finish at the top of your class this term.'

'It's not me,' said Cyril, flushing purple. 'It's St J's. It's ... it's Dr Jordan. It's, er, you.'

'I *beg* your pardon?' Margaret could feel her face heating up.

'H-he read that article and guessed what – I mean where – it was about. He wants me to transfer to a different teaching hospital. He's started enquiries.'

Margaret sat back, furious. She wanted to say *go, then*, but sensed misery under Cyril's matter-of-fact answers. After all, like Algie's father, Cyril's father controlled the purse strings and therefore his son. She willed herself to be reasonable. 'I see. Well, if I'd read that article as the parent of a student here, I might have doubts, too. What was your response?'

'That the article was three names short of libel.' Cyril's flush deepened. 'That I want to stay. That Dr Jordan follows the latest books by the letter. That neither of you is interested in self-aggrandisement or courting fame or anything but doing the job in hand, which is more than can be said of some other London pathologists. That I'm learning no less than I'd learn elsewhere under men more frequently in the newspapers, whose decisions are called into question more often, but which they refuse to revisit from arrogance. That he shouldn't think of you as a woman at all, but a highly skilled doctor.'

Margaret reflected that Cyril was clearly unconscious that his final statement might offend. 'I'm glad you want to stay,' she said. 'I hope you manage to persuade him. Are any of the other students under similar pressures?'

Cyril looked blank. 'I don't know. I don't discuss personal matters with anyone. I prefer to concentrate on my studies, doctor: I'm not interested in gossip and frivolity. I like to discuss medicine and science and surgical innovations, but it can be hard to find anyone with the time to do so.'

Margaret realised he must be lonely and yet to find a kindred spirit, and felt sorry for him. Even when she had been a student keen to prove herself, she had enjoyed more than her fair share of gossip and frivolity. Generally, she had been highly unlikely to spend much time out of lectures discussing the serious side of things. Joel had been a calm haven after an ocean of socialising. If he hadn't died, would they have fallen properly in love and then married? Would she now be bored with his quiet, soft-spoken ways?

Maude seemed to manage with Geoff. But Maude wasn't Margaret.

And Cyril was very different to Joel, who had enjoyed society and had a subtle sense of humour. It was hard to work out if Cyril had one, or understood people's spirits and personalities as well as he did the mechanics of their bodies. She very much hoped he would stay in laboratory work, where he'd excel, rather than venture into general practice where he might miss or misinterpret the vague clues patients tended to give.

'Would you like me or Dr Jordan to write to your father?'

Cyril pondered, twisting his face as before. 'Not yet. I just wanted to let you know that if I am deficient in my duties, it's because I am distressed in my mind.'

'Thank you for telling me,' said Margaret. 'And I can assure you that you haven't been deficient today, and you never are.'

'Aren't I? Good.'

He showed no signs of leaving. Soon Margaret would have to go and speak with Dr Jordan about the work they had to undertake before lunch, and time to review the two autopsy files was running out.

A thought struck her. 'I'm pleased you told your father that Dr Jordan and I are always prepared to revisit our findings to make sure nothing was missed. I wonder if you'd like to assist. I'd be interested in what you see that we didn't, or what you see that reinforces our conclusions. You can tell your father that, too.' She stood up and opened the filing-cabinet drawer where she put things ready to file properly when she had time. She vowed to herself yet again to keep her filing under control in future, since it took some rummaging to find the one she wanted, buried under some case notes and three copies of the *Lancet*. She had thought she'd left it on top of the pile she'd swept up from her desk. Perhaps Dr Jordan, the only other person with keys to the drawer, had looked at it and put it at the bottom to make a point, although that didn't seem the kind of thing he'd do. She extracted the file, irritated with herself. Since having the twins, her mind had sometimes felt less focussed at home, but not at work. She turned the pages inside to check nothing was missing. Everything was as she remembered, in order, from photographs to diagrams. Maybe she was becoming unfocussed at work, too.

'Is that the report on the maid who was found at the bottom of some stairs?' said Cyril.

'Yes.'

'The undertakers collected her on Monday, didn't they?'

'Er, yes.' Margaret wondered if, despite being told to keep quiet, Darnell or the orderly had let anything out about the loss of the body. If they had, Cyril probably didn't know.

'I hope they're more efficient than their van would suggest. The lack of attention to detail was astonishing.'

'Their van?'

'Yes: I saw them loading it up. Whoever painted their name on the side put an apostrophe before the S in "undertakers". And I'd have wanted a different number plate.'

'Would you?' Margaret tried not to sound too eager. 'I didn't know you were interested in motor vehicles. What kind was it?'

'I'm not and I don't know, but grammatical and spelling errors jump out at me. I see patterns in words and numbers that other people don't. There's probably a name for it, but I don't know what it is. Do you?'

'How interesting!' said Margaret. 'What pattern did you see in the registration number that made you think you'd change it?'

'It wasn't a pattern, it was a word. *PEST*. It seemed a bit unsavoury: more suitable for a rat catcher.' Cyril's serious face broke into a rare smile. 'But perhaps it's just me and no one else would notice.'

'Pest?' Margaret frowned.

'PE 57.' Cyril's smile faded. 'My brain turned the 57 into ST. I daresay you think I'm mad. Papa thinks I'm peculiar. Mama thinks it's endearing.'

'I don't think you're mad at all,' said Margaret. 'It encourages me to rely on you to look through those files for anything unusual. Thank you, Cyril. Could you bring them back this afternoon so I can file them properly?'

'Yes, doctor. I'll take them to the library now. I have a study day and this will be an interesting task. Thank you.'

'My pleasure,' said Margaret. 'On your way, can you drop in on Dr Jordan and say that I'll be with him shortly? I need to send a telegram first.'

***

Her afternoon at St Julia's began with a telegraphed reply from Fox's clerk, Elinor Edwards, signed with her office nickname: *Thanks. Hedgehog.* It ended with a visit from Inspector Silvermann. He asked to speak with Dr Jordan, who asked Margaret to join them. The inspector told them that Dervla's body had been found in a shallow grave not far from an archery pavilion in Surrey.

'Fully dressed, which was a nice touch. It takes some effort to get clothes on a corpse, so you have to admire them for that.'

'It's nice that they gave her some dignity,' said Dr Jordan.

'Maybe,' said the inspector.

'When are you bringing her back here?' asked Dr Jordan.

'Didn't like to trouble you again. She's at St Bart's.'

Dr Jordan removed his spectacles and polished them. 'I undertook the post-mortem.'

'Do you object to a second opinion? Either of you?' The inspector's piercing eyes speared them in turn.

'Of course not. I'd be grateful for the relevant doctor's name, however, to compare notes,' snapped Dr Jordan. 'I feel you're casting aspersions on St Julia's.'

'No *medical* aspersions are being cast, doctor. Clerical competence is another matter, of course.'

'Our clerk is fairly new to his job.'

'Is he? Well, covering for that risks clouding your judgment.'

'Utter nonsense,' growled Dr Jordan, replacing his spectacles and glaring at the inspector.

'Was there, as far as you know, any other injury on the body?' said Margaret.

'To obscure the cause of death? No. Just the sort of marks you get when a body is manhandled after death, and from being buried. And yes, I'll give you the doctor's details. It was a shallow grave but she might not have been found for a while if one of the archers hadn't lost an arrow among the trees. If more time had passed, it would have been hard to confirm your finding that her neck had been broken by hand, so to speak.'

'Possibly,' said Margaret. 'But if more time had passed, her being found would be irrelevant. She'd be unrecognisable.'

'Unless her clothes gave her away.'

'I don't understand,' said Dr Jordan. 'You took the uniform she'd been wearing away with you. How did they get it from the police station?'

'She wasn't in Olive's uniform,' said Inspector Silvermann. 'She was in nice clothes a cut above what a maid could afford, with marks from a Dublin laundry inside all but her jacket, which was unmarked. She had a very good quality handbag. Its contents were a purse embroidered *DM*, a tube containing a vicious trio of hatpins, a typed list of the haberdashery you'd need for a tropical outfit in an envelope addressed to M Malone, care of a Carmarthen hotel, and finally, a return ticket from Fishguard to Rosslare. They'd have identified her.'

'I don't understand,' said Margaret. 'The twee— I mean, between one thing and another, I thought this woman was masquerading as Olive and using Olive's things. Even if she'd kept her handbag, how did it... I don't follow.'

'Don't you? Also in the grave was a gent's fob watch which just might have fingerprints on it – presumably it fell off one of the men burying her. Interesting, isn't it, Dr Demeray?'

'Extremely,' said Margaret, trying to keep her gaze steady as her mind flitted from thought to thought. 'I'm surprised you're telling us any of this. Isn't it classified information?'

'Not from my point of view,' said the inspector. 'It'll be in the papers to see if anyone recognises any of it, unless certain people tell me otherwise. Do you think they will?'

'How on earth should we know?' said Dr Jordan. 'I suppose I should thank you for informing us about her body. I shall contact St Bart's immediately. In the meantime, what about the real Olive Nolan? Is she safe? Are you any closer to finding her?'

'She, or at least someone who says she's Olive and looks like her photograph, is safely performing "the maid" in a third-rate production of "What Every Woman Knows" playing in an unpronounceable northern town called Mytham-something. I have a good many leads and I'm following them.'

'I hope you're following the right ones,' snapped Margaret. 'Not wasting time following a trail that will get you nowhere.'

The inspector narrowed his eyes. 'They all lead somewhere,' he said. 'What have the innocent to fear?'

Sixteen

When Margaret arrived home she found Fox already there, playing with the children in the sunny upstairs sitting room. They were all lying on the floor on their fronts, Fox in the middle, moving toys just out of Alec's reach.

Edie was patting Fox on the side of his head to make him turn his face. 'Da da da!' He twisted to look at her with an expression of utter surprise and she chuckled in delight, hiding her face in the carpet and kicking her feet. Alec, half-raised from the carpet like a small blond cobra, stretched, then pulled himself onto his knees. He rocked back and forth, his left hand reaching for a ball, then lost his balance and rolled onto his back, spotting Margaret. 'Ummama!' He put his arms up and Edie, twisting round, giggled even harder. 'Mamama!'

Margaret felt as if her heart would burst.

'Come down here,' said Fox. 'Life makes a lot more sense from this angle. Look at this…' As Margaret dropped to the carpet, Fox sat up and lifted each of the twins into a seated position. Edie lolled at an angle and he tucked her into his side, but Alec sat properly, only tipping sideways when he grabbed his own foot.

'They can sit!' Margaret pulled Alec onto her lap. 'You clever darlings. That's the best thing that's happened all day.' She felt sad that she'd missed the twins reaching a milestone, but glad that they *had* reached it, given the gloomy predictions she'd received when they'd been born.

'Let's stay down here with them for ever,' said Fox.

'Let's.' She played peek-a-boo with Edie, covering and uncovering her face.

Edie tried to do the same, then reached for Alec, who was chewing on a rattle. 'Ah eh.'

'Ee ee.' He held the rattle out.

Margaret sat him next to his sister to play and moved to Fox's other side. He put his arm round her. 'They found Dervla,' he said.

'I know. They won't let us have her back. It seemed like she was dressed in her own clothes.'

'They were the ones she was arrested in,' said Fox. 'She was on remand, so in prison, she wore her own blouse, skirt, cardigan and underthings, and was still wearing them when she escaped. The rat who was working on the inside must have got her handbag to her before we uncovered him. But the overcoat she had in Pembrokeshire is still at the prison, so the jacket on her corpse is new. Very fancy, I gather.'

'She can't have been the woman on the bench,' said Margaret. 'Dervla was still in custody.'

'True.'

'The inspector says there was a fob watch in the grave which they're testing for fingerprints.'

Fox frowned. 'He's telling you a lot of confidential information, Margaret.'

'He said he was going to put it in the papers unless someone stopped him. I assume he meant you and it was an oblique threat.'

'If he thinks I or any of my men are amateurish enough to drop a watch into a grave, he should remember how his men identified the body incorrectly by asking the wrong people. What is it, young man?' Fox bent down to Alec, who was reaching for his cufflinks. 'Not all shiny things are yours, Alexander David.' He gave Alec something else to play with and shook his head. 'A fob watch ... that rings a bell.'

Margaret watched his face twist. 'It'll come to you. Did anything come of that registration number?'

'Ah yes – thank you for that. The plates were stolen from a car in Surrey on Sunday night and left in the owner's garden on Monday night.'

'Surrey again. Anywhere near where Dervla's body was found? Is he involved, do you think?'

Fox shook his head. 'He lives several miles from where she was. He's not under suspicion; it seems logical to assume the people who stole them know the area. Only someone like your Mr Purefoy would notice the plates. I don't suppose he remembers the make of the van?'

'No. It was just the numbers and the sign he noticed, as they disturb his sensibilities.'

'We can try and find the printers who printed the sign for the van, which is doubtless at the bottom of the Thames by now, but it would take years to go through them all, or even the ones with low proofreading standards. Did anyone follow you today?'

'No. I'm not sure whether to be pleased or worried. Maybe I really did convince them of the boredom of my life yesterday. You?'

'Not today,' said Fox. 'But it's worrying. I hope we can get this all resolved before we go to Brighton. I don't fancy being followed about on the beach.'

'That's not what's worrying you.'

Fox was silent for a moment, watching Edie prod his arm with a rattle. 'No it isn't.'

'Then what is?'

'I arrested Dervla and put her safely in custody, waiting for her to tell me something about someone in London. I heard about Moore seeing Gastrell and planned to see him, as did Sir Broderick. Moore dies, then Dervla escapes and somehow changes places with Olive – a born-and-bred Londoner of Irish descent – to work near someone we've had under observation.'

'Who?'

'The next door neighbour Rainer, who identified Dervla as Olive.'

'Sally thought that was because he didn't know her,' said Margaret.

'Which could be quite true,' said Fox. 'But equally, it could be deliberate.'

'What about Mr Webber?'

'Webber has no discernible connection to Irish independence,' said Fox, taking the rattle from Edie and handing her a wooden ball. 'He's a chief clerk in the Patent Office with an immaculate record going back eight years. Before that he had a photographic business which didn't take off, before *that* general clerking and, he admits, failing exams at Cambridge and leaving without a degree. But one of my colleagues has intelligence about Rainer, though it's not clear what he's involved in. He's only been there a month and we haven't tracked where he's from. His maidservants were happy enough to say that he has foreign mail.'

'Mail from Dublin?'

'No one thinks of Ireland as foreign. No, from Windhoek.'

'South West Africa?'

Fox nodded. 'Which is where the double agent Gastrell worked with went to live.'

'Where is he now?'

'Died of tetanus in 1903. Nothing sinister, evidently.'

'And too long dead to matter,' said Margaret.

'Yes. But the note in Dervla's pocket linked her to Gastrell, Moore and possibly either me or Sir Broderick,' said Fox. 'Who did it really belong to? Dervla? Olive?'

Margaret frowned. 'It's "*a* fox" not Fox and how could anyone assume that "old soldier" suggests Sir Broderick?'

'He reported Moore's suspicions about Gastrell. I investigated as a military policeman.'

'So you think it meant to imply that Sir Broderick was responsible for Gastrell's disgrace and therefore his death? That it was somehow deliberate?'

'Or maybe that though I said I was trying to save Gastrell and get him out of the river, I was actually drowning him.'

Edie gave a loud cry, leaned over Fox and reached for Margaret. 'Mamamama!' Fox lifted her and passed her to Margaret. Edie snuggled into her mother's neck, fingers stuffed into her mouth. Nellie would disapprove, but Margaret didn't care. She closed her eyes, feeling sick. 'But you didn't—'

'No, I didn't,' said Fox. 'But he had a weak arm: I injured it. There were enough witnesses to see what I did to save him, but whether they're still alive or can remember is another matter. Come along, Alec, let's take you and your sister back to the nursery. I am taking your mama out to dinner and the cinema.'

Fox got to his feet, lifted Alec and helped Margaret up. 'We can talk on the way, then lose ourselves in dinner at the Black Lion and then whatever nonsense is playing at the picture house. It'll clear our minds.'

'I don't know why we pay Vera to cook.'

'Nor do I. She's better at nursemaiding.'

An hour later, Margaret and Fox left the house on foot. The evening was warm and no one seemed to be following them.

'This is what I think,' said Fox, as they walked along the quiet streets. 'The man Moore overheard in Bishops

Park is the man Gastrell colluded with ten years ago, whom we never found.'

'The double agent?'

'No. The officer that was also supposed to be involved whom I never found. After Gastrell's death, no more intelligence went missing, the war ended and of course, I had no authority to keep looking anyway. Now, I wish I'd argued about it more.'

'Even though the intelligence stopped going missing.'

'I think he must have just laid low for a while then started to build on the network he and Gastrell created. They were selling secrets then, so presumably he's selling them now, only the secrets have changed.'

They arrived at the Black Lion and after being seated in a quiet part of the dining room, made their order. Fox fidgeted with his cutlery and then the cruet.

Margaret laid her hand over his to stop him. 'Where does Dervla come in?'

'I suspect she was offered financial assistance to her cause in exchange for smuggling information.' He shook Margaret's hand off and moved the cruet about again. 'If only I'd had enough time to get her to talk. When the murderer heard who had arrested her, he must have feared she might say something to remind me of the investigation into Gastrell and reveal his accomplice. So he arranged for her to escape, so he could ensure her silence. And put a note in her pocket which said—'

'"*Moore's dead because he knew who really killed Gastrell. Watch your neck. There's no mercy in either an old soldier or a fox.*"'

Fox ran his hand over his face. 'Is that supposed to imply that either Sir Broderick or I are happy for someone to be killed without trial?'

'Sir Broderick doesn't seem that sort of man any more than you do,' said Margaret, 'and Mr Moore died of stroke.'

'A stroke can be induced or mimicked, can't it?' said Fox. 'The man in Fulham must have recognised Moore that day and recalled him as the man who was willing to testify against Gastrell. He didn't know the old chap was too doolally to be a threat, so they needed him dead.'

'Mr Moore's doctor didn't query the cause of death.'

Fox crossed his cutlery into a star, uncrossed them then peered round the dining room. It was newly papered in a modern design and the wall-lamps cast warm light onto the other diners. Another couple eating in silence and staring in apparent boredom into a space beyond each other's heads, four men smoking and laughing, and two men chatting with intensity over brandy. None were near, or evidently interested. 'No,' said Fox. 'But if someone queries it now and something suspicious shows up, then they've got Dervla's death to link to it, and potentially to Sir Broderick and me.'

Margaret shook her head. 'Fox, this doesn't make sense. You didn't visit till after Mr Moore had had his stroke and Sir Broderick didn't go to Fulham till after he'd died.'

'You don't have to be there to have someone killed, you just have to give an order.'

'But you didn't,' said Margaret. 'And why would anyone try to make it look as if you had?'

'Revenge for Gastrell's death. Sir Broderick started that investigation. I pursued it. He's only just retired. I have been living in relative obscurity. Until now, it would have been harder to get to either of us. Maybe it wasn't supposed to happen yet, but Moore and Dervla were a risk. Both needed to be got rid of before they told anyone anything. And then Dervla's murder became an opportunity for that long awaited revenge.'

'Would a former colleague of Gastrell's care so much about his death that he'd seek revenge on Sir Broderick now?'

'Even traitors have loyal friends. Not everyone forgets easily.'

'Gastrell sounds eminently forgettable,' said Margaret.

'Obviously not by everyone. And if I'm right and his former accomplice continued what he started, they'll do anything to stop that from being found out.'

'What about the woman with the jacket?'

'Wife? Accomplice? Secretary?' said Fox, knocking the pepper pot over, then righting it. 'Has Anna found out who ordered it yet?'

'If so, she hasn't written.' Margaret put his hand over his again.

'Mmm. Well, I suspect Inspector Silvermann's men have backed off for now.' Fox squeezed her fingers.

'I was going to ask about the haberdashery letter in Dervla's handbag,' said Margaret. 'Was it from Islington? Could it be code?'

'You think there's a link between Kavanagh and Dervla Mallowan? It's possible. The problem is that I don't have that list any more: Silvermann does. All I have is Dervla's photographic case. She seemed rather blasé about it I couldn't tell if that was because there was nothing to be found, or something which she wanted to be found. I wonder if you can look. As for Kavanagh, he's gone to Ireland.'

'You know he wasn't in London? I thought you didn't know anything much about him. Why didn't you tell me?'

'Because until Anna's letter came,' said Fox, 'there was nothing to link him to this but an irrelevant argument with a striking tailor.'

'And now we need to put them together.' The waiter had arrived with their food and placed it before them, then with a tut, rearranged the cruet. 'Come on Fox, you'll feel better if you eat. What's on at the cinema ?'

'I don't know,' said Fox. 'Let's hope it's something calming.'

Seventeen

The main films at the cinema were a thrilling drama set in the future called *Aerial Anarchists,* and a somewhat nauseating version of *Pollyanna.* The following morning, Margaret woke from a confused dream in which aeroplanes attacked London with a hail of bullets and bombs and buildings went up in smoke. She rubbed her eyes wondering why her brain had latched onto the most disturbing film, though at least it wasn't sentimental. Fox was long gone.

Vera brought breakfast in bed, then Nellie delivered the children to be propped up on either side of Margaret, playing with rattles and teething rings. Juniper, having retreated to the footboard, watched in disgust before slinking out of the open window.

The upstairs telephone rang as Margaret was taking the children back to the nursery. She sat the twins on the floor and answered it. 'Hallo?'

'Hallo, it's Maude. Would you like to take me to a sweatshop for research today?'

'Er...' Margaret caught sight of herself in the landing mirror. Her hair looked as if she'd been sleeping in a bush and the circles under her eyes suggested it hadn't been a comfortable one. One of the twins whacked her bare foot with a damp rattle. 'Ow!'

'Ow?'

'Edie is battering me. I don't think I can. I'm very behind on my essay for Dr Naylor and—'

'Don't worry. Maybe we can go on Friday instead.'

'You ask me to the loveliest places, Maude, but I'm afraid I can't. Fox and I will be house-hunting.'

'How lovely.' At the other end of the line, Maude let out a deep, uncharacteristic sigh. 'Life is rather serious these days, Demeray. I wish that you, Phoebe and I could go away for a while, just the three of us. When the summer term is over, I shall hire a little cottage and make you both come with me. No husbands, no children, no servants.'

'You? Without servants?'

'You'll cook, of course. Phoebe can do the nurturing and cushion plumping. I'll be worn out from organising everything and paying for it – though I could probably rouse myself to pour the wine. Telephone me later.'

***

By ten, Margaret had been working at her desk for over an hour. There was nothing of interest in the mail.

She missed the laboratory, where she'd have things to look at, not just theoretical ideas, and there would be someone to discuss her thoughts with. From upstairs came the sound of Nellie singing as she prepared the twins for their morning walk. Now they were sitting up, perhaps they could spend time with Margaret as she worked, playing with their toys, content in their world as she was in hers.

Except that they wouldn't be, and she wasn't certain she would be either.

Footsteps sounded on the attic stairs and then the landing. 'Would you like to say goodbye to the twins, ma'am?' Nellie stood in the doorway with a child on each hip. They were dressed in their sailor outfits. Alec was leaning backwards so far that his hat was about to come off, while Edie twisted and reached out to her mother.

A vision of what would happen if they unbalanced Nellie on the stairs made Margaret cringe. 'Let me take Edie downstairs for you.'

'Oh, thank you, ma'am. They do wriggle so. What'll it be like when they're crawling?'

'Just as well we have Vera, too.'

'Mmm,' said Nellie as she went downstairs. 'I'll get the baby carriage. You'll have peace and quiet to do your book work now.'

Margaret returned to her desk upstairs. All the little noises from the hallway and kitchen were muffled, but she somehow dreaded being left with the silence that Nellie thought she craved. Finding it hard to focus, and dismissing her guilt by telling herself that she was achieving nothing, Margaret turned to the newspapers instead. Somewhere, there must be a link.

The most obvious place would be the personal advertisements or the announcements. Nothing sprang out. The usual men and women sought companions or jobs or dwellings. The usual secondhand goods were on sale. The usual kindly gentlemen offered loans on note of hand alone with no delays, fees or objectionable enquiries. The usual 'doctors' declared that their preparations would restore a distressed man's strength or a desperate woman's regularity.

In the announcements columns were the usual engagements, births, deaths, and marriages. But no clues appeared to be hidden among the strangers' names.

Then there was a small paragraph,

'Tufnell Park Maid Death - Is A Fenian Responsible?'

We have received information that a man, thought to be a member of the Irish Brotherhood, whom N Division have been seeking for some weeks has been arrested in Tufnell Park. Was this man, connected with an unexpected death in Islington earlier this month, also responsible for the death of a maid in the area, which the police believe to be murder? We await more more news.

Inspector Silvermann had found Kavanagh. And someone had told the papers.

'Wait for me!' Margaret called, then ran downstairs and bundled herself into her hat and outdoor shoes. 'I need to go into town. If you wait, I'll walk with you to the other side of the park. I can push the pram.'

Nellie looked askance. 'I can't have you pushing the pram while I'm there, ma'am. The other nannies and nursemaids will think it even more peculiar than when you take it alone.' Her face glowed. 'I'm sorry, ma'am, but it's the truth. They think it means I'm not up to the job.'

'Oh dear.' Margaret heaved a sigh. 'Very well, you push and I'll walk alongside looking like one of those mothers that can barely recognise their own children. Will that do?'

Nellie giggled. 'Yes, ma'am.'

They crossed the road and entered the sunny park. There were very few men about, but several women meandered, chatting, bustling, comparing children.

Until she'd had the children, Margaret had been unaware of how many other mothers were in the area. With twins who were born early and undersized and were only just catching up, Margaret had always felt left behind. Initially, the other women's gloomy assurances that at least one of the twins would die young and she shouldn't get too attached were distressing. Now, their inability to discuss anything other than domestic woes was simply boring.

'Apart from me professionally embarrassing you,' said Margaret, 'are you happy with us, Nellie? I know you want to train as a Norland's nanny in a few years, but I hope you're getting enough experience with us now.'

'I should say so,' said Nellie, deftly steering the perambulator to avoid a small girl with a hoop. 'And yes, ma'am, I'm very happy. But I can do more of the housework if you want me to.'

'How about cooking?' said Margaret. 'If you don't know how, I could teach you. Vera could... Vera could take care of the children.'

To Margaret's surprise, Nellie burst into a peal of laughter.

'You think she'd be offended?'

'Oh, no! And I'd rather learn from you. Your cooking is more modern, what with that maracaroni stuff you make. I like that.' Nellie paused to look around, presumably for her fellow nursemaids. Margaret realised she was probably stopping Nellie from meeting them. Or perhaps... A young man of about eighteen was sitting on a bench, smoking a cigarette.

'Nellie, may I ask you something very direct?'

'Yes, ma'am.' Nellie's expression was wary.

'Have you a follower? I mean, a best boy?'

'Me? No! *I* don't have a follower.' Nellie stuck out her chin then looked towards the bench. 'I wouldn't want a loafer like *that*... I think he's a copper, anyway. No disrespect to you and the master: Mr Fox is an officer, not a mere constable. My mum says I can do better than a flattie, and I intend to. So I told him right off, "Thanks but no thanks. I'd only walk out with a boy who goes to church regular, which I bet you don't, and anyway, I've got a career to make."'

Margaret glanced at the young man again. His well-made suit and boots didn't seem particularly appropriate for walking a beat. Was he plain-clothes police, in better disguise than usual? 'Has that man asked you to go somewhere with him?'

'Tuesday, ma'am. Only to see a band in Regents Park, mind, but even so. I'm not a fool: I expect he asks all the maids. But who wants a lad who's on shifts? That's no good to a maid who's only free in the evenings.'

'I don't mind if you *do* have a young man, but I'd like to know. Apart from anything else, I don't want to get on the wrong side of your mother.'

'You and me both, ma'am.' Nellie gave a surreptitious wave at another young nursemaid. She seemed unconcerned about the young man, more interested in Margaret leaving so that she could meet her friends. 'Vera says if he troubles me again she'll set on him with the rolling pin.'

'Please tell me, too,' said Margaret. 'I'll join in with a saucepan. Seriously, Nellie, I wouldn't like you to feel afraid here.'

'I feel quite safe, ma'am. It's a happy place. Even if it's a bit funny, what with the master coming and going and that Bert and Mr Pigeon and their machines.'

'Stay with your friends, all the same,' said Margaret. She bent down and kissed the twins goodbye. 'I'll be back in plenty of time for dinner, Nellie. Tell Vera I'll show you how to make the macaroni dish once the children are settled. Then she can get away early for that bazaar meeting she wanted to attend.'

'Mmm,' said Nellie, her face expressionless.

Margaret was puzzled. By preference, Nellie went to a lively Baptist chapel rather than staid St Matthew's, but maybe she'd like to be involved with a fundraising fete, despite the possibly heretical Anglican surroundings. 'Did you want to join her?'

'No, thank you,' said Nellie, with the firmness of nonconformist scruples. 'Goodbye, ma'am. Have a lovely day.' Without further ado, she turned the pram and marched towards the other nursemaids.

Margaret glanced at her watch: she could spare a few minutes. She walked directly to the bench and sat down next to the young man. 'Good morning.'

He blinked at her, touched his hat, then ran his finger round his collar. 'Morning?' he mumbled through the cigarette.

'I don't have long,' she said, scrutinising his face. 'That's a shame. I'd like to sketch you, in case I forget your face when I do it later, from memory.'

'W-what?'

'I'm very accurate,' she said, leaning a little closer to gauge the exact blue of his eyes and chart the pattern of freckles speckling his cheeks. 'In case you don't know, though I suspect you do, I'm a doctor. Maybe you don't realise that I'm surgically trained, too. I know exactly how the muscles and bones lie under your skin. I can draw a face as accurately as I can dissect it. Sometimes I do both.'

The young man turned what sounded like a retch into a cough. Ash exploded from the cigarette and drifted onto his knee.

'Maybe you're here because you have nothing to do but proposition young women to whom you haven't been introduced,' Margaret continued.

'Do what?'

'In which case, if I see you here again, I shall report you to the police.'

'Hang on...'

'But if you're on a job now, please tell your employer that my maids are trained in ju-jitsu. You might like to ask him who will pay to get the grass stains and blood out of that nice suit if you try to lure one of them away.'

The young man removed his cigarette and licked his lips. 'Think there's been a misunderstanding, madam. I'm just taking a breather before going into town.' He rose to his feet and made briskly for the park gates, where he hailed a taxi.

'I hope so,' said Margaret, following at a more leisurely pace. 'I'd like to say "See you around", but for your sake, I sincerely hope I don't.'

For all her words, as she waited for the cab to drive away she felt a deep, uncomfortable dread. The man could easily have turned on her, but her direct action and the busy park had surprised him too much to act. Now she thought about it, had the back of his head been familiar? Perhaps he had followed her before.

It was true that she'd trained both Nellie and Vera in ju-jitsu, the latter turning out to be an unexpected natural, and Nellie, who never ventured far with the children, enjoyed the company of girls of her own age so was rarely alone. Even so, if someone were watching the house, was this man's interest in Nellie coincidental or significant? And the children were caught in the middle.

Margaret stopped at the telegraph office and sent a telegram to Fox: *Different house viewers today. Await suitable response.*

She hurried to the tube station. It had felt dangerous enough when she'd first worked with Fox and there were only the two of them to worry about. Now, she felt responsible for the world. They couldn't take Nellie, Vera and the children house-hunting the next day. Somehow, she'd make sure they were elsewhere.

But right now, she had a police station to visit.

Eighteen

The Walrus entered Inspector Silvermann's room shortly after Margaret had been handed a mug of strong tea from a battered tray.

'Hallo,' she said. 'Did you find anything you fancied in the babies' section?'

The Walrus handed a file to the inspector and said, with a smile, 'Yes, thank you, doctor. A nice bonnet. My missus was very pleased.'

'Perhaps you should have visited homewares. They have a nice line in Thermos flasks. You could have filled one with tea, in case you felt the urge to hang around in parks all day.'

'What goes in gotta come out,' said the Walrus, 'and park keepers get funny about how their plants are watered. Anyway, here's the file, Inspector. Anything else?'

'Not for the moment, Davis.'

The inspector waited till he'd gone, then said, 'If your husband did his job properly, I wouldn't have needed to send him.'

'*Them*,' said Margaret. 'Two men followed me. The one who just came in, and another whom I left on the tube. And what do you mean, "if my husband did his job"?'

'Protecting you.'

'I don't need protection.' Margaret remembered she was trying to get the inspector on side, but his words rankled. 'And how dare you send someone else to accost my maid?'

'I didn't.' Inspector Silvermann frowned. 'What sort of man?'

'This sort.' Margaret handed over the sketch she'd made while on the underground train. Her nausea deepened. Her instinct had been right.

'He's too well dressed for your average copper and I wouldn't use anyone that sneaky-looking. Sure it's you he's after? And what has that to do with Kavanagh? I'm guessing he's why you're here, though I'm not sure why.' His eyes were shrewd. 'What do Abram Cohen and a Whitechapel sweatshop have to do with a murdered maid carrying a note which might be about your husband?'

'She also had a list of haberdashery in her handbag,' said Margaret. 'Mr Kavanagh is a haberdasher. Perhaps we should ask him about it.'

'We?' The inspector scowled. 'Look, doctor, I can see you're annoyed about me sending men to watch you, but it was for your own good. Whatever your husband's got caught up in, there's no reason why you should be, too.'

'Isn't that part of being married?'

'Not in my book.'

'In case you hadn't noticed, Inspector, I'm not the type to sit around. I have a career of my own, which you've hindered by sending Dervla's body to St Bart's.'

'I'm not stopping you from visiting her,' snapped the inspector. 'Why not do that on your day off and let us professionals do our job.'

'Your men are too incompetent to keep themselves hidden.' Margaret heard her voice rising and paused before continuing. 'Mr Cohen's death was, regrettably, waiting to happen. The article that near enough libelled me implied that we said the cause was overwork. We didn't, but overwork wouldn't have helped, and neither would an argument. I have a professional interest in the pathology of the case. Right from the start, you discounted Mr Kavanagh. Now you're holding him. Why? Because of haberdashery samples?'

The inspector raised his eyebrows. 'Hope your husband never tries arguing with you.'

Margaret ignored the jibe. 'I won't question Kavanagh. But I'd like to see him.'

'He's a very sick man.'

'Then I can examine him and give my professional opinion.'

'You won't give up, will you? All right. I'm still not satisfied about that row at the Angel.'

'Why? Because of a heated discussion between colleagues who'd perhaps become friends?'

'Very recently if so. Kavanagh's been selling his wares for only a few months. Mostly to Sullivan.'

'Everyone has to start somewhere.'

'Yes, but it's funny how an Irishman starts up in Whitechapel just when there's rumours that someone's hiding arms there in case there's trouble over the final decision on Irish Home Rule.'

'Isn't that a job for Special Branch?'

'If you don't like St Bart's snouts in your trough, how do you think I feel about Special Branch snouts in mine?'

'Couldn't you all work together?'

'Couldn't you go to St Bart's and work with them?' Inspector Silvermann rolled his eyes and stood up. 'I suppose you might be useful. Do an examination and listen, but don't ask questions. The division surgeon leaves a spare stethoscope here; I'll have someone collect it for you.'

***

Joseph Kavanagh sat in a small side room with the policeman Margaret had left on the train.

The room was panelled in oak that was almost black from years of smoke, dirty hands and greasy clothes left by anyone unlucky enough to be giving a statement. Sunlight barely made it past the window: the room was so full of smoke that it was like being engulfed in thick, choking fog. The policeman held a smouldering cigarette in his left hand while he wrote in a notebook. He held Margaret's gaze for a few seconds, then looked at Inspector Silvermann, expressionless.

On the other side of the table, Kavanagh took a deep drag on his own cigarette, coughed a painful, hollow cough that seemed to come from his boots, squashed the stub in a full ash-tray, then lit another. He offered a cigarette to Margaret, and when she refused, Inspector Silvermann. The inspector waved his own packet of cigarettes and lit up too.

Margaret's eyes watered. She wondered if a penknife could cut an air hole round her head big enough to breathe in.

Kavanagh was in his mid forties, his hair and moustache dead black, his eyes blue, and his skin very pale, both from nature and ill health.

'See what I mean, doctor?' said Inspector Silvermann.

'Doctor, is it?' said Kavanagh. He leaned back in the chair and scrutinised Margaret, making her wish she were wearing something more professional than an outfit with daisies on the lapels.

'I'd like you examined,' said Inspector Silvermann. 'Dr Demeray is something of an expert in chest ailments.'

Kavanagh nodded. 'Good for you, doctor.' He made no move to remove any clothing, just took another drag on the cigarette and coughed. The policeman put his pen down and followed suit, his cough quieter, briefer, less worrying.

Inspector Silvermann cleared his throat. 'I should add that Dr Demeray is one of the pathologists at St Julia's Hospital. She was involved in the post-mortem on Abram Cohen.'

'Ah,' said Kavanagh. He stared at Margaret without blinking for a while, skimming her from summer hat to blue kid shoes, pausing at her white-gloved hands. Nothing could be ascertained from his expression.

Margaret waited.

With an effort, Kavanagh removed his jacket. 'Go on then, listen away while the inspector tells me what he's going to do.'

'I'll let the lady finish first,' said Inspector Silvermann.

Margaret listened to Kavanagh's heart and lungs and timed his pulse. His wrist was bony, his skin fragile under her hands. The blueness of his eyes couldn't disguise the yellowness in the whites, or the greyness of his skin. He must have been very sick for some time. 'You should go to hospital, Mr Kavanagh,' she said, 'and have a full examination and maybe an X-ray.'

He raised his eyebrows. 'And how much would that cost?'

'It's a charity hospital. It would come from the fund, which you're welcome to contribute to. In the meantime, maybe reduce your smoking.'

'My doctor says it's good for clearing the lungs.'

'Many do,' said Margaret firmly. 'A small number believe the opposite, and I'm one of them.'

'Ha,' Kavanagh gave a mirthless laugh as he shrugged his jacket back on.

'You recently arranged lodgings in the Tufnell Park area,' said the Inspector, 'near a house owned by a couple called Webber.'

'I arranged lodgings. Haven't had time to meet the neighbours.'

'One of their maids is dead.'

For the first time, Kavanagh appeared genuinely startled. 'Dead? Since when? Who?'

'A few days. A Miss Dervla Mallowan. She might have been mistaken for a Miss Olive Nolan.'

Kavanagh frowned, his expression a little more guarded as he stubbed out his cigarette. He gave into another violent bout of coughing. When he was eventually able to speak, his voice was hoarse. 'Poor girl.' He shook his head and stubbed out his cigarette. 'Are you going to arrest me then, or send me off to have whatever bedevilment an X-ray will do to my chest?'

Inspector Silvermann turned to Margaret. 'If he goes to St Julia's, would you recommend he be confined to bed for a few days?'

'Yes.'

'Fine by me,' said Kavanagh. 'I'm fit for nothing just now. But here's the thing. The Webbers' property is worth looking into. But as for this Olive Nolan – never heard of her. There'll be a boy behind it, you wait. There usually is.'

***

But he was wrong.

At the hospital, helping to explain to the doctor in charge why Kavanagh should be admitted, Margaret felt frivolous in her pretty summer clothes and steeped in nicotine. When she visited the mortuary wing before going home, a message was waiting: Elinor Edwards, suggesting a late lunch in their favourite haunt, where she'd be until two.

Elinor was waiting in the Gardenia Restaurant near Covent Garden. Her tight curls were crushed under a beige toque which matched her simple outfit. 'I left a message at your home and St J's as a gamble. I knew that if you missed me we'd make other arrangements, but I felt you wouldn't.'

'Is there witchcraft in your blood, Elinor?'

'I've been accused of worse.' Elinor signalled to a waitress. The restaurant was as full of suffragettes as ever, intent on their campaigns rather than other diners.

'I managed to speak to the tweeny, as you suggested,' said Elinor. 'I didn't get much out of her, if it makes you feel any better. But she did tell me that Olive had always wanted to go on the stage. Out of the blue, this company made her an offer, so she gave notice and went.'

'Without questioning it? Is she all right?'

'Fox found the location of the theatre troupe and Hare sent me up to speak to her before the police did. It's been exhausting. I still feel as if I'm on a train.'

'Is she…?'

'The company's legitimate. The person who runs it is highly creative, so rather vague, but said that a mystery benefactor provided much-needed capital in exchange for offering Olive a role. He was asked not to explain the real reason to Olive, as it was a gift.' Elinor paused as Margaret gave her order to the waitress. 'He told her she'd been recommended by a music-hall manager who'd seen her audition but hadn't been able to give her a job.'

Margaret raised her eyebrows.

'The tweeny said Olive knew it was a risk,' said Elinor, 'but she had an escape plan if necessary. It wasn't, fortunately: she's having the time of her life. I asked Olive why she was so keen to go, apart from getting the chance to perform, and she said it was good timing. She didn't want to stay on after she'd heard someone in the study talking about "sorting the girl out".'

'Her master?'

'I don't like that word,' said Elinor, scowling. 'If you mean her employer, no. It was a new neighbour whom she didn't take to. She planned to give notice and tried to get the tweeny to give notice too, without explaining why, but the tweeny – too dim and with nowhere to go – wouldn't. When Olive got the chance to do what she'd always wanted to, she upped and left.'

'But if she overheard something, is she really safe?'

'If anyone knew she'd overheard anything, Olive would be dead,' said Elinor. 'I think they wanted to get her away so they could replace her with Dervla at short notice, and they were pleased she swallowed the bait so easily. While in the north of England, Olive would never hear about the death of a maid in London, when it was barely mentioned in London itself. By the time she heard about it, the fact that there'd been a mistaken identification would also be known.'

'So what was the point? They could have killed Dervla anywhere and disposed of her body without anyone finding it, and kept the focus away from the Webber house'

Elinor took a sip of tea and pondered. 'So it must have been deliberate. The false identification would muddy the waters just long enough to cause confusion. The police would have worked out all the connections eventually and Fox would have found out even without your telling him about the post mortem.'

'And you think that in the meantime, they'd abstract the body,' said Margaret, 'and bury it where it was likely to be found early enough to be identifiable, bearing items linking it to Fox.'

Elinor nodded. 'They'd know that Fox would ask for the body's real identity to be suppressed to protect the original investigation.'

'Surely that's a perfectly common request.'

'Normally,' said Elinor. 'But it's a suspicious one when the person asking might be implicated in the death. Here's an Irish girl, presumed to be a revolutionary, arrested by Fox for gun-running, despite having insufficient evidence for a safe conviction. Somehow, she's allowed to escape and is then murdered, when he should have been keeping her under lock and key. Is he incompetent? Or did he do it to ensure her death? Don't look at me like that, you know I don't think either of those things. But it's easy to make it look that way.'

Margaret swallowed. 'All right. I accept that premise. I can see that they must have sent Olive away so they could house Dervla in an anonymous sort of way. I suppose killing her there makes a sort of sense, but why not move the body so there was no connection? I think it was a mistake. If the delivery boy hadn't come early, they could have moved Dervla's body, dressed her in her own clothes and put her somewhere else. That's why they had to steal her from St Julia's.'

'But wasn't there a note in Dervla's pocket implicating everyone?'

It sounded as if Elinor hadn't seen or read the note, and Margaret thought back to what it had said.

Moore's dead because he knew who really killed Gastrell. Watch your neck. There's no mercy in either an old soldier or a fox.

'Maybe it was also one she received herself so she knew what was threatened, but not who to turn to. Poor Dervla.' Margaret crumbled the piece of cake on her plate. 'You said Olive overheard something. Was it any help at all?'

'If anyone can make sense of it.' Elinor flicked through a notebook full of shorthand. 'She reported that the man was on the telephone and said "when the girl's shut up for good, like the quartermaster, make sure the fox and the Irishman get the blame." Then he laughed and added "Revenge if you like. Mentioning gas'll do the job." Olive said she's been putting up with people demeaning the Irish since she arrived from Belfast, but it made no sense. She doesn't know what a quartermaster is, they don't get foxes in the garden, and if they did and wanted them dealt with, the local vermin catcher's English. Also, the Webber's house is on electric light now, though the neighbour's might still be on gas.'

Margaret was uneasy, it seemed Elinor knew nothing about Gastrell.

'Who is the Irishman who's supposed to be blamed, though?' said Elinor. 'Could it be Olive's father or Dervla's?'

'Maybe it's neither,' said Margaret. 'Perhaps the key thing is to discover what an Irishman did that deserves revenge.'

Nineteen

Early the next morning, with Bert driving, Fox and Margaret went house-hunting.

They were silent for the first mile or so, daunted by their plans for the day. They had to cram three house viewings into the morning, then find the village northwest of London where Norris Gastrell had been born.

'Did you remember that Moore junior wants to take you out for a beer?' said Margaret, eventually. 'Lucy said when she wrote.'

'Yes and it's a shame, but it will have to wait. I don't want to make him look more involved than he is.'

'Do you ever wish you could swap places with someone who has a simpler life?'

'Do you?'

'Not often, but maybe today.'

'Any closer to finding the Webbers' neighbour or a link with Kavanagh?'

'Not yet. Rainer, if that's his name, arranged the tenancy of the house through an agent who paid upfront for a six month lease. As the house needs a good deal of refurbishment, the absentee owner didn't ask too many questions. We don't have a first name, just the initial K. The address the agent gave for him was the same as the one for Bythersee undertakers, but nothing was ever posted there, so it was never revealed as false. Rainer invited Webber for card nights, and occasionally he went to play cards at Webber's. The maids describe him as good-looking, tall, slender and fair-haired. In his thirties perhaps, though they say he's tanned so his skin seems older.'

'Attractive then.'

'See for yourself.' Fox reached into an inner pocket, extracted a small piece of paper and handed it over.

'This is a copy of a sketch the observer made. Yet another more or less average sort.'

Margaret considered the simple but skilled drawing. 'Yes. He's attractive. And somehow familiar.'

'Really? Where from?'

'I don't mean I know him.' Margaret shrugged. 'There's not really enough detail to tell.'

'Well my man could hardly go and ask him to sit for a portrait. He made a quick sketch and he took a photograph, both from some distance, and later visited as an insurance salesman in the hope of getting a closer view. But Rainer wasn't interested, or didn't fall for it, depending on the point of view.'

Margaret handed the paper back. 'I think he's familiar because he has a certain look. That colonial arrogance where someone who lives out in India or Africa treats native servants like they're a lesser species and junior staff of their own race not much better. I've rarely had a lot to do with that sort of person, thank God. It may be a clichéd image, I'm sure they can't all be like that, but I think that's what his face must make me think of. I've certainly never met him. On a superficial physical level, his face is attractive apart from that suggestion of arrogance, but that's not evidence of character. Do you know what he's like as a person?'

'The servants are pretty cagey - he's paying their wages after all, even though he's not there - but I had the impression they don't like him.'

'Because?'

'Hard to say. There's a rumour going round the neighbourhood that he waited till Webber was away and killed the girl they know as Molly for resisting his advances.'

'So he molests maids?'

'There's no evidence of that. Rainer's own staff wouldn't tell a man that sort of thing, but to be honest, I had the impression that they don't like him because he was exactly as you described - arrogant and demanding. I don't think the rumour came from his own maids, I think it's just local tittle-tattle because Rainer's an incomer, who disappeared immediately after the murder. No one wants to think a killer who's living unrecognised within their neighbourhood killed Molly. It's easier to blame an outsider who kept himself largely to himself apart from playing cards with a man wetter than a January Sunday and has since gone away again.'

'Kavanagh has lodgings nearby.'

'Which appear quite legitimate,' said Fox. 'It's the sort of area where rich, middling and poor could lean out of windows and shake hands if they wanted to. But he arranged the lodgings in March and left the country the day before I brought Dervla to London.' Fox leaned forward. 'Here we are, Bert. This is the first.'

Bert stopped the car outside a large square villa. The ivy growing on it was so symmetrical that it looked like a severe haircut. A regiment of rose bushes guarded the front garden and a sign on the gate said, 'No tradesmen at *this* entrance'. A didactic hand pointed towards a narrow entrance to the left.

'Any good?' said Fox. 'It's close to a main line. There are trees at the back. The pub nearby is allegedly decent and there's a twee tea shop for you.'

'Honestly?'

'No good, then.' He squeezed her hand. 'I'm not suggesting we take any of these seriously. We have to be seen doing what we said we'd do, so we're looking at the outside of two houses and the inside of one.'

Margaret resisted the urge to turn and look. 'We're being followed?'

'I don't think so, but one can't be certain. Bert can keep an eye out.' He leaned forward and tapped on Bert's shoulder, said 'On to the next', then turned to Margaret. 'I doubt you'll appreciate the second house either, but it's on the way to Gastrell's home town and we may as well appear logical.'

They dealt with the second house much as they had the first, and arrived at their third destination a little after noon. The creeping edge of London was ten miles away. The railway was a branch line, the village sleepy.

Margaret was starting to feel hungry and looked with longing at the small thatched pub which stared across the obligatory duck-pond at a small Saxon church. They were both short and stubby, personifying an understanding between landlord and vicar that each was important to their parishioners and sometimes performed a similar function.

The house where Norris Gastrell had been born was Georgian. Other, larger houses, dating from Tudor to early Victorian, were dotted about, with large gardens and paddocks between them. A few thatched cottages, of the picturesque but doubtless dark and insanitary type, also lurked, but it seemed as if their days were numbered. One row was in the process of being demolished and replaced by small villas and modern cottages.

The Georgian house looked none too happy about developments. Bougainvillea dripped like tears from its windows, and its front door was a depressed grey.

'Like it?' said Fox.

'No.'

'Nor do I. Maybe it's because it spawned Gastrell, but no, I don't like it.'

'What are we going to say to his family?'

'Gastrell's parents died within a year of him. The heir to the estate sold the house to someone who's never lived there and is now selling it. Maybe something inside will help.'

'If someone *is* following us—'

'How were we supposed to know this was Gastrell's family home? We're just looking for a house, and then going to meet the verger in the parish church.'

An agent showed them round the house while Bert waited in the car. To Margaret and Fox's chagrin, it was almost entirely unfurnished, with nothing of a personal nature left anywhere. Anything that might have remained of the Gastrell family was long gone, which left only the parish records.

The church was pleasantly cool and quiet after a house which had been shut up for months. A wedding had taken place earlier. Drifts of confetti fluttered as they passed, and inside, the flowers and ribbons tied to the pews were still fresh and fragrant. Bert made a quick tour of the interior, then came out, saying he liked to read old gravestones.

The verger, a man in his late fifties, showed them round the building with pride. It was an unostentatious country church, with only its east window resplendent in stained glass. He was excited to show them a dark corner of the nave, where years of whitewash had fallen away to reveal the pale ochres and greens of a medieval painting which an expert was going to restore. On one side of the nave, three huge boards were fixed to the stone wall. Gold lettering declaimed the commandments, the beatitudes and eighteenth-century bequests left by the local rich to benefit the local poor. On the opposite wall, ragged military colours from Waterloo to the South African war hung from brass holders. Scattered about the walls were memorial plaques. In a prominent place, a brass one commemorating victory in South Africa was engraved with the names of five men from the village who had died there. The deceased were ordered by social rank, with Captain Norris Selwyn Gastrell, aged thirty-four, at the top. Even in the low light of a church interior, it was possible to see that someone had tried to scratch his name out.

'I gather there's a story there,' said Fox. 'We've just viewed the house which it turns out was once his. It seems ... an unhappy place.'

The house had felt nothing but uncherished and stale, but this judgement livened up the verger.

'It was,' he said. 'It seems all wrong to me to have his name at the top because he was gentry, and my youngest lad at the bottom just because he was a private. We're all equal in God's eyes, aren't we? There's no pockets in shrouds. Why not just do it alphabetical?'

'I'm terribly sorry,' said Margaret.

'I am, too,' said Fox. 'And as wars go, it was a horrible one.'

The verger heaved a sigh. 'My son died saving a friend when they were ambushed. Word was that the ambush only happened because Gastrell sold secrets to the enemy. And Gastrell himself drowned afore it could be proved. So why's *he* a hero? The rumours benighted that family. But then they were the ones who spoiled him.'

'Ah,' said Fox.

The verger nodded.

Ah, what? thought Margaret. *Aren't you going to ask anything else?* She opened her mouth to speak, but Fox put his arm round her and squeezed her waist.

'That's my son at the bottom,' the verger reiterated. 'Nineteen, he was. At the bottom. And the man who killed him is at the top.' There was another pause, during which the verger seemed to come to a decision. 'You want to know the story? Maybe I shouldn't. But it might help you decide whether to buy that house.'

'If you've time,' said Fox, mildly.

'Come and look at the registers, then.' The verger took them to the cupboard where the marriage register lay, put a piece of blotting paper on the latest page, and turned the heavy pages back. Thirty-nine years of weddings passed in a whisper of thick paper and little clouds of dust puffed into the air. 'Here's Gastrell's parents getting married in 1862.'

'Did you know the family?' asked Fox.

'I should think so. Born and bred, I am. They're incomers, acourse.'

'When they married?'

'No, bless you, sir. My folks have been buried in that graveyard since before the Conqueror. The Gastrells only came here in 1760 or thereabouts. Maybe a bit before. Not sure where they were from. France, perhaps, with a name like that. All gone now.'

'I see,' said Margaret. 'So Norris Gastrell was the last of them.'

'In a way.' The verger stood there, smiling, but said no more.

Margaret wanted to scream. She could have gauged how to make a Londoner continue, but faced with this country insouciance, she was stumped.

'Ah,' said Fox, then fell silent. He studied the interior of the church. 'This is a beautiful place. Have you a collection for its upkeep?'

'Bless you, sir, we do.' The verger produced a small box as if by magic, put it next to the marriage register and watched Fox put half a crown into it. 'Well now, here you are.' He extracted the baptismal and burial registers from the cupboard and laid them on the table, turning their pages back and forth, tracing names from volume to volume. Gastrell's parents' marriage in 1862, the baptism and burial in infancy of two children, Gastrell's birth in 1868, then three more doomed children.

Years passed under the verger's hands until he arrived at 1902 when Mr Gastrell senior and his wife were buried a few months apart, within a year of their son's death. 'Near enough killed them he did with his shameful death, for all his name's high on that plaque his mother paid for.' He pointed at the wall, the names equal in indecipherability from where they stood. 'She invited his cronies to see it unveiled and it was in the papers and everything, but there was disgruntlement, I can tell you, among those local lads who came back. Mrs Gastrell left the estate to some cousin, but he sold it to someone else who's selling it now. So that was *in a way* the last of them.'

'In a way?'

'Depends on how you look at things.' The verger tapped his nose and turned the pages of the baptismal register back to 1892.

8th August 1892
Child's Christian Names: Carl Gastrell
Christian Names of Parents: — & Lena
Surname of Parents: Father: — Mother: Webber
Quality, Trade or Profession of Father: —
By whom the ceremony was performed: L H Fairbanks

'What do you think of that?' he asked.

'Webber...' Fox added a florin to the collection box. 'Interesting. How did the Gastrells feel about their surname being used as an illegitimate child's middle name?'

The verger chuckled. 'What do you think? When they heard, they came to argue with Reverend Fairbanks that Gastrell wasn't a Christian name and shouldn't be allowed. He said it wasn't for them to object, and asked, in his cunning way, weren't they honoured that Lena Webber had thought so highly of them that she'd chosen the name for her son? Surely they had nothing to hide? And there was plenty of time for a wedding, if the father chose to make an honest woman of her and own his child. But Mr and Mrs Gastrell put their noses in the air and walked away. Or so I've heard.'

'Was Lena Webber one of their servants?' asked Margaret.

'No, bless you, madam, she was the doctor's daughter. Never worked a day in her life. Very respectable. Just eighteen when the lad was born. The Gastrells had eyes on a higher-born girl, I imagine. And one who didn't fall so easily.'

'That's unfair,' said Margaret. 'She may have only been seventeen when Gastrell made her pregnant, but he'd have been twenty-four.'

'Her father should have kept better control of her,' replied the verger. 'I wasn't much older than Lena Webber at the time, and I remember the scandal. Perhaps she hoped Norris would do the right thing before it was too late, but he didn't. So maybe she thought she'd shame him into it afterwards by naming the child as she did.'

Margaret felt her heart race. 'But it didn't work.'

'Not here, it didn't. And if it did later, she made a worse bargain by marrying him than being seduced by him. Her family shuffled her off just outside London soon after the baby was born. There were that many rumours going about: that she pretended to be a widow, that she had the child adopted and started again, that – and I hope this wasn't true – that Gastrell kept her without marrying her. The rest of the Webbers moved away, and we never heard any more.'

'The rest of the family.' Fox nodded wisely. 'A younger son?'

'That's right, John. A year younger than Lena, or thereabouts. You heard of him?'

'Maybe,' said Fox.

'Looked up to Gastrell. Did little errands for him. Played tricks on people for him, which no one could mind because the Gastrells were too important.'

'Wasn't John angry about his sister?' said Margaret.

'He thought her a fool at best and a harlot at worst, and Gastrell a fine fellow of a man for following his instincts. But that's a common enough view, isn't it?'

'It's an appalling view.'

The verger nodded. 'I shouldn't speak ill of the dead, but there was a rumour Gastrell's death wasn't accidental and maybe he asked for it. Gastrell was a wrong 'un from early on. Thought he had a right to anything he wanted and didn't care how he got it. Shouldn't say it, but—' The verger looked towards the font. 'I think it takes more than holy water on a baby's head to make a Christian. Gastrell chose a different master. Even the old reverend was glad we didn't have to bury him in consecrated ground.'

'And Lena Webber?' persisted Margaret. 'You say she moved near London. Do you know where?'

'Your wife's a true Londoner, isn't she?' said the verger to Fox with a chuckle. 'Always in a hurry. Can't let a story tell itself.' He scratched his head. 'There was a castle there. Or a palace. Now let me think…'

'North? South? East? West?'

'South. Or west. One of them. Both, maybe. The name always makes me think of a good meal. Fulham. That's it, Fulham. Funny name, that. Full … Ham. Wonder if the person who named it was hungry. What d'you reckon?'

Twenty

The verger told them the village pub didn't serve meals suitable for ladies, and the nice little tea shop was closed to prepare for the holiday weekend. He reluctantly suggested a nearby town, where the offices of the newspaper which had reported on the memorial service were situated. Wondering what sort of meals were unsuitable for women, Margaret tied her veil over her face.

The journey to the market town was painful and dusty. The country lanes were unsurfaced: horses and cartwheels had dug holes and grooves which had turned into ruts when dried by the sun.

Aching from the juddering of the wheels, Margaret felt frustrated. Even if they could get word to Elinor, the chance of her obtaining access to records tracing Lena, John or Carl Webber, on a Friday afternoon before a holiday weekend, was almost nil.

'John Webber rings a bell,' said Fox, once they were on a better road. 'I think he was the one Sir Broderick described as a milksop, who sucked up to Gastrell. He seemed too young and unreliable to be Gastrell's accomplice.' He extracted a notebook from an inner pocket and despite the jolting of the car, began to write. 'In 1892, when the scandal with Lena Webber happened, Gastrell was twenty-four and she was eighteen. The verger said Lena's brother John was a year or so younger than her, so he'd have been sixteen or seventeen. Therefore he was in his mid twenties in South Africa and mid thirties now. So far, we've discounted Mr Webber, who owns the house where Dervla died. Could he actually be this Webber?'

'All the better,' said Margaret. 'If anyone digs, he can just say he wanted to distance himself but not conceal anything. But surely it was a huge risk to have her die there.'

'The evidence points at the neighbour and me. He's being used. Damn, I'll have to go back to regimental headquarters and find out more.'

'You could ask Sir Broderick.'

'Of course, yes'

'At least you might find something out about him,' said Margaret. 'Finding the others will be hard. Even if we assume Lena stayed in Fulham and get access to electoral rolls, that won't help. Carl Webber is too young to be on the roll and Lena *won't* be on it because she's a woman.'

'I might write to the prime minister and argue for universal suffrage just for that reason,' grumbled Fox.

'You do that, but it won't help now. Can you get access to last year's census?'

'We can try,' said Fox. 'But Lena might have boycotted it. Tax records are even harder. I suppose there's Somerset House, in case Lena married or died. The newspaper which reported on the memorial ceremony might give some clue, if any of them turned up. Though I can't see why they would. It'll be a job for Elinor, talking to all those clerks and convincing them to hand over records.'

'I don't know how she does it.'

'We don't call Elinor Mrs Hedgehog just because she's prickly. I've often suspected hints of violence. Probably a covert operation to disorganise their filing under cover of darkness.' Fox's face, though obscured by driving goggles and road dust, was grim despite his words. 'It's a damn nuisance that nothing can be done till Tuesday. I hope to God Sir Broderick has found something in his diaries, or knows if Webber in Tufnell Park and Webber who knew Gastrell are the same man.

Remind me to wire him when we're home and arrange a meeting.'

In the town, a market filled the main thoroughfare, forcing Bert to slow to a crawl as they drove through. The pub was crammed with beer-drinking men, the tea shops with gossiping women.

The entrance to the newspaper office was obscured by a large delivery vehicle, but its name was boldly painted on the wall above its third-floor windows. To their relief, they found it still open.

'Access to the archives from ten years ago?' said the clerk, blowing out his cheeks. 'Of course you can see it. But you'll have to give us a bit of time. Most of us are flat out on the evening edition.'

'Go on and get Mrs F some lunch,' said Bert. 'I'll wait here.'

'I'm not hungry,' said Margaret.

'I want to get on, too,' said Fox. He stood, arms folded, jaw set. 'But we're stuck.'

'You could just go home,' said Bert. 'I'll come on by train. If Mrs F drives, I'll probably beat you.'

'Very funny, Bert.'

'Well, there's no point in three of us waiting here,' said Bert. 'If you prefer, Mrs F, you can stay. Fox and me'll go to the pub and buy some sandwiches for when you suddenly indicate you're starving by taking our heads off in about…' He consulted his watch. 'About an hour.' He bestowed a slow, insolent grin on her.

'Thank you for your unquestioning subservience, driver,' said Margaret, 'but I'm not sitting here while you two go to the pub. I've got a much better idea. If the library's still open, Fox and I can go and—'

'What kind of person prefers a library to a pub?' said Bert.

'One who doesn't want to fight to be served because she's a woman, and who wants relevant information ungarbled by alcohol.'

'That's the trouble with you, Mrs F. You have no idea how to have fun.'

'Stop arguing,' said Fox. 'We can't gain much by leaving you behind, Bert. Margaret, I spotted the telegraph office a few doors along. We'll send a wire to Elinor to get the ball rolling, and another to Vera, to let her know we might be late. Then you can explain why a library would be any use.'

'If only somewhere this far out in the wilderness had a public telephone, I could telephone Vera,' said Margaret, as they left. 'It might be quicker and I'd know everything was all right.'

'One day I'll find you a real piece of wilderness and dump you there. But even if there is a public telephone, it would be more expensive than a telegram and take ages. Who knows how long it would take to connect all the exchanges between here and there? The children are all right.'

'How do you know?'

'Why shouldn't they be? Let's get this job done.'

She was about to retort when she caught his expression. He was looking at somewhere into the middle distance, his eyes unhappy, his mouth a thin, angry line.

'I didn't mean to sound facetious,' she said. 'I'd just like to be sure. I know you want to live somewhere like this.'

'What?' He focussed on her. 'No, I don't. Did I snap? I'm sorry, I'm just thinking. Here we are. At least it's not busy.'

Inside the telegraph office, no one paid any undue attention as Fox filled in a form with what would look like an innocuous message, then asked for directions to the public library.

The library was as busy as the market square, as people took the opportunity to secure books for the long weekend. But it was quiet: the only noise louder than the shuffling of paper and muttered exchanges was the thud of the date stamp. The bookshelves Margaret wanted in were in a dark corner.

The librarian grimaced in a refined manner, and breathed rather than whispered. 'Yes, I've heard of the Gastrells, but they weren't real gentry. Not *county*. They won't be in *Who's Who*. They lived in this town for a while before buying a fancier house in the country.'

Margaret blinked at the thought that the librarian didn't consider the tiny town to be in the country too, then pulled herself together. 'I thought they might be in a book about local history.'

'The Gastrells?' Again, the dainty face-pulling. The librarian bent to a low shelf marked *History – Local*.

'Perhaps they came here from France,' said Margaret. 'I'm of Huguenot stock myself.'

'How fascinating,' said the librarian, sounding supremely disinterested. 'But the Gastrells, as far as I've heard, came from Gloucestershire.'

'Ah.'

'This might do.' The librarian held out a slim volume about the village. 'Published in 1895. There's information about the history of the church, the houses and their inhabitants. It was written after they put in the branch line, but before they started all the new houses.' She peered over at Fox, who was delving in the Military section. 'Is your husband all right? Does he know what he's looking for?'

'Information about any local men who took part in the South African War,' said Margaret.

'Mmm,' said the librarian. 'It'll be dry, factual and general, I imagine. What about...' She moved along the shelves and bent down. 'This is a little volume which a rather nice local chap wrote about his experiences. He was far too old to be fighting – sixty-five if he was a day – but refused to give up till afterwards. Isn't it curious that he survived while younger men died?' She extracted a thin volume in a dark-green cover. 'He had it published privately for his family but his daughter handed her copy in when he died. She said she couldn't bear to read it but it ought to be available to anyone who wanted to. Of course, no one's interested, but...' The librarian flicked through the pages. 'Oh my! What a funny coincidence! Here's the name Gastrell! They must have served together.'

'May I see? I have membership.' *Of an entirely different library*, Margaret added to herself.

'Of course you may. I'll have to leave it with you for a moment: I'm needed at the counter. We'll be closing for lunch in five minutes. Do take notes, but I'm afraid that, membership or no membership, we don't allow reference books to be borrowed.'

'Ah. Thank you.'

The librarian nodded and swept to the counter.

Margaret turned the pages of the book. *They say that the devil knows his own*, it said on a page towards the middle. *If it were not true of Gastrell, then it is not true of anyone.*

She hissed at Fox. 'Psst. Come and look.'

Fox looked up from the tome in his hands just as Bert walked in, flourishing an envelope. 'Here you go, guv'nor!' He said loudly. 'We can go!'

At least twenty people said 'Shhh!'

Everyone glared at Bert, apart from a librarian who was checking his watch against the clock and a woman in a large hat immersed in a novel in the Romance section. It was twenty-five past one.

The librarian who had been helping Margaret returned, snatched the book before Margaret could tighten her grip, and smiled cheerfully. 'Do come back later, madam, but please don't bring your chauffeur, unless he's learned to speak at an appropriate volume.'

'Yes. I mean, no. I just wanted to write down the details of that book, including the publisher. I should like to find another copy, if there is one.'

'I'm sorry, madam, but we are about to close. If I let you dilly-dally, everyone will dilly-dally. Do come back after lunch.'

Margaret glanced at Fox, who was frowning from the doorway. 'I'm afraid that's not possible.' She extracted a calling card from her purse, together with a blank postcard and a stamp. 'As a favour, could you post me those details as soon as you can today?'

'Very well,' said the librarian, with a sigh. 'Now will you go, madam?'

'What was all that about?' asked Fox, as they left.

'A book by a local soldier about his experiences in South Africa. It includes reference to Gastrell,' said Margaret. 'I didn't have time to read it. I don't know if it's libellous or not, but it didn't look complimentary.'

Fox stopped. 'Why didn't you borrow it?'

'She wouldn't let me. But she's sending me details so I can look for another copy. The publisher must know if there is one. Hopefully the card will arrive this evening.'

'Thank you, Margaret,' said Fox. He resumed striding towards the car. Once they were settled inside, he said 'Bert, what do you have?'

'A transcript of the article, and a photograph of the photo they used for it.' Bert lifted a folding camera from his pocket. 'They said they'd send a proper copy if they can find the negative, but my photograph will do for now. I'll get our chap to develop it this afternoon.'

'What does the article say? Who's in the photograph?'

'It was simple enough: a description of the ceremony, a list of the dead soldiers' names, ranks and ages, with a sentence about each one, and a list of the attendees' names. There were about fifty of them.'

'Fifty?' Fox took the envelope and extracted the transcript. 'How long will it take to wade through them all?'

'If you'd let me finish,' said Bert, 'Anyone from outside the village is listed with where they came from. There are a few people who appear to be relations, but also Second Lieutenant Webber from Hammersmith, Mrs and Master Gascon from Fulham, Captain and Mrs Selkirk from Harrow, and Mr Punifoy from Shepherd's Bush.'

Margaret leaned over Fox's shoulder. 'Purefoy? Oh, Punifoy. I've never heard of that name.'

'The Selkirks?' said Fox, ignoring her. 'But Sir Broderick loathed Gastrell. Having a traitor under his command nearly destroyed his career. What on earth was he doing there?'

Twenty-One

The return home, even with Bert breaking the speed limit, took two hours.

They stopped for a simple lunch while Fox reread the article. He was unresponsive when Margaret put her hand out, replacing the transcript in its envelope without showing her. Irritated, she sensed Bert watching them.

Annoyed as she was, she wasn't going to argue with Fox in front of an audience. She took a final mouthful of warm cider, stood up, then shrugged herself into the hot, dusty motoring coat. 'Let's go.'

They continued the journey in silence and arrived at four-thirty.

The twins were settled in the nursery with Nellie, who said 'Would you like to help with the feeds, ma'am?' She gave the distinct impression that she'd prefer to manage alone, but Margaret helped anyway.

'It's a shame you didn't see the printed photograph,' said Fox, when she went to find him with the post at five. 'You could have sketched the people in it so that we didn't have to wait for Bert's photograph to be developed.'

'Then I wouldn't have been in the library to find that book,' she snapped.

He looked up. 'What's wrong with you?'

'What's wrong with *you*? You've been rude and – and secretive all afternoon.'

He blinked at her.

'This is like an obsession, not a mission,' she said. 'You ask for my help, then shut me out and treat me like a nobody in front of Bert.'

'I don't.'

'You did today. You wouldn't even let me look at the transcript of that article.'

'I thought you heard what I read out.'

'I've lost any sense of whether this mission is about Germans, Fenians or something else entirely.'

'Shhh.'

'Vera's at the bazaar. There's no one in the house but you, me, and Nellie three floors up, singing lullabies!'

'What came in the post?'

'What does it matter?' Margaret muttered as she slammed letter after innocuous letter on the table, then scowled at a small parcel postmarked two hours earlier, the name of the post town blurred. She opened it. Inside was *A Lance-Corporal's Life Under Fire,* the book she'd found in the library, and a note on a postcard.

Dear Dr Demeray,

The chief librarian says you may have difficulty finding a copy of this book, as this was the only one printed for distribution and the publisher may not have proofs any more. Given that you are clearly a woman of good standing and the only person who has been interested in it for years, he is prepared to lend it to you for a month in good faith.

Yours,

An illegible squiggle for a signature. 'How did the post beat us home?' she asked.

'Came by train,' said Fox, taking it from her.

'Don't snatch! Do you think a woman can't understand a book about warfare?' snapped Margaret. 'If you didn't want my help, why ask for it? And when I give it, don't treat me like someone too stupid to be trusted!'

He got up and moved close to her. 'I'm sorry.' His eyes were troubled, his mouth downturned. 'It's not personal. I'd be the same with anyone.'

She took a breath, then cupped his cheek. 'Just explain. If you can't, then please tell me why not.'

'I want to read this book first,' he said, leading her to sit next to him. 'I know you found it, but if it refers to Gastrell's death then it'll mention me, and I want to know what you're going to read.'

Margaret stared into his eyes. The contradiction must haunt him. He had tried to save the life of a man he'd wanted hanged for treason and he would always wonder whether he hadn't tried hard enough because Gastrell didn't deserve to live. 'Why didn't you say earlier? I'd have understood.' She sighed. 'I'll put something soothing on the gramophone and get us a drink.'

'I'm still puzzled about why Sir Broderick went to that memorial.'

'For the sake of another soldier from the village, perhaps,' said Margaret. 'Or, since Gastrell was never formally charged, it might have looked odd if his commanding officer didn't attend.'

'True. I wonder how long it'll take to find the right part of the book.'

'You're not reading from the beginning, are you?' said Margaret. 'I'd go straight to the relevant bit if it were me.'

'Some of us are patient.'

'Some of us like getting nasty things over with.'

After finding a bottle of beer at the back of the pantry, Margaret made tea for herself and Nellie. Vera entered through the side door just as she'd laid out two trays.

'I can finish that, ma'am,' said Vera. 'It's not for you to do.' For someone who'd been preparing for a bazaar she seemed downcast, her eyes a little red, her shoulders slumped.

'What's happened?' Margaret cursed herself for being too self-absorbed to notice whether anyone was lurking outside.

'It's n-nothing.' Vera looked round the kitchen as if it were a prison and sniffed. 'I miss having my own place, that's all. I suppose I could stop renting out my place, live there and get a lodger, and work here in the daytime like Dinah does, but I couldn't leave you and Nellie in the lurch, ma'am. Not with the way things are.'

'I'm not expecting a baby, Vera, if that's what you mean.'

'You aren't?'

'I just don't like boiled beef.'

'Oh.' Vera's face reddened. 'But maybe—'

'We're not planning it,' said Margaret. 'Sit down and let me pour you some tea.'

'It's not right, ma'am.'

'Nonsense.' Margaret handed a cup over. 'Please don't feel trapped. I can understand you missing your own place.' *I miss my own little flat just for me, too,* she wanted to say.

But maybe it wasn't time alone that Vera missed. Something Nellie had said slipped into her mind. *I don't have a follower.* 'Vera, can I ask you …have you a young man?'

Vera blinked, then her face relaxed into a relieved grin. 'Not exactly young,' she said. 'He's pushing forty, but then I'm thirty-four.'

'Is he … is he someone you've known for a while, or —?'

'Lord bless you, ma'am, you know my Norbert. He's a ticket clerk at the tube station. A little thin on top, and shy. But I don't mind.' She chuckled. 'Cos he *likes* my boiled beef.' She sobered again. 'He's widowed, too. Just like me.'

'That's wonderful,' said Margaret. 'I don't mean being widowed. I mean—'

'I know what you mean, ma'am. Thank you. I'm glad you don't mind.'

'Of course I don't,' said Margaret, rising. 'And if you marry, Nellie and Dinah and I can manage till we find someone to replace you.'

Vera went pink and Margaret grinned. 'So he's asked. Don't wait too long to say I do accept.'

'No, ma'am,' Vera became businesslike. 'Will salad do for dinner tonight, ma'am? Or shall I go back to the shops so I can make something more substantial?'

Margaret thought of the brief, bad-tempered lunch of warm cider, sweaty cheese and dry bread. 'I think we'll eat out. You and Nellie can finish the salad.'

'Very well, ma'am. And thank you, ma'am. And, er, please don't tell Norbert about the ju-jitsu. He likes me to be ladylike.'

'I won't,' said Margaret. 'But maybe tell him anyway. Marriage is better without secrets.'

She returned to the sitting room. The music had come to an end. Fox was staring at the book as if it had turned him to stone.

'What is it?' she said. The oasis of domestic normality she had shared with Vera was engulfed by foreboding.

He looked at her, eyes wide. 'I took your advice and went straight for the part about Gastrell's death.'

Margaret dropped into the chair beside him and put her hand on his arm. 'If it lies and blames you for letting him drown, no one will ever read it.'

'I have no idea whether it does or not.' Fox handed her the book. 'Read from halfway down.'

Margaret did as bid, reading aloud from the end of one page and then the beginning of the next.

'Stay where you are, men,' ordered Lieut. Gastrell to our surprise, nay irritation. We did as commanded, even though we were none of us on duty. Or rather, we did not move from where we sat by the river. Lieut. Knox had already told us to stay put and wandered off as was his way, and he would not have heard Gastrell, being some time out of sight beyond the trees. Moore and others of the younger chaps grumbled, feeling it was not for him to order us about when we were not under his command, and moreover, were on a half day's leave. But it wastes energy to be upset by officers' little ways.

It was most interesting to see what occurred next, for who should appear but Lieut. Foxcroft-McSionnach, walking apace. He walked quietly and said nothing, simply nodding as he passed. The younger fellows took this to mean that we were again being commanded to stay put, but I did not see it that way. Lieut. Foxcroft-McSionnach had little direct authority and had, as you have read, been courteous in all his dealings with us. Yet for some reason Lieut. Gastrell turned, and seeing the other man nearing him, began to run.

It was at that moment that we were asked what we had seen of his final moments, which of course was not a great deal, other than Lieut. Foxcroft-McSionnach's frantic attempts to revive Lieut. Gastrell to no avail, until he was quite exhausted, himself nearly drowned too. There is little else to be said on the matter, and we did say among ourselves that it had saved the army a good deal of disagreeable shame, aught else being but rumour. strongly believe, however, that in the end, justice will somehow prevail.

Margaret stopped reading. 'That doesn't make sense. One minute Gastrell is alive, the next the men are being asked about his final moments.'

'Look at the page numbers.'

On the left was page ninety-six, ending in the words *'It was at that moment that'*. On the right, page ninety-nine started mid-sentence: *'we were asked what we had seen...'* In between, it was just possible to see that the intervening page had been cut out, very close to the stitches holding the book together.

'Why... who...'

'And what,' said Fox. 'I've checked the other pages and they're all there. It's just that one, giving the details of his death. Did you notice anything else?'

Margaret read it through again silently. 'Who is Lieutenant Knox?'

'I don't remember anyone of that name. We'll need to go back through it to see if he's mentioned elsewhere.'

Margaret flipped the pages, glancing at Fox. He poured out the beer but didn't drink, staring at his notebook as he drew angry little star after angry little star, the ink blotting and the nib scratching as he stabbed. Whether his subconscious was trying to excise something from the paper or slash it to ribbons was unclear.

'Maybe the page was taken out by someone in the Gastrell family,' she said.

'I doubt it. They didn't cut out the pages where he's effectively libelled.'

'Then...' She held his hand to stop it stabbing. 'Even if that one page said the most terrible things about you, no one will know. It's just one book published by one man for one family.'

'Is it?'

Margaret turned back to the book. A name jumped out at her from the middle of a page of dense prose, then another. 'Fox, look. This is from 1900. "In the sick tents, once he had recovered enough to speak to me, Lieut. Mallowan declared he was disgusted at what Lieut. Gastrell had done, and saying that Boer women were worthy opponents, fighting to protect their homesteads as fiercely as any man would and deserved better treatment."'

'Mallowan? I didn't interview a Mallowan when I was there.'

'A sick tent in 1900 might have mixed up the regiments,' said Margaret. 'This can't be a coincidence.'

'Which indicates a link between Mallowan, Gastrell and this Knox person. I'll bet you anything—'

The doorbell rang and Vera answered it. A thought came to the edge of Margaret's mind, then dissolved as Vera entered. 'Sorry to disturb you, sir, ma'am. It's a telegram for the master. The boy's waiting for a reply.'

Fox opened the envelope. 'It's from Sir Broderick. He says many apologies for the short and informal notice, but would we care to spend the evening with them from seven thirty, as there are matters which Sir Broderick wishes to discuss.' His face was weary but his eyes were bright as he scribbled on the back of the telegram. 'Please give this and the fee to the boy, Vera. And as you may have guessed, the mistress and I may not be home till late. We'll have to pack for Brighton tomorrow morning.'

'You're exhausted, Fox,' said Margaret, as Vera left the room. 'We both are.'

He shook his head. 'Sir Broderick has found something and we have a prompt if it's not enough.' He smiled. 'We have an hour to get ready if we're to arrive on time.'

'I know you think I'm being oversensitive,' she replied, 'but I'm scared.'

'We'll take Bert as our chauffeur. Then you'll have two knights in suits to protect you.'

She feigned a humour she didn't feel. 'I might have to protect you.'

'Better wear sensible shoes, then.'

'I can't go to dinner in sensible shoes.'

'Then you can either bring a handbag with a brick in it, or submit to be protected.' He kissed the top of her head. 'I'm not letting this opportunity go, Margaret. On Sunday we can sleep all day if we want. I'll speak with him and contact Bert. You go and get ready.

Twenty-Two

As they turned into the drive Archers Steading was shadowy, its lower windows glowing like watchful eyes.

Margaret cuddled closer to Fox. The sun was low, the breeze cold. She felt chilly, but mostly from the anxiety that had ebbed and flowed all day.

The car lurched over a pothole and stalled. Bert took the opportunity to get out, check the wheels, then speak to Fox and Margaret, his voice very low. 'Followed halfway along the busy roads by a chap on a motorcycle, then up to the last turn by a series of motor cars, each overtaking shortly before another pulled out behind us. Agreed?'

'And there was that man on the bay horse,' said Fox.

Bert grimaced. 'How'd he know when we'd arrive?'

'How could the cars?' said Margaret.

'No one notices a car hanging around,' said Bert. 'Cars break down. They run out of fuel. Drivers stop to admire the view. A horse-rider standing about is something else, and horses get spooked, especially at dusk. Anyway, I reckon we'll be safe here till we leave. You should have taken up that offer of a bed for the night.'

'I want to be home tonight,' said Fox, squeezing Margaret's hand. 'I imagine all anyone wants is to know where we're going. If they followed us earlier, they'll know the oddest thing we did was visit a newspaper office and it's not as if that yielded much.'

'Sorry you're disappointed about that photograph,' said Bert, cranking the engine back to life then getting into the driver's seat. 'I should have told you that almost everyone was looking at the memorial. The original photograph might be clearer than a snapshot, but it won't be easy to identify anyone from the back of their head.'

Fox grunted. 'I'll see what Sir Broderick has remembered, and you can see if the staff have anything to tell you.'

'Yes.'

'Yes, *sir*. You're supposed to be my chauffeur.'

Bert chuckled. 'We ain't there yet.'

The black cat stood watch on a fence post as they passed. Once again, the groom appeared from the left and the Selkirks from the right. The sense of being in a play returned, but this time a different, more melancholy act. Lady Selkirk's face was grey and she stumbled a little on her greeting. Margaret, suspecting a migraine, wished they were close friends so that she could tell her to retire while she and Fox chatted with Sir Broderick.

'How are you?' she said as they shook hands, wondering if the older woman would take the prompt.

'The weather makes one a little headachy, my dear,' Lady Selkirk responded. 'But it's nothing to make a fuss about.'

Dinner, while delicious, was frustrating. Margaret had hoped that Sir Broderick would say something about his findings during the meal, or that Fox would drop names into the conversation, but neither happened. Small talk continued through celery soup and croquettes de volaille, and when succulent beef was brought the conversation turned to current affairs. Lady Selkirk's colour seemed to have improved. Perhaps, after all, it was merely a headache.

'Do you read *The Globe*, my dear?' she said to Margaret. 'An excellent summary of my views on the cruelties I must force on my maid from July.' Seeing Margaret's alarm, she added, 'I mean the Insurance Act: Mr Lloyd George's iniquitous tax.'

'Oh, I see. I'm afraid I disagree. I'm glad that servants will know they can retire at sixty with a pension to look forward to.'

'I encourage my servants to save,' replied Lady Selkirk. 'And I give anyone who retires in my service a small gift with which they may buy an annuity if they choose.'

'Sadly, not every employer is so generous,' said Margaret, trying not to catch the eye of the butler, who was at least sixty-five.

'I consider it my duty to help provide for their future, but I find it very annoying to have the government tell me I must do it. I quite took the *Globe*'s point that, given the current fashion for all these wretched strikes, it would not be surprising if servants rose up and did the same. Or perhaps their mistresses. The very *thought* of all those stamps and paperwork.' Lady Selkirk took a tiny sip of Bordeaux, cut a sliver of beef and smiled. 'We shall have to agree to disagree, my dear.'

'We shall.'

'Never mind stamps, Ailsa,' said Sir Broderick. 'We should be more concerned about the situation in Morocco. If the French don't enforce their colonial authority, it will bode ill for all the other European colonists in Africa. There's already a disagreeable amount of anti-European feeling and a risk of the natives rising. And who's keeping an eye on Turkey? Constantinople is in disarray, isn't it, Fox?'

'Everything is,' said Lady Selkirk. 'I don't know if you'll *ever* get that suit you ordered, Broderick. You'd think the tailors would feel they'd made their point by now.' She heaved a sigh. 'Never mind. How is your essay progressing, my dear?'

Margaret thought of the blank pages shoved aside, the needling by Inspector Silvermann, the empty trolley where Dervla Mallowan's body had lain. It seemed a long time since she'd had a normal week. 'Slowly. A young maidservant was murdered—'

'No common sense, these girls,' said Lady Selkirk as a maid of about fifteen removed the plates. 'And you want them to have the vote.'

With an effort, Margaret kept quiet. It would be a waste of breath, and might make Fox's conversation with Sir Broderick harder.

After the cheese course, she and Lady Selkirk left the men to their port and cigars. 'I realise that younger, more modern hostesses like you and Mrs Holbourne would probably stay,' said Lady Selkirk. 'But I'm old-fashioned, and besides, I find it nicer to sit comfortably on a sofa.'

'I'm not terribly fond of smoke,' said Margaret. 'I really don't mind.'

They settled in the drawing room and waited for coffee. 'Are you going away for Whitsun?' asked Lady Selkirk.

'Brighton for Sunday and Monday. You?'

'We're staying at our place in town for a week. I shall be rather bored, as Broderick has matters to attend to. I wonder if you and Mrs Holbourne would like to join me for morning coffee one day?'

'I'd be delighted and I'm sure she would too.'

'Would Thursday suit? I think you said you didn't go into the hospital on that day.'

'I don't normally, but I will be this week. Would Friday be acceptable or will you have come back home?'

'Friday would be perfect.'

Margaret hoped Lady Selkirk would explain what Sir Broderick's business was, but the other woman merely chuckled. 'What mysteries do you suppose our husbands are talking over?'

Margaret gave a tiny shrug. Lady Selkirk's expression suggested she was trying to gauge what Margaret knew. It wouldn't hurt to give a logical answer. 'I imagine it's to do with South Africa. Is Sir Broderick writing his memoirs?'

'He's always talked about it,' said Lady Selkirk, 'and since becoming reacquainted with your husband he's been spreading papers all over his desk. But I can't see him actually writing one. Men of action are rarely men of words. What do you know of their first meeting? I only know that your husband went out there with the military police. There are always those soldiers who misbehave, I suppose. Boredom, drink, being a long way from home. But I've never understood why misdemeanours can't be dealt with by regimental officers.'

'Perhaps so that afterwards, any bad feeling is directed at the military police rather than within the unit,' said Margaret. 'Or, maybe, because of who's under suspicion.'

Lady Selkirk went very still, her pale face flushed. 'An officer? Like Lieutenants Morant, Handcock and Witton? They were irregulars.' Her words fell over each other. 'That trial should *never* have been made public knowledge. The conduct of a few should never be allowed to bring our army into disrepute. And even then, something about the whole thing wasn't quite....'

She knows this is about an officer, thought Margaret. *Even, maybe, that it's Gastrell. But I wasn't expecting her to mention Morant and the others. They weren't spies, but murderers. What does she think Gastrell did?*

Lady Selkirk rallied herself. 'I don't pry into Broderick's work. One isn't that kind of wife.'

'Of course not,' said Margaret in shocked tones. 'One wouldn't want to be.'

'That's good to know,' said Lady Selkirk, her shoulders relaxing a little. 'It was a brave campaign.'

'There were a lot of sad deaths.'

'That's the nature of war. A soldier's wife and m-mother has to steel herself for it.' Lady Selkirk turned to the walls, where photographs were grouped among the watercolours and sketches.

'Maude – Mrs Holbourne – told me that you'd lost your children,' said Margaret. 'I'm so sorry. I can't imagine how terrible that must feel.'

The other woman rose to her feet. 'Come and see us in happier times.' She gestured to the photographs. One was a family group from the early 1880s. Lady Selkirk, a young woman with a baby in her arms, sat with her uniformed husband behind her and a little boy to her side. A second family group showed only three, the boy now around twelve, standing with a hand on his mother's shoulder. Then the son was in his early twenties, and both he and Sir Broderick wore uniform. A fourth showed a platoon of soldiers, the younger Selkirk sitting with other officers, and a fifth, a similar arrangement with Sir Broderick in a more senior position.

'Broderick and Len were in different platoons,' said Lady Selkirk. 'But the same battalion.'

Margaret scanned the photographs, looking for a familiar face. The men, in their uniforms and rigid poses, all looked so similar. She could just pick out the Moores in the photograph with Sir Broderick. The younger Selkirk, tall and with a youthful arrogance in his face, reminded her of Darnell, even though when the photograph was taken Darnell would have been a schoolboy. 'I suppose you remember the names of all the men who served with your husband and son,' she said.

Lady Selkirk sighed but sad nothing.

Margaret made a final attempt. 'I suppose there were memorial services afterwards.'

'A few,' said Lady Selkirk. 'They were sometimes sad, sometimes... As I said, one doesn't ask questions. Nevertheless, one heard things which made one think one wouldn't have much liked the deceased, and it was hard to hear them eulogised as positive saints. However, one has to think of their poor mothers.'

Thwarted, Margaret decided to put the subject aside. 'I hope you aren't offended that we couldn't take up your kind offer to stay,' she said. 'I'm not quite as used to leaving the children as Maude is yet.'

Lady Selkirk turned to her. 'Don't get used to it, doctor. Don't.' Her eyes were troubled. 'Will you ... will you excuse me a moment?'

'Of course. I'm so sorry: I didn't mean to upset you. I—'

'No, it's not that, dear. I have to tell someone something, and my headache is still hovering. I need to get a *cachet faivre* and ask where the coffee is.' She hurried from the room.

Mortified at her lack of tact, Margaret pulled a face at herself in the mirror over the hearth, then examined the photographs in case any names were written on them. There was nothing except a place and year. The faces remained as average as ever.

She toured the room, looking at the paintings and drawings. A few were very good, but most were mediocre watercolours signed *AR*, in the style that had been taught to nice young girls fifty years earlier. Two of the sketches, however, while not particularly skilled, had more modern energy and composition. They were signed *L Selkirk*.

She returned to the photographs and looked at the younger Selkirk in his uniform, then went to sit down while waiting for her hostess – or better still, Fox – to return.

Fox entered the room just ahead of the maid and sat down next to Margaret. As their coffee was poured, he said brightly, 'Our hosts have to deal with an unexpected matter and will be here in a second.'

'I hope it's nothing serious,' said Margaret as the maid withdrew.

'I don't believe so.'

'Have you had an interesting time talking over the old days?'

Fox's nose twitched. There was a flash of irritation in his eyes. 'A memory that's important to one person may be trivial to another.'

'Trivial?'

'Forgettable, perhaps.'

'Names and places can be hard to remember.'

'Not so much the places,' said Fox. 'Names may require effort to recall.'

'Come and see these photographs,' said Margaret. She pointed out the pictures of the two Selkirk men with their fellow soldiers. 'He was called Len,' she murmured. 'What rank was he?'

'First lieutenant.'

'Is he in the book?'

'I haven't found him so far. I knew he was around at the time, but never met him. He and his father were in different platoons, so there was no reason to.' He leaned in close, and whispered, 'That's Gastrell there on the left. The Moores at the front. Webber to the right. Is he the Mr Webber you met?'

'I can't tell. Mr Webber is older, plumper, balder and has a beard. Was your conversation with Sir Broderick totally hopeless?'

'Pretty much. But he's upset. He's making out this was nothing and is best forgotten, but I think I've raised a ghost.'

'Mallowan?'

'He said, "That's the name of the Irish chap I had doubts about. Potential republican. He was with my son in a hospital tent in Kimberley once." That's what he said. It's what he *didn't* say that intrigues me. We'd better stop whispering and look like good guests.'

'Aren't we good guests?'

'I don't suppose you feel like doing any thieving? That photograph would be very useful.'

A few moments later, the Selkirks entered. Lady Selkirk seemed composed but pale, patting Margaret on the hand and giving her an apologetic smile.

'I hope you're feeling better, Lady Selkirk,' said Margaret.

'Oh yes, the *cachet faivre* is working already and the coffee will be here shortly. Now, shall we play a few rounds of bridge? You surely needn't rush home.'

'We'd be delighted,' said Fox, but his hand, holding Margaret's under cover of the edge of her skirt, tightened its grip. 'There's no rush whatsoever.'

Twenty-Three

They left soon after eleven, the car roof raised. 'Something's troubling the Selkirks,' said Fox.

'I think they had an argument.'

'I agree.'

'Lady Selkirk really didn't want us to leave. Did you find out anything more from Sir Broderick when you played billiards?'

'He said that some stones are best left unturned. When I mentioned Mallowan again, he turned puce and said that no reasonable, educated Irishman would prefer the control of Rome.'

'And Webber?'

'He resigned his commission under a cloud of incompetence and disappeared into obscurity. Sir Broderick gave no indication of knowing about Gastrell's illegitimate son, but I could only hint. I asked about memorial services and he said Gastrell's was repugnant, but as he had apparently died blameless, Sir Broderick didn't feel he could disappoint the man's mother.'

'Lady Selkirk said much the same.'

Around them scattered houses slept in darkness, while a cluster of streetlights showed where the village was. Margaret fixed her gaze on the distant glow of London, longing to be secure in its insomniac streets. She didn't ask if anyone was following; Fox's tension made it unnecessary.

Thirty minutes after leaving, the car made a peculiar noise and they halted between two high hedges.

'I need to look under her bonnet,' said Bert, 'only not here. You two should go on. Archers Steading's ten miles back. The nearest station's less than three miles ahead but I don't know if the car will get there.'

'The people following are swapping again, aren't they?' said Fox.

'Yeah. They'll catch up soon and I expect they'll be driving without lights when they do. I had a feeling this would happen. That's why I put the roof up, so they wouldn't know if you'd got out. Best go now. Hide behind the hedge till the next car passes, then walk along the edge of the field. I'll try to get the car somewhere I can hide it. If they catch up with me, they'll assume you're still inside. If necessary, I'll get out and leg it too. If they corner me, I'm equipped.'

'There must be somewhere we can leave Margaret,' said Fox.

'I'm not a package!'

'I'm not having your blood on my hands, Mrs Fox,' said Bert. 'They're not far behind. Look.'

The tiniest speck of light could just be made out through the hedges, moving towards them.

'Very well,' said Fox. 'Get somewhere safe, Bert.'

'I'll meet you at the station if I can. If not – you know what to do.'

Fox and Margaret were barely out of the car when Bert drove off. 'Quick,' said Fox, pulling her behind a tree. A car passed slowly by.

They were about to step out again when a second car, driving without lights, pulled up and stopped. The driver shone a flashlight around the verges, then drove on.

'Instead of the field, we could take the lane back there,' whispered Fox. 'It'll take us to a parallel road that leads to the station.'

'Are you sure?'

'We looked at the map earlier just in case. I'm not convinced we've fooled them.'

'And Bert?'

'Bert can take care of himself.'

Margaret looked over the gate into the field. The shadowy grain was taller than she was, an army of ghosts. 'Let's take the lane.'

'If there's a farm, we might be able to some help.'

'Why didn't you suggest that to Bert?'

'We needed to split up. Come on.'

'Who *are* they?'

'Not Inspector Silvermann's men. The Met doesn't have that sort of money.'

'This way?' said Margaret, trying to keep the anxiety out of her voice. Her weak ankle ached as her feet twisted on the uneven ground. An arch of trees overhung the pitch-dark lane like hunching judges. Somewhere, something screeched. She felt a desperate longing for Whitechapel. At least you could reason with the monsters there.

Half an hour later, her feet had passed through agony into excruciation and the farmhouse was a welcome sight. Lamplight shone from a front window, suggesting that someone was awake.

'They won't have electricity,' said Fox. 'No hope of a telephone. But they might lend us a horse.'

Margaret huddled closer. 'It's a funny time to be up.'

'It's a farm. Animals don't worry about the clock.'

They passed through the gate into the yard. From the shadows of outbuildings they could hear soft, inquisitive woofs and gentle shaking of chains.

Nothing happened at the first knock, but after a second the light moved, as whoever was inside presumably picked up the lamp and made their way to the door.

Fox tucked Margaret behind him. She bridled. 'I—'

'I'm taller than you,' whispered Fox. 'My clothes are thicker than yours, and I've got a flask in one inner pocket and a revolver in the other. If someone shoots, I *might* be all right and you'll definitely have a chance to escape. But if you stand in front, wearing that ridiculous flimsy dress, the shot will go through both of us.'

'Do forgive me. Next time we go out for dinner, I'll put on my suit of armour. What if someone shoots from behind?'

'They can't see us. I'm in black, you're in navy blue.'

'Indigo. And if we don't get shot, I get first sip of whatever's in that flask. It had better not be tea.'

'Shh.'

The door creaked open and a sliver of light illuminated an elderly face. A dog pushed its nose through the crack, then its body. It woofed a soft welcome and herded Margaret and Fox towards the door, its tail wagging against their legs. The old man inspected them in the lamplight, taking in their smart clothes and inadequate shoes.

'We're sorry to disturb you, sir,' said Fox. 'We're trying to get to the station but our car broke down. Is there any way you could help us?'

'Won't be a train till five.'

'But we can telephone or telegraph from there, perhaps. It's a matter of urgency.'

'Life or death?'

Fox's arm tensed against Margaret's back. 'Possibly.'

'You knock someone down?'

'Nothing like that. I wondered if you could lend us a horse.'

The farmer grunted. 'Dog likes you. I've just made tea. Come and have some while I decide how I can help.'

We don't have time, thought Margaret, *and what is there to decide?* But there was no choice but to follow.

The kitchen was warm. A teapot and cup and saucer waited on the well-scrubbed oak table. The farmer went to the dresser for more cups and saucers. His gait was sprightly but there was something awkward about the way he moved his left arm.

'Are you hurt?' said Margaret.

'This?' The farmer reached to touch his shoulder and winced. 'Caught it on a hay hook. My son and daughter-in-law are away till late on Monday. When they come back, she'll see to it.'

'I'll look,' said Margaret. 'I'm a doctor.'

The farmer stared quizzically at Fox, then down to the dog, which had sat down beside Margaret and was leaning against her leg.

'She is,' said Fox.

The dog gave a soft, approving woof.

'All right, then.' The farmer removed his shirt and hunched himself out of his vest, swallowing a curse as he did so. 'I don't hold with women doctors, but it's in an awkward place and I couldn't get the powders on right.' Just below the clavicle, his shoulder was red and hot to the touch. The gash was oozing: blood and pus had dried into his vest.

'I'll clean and dress this for you,' said Margaret. 'But you must go to the doctor as soon as it's light and have him stitch it up. Where are the powders? Have you bandages?'

'Thought you were in a hurry to get to the station,' said the farmer, nodding at a cupboard.

'We are, but I can't leave that wound. You'll get sick. Er, darling, will you put the kettle back on to boil?'

'It's a shame my son's away,' said the farmer, watching Fox do as he was bid. 'He's got the trap. He coulda taken you both nice and comfy. But he's off seeing about a farm further west.'

'For himself?' asked Margaret, cleaning out the wound and longing for the bright electric lights of the hospital.

'For all of us. They say we'll be surrounded by houses in a few years. I won't be able to breathe. Might as well sell up and move.' He winced as Margaret secured the dressing.

'All done,' she said.

The dog stood up, wagged his tail and flopped down in front of the stove. The farmer went to peer outside, then turned back to the room, frowning. There was a pondering silence that made Margaret want to scream. Her children were at home, with no one but Nellie and Vera to protect them, and no one to protect Nellie and Vera. And somewhere in the dark, Bert might be injured or worse.

The farmer had just opened his mouth when the dog pricked up its ears and started a low growl. From the farmyard came a cacophony of barking, then a bang on the door. 'You got pals?'

'None that know we're here,' said Fox.

'Next time I can't sleep, I'll make tea in the dark.' The farmer took a shotgun from a dark corner next to the dresser then jerked his head at the dog. 'Come on, if you've a mind to. Let's see who it is you don't like.'

Fox drew Margaret into the shadows and extracted his revolver. 'If anything happens to me, don't run. Stay in the shadows and hide.'

'I'll be too busy killing them.'

'Shh.'

She could just make out the creak of the front door and voices.

'Hello, my good man. We're looking for a friend. A gentleman. He'll have said he's lost.'

'On his own?'

'Yes. Is he here?'

'What's he done?'

'Nothing.' A laugh. 'Good boy! Good boy! You needn't growl at me. Lively dogs you've got, old fellow.' Another laugh.

'Dogs know their own minds.' The farmer's previously clipped tones slowed and drawled, his accent broadening.

'Ha ha! Sure you haven't seen our friend? Middle height, reddish hair, evening dress?'

'What would a gent be doing wandering alone in the countryside at midnight? Loony, is he?'

'A little confused, perhaps.'

'A bloke like that was heading west.'

'West?'

'You'd best get going.'

'Could we perhaps check your outbuildings?'

'You've done that already. I saw the light.'

'Maybe you could let us in.'

'What for? Your friend's a-wandering all alone. He'll be lying in a ditch, shot by a farmer who doesn't like strangers on his land rummaging through his barns with torches likely to set them afire.'

'It has a battery, you old foo— It has a battery, man.'

'Glad to hear it. Good night to you. If an anxious gent wandering alone comes back this way, I'll be sure to say you were looking. What's your name?'

The briefest of pauses was filled with the dog's intense low growling.

'Gastrell.'

'Gasket, is it? If I sees him, I'll tell him.'

The door slammed. The farmer came through to the kitchen, ignored Fox and Margaret, and went to peer through the window again, his shotgun still cocked. After a while, the barking outside came to a stop.

'They've gone. Who were they calling a fool?' He turned back into the room and uncocked the gun. 'You meet their description except you're not on your own and the dog likes you better 'n them. Is this Gastrell anyone you want to meet?'

'Hardly. He's been dead for ten years. Thank you for misdirecting those men.'

'I didn't say I saw a loony man heading west *tonight*, just that I'd seen one once. If they didn't check when, it's no skin off my nose. When you said someone's life might be at risk, is it yours and your wife's?'

'Maybe. It's certainly a friend's. I assume they think I found somewhere safe for my wife a while ago, which I would have if I could.'

'If she'd let you,' added Margaret. 'We'll go. We won't trouble you for a horse.'

'You can't walk any further in those shoes. Anyway, I owe you for this.' He tapped his arm. 'Even if you've not been quite straight, the dog likes you and you're polite. "My good man, old fellow, old fool." Tsk. We've a couple of bicycles, one my daughter-in-law's, and the meadow's mown which cuts off a big corner. Leave 'em at the station and say Ezra Ivory'll collect them later.'

***

Ten minutes of cycling seemed never-ending, and when they finally arrived at the railway station, the only human presence was a youth in a threadbare suit asleep on the bench. The police station's blue light glowed, but there was no sign of Bert's car.

Fox propped their bikes near a motorcycle and reached for Margaret's hand, then ushered her up the steps. *He's not here,* she thought. *There'll just be the desk sergeant dozing with his feet up, and Bert...*

But the sergeant was alert, and a constable in motorcycling clothes said 'These who you're after?'

Margaret's heart missed a beat. Then a familiar voice said 'Yes, thank God.'

Bert shook hands with them, smiling in an insolent way that she knew hid relief. 'You look a bit tousled, Mrs F.'

'Pleased to see you too, Bert.'

'Where's the car?' asked Fox.

'In a ditch. I decided to double back towards Archers Steading. I thought that even if I only got so far, I could walk on and get help from the Selkirks. Then the brakes and steering went. I was in the ditch for a bit, too.' He rubbed his head.

The sergeant was joined by a uniformed inspector. 'Superintendent Foxcroft-McSionnach? Pleased to meet you. Your man Sergeant Ainscough here asked us to telephone your chief and confirm what he said.'

'Ainscough?' whispered Margaret. 'That's you? I thought Bert was your last name.'

Bert winked.

'I bet Hare wasn't impressed,' said Fox.

'No, but it was necessary. We'd had reports of an unusual amount of traffic all evening, so I sent one of my constables out on his motorcycle to see what's what. He found Sergeant Ainscough limping about the lanes and brought him back. For all we knew he was up to no good, but he said someone was pursuing you with criminal intent. It all sounded a bit odd, but I've got a mate in Special Branch and I've heard of Chief Superintendent Hare. Who's after you? London villains?'

'Yes,' said Fox. 'It seemed wiser to split up: I wanted to keep my wife and the Selkirks out of things. A farmer called Ivory lent us bicycles for the last mile.'

'Ah,' said the inspector. 'The Ivorys are a good family. The first train to London's not till after five. If you can't wait, a chap in the village has a motor taxi, believe it or not, but it'll cost you. Or will it cost Special Branch?'

'Me,' said Fox. 'Hare won't pay. In fact, he'll probably try to charge me for the damage to the car.'

Twenty-Four

Margaret felt as if she'd barely put her head on the pillow, but when Vera came in with a tea tray it was past nine o'clock. Juniper sprang from Fox's empty side of the bed to Margaret's nightstand, where she tidied herself into a smug Egyptian deity, tail tucked round her paws.

'Mrs Holbourne telephoned a few moments ago, ma'am,' said Vera, 'but you were dead to the world. She said she hoped it would be all right to visit at half past ten.' She busied herself with the tea tray then tidying the small amount of mess that Fox had left on the dresser, never quite looking at Margaret. 'I don't like to say it, ma'am, but you look quite done in and you ought to stay in bed. Nellie says it was after two when you went into the nursery to kiss the twins.'

'I didn't mean to disturb her. The car broke down and it was rather a convoluted journey home.'

'I'm sorry to hear that, ma'am.'

'I take it there was no trouble in the neighbourhood yesterday evening.'

Vera shook her head. 'Nice and peaceful, ma'am. Is that a note from the master on the floor? I reckon the cat's pushed it off.'

'Prrp,' confirmed Juniper, then jumped onto Margaret's lap as she opened the envelope.

Dear M, I didn't like to wake you. We've posted someone outside as we did yesterday. He may not be the only one watching. You said someone had said something that made you think of something. I'm sure it'll come to the surface. F

'I don't suppose you saw the master before he left?' she asked.

'He was making toast and coffee at six thirty, ma'am. I offered to make something more substantial if he'd wait but he said no. And he said not to expect him for lunch.' Vera eyed her narrowly. 'Can I expect *you* for lunch, ma'am?'

'Of course, Vera. And don't worry, I can manage a visit from Mrs Holbourne and I'll return her call to say so. I expect she wants to see us before we all go away for Whitsun.'

'Yes'm.' It was hard to be sure, but Vera seemed less than enthusiastic about two days at the seaside, but Margaret didn't have the energy to ask why.

'Hallo, Demeray,' said Maude, when she arrived an hour later to find Margaret playing with the children. 'I telephoned yesterday evening but Vera said you were visiting the Selkirks. Nice time?'

'Apart from the car breaking down on the way back, yes.' The distress of the Selkirks, her fear during the drive, the night, the darkness, the noises from trees and hedges, the farmer's wound barely visible in the lamplight, the strangers at the door, Fox with a revolver at the ready... Her mind had turned it into a horrible dream. 'We were late back and I'm very tired. I thought you were going to Boulogne.'

'Not till much later,' said Maude. 'When are you leaving for Brighton?'

'Tomorrow morning.'

'You don't look too thrilled at the prospect.'

'I'm just rather tired.'

'The ozone will buck you up,' said Maude. 'And so shall I. Thanks for letting me visit. My children are overexcited and I could do with a rest from them.'

'Your poor nanny will probably run off the moment you get to France.'

Maude chuckled. 'I can run faster. Which is more than you look capable of doing.'

'You're probably right.'

Margaret was sitting on the sofa with Alec. Edie had been miserable from the moment that Nellie left the room, and nothing Margaret could do would comfort her. Worn out from crying, she lay on the floor, turned away from Margaret, knuckling her eyes. Juniper, who had slunk in with Maude, padded over, sniffed Edie's damp face, rubbed her own against it, then stretched alongside, letting the curious little hand stroke her. Edie put her arm across the soft fur. She slipped into a doze and Juniper purred loudly.

'How charming!' said Maude. 'Our cat won't stay within ten feet of my children.'

'Edie's been sobbing for Nellie and wouldn't let me cuddle her.' Margaret sighed. 'Now there's someone *else* she prefers to me.'

'Chin up, Demeray. If you ask Nellie, I bet she'll say Edie cries when *you* leave.'

'I'm hardly ever here at the moment. I'm surprised Edie recognises me.'

'Nonsense.' Maude knelt by Alec. 'Look what I have for you and your sister, young man!' She took two painted wooden dolls from her bag: a woman in a long white coat over a white dress and a soldier in a uniform with gold buttons. 'Here's your mama and, sort of, your papa.'

'Fox isn't a soldier,' said Margaret.

'I couldn't find a plain-clothes policeman. The woman's a suffragette-doctor. It took ages to explain that I wanted her repainted. She was all over flowers and frills before.'

'Thank you. I hope you realise they'll be chewed.' Margaret lifted Alec into the baby cage and he played with the wooden dolls, chattering at their cheerful faces.

'A little paint never hurt anyone,' said Maude. 'And at least they're not noisy toys, unless he bangs them together. Come along, Demeray, let me tell you about my interviews with sweatshop workers. Oh, and here's your post.'

She handed Margaret an envelope addressed in Anna's careful print, then poured the coffee. 'Interesting handwriting. One of your patients?'

'A friend.'

The note inside was simple: the first half presumably copied from a ledger, the second half Anna's own words:

Mrs Norrice Gascoigne, 42a Flora Street, Fulham SW. One dress with matching jacket in ivory linen with embroidery pattern A in Saxe-Coburg blue. 6 guineas including 2/ for expedited completion. Date of order April 30th 1912. Date of payment and despatch May 3rd 1912.

Sale 6 guineas. Cost of material, threads and silks 11/6. 50 hours work over 5 days for the tailoress who was paid 7/6-. 8 hours work for each of the piece-work embroiderers working at home. 8d each, total £1/4/8. Profit £5/2/4. These are better wages than some.

Margaret read the second paragraph aloud. 'Is this part of the research for your essay?' asked Maude.

The essay and Dr Naylor seemed to belong to someone else's life, but Margaret nodded, telling herself that she might use the information somehow.

'I heard similar figures when I was interviewing seamstresses yesterday,' said Maude. 'Once the strike's over, I shall visit the businesses Geoff and I patronise and demand to see their workshops. If they don't convince me they're improving conditions and wages, I shall move our custom.'

'Good,' said Margaret. She folded the note back into the envelope. She'd grown up in Fulham and couldn't recall a Flora Street, only a Floral Gardens.

Maude summarised her experiences while Margaret sipped coffee. The passion for justice which she usually expressed for suffrage had found an additional cause. 'Whitechapel is quite the warren.'

'I know. Half my patients come from there, remember?'

Maude wasn't listening. 'One of them said that when they had time to play, the children used to dare each other to look for blood where Jack the Ripper's victims had been found. I expect she's teasing.'

'She might not be,' said Margaret. 'There's little space for sensitivity in that kind of youth.'

'It sounded more fun than my childhood till I looked at the environment and realised they barely had one.'

'Quite. I've been trying to get you to write about all this sort of thing for years.'

'I might have to start another magazine for that. The only time we mention blood to the readership of *Athene's Gazette* is in the hints and tips column, under the heading of removing it from one's white suffragette outfit after a battle with police.'

'I meant about the social situation, not the blood.'

'The same thing applies,' said Maude. 'You look exhausted. You're not expecting again, are you?'

'No.'

'I suppose if Fox is at work all the time...' Maude winked but her expression remained thoughtful. 'I don't know what's bothering you, but I hope it's not just Edie crying. You're a wonderful mother and the twins love you, but they're at a very boring age. They can't move much, they can't talk, they can't hold on to anything, their gums hurt. You'll feel better after some time at the seaside.'

They embraced. The familiar scents of perfume and cigarette smoke in Maude's hair comforted Margaret, taking her back to the days when the most distressing thing they had to deal with was attention, or lack of it, from the young men they knew. Her memory stirred and so did Edie, waking with a jolt. 'Mama?' She looked round for Margaret and grinned.

'Mama! Dada!' echoed Alec, waving the soldier and the doctor.

Joel, thought Margaret. *Joel was an army medic working in Kimberley around the time that Len Selkirk was there. What if there's something useful in the letters that I haven't read for twelve years?*

'Thank you, Maude,' said Margaret, kissing her. 'I don't know what I'd do without you.'

She waited till Maude had gone, then read Joel's letters. He came into focus again: a shy young man with glasses, passionate about science and caring towards his patients. He had Cyril's drive, balanced with sensitivity and compassion.

The first few letters were no use. Joel described the strange beauty of South Africa, the heat, the men suffering in their woollen uniforms. Then ambushes, sieges, injuries, deaths and the beginnings of disease. He hinted at the arrogance and incompetence in the senior ranks, who assumed that enemy brigades of farmers posed no threat. Then he spoke of the camps in

Pretoria and Bloemfontein, where they held the captured white Boer women with their children and a few Black maidservants.

Where we have insufficient rations, they have less. Where we have disease, they have more. Things are improving, but too slowly. People die too fast to be saved.

The officers who say it's honourable to protect the weaker sex allow Boer women to turn into wraiths before them, on the grounds that the enemy counts less. The black people count less again. At least the white women don't have to pay for their rations. From separate camps, we recruit black men to work for us, then make them pay for the inadequate food their wives and children need.

Boer guerrillas lie in ambush to slaughter our troops, and in turn we capture Boer women who fight to protect their farms. We burn their houses and slaughter their livestock so that there is no shelter or food for their men when they pass through.

What will be the legacy of this war? Good men dying for the sake of diamonds and gold. When pointless pieces of mineral become more important than human beings, human beings become less than human.

Initially, Joel referred to his patients and cases by initials, but then a full name appeared: *Mallowan*.

Margaret started to make notes.

An officer called Mallowan was admitted with typhus yesterday. He is thirty-three and not expected to live. His friend Selkirk visited against advice and called Mallowan a typical Irishman, although I couldn't say what he meant.

When Gastrell, a man they said was Mallowan's other friend, was admitted, I confess I wanted to weep to see one more man in his prime likely to die so pointlessly. He's a country squire's son from some village north-west of London. Like Mallowan, he is in his early thirties, but in sickness both look older. And I, who am not yet twenty-seven, feel older again. Selkirk is a younger man, just twenty-one, and full of the arrogance of youth.

Listen to me, writing as if I were in my dotage.

I wouldn't normally name my patients, but I grieve to see these three friends die in such indignity, to be buried on foreign soil so far from home and feel that I wanted to share it with someone without making them near anonymous as if they aren't real people. I don't think I am saying anything that will incur the wrath of the censor.

The next few letters made no mention of those specific men, but then came one which seemed to refer to them, though only by initials. Perhaps the censor, without redacting anything from the previous letter, had warned Joel about including names again.

G recovered some days ago. W, a junior officer who'd known him in childhood, came to see him a few times. He was almost in tears at the sight of a man eight years his senior. It's strange that he should care so, since I've heard unpleasant rumours about G mocking and manipulating W, and about his unjust treatment of Boer prisoners.

S succumbed to typhus eventually, too. I asked him about the prisoners' deaths when I could, but he was in a different squadron and seemed unconcerned. 'Self defence,' he said. 'Boer women don't surrender without a fight. Why should they?'

G and S recovered and went back to their squadrons. But M took longer. When he recovered, he angrily called this a dirty war, and I couldn't disagree. I told him Gastrell had recovered and was asking for him.

'Is he now?' he said. 'The only reason to be glad G didn't die is to pray he's got worse coming. And then there's Knox, the slimy little weasel...' But he said no more. I had thought from what S said that G was M's friend, but at that moment I realised I'd been very mistaken. I don't know who Knox must be. I've tried to find out the truth about the Boer prisoners, but I am weary, not only in spirit but body, and it's hard to find the time.

Your most recent letter reminded me of a night when you and I dashed between cab and restaurant in the pouring rain and you complained bitterly that it was ruining your dress. Blue, wasn't it? Was that the same blue dress? You wrote that it was stained in a downpour, and how you longed for sunshine. It was a little aside between writing about your cases and the latest research reports in the Lancet. I can't work out the connections between the three bits of news at all. Were you writing things down as they came to mind, the way you talk sometimes? You only do that when you're worried and want to block it out with chatter.

Please say what's worrying you, but remember it's cruel to read about rain! My pen slips in my fingers, sweat soaks these 'proper' clothes that 'civilised' humans wear. I wish the sun would stop blazing. It makes every smell a stench, and every death more of a horror.

I'm longing to see you again under cloudy, chilly English skies. I'll teach you to love the rain and never wish it away again.

Dear me – how poetic! You must think the heat has curdled my brain. I'm so sorry! About that article in the Lancet...

There were only two more letters and neither mentioned Gastrell, Mallowan, Selkirk, or Knox. She'd read them in 1900, unaware that as she did so he was perhaps dying in his own hospital tent, never to see grey English skies again.

I did it, Joel, she said in her mind. *I landed the job everyone said a woman would never land. I just wish you'd lived to do all the things you wanted to.* She wiped away a tear and tied the letters back up.

The book mentioned Knox going for a walk along the river where Gastrell died. Could he be the same person as Joel's Knox? And if so, was he relevant?

Margaret telephoned a coded message to Fox's office to summarise what she'd discovered. Then, while the children dozed, she read the old soldier's book from beginning to end.

Twenty-Five

Margaret was skilled at reading quickly and taking in the salient points, but her eyelids drooped over battles which sounded less exciting than wallpapering a parlour. The author skirted round the realities of typhus and didn't mention the camps at all. His distrust of anyone he couldn't understand was clear – from the white Boers 'jabbering in Afrikaans' and wanting to kill him, to the black African wagon drivers 'talking in heathen tongues' and wanting who knew what. And then...

Lieut. Gastrell's view was that after we had got the womenfolk out of every farmhouse, we should take anything that would go to waste before the place was mined or burned. I just took food. I was tempted once by a pretty photograph frame: I thought it could hold a picture of my darling granddaughter. But it already held one of a little girl. I realised she could be the granddaughter of the old couple being loaded on a wagon to go to the prisoners' camp. All their lovely things would be destroyed and I felt ashamed.

I took the picture and gave it to the woman. She was crying because she and her husband could not stop us from taking the farm. She looked as if she would spit on me if she thought I were worth the spittle, but she took it anyway. Lieut. Gastrell mocked me with words which I shall not repeat, and I took against him then as heartless. I was never tempted to loot again.

I should have asked to go under a different command, although I do not know what would have happened if I had. It was not just the looting which made me despise him, though, but another event I feel polluted by witnessing. Two of us reported it to the major afterwards and he said they'd investigate, but we were never asked for our statements, not even when the military police turned up about something else. Maybe it would have been dealt with after the war if Gastrell hadn't died. But he did, and no one told, so I shall tell the story now.

Eight of us had got separated from the others and we had been under fire on and off for hours, though we could not see from where. Lieut. Gastrell was agitated. What a coward he was when he didn't have Captain Selkirk to take charge. It was clear he had no plan.

We came across a small farmstead and he said we must requisition it as shelter till the others caught up with us. We said someone was bound to be guarding it and he replied, 'Then they will surrender or get rough treatment'.

The sergeant said that if we had to take any prisoners with us it would slow us down, and we should just hurry on, since whoever had gone before us hadn't done anything. Gastrell ordered us forward.

As we neared the house, a young lad ran out brandishing a shotgun. A smaller boy of maybe four years old ran out after. He was followed by a young black girl, who I assume was a nursemaid, and a woman, presumably the boys' mother, also bearing a gun. The mother cried to everyone to stop, but the older boy raised his weapon.

Gastrell shot the lad between the eyes. He dropped dead where he stood. The little boy screamed in terror and ran forward and the maid swept him up in her arms. The mother, white as a sheet, tears streaming, also raised her weapon. Lieut. Gastrell shot her before she could even take a step.

The maid turned to run to the house and Lieut. Gastrell ran after her and caught her arm. I was not close enough to hear what he said, though he said afterwards that he was asking her to surrender so we could care for her and the child. But she pulled away and started to run again, so he shot her in the back of the head. When she fell, he also shot the little boy.

The sergeant remonstrated, but Lieut. Gastrell said the older boy and the Boer woman were about to fire and at close range their shotguns could have killed or fatally injured more than one of us. The girl had told him she would get a third gun and send a signal to the guerillas. It was then that I noticed only the boy had a rifle. The mother had naught but a broom.

'And the child?' asked the sergeant.

'The gun misfired,' said Lieut. Gastrell. 'But all's fair in war. How would we get to safety if we had to take a child with us? Now, set fire to the house and fields and we'll get on before they catch up with us.'

'We should bury them.'

'There's no time. And if anyone else tries to argue, they'll be on a charge when we return.'

I can't say why none of us intervened, except that it took less time to happen than to write. We were trained to follow an officer, not overpower him. And he was right: the older boy could have killed at least one of us. But a girl no more than sixteen and a child of four? We were all horrified.

At that moment, what little respect I had for Lieut. Gastrell vanished altogether. We had seen slower, more undignified deaths. We had seen women and children caught in the crossfire before. But of all the things we'd seen, that was the worst. It was a stain on our squadron, on the army, on everything we stood for and everything we were fighting for.

We all felt cursed by seeing it. Afterwards, when one of us died, the rest of us thought we would be next because of what we had let happen, even though none of us knew how we would have stopped it. After that, we all said that Lieut. Gastrell deserved whatever befell him, but what he most deserved was the noose.

The book became leaden again. After the page which had been removed, the book said nothing more about Gastrell or Fox and trundled towards the soldiers' triumphant reception when they arrived home. But an elaborate description of victory parades couldn't erase those few vivid paragraphs.

When Fox walked in at dinner time, she was once more staring at the book's dull green cover. 'Have you read it?'

'Now I understand why most people hated Gastrell. What I don't understand is why some didn't.'

'Some thought he had done the right thing in the circumstances, or he persuaded them that he had.' Fox sat beside her and put his arm round her shoulders. He seemed tense. 'I'm sorry you had to read it.'

'So am I. I've seen industrial injuries from explosions, fires, and failing machinery. I've seen people beaten senseless, with broken limbs – sometimes inflicted by people who should have cared for them. I've been involved in police post-mortems for two years. I've seen worse injuries than what he describes. I just … I haven't read a description of a cold-blooded murder outside a novel. Those children…' She felt her voice choke.

'Gastrell's argument was that a fifteen-year-old boy wasn't a child. If he and his mother hadn't threatened the soldiers, they wouldn't have been shot, and the smaller child and the maid shouldn't have rushed into the line of fire.'

'There's no description of anyone getting into a line of fire, though. The older boy and the woman were shot in the forehead, the maid in the back of the head, and I don't know about the little boy. I can't begin to express what I'd do if anyone even threatened to shoot—' She cleared her throat. 'They were shot one by one, like tame ducks. I can't believe the soldiers stood by and did nothing.'

'Soldiers are a superstitious lot. Two of the witnesses died of typhus, another two in an ambush: the verger's son was one of the latter. The sergeant and the two privates who survived weren't sure whether to salve their souls by accusing Gastrell or push it into the past. Gastrell and Webber were the only two indifferent to what had happened.'

'Webber was there?'

'Yes, and he backed up Gastrell when asked.'

'Even the child's murder?'

'A regrettable accident.' Fox sighed. He was black under the eyes, his face unshaven. 'Changing tack, thank you for Mrs Gascoigne's name and address. We'd been looking for Gascon and getting nowhere. Either that damn memorial article had it wrong or Bert copied it wrong.'

'It's right now.'

'Did you put the original in the safe?'

'Yes. Did you get the message about Joel's letters?'

Fox looked blank for a moment. 'Oh, *that's* what you meant. He was your doctor friend serving in South Africa. Of course. Where was he?'

'In 1900 he was in Kimberley, treating Gastrell, Len Selkirk and Mallowan.'

'What did he say about Mallowan?'

'Initially he thought they were friends, but when Mallowan recovered, found out they weren't.' Margaret gave a summary of what she'd read.

Fox nodded. 'The murder investigation was far above me, but I've looked into other allegations against him recently. The destruction of farms and homesteads was policy. The looting wasn't. Mallowan clearly loathed both and reported every action he considered beyond the call of duty. Time after time he reported Gastrell – looting, unnecessary destruction, assault of prisoners. He even reported suspected treachery but there was no evidence. No one told me about that in 1902, or I'd have taken his statement. He sounds like a man I'd like to know. His record and history was exemplary, except that his Irishness was given as the reason for his sentimentality about Boer farms.'

'Sentimentality? Wasn't he demonstrating the fairness we're supposed to pride ourselves on?'

'According to records, he's from a long line of Dubliners with city jobs, but they'd have known about the evictions that took place in the forties during the famine. His grandparents might have known people who died or emigrated then. They'd certainly have seen the emigrants waiting to sail. And maybe Mallowan saw those who emigrated during the famine in seventy-nine. How could all of that not influence his thinking? After the South African war he resigned his commission, joined the Irish Brotherhood, then left for America with his family – twelve-year-old Dervla included – where they disappeared into obscurity. On every level, a man so sickened by what he'd witnessed that he wanted his country to be independent of Britain.'

'And Dervla?'

'She came back to Ireland alone in 1909 and joined the Daughters of Ireland, where she became involved with a group of gunrunners and activists. Mallowan himself is dead, so how Gastrell's gang found her, and what the point of revenge is now, I can't work out.'

'Can you find out anything more over the weekend?' said Margaret. 'With everything shut tomorrow and Monday, and going to Brighton tomorrow—'

'I'm afraid you'll have to go to Brighton without me,' said Fox. 'I need to go away on Monday. You *can*,' he said, as if Margaret had argued. 'We agreed to behave normally. You're working at St J's on Tuesday in lieu of Whitsun Monday, so you can still have the holiday. I'll see you to the station tomorrow morning and—'

'*We* have to behave normally,' said Margaret. 'Either we all stay here or we all go to Brighton. Otherwise, if anyone is watching us and sees you don't come with us, they'll know we suspect something about the car breaking down and they'll definitely follow you. But to be honest…'

'To be honest?' Fox prompted.

'Even without all that, the prospect of getting all six of us on the train, then staying in a hotel and managing a crowded beach and promenade with two small babies is terrifying. I'm quite happy to stay here. On Monday we can all go out for the day and if we come back in the dark, maybe you and Bert can swap places and he can leave by the back door. So if they're watching, they'll never know you didn't come home.'

Fox scratched his nose. 'Won't Vera and Nellie be disappointed?'

'I think Vera will be thrilled, and Nellie was worried about disrupting the twins' routine anyway. I could give Vera leave to spend Monday with Norbert. Nellie could go home, and we could manage the twins together.' She saw panic flicker in his eyes and gave a rueful chuckle. 'Maybe not, then. I'll make it up to her another day.'

'Good,' said Fox. 'But actually, I wanted you out of the house tomorrow anyway. There's a huge demonstration in London, so a good deal of our resource will be there, watching for suspicious activity among the crowds. And Webber's visiting his wife in the country for the weekend. We haven't anyone to watch this house.'

'What demonstration? I thought the tailors' dispute was nearly over.'

'The dockers. They'll bring the London docks to a halt. The demonstration is likely to be massive.'

'And that will make it harder to track anyone else down.'

'It will...' Fox pondered. 'You may have a point about staying here and looking normal. What reasons have we to stay home rather than go to Brighton?'

'The children are teething and a little feverish, and therefore unreliable in their, er, hygiene. That makes being far from home complicated and unpleasant.'

'We're definitely keeping Nellie, then, if "unreliable" means what I think it does,' said Fox. 'Very well. Perhaps the maids can pass that on to their friends. Tomorrow, we can be normal citizens: go to church and spend the rest of the day at Katherine's, on the understanding that she and James won't mind if I disappear for a few hours.'

'I expect James will disappear, too. He'll want to report on the demonstration for his newspaper.'

'True. I suppose he's reporting nothing but strikes these days.'

Margaret shrugged. 'I'm not sure. There are so many of them just now, they're not precisely news, just a fact of life. James tries to concentrate on the reasons behind them, to keep a balance. But as for what you're suggesting, it's a good idea. And on Monday we can picnic in Green Park with a million other Londoners, send Nellie and the children home in a taxi, and go to a nice, quiet picture house till it's dark. Bert can see me home.'

'It won't be Bert. He's coming with me,' said Fox. 'And it won't work: it's dark too late. Tell you what, Nellie's always talking about taking the children to see her mother. Why can't she do that on Monday while I take you to Brighton for the day? The room we booked gives us somewhere private to be. In the evening, when we get back to London, you can switch me for someone at the station and go home by cab. It'll be expensive, but it should work, and you and I can think in the fresh air for a few hours. I could do with cleansing right now.'

Twenty-Six

Margaret was aware of Fox's frustration throughout Sunday. Even when he returned after the demonstration and they went home, he had little to say. He barely slept, his body turned away from her, rigid with tension. With all his men watching for troublemakers, there was no time to look for anyone or anything else.

Monday morning was a flurry of rushing from place to place, the train to Brighton so full that they could barely breathe, let alone talk.

Brighton itself was awash with holidaymakers, noise and heat. It was nearly two years since she had walked along the promenade in Eastbourne, wondering if she'd ever meet Fox again, and now he was her husband. She had been in danger then: now he was. Then he had teased and joked, now he was silent and distant.

There were far too many people about to know whether anyone had followed them, and after a short walk in the sunshine they went to the Curzon, ate lunch and retired to their suite. She cuddled up to him on the sofa and kissed him softly, but he didn't respond. After a while, he withdrew his arm from her shoulders.

'What is it, Fox?'

'I need to tell you something. I don't think any of this will come clear till I do.'

'What?'

'I didn't let Gastrell drown, but that doesn't mean I didn't kill him.'

'I don't understand.'

'A while ago, you said I'd never shoot anyone in the back. I said that under the right circumstances, I would. Well, I certainly shot *at* Gastrell that day. He thought he'd got away with everything. Murdering women and children. Selling secrets. He knew he'd have to resign his commission, but he was preparing to carry on with his espionage somehow. We had intelligence that he had one last piece of crucial information to hand over to someone. I was ordered to stop him rather than intercept him.'

'But surely—'

'Yes. If I'd intercepted him, I'd have got two traitors instead of one. But the orders were to bring Gastrell down and stop him from handing over whatever it was. When he realised I was on his tail, he ran. So in the end I did shoot him, Margaret. I shot a man from behind as he was trying to get away. I did what you thought I wouldn't do. And I'd do it again in the same circumstances.'

Margaret said nothing, conscious not only of his distress but her own shock. It made perfect sense in theory that a policeman might have to fire at a criminal's back to stop them, but knowing someone who'd done it was different. She wished she could change the subject, but all she could say was, 'I can't see what choice you had.'

'I should have been better prepared,' said Fox. 'I should have asked for someone to be stationed ahead. I should have questioned orders.'

'But no one's said that Gastrell died from gunshot wounds.'

'The inquest concluded that he drowned, but it was cursory. They knew he was a traitor, but unconvicted, so it was kinder to his family to say it was an accident. The point is that maybe he wouldn't have drowned if he hadn't been injured. He faltered when the bullet struck but staggered on, then slipped and fell in the river. I'm not pretending that I didn't think he should die, but I thought he and his accomplice should face trial first. By injuring him, maybe I killed him. The river wasn't as full as it might have been – it was summer, after all – but he was weighed down by clothes and boots and struggling. I went in after him to save his life for the trial and get hold of whatever he was going to pass over. But I couldn't save him and his pockets were empty. I killed him.'

'Oh, Fox. Why haven't you told me before? You needn't have carried this alone.'

'I told you it was a memory to burn. It's like grief, buried so deep that it ought to have been smothered years ago, but sometimes it bursts through the surface and cuts you open again. It's a face that never faded, and one sleepless night in a million it presses nose to nose with yours until hatred, guilt and justification entwine and you're ready to vomit.'

Margaret pulled him close.

'I can feel your brain churning,' said Fox. 'Are you ashamed of me?'

'Of course not,' she said. 'I didn't realise it was so deeply personal. I thought it was mostly business.'

Fox was silent for a while, then kissed her and stood up. 'I've let this become far too personal when I should be concentrating on the business side. How unprofessional. I'm very sorry.'

'You did what you had to.' Even as she said it, Margaret felt the conflict in her mind. *He did what he had to. He shot a man from behind. He couldn't get a conviction. He's a decent man. But ... he's a man who shot someone from behind.*

'I did as I was ordered,' said Fox. 'Wasn't that Gastrell's excuse about the women and children The old soldier's excuse for not stopping him?'

Margaret shook the treacherous thoughts from her head. 'It's not the same. Most of the people who knew Gastrell would have paid you to do it.'

'But not all, Margaret. Not all. And I think that's what this is about.'

'No one has bothered you about it for ten years.'

'I haven't been easy to find,' said Fox. 'And until now I had no idea that anyone was carrying out the same dirty tricks. But now I do, and I'm digging where they'd rather I didn't. But without knowing who I'm up against, it's not enough. If I don't move faster, they'll get me before I can get them.'

'Webber's missing neighbour who receives foreign mail had the initial K. Could he be Knox?'

'It's an odd first name. But possibly.'

'Joel mentions someone called Knox. Is it the same person? Could it be Mr Webber? Does he have a middle name?'

'Yes, but it's Tristram.' Fox frowned. 'The book writer says Knox walked on ahead. The only person I saw doing that wasn't a lieutenant. He wasn't even a soldier.'

'Is the person you saw important? The author only mentions soldiers.'

'It depends on your point of view. To me he was. To the writer, probably not. He was a captured Basuto farmhand whom the army had hired to work as a spy, under cover as a wagon driver. His wife was a Boer woman's maid, just like the one Gastrell shot. Half his wages went to keeping her and his children alive in their camp. But was he called Knox? No. He's called Amose.'

'So he's alive?'

'Yes,' said Fox. 'His family survived. The army moved them to Basutoland after the war and got him a job with the police. But I don't think he knows anything we need to know now. He was there. He put Gastrell's body on the wagon – threw, I should say – and shook my hand afterwards. He's a good man, an asset: a missed opportunity. I'd wanted him to work for me in London but Hare wouldn't have it. Amose wasn't involved.' Fox leaned forward and rubbed his temple. 'What else did Joel say about this Knox?'

'It was just Mallowan's disparagement, really. He called him a weevil or something, and thought him worthless.'

'What did he say about Webber? Was it in the same letter?'

Margaret took her notes from her bag and looked through them. 'Yes. He described Webber as nearly crying over Gastrell even though Gastrell allegedly bullied him. Reading between the lines, I think Joel thought it an unhealthy friendship. Mentally, I mean: the younger man being manipulated by the older one and not realising, or not admitting it to himself.'

'I'd discounted Webber. Even Olive described him as wet.'

'Maybe Olive isn't the only one who can act.'

'You could be right!' Fox started pacing the floor, then extracted his notebook. 'Let's see...' He flicked through its pages.

'What did you find out about him?' said Margaret.

'Apart from the lie about Cambridge, which he uses to cover up leaving the army under a cloud, he seems quite legitimate. In late 1902 he set up as a portrait photographer but failed to thrive, although he occasionally sells photographs to newspapers and magazines. He married in 1904, but his wife generally lives in the country. Since 1906, she has seemed disconnected both from him and from anything he does. Around the time of his marriage, he took up new work: first for an engineering company, for which he's still a board member, then as a chief clerk for the Comptroller of Patents.'

'All very respectable.'

'The only dubious thing, apart from his sudden friendship with Rainer, is that according to one of his neighbours he's been seen visiting the East End. The neighbour doesn't know why but assumes it's for the usual reasons, especially given the absence of his wife. He hasn't done it for a while, though, possibly because of the volatility there – and definitely hasn't since we've been watching. It's possible that it *wasn't* for the usual reason, but we can find no link between him and the Whitechapel anarchists or any other undesirables.'

'And Rainer?'

Fox sat down next to her again. 'I have a lead on him. One of the few things that led us to looking for Dervla in the first place was a business in Berlin which appears to receive more innocuous trinkets from German West Africa than it sells. It seems likely that documents are being sent too. We've been watching it ever since, which as you know, is a risky business these days. One of my men is currently in German custody.'

'Is he one of those alleged spies the papers say the Germans arrest every second day?'

'Well there's no "alleged" about it. Of course he's a spy, but we're hardly going to admit it, so the Germans have no evidence against him. Therefore for them, it's more of a point-making exercise and they'll release him soon. His colleague on the other hand, has managed not only to evade capture but intercept some mail. There were no documents of interest, but there was a letter saying to expect Herr Rainer on 30th. It's why I need to go to Germany, to be there when he arrives.'

Margaret swallowed. *Of course he's a spy.* Fox had said it as if describing a bank clerk. It wasn't that she didn't know. It was just that she didn't know this agent who worked for Fox. She only knew Fox, and even if she was struggling with the image of him shooting someone from behind, she struggled even more with the image of him in a German prison.

Fox was oblivious. He'd stood and was pacing the floor. 'Could Webber be behind this after all? I had him down as a follower, not a leader, in 1902, and thought he'd shaken it all off since. But…' He looked around the room. His gaze settled on the small case Margaret had brought to carry a wrap and her vanity items which were wrapped in a specially designed roll of fabric tied with ribbon, and he frowned. 'Is that the case Dervla used for her camera equipment and so on? It's very like it.'

'You brought it home for me to look inside, remember. I haven't had time, so I thought I'd bring it today with my things inside. I doubted anyone would think it was anything but a valise that way.'

'But won't your things —?'

'They're in a separate bag inside. Everything else is as it was and your people went over it before you brought it home anyway.'

The case was compact, covered in shiny black leather. The silver catches opened without difficulty. Margaret removed the silk bag containing her wrap and vanity case from the middle of three compartments lined with soft cream tissue paper. She ran her fingers round each one.

'Anything?'

Margaret lifted out a piece of tissue and unfolded it. It was plain but for the edge of a pattern in one place. It was hard to be sure what the pattern was – a fan? A bunch of flowers? There was dust on her fingers… no, not dust, tiny fibres, perhaps from feathers. Did photographers use feathers to clean lenses? She didn't know. 'Nothing… Wait a moment. There's something trapped between the lining and the outer case, something small... Can you get my tweezers from my vanity roll? It's inside my wrap inside that bag.'

Fox handed them over and watched her fiddle.

'It's tiny. It's... Without a lens I can't be sure, but...' Margaret carried the case to the window, and inspected it. 'I *think* the stitches here are different. It's as if someone snipped a couple and then resewed them with something trapped in place.'

'Why didn't my men find that?'

'You'll have to ask them,' said Margaret. 'And I might be wrong. Do I have your permission to snip a stitch on this piece of evidence?'

Without answering, Fox passed over her nail scissors.

Margaret cut the stitch then fiddled once more, probing with the tweezers. Was there something white? She pulled out a tiny roll of tissue, twisted tight. When unrolled, it said WEBBER (KNOX) in faint pencil, with John Webber's address underneath.

'Knox must be a nickname,' said Fox.

'That's what Joel thought, but meaning what?'

Fox shrugged. 'Who knows? Perhaps it was from when Webber was a child, following the adolescent Gastrell around and being mocked by him. Noxious? Willing to take knocks? Or something else entirely? Nicknames don't always make sense. Mine at school was Snowy and I can't remember why. Is there anything else written on it?'

Margaret held the paper up to the window. The creases in the twisted paper made it hard to make out, but something else was written faintly in script. 'I think it says *Gascoigne Street, Angel, Whitechapel*'

'It doesn't say *street*, it says *ST*.' Fox peered over her shoulder. 'And there are no commas. Can we be sure ST means street?'

'No. It could be *Gascoigne SAINT Angel Whitechapel,* although even then I'm not certain. There might be an extra letter or two. It might be names, places or both. You need someone with a really good lens for this, Fox.'

'Yes, but you found it. Thank you.' Fox smiled. 'And here's Gascoigne again. Elinor's looking into that connection, but apart from trailing the streets of Fulham it's impossible to get far with every office in the country closed. How can a wretched fancy jacket mean anything?'

'It probably doesn't,' said Margaret. 'But the woman on the bench in Fulham that day must have been Mrs Norrice Gascoigne. That has to be his sister Lena, who moved to Fulham and renamed herself to give her son legitimacy. Maybe Webber has her son Carl working for him now, too: he'll be twenty. Maybe...'

'What?'

'Maybe the young man who tried to lure Nellie was Carl Webber, or rather Carl Gascoigne. If Lucy hadn't noticed the design on the jacket, it wouldn't have mattered. Through what Mr Moore said, we'd still have found Webber and ultimately his sister. This has just speeded things up. Elinor will find her.'

'The main thing is that we now have a definite connection between Webber and Dervla,' said Fox, slipping the piece of paper into his wallet. 'If I put someone onto him today and track down Rainer in Germany, we can close the circle. I need to send a telegram, and then we'll spend the afternoon doing something innocuous and highly public before going back to London.' He looked towards Margaret, putting her things back into Dervla's case, but his gaze was unfocussed. 'One thing we haven't looked into is Webber's ancestry. All we established is that his father was a country doctor, but Webber's as German a name as it's English, just as Rainer is. He must have been behind this all along. Maybe he was even running Gastrell. It just goes to show, you should never overlook the apparently insignificant man.'

'Or woman.'

'There's nothing insignificant about you,' he said. 'Thank God. And thanks to you, we're back on track.'

Twenty-Seven

On Tuesday morning the area around St Julia's was uncannily quiet. There were no vehicles going to and from the docks, no workers rushing about. A fruit seller sat hunched at her half-empty stall, hands folded, expression pensive. Margaret paid over the odds for a small bag of unripe gooseberries, even though they looked dusty and pale.

At the front of the hospital, she was assailed by newspaper boys waving their wares and shrieking headlines. *The Daily Mirror* had a full front-page photograph of soldiers crossing picket lines at the docks to collect their own food and their horses' fodder. The tone of the various newspapers' headlines ranged from concerned to fear-mongering:

> *Will All Europe Strike?*
> *Will Britain Starve?*
> *Hooliganism Rife!*
> *Docks Idle, Factories Idle!*
> *Meat Already Dearer!*

She couldn't bear to buy one.

Near the front steps, the usual flower seller sat with her buckets and jars, making up boutonnieres and corsages. The strike seemed to be having little impact on her, as the containers were full and she had a helper. But who knew how it would affect her if members of her family were striking? Maybe the helper was one of them, hoping to increase the day's income. Despite not wanting to be late for work, Margaret decided to buy some flowers. A few pennies would make little difference to her, but a good deal to the flower seller.

With a small bouquet of red roses, Margaret hurried to the mortuary wing, slowing to a normal pace as she entered.

Mr Baines, one of her least favourite governors, stood there, hands in pockets, glaring at Dr Jordan. 'I appreciate you may not think it a concern on this wing, but— Ah, good morning, Dr Demeray. Nice to see that you feel you can go shopping before work. I suppose you're in favour of this latest strike.'

'I haven't formed an opinion yet, Mr Baines,' said Margaret.

'Really? Your husband's a police superintendent, isn't he? There's genuine concern that food will run short if it goes on as threatened, and if, God forbid, it spreads to the continent. We need the police to ensure that supplies get through to hospitals. What are they doing about it?'

'I really can't speak for them, Mr Baines. I'm sure everything possible will be done, but I hope that won't include violence.'

'Do you? I thought you agitators actively welcomed violence. Or is that just suffragettes?'

Margaret stayed silent.

Dr Jordan frowned. 'As you can see, Mr Baines, Dr Demeray has come in to work today rather than yesterday, to assist with work that's accumulated over the holiday weekend, and she'll be working Thursday instead of tomorrow, so not missing any days. As for the strike, hopefully it won't come to violence and there won't be real shortages for any length of time. Meanwhile, the bursar will ensure that strict controls on waste are applied.'

'Even in the short term, this situation will bring more patients,' said Mr Baines. 'They're badly enough nourished in the first place. Once they're starving, they're more vulnerable to their ailments. And then, before we know it, they're *your* customers, and—'

Dr Jordan cleared his throat. 'Don't speak so lightly of their deaths. Each one is its own tragedy.'

Mr Baines scowled. 'At any rate, the strike is the reason for the emergency board meeting, Dr Jordan. I daresay Dr Demeray can manage in your brief absence, provided she can remember what she does after so many days away.'

Margaret raised her eyebrows. 'I can remember what all the scalpels, saws and pliers are for, thank you,' she said. 'Good morning, gentlemen. I'll be in my office, Dr Jordan.'

'Goodbye, Mr Baines,' said Dr Jordan. 'I'll join the meeting shortly. I need to speak with Dr Demeray first.'

Mr Baines grunted and stalked off towards the internal staircase.

'Have you spoken with St Bart's about Dervla Mallowan?' asked Margaret. 'Has Inspector Silvermann been back?'

'Yes, and not yet,' said Dr Jordan. 'The former confirmed my findings. The latter telephoned on Friday to ask if I knew what your weekend plans were and when you'd return. I told him your free time was your own and you'd be back today. Then he wanted to speak with you about a patient called Kavanagh on Bibury Ward. I understand that you helped admit him. I surmise that he was suspected of Abram Cohen's murder before it was proven to be natural causes.'

'Has Mr Kavanagh died?' Margaret's mind began to race. 'I didn't think that was imminent.'

'No. They plan to discharge him, but not until after Inspector Silvermann has visited us today. He wants us to do something but he wouldn't say what.'

'Why us?'

'I have no idea.'

'Honestly, I'll never understand how the inspector's mind works.'

They reached Darnell's desk and Margaret greeted him.

'Message from Inspector Silvermann to expect him at ten, doctors,' he said. 'Letters are on your desk, Dr Demeray, and Mr Purefoy telephoned to say he has left a report for you but will be delayed this morning.'

'Ah, yes,' said Dr Jordan. 'He went home for the Whitsun weekend and I gave him permission to start a little later today.'

'I hope everything's all right.'

'He does tend to overwork, so I thought it good for him to have a little longer with his family. I doubt he'll be very late. He's the punctual sort, and hasn't far to come.'

'Where's "home"?'

Dr Jordan frowned. 'Ealing? Shepherd's Bush? Hammersmith? Somewhere round West London. Anyway, Dr Demeray, I'll join you when the inspector comes, whether the meeting has finished or not.'

'Thank you, sir,' said Margaret.

In the laboratory she filled a clean jug, put the roses inside and took it back to her office to put on the windowsill. She placed the gooseberries on her desk, beside a small pile of correspondence and a large envelope with Cyril's scrawl across the front. Inside were the two files and a near-illegible note.

Dear Doctor Demeray,

Without having been involved in the post-mortem, my view from the evidence presented is that its conclusions were correct. In the case of the body falsely identified as Olive Nolan (and later noted to be a different woman

living under an alias), having referred to a number of texts, the mode of death appears to be that used by an assassin or spy, which is somewhat peculiar.
Yours sincerely,
Cyril G. Purefoy

His writing was forming into a classic doctor's script, the letters irregular and misformed. Even his own name appeared more like Cycil Punifoy.

Punifoy: just like the name in the newspaper article about Gastrell's memorial service. Only hadn't that been a *Mr* Punifoy?

Could it be a misspelling, like Gascon/Gascoigne, from a bored reporter dashing off an article that only the Gastrells would care about?

Dr Jordan had said that Cyril was from West London, which included Fulham. In 1902 Cyril would have been around ten, the same age as Carl Gastrell Webber when he attended the memorial. Long before that, Lena Webber had moved to Fulham and presumably renamed herself Mrs Norrice Gascoigne while she was kept by Gastrell. Had she been connected with the Purefoy family? And if so, had the link been kept up?

Cyril's father was a doctor. Lena and John Webber's father had been a doctor. Their families might not be on the same social level as the Gastrells, but they were on the same level as each other. And presumably the Purefoys did know the Gastrells, otherwise they wouldn't have attended the memorial. A rung or two on the ladder didn't always matter. Margaret was on a lower social level than Phoebe and Maude, yet they were the closest of friends.

Margaret put the note back in the envelope then paced. She straightened books and dusted the skull which grinned from the top of the cabinet, its cranium a cheerful pink from the light shining through the roses. She took a rose and clamped it in the skull's jaw to relieve her tension. It didn't work.

Presumably Elinor was knee-deep in records looking for Lena Webber, later Gascoigne. Fox was on the way to Germany, following the trail of Rainer, while his men closed the net on Webber. Margaret wished she had more contacts. There was Inspector Silvermann, of course…

She scrawled sentences in a notebook. It was probable that she wouldn't be able to decipher them later, and certainly no one else would. There was nothing else she could do but concentrate on work.

The schedule, when she returned to the laboratory, included tests on samples from various patients on Bibury Ward. None were Kavanagh's, but when she checked the records, they showed that tests on Kavanagh undertaken the previous Friday showed no sign of tuberculosis, but damage from repeated bouts of bronchitis and a shadow on one lung. That didn't surprise Margaret, but it saddened her. She set to work, and had lost track of time when the door creaked and Cyril walked in. 'I'm sorry to be late, Dr Demeray. I hope Dr Jordan explained.'

'He did. I hope all is well at home.'

'I'm sure it'll be fine, thank you. Here's a telegram: Mr Darnell was about to bring it in but I said I would.'

'Thank you.' Margaret peeled off her gloves and went to take it from him.

A stroll by the river at one to discuss what's awry. Elinor.

Margaret put the telegram in the pocket of her dress. What was awry? Fox had left the station the previous evening confident and ready to meet Bert and travel to Germany. She'd had word that he had reached his stopping points safely both that evening and first thing in the morning.

Cyril's expression was as neutral as usual as he checked the work schedule and peered at what Margaret was doing. His face was unremarkable, neither handsome nor ugly: light-brown hair made dark with oil, small blue eyes behind round glasses, a straight nose, slightly rosy cheeks. It didn't make her think of anyone in the photograph on the Selkirks' wall, but like Darnell, she felt she'd seen similar features somewhere. Conscious that she was staring, Margaret picked up her gloves. What could she ask him to gain more information, either way?

'Oh, and Inspector Silvermann's here,' Cyril added. 'Mr Darnell told him to wait in the corridor.'

Margaret glanced at the clock. He was early. 'I'd better speak with him; I might be away for a while. Will you concentrate on these tasks, please.' She pointed at items on the schedule. 'Leave the others till either Dr Jordan or I have returned.'

'Yes, doctor.'

'Oh, and by the way…' Margaret hung up her lab coat and collected the envelope with the post-mortem reports inside. 'Thank you for this, Mr Purefoy.'

'It's really a note of observations.'

'Indeed. Very succinct. I never imagined you had an interest in detective stories.'

Cyril looked startled. 'I don't read fiction at all. Some students waste time on novels, plays and moving pictures, then talk about them when we should be discussing our lectures. I don't understand the point of them at all. Why do you mention it?'

'I wondered where the reference to assassins came from.'

'Oh.' Cyril raised his eyebrows. 'I referred to books and articles about how to tell a trained intelligence officer's actions from those of a spontaneous murderer. This morning, I heard about an assault which backs up the theory.'

'Really?' said Margaret. 'A murder among the dock strikers? I know there's talk of violence, but—'

'It was nothing to do with the strike,' said Cyril. 'Or the docks. It was Olive Nolan's employer. Yesterday, someone tried to do to him what they'd done to her, but he managed to get away. The man who attacked him is wanted for attempted murder, and though he hasn't been named, I believe he's a known assassin. An intelligence officer, though I'm not sure for which country.'

'How do you know that? Surely that wasn't in the newspaper.'

'Newspapers surmise things,' said Cyril. 'You know that as well as I do. Sometimes, they're correct.' He was pale, staring at his clenched hands. 'It shocked me. You always say that these bodies are people with stories behind them. Comparing this attack with that postmortem was the first time I've realised that what you say is true. He'd just come home, they say. How victimised he must feel, Dr Demeray. First, in good faith, he employs a girl working under a false name, then a few days later he's implicated in her murder even though he was elsewhere at the time. At least now, he's completely exonerated.' He looked up. 'Why would an intelligence officer want to kill an innocent householder? What could he know? And apart from efficiency, what's the difference between an intelligence officer and a murderer, at the end of the day?'

'Intelligence officers aren't necessarily murderers.'

'Some are,' said Cyril. 'And they should pay for it.' He held her gaze for a moment, then rolled his shoulders and picked up a scalpel. 'I don't want to keep you, Dr Demeray. Do go and meet the inspector. I'll make a start on these tasks.'

Twenty-Eight

Margaret stepped into the corridor, sure that the paleness of her face must give her away. Had Cyril been making an observation, a judgment or a threat?

No, she was being ridiculous. Cyril was voicing the clinical judgment she prized him for. He had assessed the available evidence and come to logical conclusions, which was more than most were capable of. She pinched her cheeks and bit her lips to make herself look less pale, and walked on.

Inspector Silvermann was reading a newspaper. Darnell watched Margaret approach, his face smug as he waited to witness their conversation. He clearly wasn't so much of a gentleman that he'd learned to hide his emotions the way the elite did. She gave him a bright smile, greeted Inspector Silvermann like a long-lost friend, and asked if he'd mind waiting until Dr Jordan joined them.

'Of course not, doctor. I trust you had a pleasant holiday weekend.'

'Delightful,' said Margaret, hoping her face could lie as well as her voice. 'You?'

He shook the newspaper. 'I spent most of Sunday in Trafalgar Square.'

'People are allowed to protest.'

'Yes, but there's always a pickpocket in the crowd, though God knows there isn't much in those poor blokes' pockets. Then there are those who stir things up and make sure blame lands in the wrong place.' He folded the paper.

'You think the strike's being stirred up?'

'No. People are undereducated, undersized, undernourished, underpaid, and unlikely to live long enough to get this old-age pension they've brought in.

But if there's a war, the country will expect them to do their part. Why shouldn't they have a life worth living before they lay it down?'

'And the vote.'

'Food on the table trumps the vote every time.'

'Maybe they go hand in hand.'

'Do they? I don't blame them, doctor. No more than I blame the tailors, the miners, the railway staff or anyone who's been striking this last couple of years. I think things have come to ... bloom? Ripen? No, those are too pretty. They've come to a head and now they've gone pop. But that doesn't mean *other* people won't use it for cover, does it?'

Margaret glanced at Darnell and realised that he couldn't have been listening harder if he'd been embracing them both, but just then the telephone on his desk tinkled with its internal ring, making all three of them jump. 'Mortuary Wing... Hallo, sir... Yes, the inspector is here... Yes, she is too ...Yes. Goodbye.' He replaced the receiver and opened his mouth.

'I take it that was Dr Jordan,' said Margaret, before he could speak, 'and he wants the inspector and me to join him. Or did he want the inspector and the cat's mother?'

'Sorry, doctor. Yes. I'll have some tea sent—'

'No time for tea,' said Inspector Silvermann. He stood up, gave Darnell a bland smile and strode along the corridor. 'I hope that young man never tries to get a job as an undercover detective,' he whispered to Margaret. 'Too snooty by half and subtle as a pink penguin.'

'He's come down in the world and feels affronted that he has to work,' said Margaret. 'His brother was on the way to make a new life for them in America but he died when the *Titanic* sank. So sad.'

'It would be, if he had.'

'What?'

'A body went missing from this hospital and the clerk let it be taken. Didn't you think we'd look into Mr Darnell's background?'

'Then—'

'He had a nice enough family, it's true. But his late father frittered away all the money long ago, and a gambling brother was sent to America in 1910 to get him out of trouble.'

'Maybe he came back, then returned on the *Titanic,* and—'

'What was happening when Darnell told you his brother had drowned?'

Margaret considered. 'I was about to say that I wanted him fired.'

'So he told his tale of woe and you felt sorry for him.'

'Yes.'

'His brother resides in a Chicago hotel where he's the friendly English lord: delighted to join in a card game or ten and be attentive to rich, lonely, older ladies.'

'Darnell's brother is a lord?'

'Of course he isn't, but "Lord" Darnell is as good at making people believe him as he is at being a card sharp. Gambling's illegal in Chicago, but when did that ever make a difference?'

'I feel such a fool for believing him.'

'Spinning yarns is obviously in the family. I don't suppose you're used to your clients lying to you, not the way I am. You're lots of things, but you're no fool. Changing the subject, I guess your old man was in Trafalgar Square too on Sunday afternoon.'

'I couldn't say. I was having tea at my sister's.'

'Did you stay put this time?' The inspector chuckled, then was serious again. 'With the docks largely out of action, there'll be a reduction on what can go to and from the continent, including things that ought to stay put. That'll make Special Branch happy, won't it? But maybe not the people who want them shifted.'

His eyes bored into hers and Margaret swallowed. So he also suspected that information, plans or secrets were leaving the country. That must be why he'd pursued Kavanagh. And even if he was looking in the wrong direction, he was right otherwise. The dockers' strike would hinder transport and traitors would have to find an alternative solution. She still didn't know what to tell him, but she could start somewhere. 'About Dervla Mallowan's employer…'

'Mr Wet Weekend Webber?' The inspector scrutinised her. 'What about him?'

'My assistant said he's been attacked.'

'Really? I'd love to know how news gets out sometimes, though Mr Webber's the sort to tell someone just to sound like a hero. His neck's very colourful. He'll be wearing high collars for a while.'

'Do you have a suspect?'

'Maybe. But Kavanagh first.'

They'd reached Dr Jordan's door and Margaret knocked. 'Come in!'

They entered. 'I just want to ask a couple of simple questions and then borrow one of you,' said the inspector. 'Preferably Dr Demeray. I don't suppose you have the post-mortem on Abram Cohen handy, do you?'

'Yes,' said Margaret. 'I was bringing it back.' She put the envelope on Dr Jordan's desk. 'Why?'

'No external injuries? No signs of poison?'

'None.'

'But he died like Wallace Moore. Remember him?'

'No,' said Dr Jordan. 'Who is he?'

'I think I might,' said Margaret. 'Someone of that name was an old soldier my husband once knew. He died of stroke a few weeks ago.'

'Sad as that is,' said Dr Jordan, 'what is the connection to St J's, Inspector?'

'A note in Dervla's pocket mentioned a Moore, and I've investigated recent deaths that might fit,' said Inspector Silvermann. 'It may not have been just a stroke. Mr Moore had a head injury. His doctor determined it was caused by the fall when he had the first stroke. But what if the stroke was caused by the blow and the fall was incidental?'

Margaret and Dr Jordan exchanged glances. 'Without a post-mortem, it's impossible to tell,' said Dr Jordan.

'I've applied for an exhumation.'

'How many weeks since he died?' said Dr Jordan. 'And what sort of soil is in the graveyard? The brain may have degraded too far by now.'

'Maybe,' said Inspector Silvermann. 'If that's what I'm after. But what if someone finished him off another way? Then it would be another execution.'

'Execution?' exclaimed Dr Jordan. 'If you asked me to confirm that Dervla Mallowan's death was one, I'd say that the evidence points that way. If you're asking me the same regarding Abram Cohen, I'd say not. Would you agree, Dr Demeray?'

'I would.'

'Someone of Kavanagh's description was seen in Fulham the night Wallace Moore collapsed, and possibly the day he died.'

Margaret frowned. 'I don't follow. Why would Kavanagh hurt Mr Moore?'

'Maybe he didn't,' said the inspector. 'That's partly what I need to find out. I'd like to pay him a nice, friendly visit.'

'The wards don't allow visits,' said Dr Jordan. 'There's always a risk of cross-infection.'

'But a doctor could take me. May I borrow Dr Demeray?'

'He may not be fit for questioning,' said Margaret.

'He can't be too unfit or he wouldn't be leaving tomorrow.'

Dr Jordan removed his glasses and polished them. Redness crept up his neck to his jaw. 'Dr Demeray is her own woman, but her work is in this wing.'

'It won't take long,' said Inspector Silvermann.

'If you give me leave, doctor, I'll go,' said Margaret. If nothing else, she didn't want Kavanagh bullied into a confession when he was too weak to argue.

The inspector smiled. 'Have you got Dervla's file here, too?'

'Yes,' said Dr Jordan, 'What has that to do with Kavanagh?'

'Maybe Dr Demeray should bring it with her.'

Dr Jordan took the file from his cabinet and turned its pages. The photograph of Dervla's dead face came loose and slid across the desk.

'Or maybe just that,' said the inspector. 'Shall we go?'

Margaret picked up the sketch and led the inspector out of the room.

'You seem very on edge, doctor.'

'Why are you following me and my husband?'

'I haven't got the resources to follow your husband. He's like a phantom.'

'Me, then.'

'Davis and Dibbs were trying to protect you. Might as well try to protect an eel. An electric one, at that.'

Margaret continued walking, ignoring her desperate urge to check her pocket for Elinor's telegram.

'Is this the ward?' said the inspector. 'Before we go in, let's have a squint at that drawing again.'

Margaret looked at it too. There was Dervla, newly dead, with barely a blemish on her narrow face, pale eyes, her lips parted to reveal her upper front teeth, and strands of fair hair coming down from her cap. 'Oh, God.'

'Didn't strike me either at first,' said Inspector Silvermann. 'Kavanagh's got black hair and a different name. But it's easy to get new hair from a bottle and use your mother's maiden name.'

'So he's really Mallowan.' Margaret turned to the door, her thoughts whirring, conscious of the telegram in her pocket even though it was impossible to feel.

'He took the Queen's shilling in 1891. Fought in both Boer Wars. Handed the shilling back to King Edward in 1902. Joined the Irish Brotherhood. Disappeared.' The inspector paused. 'Dervla was a captured member of the Daughters of Ireland. My theory *was* that Kavanagh is a gunrunner using the rag trade as cover, and Abram Cohen had figured it out and threatened to expose him. I thought maybe Kavanagh had killed Dervla as punishment for being captured, or to avoid her sharing information. That doesn't seem so likely now, does it?'

'No.'

'If you know something, tell me. It might save your old man's life.'

'What?'

'Dervla Mallowan was a Fenian, to all intents and purposes. He'd arrested her. She'd escaped. A word which might be your husband's name was on a note in her pocket, along with Moore's. That suggests she needed to watch out because he was coming for her. What if she was running because she thought she'd never have a fair trial?'

'Fox would never send an innocent person to the gallows. Never.'

'I want the right man charged for the right reason, else I'd have Kavanagh in a prison hospital wing on remand right away,' the inspector muttered. 'I have my standards. But at the moment the evidence for Dervla's murder and possibly Moore's too points one way: at your husband. And then there's the assault on John Webber. If you know something that'll help, spit it out.'

Margaret swallowed. A nurse slowed down as she bustled along and two doctors consulting in the corridor paused to watch her. 'A soldier named Mallowan knew another called Gastrell who himself knew someone called Webber,' she said. 'Moore gave evidence that Gastrell was crooked and my husband was investigating that. I'm surprised you didn't know.'

'Thank you. I'll look into it.'

'Give me a piece of paper from your notebook.' Margaret sat down on the bench outside the ward and copied the sketch, softening Dervla's angry, lifeless glare, making the mouth smile a little, tidying the hair. 'Do you think this will pass? It seems kinder not to show him a corpse. If he killed her he wouldn't care, but if he didn't, he wouldn't want to see that.'

'Sentimental?'

'Parental.'

***

Kavanagh perused the hasty sketch and faded into himself. 'This was drawn after death. The life's not shining from this girl.'

'You're right,' said Inspector Silvermann. 'This is the woman we told you about at the police station. The body initially identified as Olive Nolan was actually once someone called Dervla Mallowan.' He paused, but Kavanagh made no sound or gesture. 'Miss Mallowan smuggled for the Fenians,' the inspector continued. 'Documents for certain, guns maybe. I have reason to believe that you were receiving such things in London.'

'Why would I be doing that?'

'In case the Home Rule Bill fails, perhaps.'

'I'm sure the Lords will see sense eventually, so why the need for bloodshed? No reasonable man wants that.'

'Maybe you were sending things to Germany.'

'Not me. I'm not a traitor.'

'Some would say Fenians are traitors.'

'Would they, now? And what proof have you about any of your allegations?'

'Among other things, I know who you are, and I know this was your daughter.'

'Ah, what it must be to be a man who knows,' said Kavanagh. He sighed, then slumped against his pillows. A fit of coughing made his face red, then grey again. 'I could feel it in the very bones of me when Dervla died. I can't explain how, but I did. I've been trying to find her. She'd been in some trouble, but sent word she'd tell me where she was as soon as she was safe. I assumed she'd gone back to Ireland but when I went there was no trace, and I heard nothing more until one day I felt as if something had been cut from my heart and I knew and I returned to London. Then... Well, I came to this hospital and there's gossip on the ward. Something about a blonde girl found murdered and brought here under a false name. And the grief came on me again.' He touched his daughter's sketched face. 'How did she die?'

'Her neck was broken,' said the inspector. His words were blunt, but his voice soft.

'Clean? Quick?'

'We believe so,' said Margaret.

'If you have nothing to hide about what the two of you were up to,' said the inspector, 'why didn't you admit she was your daughter before?'

'In case you added two and two to make five, just as you're doing now.'

'Do you know a Mr Wallace Moore?'

Kavanagh shook his head. 'No, but I can see you do, inspector, so on the grounds that's another thing to add to your badly worked sum, I suppose you'll be arresting me. So be it. But I'll say nothing about what Dervla might or might not have been doing. I was looking for her, nor working with her.'

'I'll need to make arrangements for a bed in the infirmary wing first,' said Inspector Silvermann.

Kavanagh gave a cold, wheezing chuckle. 'You mean you've yet to obtain a warrant and I haven't confessed, so you can't take me in.' He turned to Margaret. 'Is there a Roman Catholic chaplain here, doctor? I'd like to see him and say prayers for my girl.'

'I'll arrange it.'

'Thank you.' Kavanagh took a deep breath, then coughed for some time. Eventually, he said, 'What else do I need to know?'

'What does the name Gastrell mean to you?' said Margaret, before the inspector could speak.

'Gastrell?' Kavanagh straightened up. 'It means unfinished business. And that, my dear, is all I'm saying.'

Twenty-Nine

Elinor was waiting outside the tube station near the river. Separately, they walked towards the shore. Margaret sat on the low wall and began to sketch. After a while, Elinor sat beside her.

Men and boys were working on the decks of boats, or ankle-deep in mud near the water's edge. One of the boats cast its moorings and steered away, nudging and tipping another. A boy on its gunwales lost his balance and fell into the river. He floundered for a bit, doggy-paddled back, then hauled himself aboard to the derision of the others. After an explosion of bad language followed by laughter the boy shrugged and returned to his work, his clothes steaming in the sunshine.

'It's surprising how many sailors and fishermen can't swim,' Elinor said casually.

Margaret's pencil paused, making a darker mark on the paper than she'd intended. 'More fool them,' she said. 'Has he gone? Have you found anything out?'

'I can't swim at all,' said Elinor. 'and I grew up in Tiger Bay.' She leaned over the wall and picked up some shingle, keeping the flat pieces and discarding others. To anyone watching from a distance she'd appear nonchalant, but Margaret saw tension in the fingers that let perfect skimming stones slip, mirroring the tension in her own which made mistake after mistake in her drawing.

'Please, Elinor. I haven't much time. I have something to tell you, too.'

'We set a man to watch John Webber in the country, but he got back to London somehow without being seen. Allegedly, someone attacked him there.'

'Allegedly?'

'He ought to be badly injured but he's just dripping about, being a martyr. However, the finger is firmly pointing towards a professional killer again. And you know what that means.'

'But surely…'

'Someone's not stupid. Whether it's Webber is another matter.'

'Have you found out about his background?'

'We believe his widowed mother moved to Germany to rent a house owned by someone calling himself Rainer. But to confirm that and get more detail, we need information from German records, which are rather difficult to obtain just now.' She pointed at Margaret's sketch. 'You've missed a rope. That boat will drift away if you don't moor it.'

'I wish I could drift away,' snapped Margaret. 'What about Mrs Gascoigne?'

'42a Flora Street, Fulham is as real as Paradise Road, Islington.'

'I thought it sounded wrong. So nothing sent would get there?'

'It would. It's a sort of *Poste Restante* address at the local post office. Someone collects mail on a regular basis. How regular and who set it up they won't tell us without a warrant. We need to place someone there as staff. That's not simple or quick. And a cursory search of the records hasn't turned up the person we think is the right woman under the name of Gascoigne, Gascon or Webber. Not getting married, dying, giving birth, or paying tax. I suspect Lena's gone under all sorts of names. It takes time.'

Margaret pencilled in the shadows under the jetty. She'd made them too dark and ominous. The pressure of her pencil had surely indented the next page as frustration made her gouge the paper. 'Where's Fox?'

'He's sailing to Antwerp. He should be there about six o'clock. He'll telegraph from there before heading on to Berlin.'

The newspaper representations of the sinking *Titanic* came into Margaret's mind, and then she saw someone shoving Fox over the rail to flounder in the black, churning sea. *Fox is only crossing the channel*, she thought. *He can swim. Please God he won't need to, but he can.* 'Was anyone following him?' she asked.

'He can look after himself, Margaret. What was your news?'

'Dervla Mallowan's father is in St J's. He's been going by the name of Kavanagh.'

'Really? Fox would want him questioned.'

'They'll have to be quick,' said Margaret, scribbling across her sketch and standing up.

'Because he's about to die?'

'Because Inspector Silvermann will arrest him the moment he gets a warrant. He thinks Kavanagh has a connection with Wallace Moore's death and he has applied for an exhumation. I think their difficulty is that unless Special Branch or Hare provide it, they don't have enough evidence.'

'Bureaucracy is wonderful if you know how to work it properly,' said Elinor. 'You can find out a good deal, but you can hide so much more. Your inspector may be disappointed for a while yet.' She winked, then threw her last stone. It skimmed, bounced once, then sank. 'What are you planning to do? Sit tight till Fox is back?'

'See if I can find out more from Kavanagh, perhaps.'

'I'll telephone you as soon as we hear from Fox,' said Elinor. 'Keep your wits about you.'

***

Her next visit to Kavanagh was fruitless. He simply said 'Sure, you know what modern women are – in a rush to be independent, never minding their father's worry. I bet you're the same,' then closed his eyes in dismissal.

Margaret arrived home at five thirty. There were letters waiting and a postcard from Maude, with a woman and a horse on the front, and a message that simply said 'Coffee with Lady S on Friday and riding at Archers Steading on Sunday all fixed. What larks!'

Margaret wished she could feel the same excitement rather than guilt and dread. She sifted through the letters. One was from Helene's, asking her to come for a fitting as soon as she was able. Two were bills. She took the last, in Lucy's writing, upstairs.

'Shall I bring you some tea, ma'am?' said Nellie, when she arrived in the nursery. The twins were sitting with more confidence and bending to reach for things – or in Edie's case, more often than not, pointing at things she wanted Alec to pick up for her.

'Yes, please,' said Margaret, sitting on the carpet with the children. 'But don't rush. If the telephone rings, please come for me. Otherwise, have a rest with Vera.'

'Thank you, ma'am.'

As she left, Margaret sat down between the children. She could see by the way that Alec twisted, bent and half-lifted himself from the rug that he was eager to be on the move. She sensed his impatience as his mind tried to work out what he needed to do and how to do it. Edie seemed content to watch him, perhaps deciding that she might as well let him make a fool of himself while working things out, then follow his lead as if she'd known what to do all along. It seemed a sensible approach.

'Alec will be black and blue from trying to run before he can walk, just like I was,' said Margaret, closing the case and tousling her daughter's head. 'And you'll sit all serene and wise, weighing things up before taking action. You really are Daddy's little girl, aren't you?'

'Ummmamma.' Edie nodded and tipped sideways as Margaret read Lucy's letter.

Dear Margaret,

I believe I saw that outfit again, or something very similar, yesterday in Fulham. I can't be certain, because I can't recall the original lady's face exactly, but this one is maybe your age with fairish hair. However, I recognised the embroidery. I was with Mother, walking towards the post office, and she was coming out. Mother saw her too and said 'Oh!' It was one of those times when one is just too far away to make a normal greeting and have to pretend one hasn't seen one another until one is close enough to speak. As she came near Mother said 'Good day, Mrs Gascoigne, how lovely to see you. How do you do. I mean…' Then Mother started to blush.

The other woman gave her a frosty smile and gave me a normal one. If she had been on the bench that day and recognised me as the person with Mr Moore, she gave no indication whatsoever. She said 'Very well, thank you, Mrs Frampton. And you too, I trust. I'm afraid I'm in rather a rush. Good day.' And off she went.

I asked Mother who she was and Mother said that several years ago Mrs Gascoigne had been a parishioner of a different church, and they'd met occasionally at joint sewing parties. Mrs G was something of an enigma, apparently. She appeared quite respectable and had a little boy whom she was bringing up very nicely, but there was some question about her marital status. Her husband was mostly abroad with the army, she said, and could only visit occasionally. He certainly never went to church and no one could describe him.

Mother said Mrs G was an excellent seamstress and everyone thought it was a shame that she had no daughters to sew for, only foundlings and foreign missions.

Apparently the husband, if that's what he was, was killed in South Africa when the little boy was nine or ten and poor Mrs G was beside herself with grief. Worse still, he left her no money, which the old cats in the sewing circle took as proof that they'd never been married. She moved away and started a business in Islington (cheaper than Fulham), which shows she had some sense, even if she made a bad choice of husband. As I suspected, the old cats thought that she'd gone beyond the pale and an honest woman would have stayed poor till she found someone rich to marry. So no one kept in contact with her, although there was always someone happy to pass on gossip.

Mother thought it all very unkind, but she'd never known Mrs G beyond a vague acquaintanceship, so had no reason to keep up with her herself.

I suppose Mrs G's son must be a little older than I am now.

Edie reached for the letter and Margaret lifted it out of her reach. *Yes, Carl Gastrell Webber must now be twenty, compared to Lucy's eighteen. His mother was eighteen when he was born, so must be thirty-seven or eight now.* She moved Edie back a little and continued reading.

Mother said that as far as she knows through gossip, the business does excellently, with trade on the Continent and in the colonies, though she had no idea whether Mrs G is still running it. She'd heard that Mrs G had remarried (or married, I suppose) two years after her husband's death and moved back west, and had no need to work for a living any more.

Mother said that was why she was embarrassed. She couldn't recall the new surname, only that the new husband had been very much older than Mrs G: perhaps over fifty when they married. So he can't have been the man I saw her with that day in Bishop's Park, as that man looked younger than Fox.

If Mrs G didn't sell her business and has goods going to the Continent, perhaps that's all they were talking about. Maybe what Mr Moore heard as 'He has what the Germans want and he can kill two vermin with one dose of poison' was actually something like 'We have what the Germans want and we can sell two of them for one sovereign'. That seems so much more plausible, and what you said in the first place.

Margaret put the letter in her lap and pulled the children close, annoying both of them, too busy with toys to want to be fussed over. Mrs Gascoigne, who was really Lena Webber, had married as soon as she had the opportunity, which was hardly unusual. Brother and sister would have kept in touch. Lena had been strong enough to hold up her head against gossiping matrons and start a business. What had she really thought of the man who'd left her with a child to bring up alone?

At a quarter past six, Elinor telephoned. 'All well. But he's on the way back.'

'Why?'

'On the one hand, a cold trail. Or perhaps hot, depending on how you look at it. And on the other, maybe a warrant *should* have been issued before

Kavanagh discharged himself three quarters of an hour ago.'

'What?'

'It's being kept under wraps. There will be nothing in the press.'

'But everyone knew he wasn't to leave till the inspector returned. All his clothes and belongings were locked away so that he *couldn't* leave.'

'Well, he left regardless,' said Elinor. 'I'd admire him if Hare wasn't worried. Serves your inspector right for not being better prepared.'

'I'm...' Margaret bit her lip. She wanted to say, *I'm glad Kavanagh has escaped. He just wants vengeance for his daughter.*

'He's a risk,' said Elinor, perhaps reading her mind. 'Even if he hasn't killed anyone in the name of the cause so far, that doesn't mean he won't.'

'I feel there's only one thing he cares about now and he hasn't long to do anything about it.'

'If he thinks one of us is responsible for Dervla's death, because of her political leanings, he's a risk.'

'But we're *not* responsible,' said Margaret.

'I wasn't including you.' Elinor paused. 'He might never have met Fox in 1902, but if he was trying to report treason he'll have heard about the investigation. Hopefully from what you told us Anna said, he knows Fox is honourable and someone else is responsible. But while the risk may not be to us, any action he takes in revenge may impede us or put us in danger.'

Margaret hadn't thought of that.

'Thank you for what you found in Dervla's case,' Elinor added.

'Did you find anything else?'

'No. But the second set of words say Gascoigne St L'Argel, Whitechapel. Argel not Angel and there's an L apostrophe in front of the A.'

'French?' Margaret picked up a pencil and jotted it down on the notepad by the telephone.

'Just meant to look it, we think: French always sounds more sophisticated than English. We haven't found any business in Whitechapel with that name yet. I admit that I too could have sworn it was Angel at first, but that's probably because of the feathers on the tissue.'

'On the tissue?' said Margaret.

'Yes, the pattern.'

Margaret's mind whirred. She closed her eyes and recalled the image on the tissue lining the case. Of course: it wasn't flowers, it was a plume of feathers. There had been boxes in the Ravel Street sweatshop with a similar symbol – or maybe the same? Sullivan was providing goods for Mr W to export. Was that John Webber? She hadn't seen him properly the day Abram Cohen was found. The doorway was too dark, the room darker still. 'Will you telephone tomorrow afternoon, Elinor? I'll be away in the morning.'

'Where?'

Margaret paused, checking that neither of the maids was in earshot but dropping her voice all the same. 'I'm going to inspect the sweatshop where Abram Cohen died.'

'Ravel Street?' said Elinor. 'Are you sure? I'm uneasy about this.'

'It's not just Fox who can take care of himself,' said Margaret, catching sight of herself in the mirror, standing straighter and fixing a cool expression on her face. 'Goodbye.'

Thirty

In the morning, Margaret hovered around the telephone until eight thirty then rushed out to hail a cab, only to have the postman thrust a letter addressed to Fox into her hand. A pigeon sitting in the road lumbered into the air as the motor taxi pulled up.

'Ravel Street, Whitechapel,' said Margaret.

'Blimey,' said the cabbie, as a pigeon feather drifted down to the taxi's bonnet.

'Just a moment,' said Margaret. She shoved the envelope the postman had given her into her handbag, on top of the folding camera she'd put in there in case she could photograph evidence, and pulled out Helene's letter about a fitting. Of course – how could she have forgotten? In the shop there were items made of ostrich feathers everywhere, and at the top of the letter an embossed image of... Margaret held the letter up to the light. A plume of feathers.

'Islington!'

The cabbie raised his eyebrows. 'What you say, madam?'

'Affpuddle Street, Islington.'

'I thought you said Ravel Street, Whitechapel.'

'I've changed my mind.'

'Thank Gawd for that.'

Helene, thought Margaret as the cab gathered speed. *I should tell Elinor. Is Helene really Lena? Or does she still run the business from a distance? Either way, why order a jacket and put it through the books? Helene seemed nice... but anyone can seem nice.* She rapped on the window again. 'Can you stop at the next telegraph office with a telephone sign?'

'This is gonna cost you.'

'I know.'

When she got through to Fox's office, she said 'Mrs F speaking. Is Miss Hedgehog there?'

'Gone out digging.'

'I have more information. Can you get it to her?'

'Yes.'

'Any news from F?'

'Overland now. Where are you? Home or public place?'

'Public.'

'Anyone in earshot?'

She glanced around. 'No.'

'Miss Hedgehog said you're going to a certain business. I'll get someone to meet you there.'

'I'm going to a different one first. She needs to know about that, too.'

'Businesses are in another house and even harder to dig up.'

'I can imagine, but it's relevant. Shall I telegraph?'

'Yes, in the usual way. Goodbye, Mrs F.'

Margaret replaced the receiver, collected a telegram form, and wrote: *Darling, don't forget Lena's wedding anniversary at Helene's, Affpuddle St. It'll be near to angelic. Where have eight years gone? She h*anded over the fee and the address and returned to the cab.

'Still Islington?' asked the cabbie.

'Still Islington.'

Margaret settled back, then noticed that the letter the postman had given her at the gate had fallen out of her bag. The envelope was typed and quite bulky. The stamp had been scribbled through rather than franked, as if someone had wanted the recipient to think it had been posted when it hadn't. Now that she thought about it, the postman had been either late for the first post or early for the second. She hadn't looked at him properly, or even registered his uniform.

She turned the letter over. The flap was bent open at the left corner so that she could see part of the contents. It was typed – no, printed – on the stiff paper used for books:

> *saw Lieut. Foxcroft-McSionna*
> *without warning, shot as he m*

Margaret and Fox never read each other's letters unless asked. Never.

She ran her fingers along the badly-sealed flap, then over the name and address on the other side, and pushed it deep into her bag. They never read each other's letters. Trying to ignore the sensation that the unread words were whispering inside the envelope, she distracted herself by turning every so often to see if anyone was following.

Eventually, the cab stopped outside Helene's. No other vehicle stopped. No one seemed to be waiting for her. Margaret climbed out and went to speak with the cabbie. 'You can leave me here and I'll get another cab to Whitechapel.'

'You still going?'

'Yes, but I don't know how long I'll be here. I may have to have a fitting.'

'Please yourself,' said the cabbie. He eyed her narrowly. 'You look you need a cuppa. Tell you what, so do I. What say you pay me what you owe so far, and I have one in that café across the road. I'll leave the car here. If I see you come out in the next five minutes I'll take you to Ravel Street. If I don't, I'll go and get the next fare.'

'Thank you. I'd appreciate that.'

Margaret hesitated, her hand on the door handle. If her suspicions about Helene's business were right, she still had to work out what connected it with Lena's brother's exports through the Ravel Street sweatshop.

She opened the door and stepped in, wondering what she was going to say to the woman who called herself Helene. But a shorter, younger woman was behind the counter, apparently comparing a ledger to some correspondence. She put both away when Margaret walked up and smiled brightly. 'How may I help you, madam?'

'Is Mrs Gascoigne here today?'

The young woman frowned a little. 'Do you mean Helene? No, I'm afraid not. She only comes in on Mondays and sometimes Saturday afternoons. She was in more frequently over the last few weeks, of course. May I help? I'm Miss Price, her deputy.'

'Oh. I see.' So was Helene really Lena, or not? 'I understood a Miss, er, Balodis would like to do a fitting.'

Miss Price reopened the ledger. 'Miss Balodis has taken a day's leave to visit a sick friend.' She pursed her lips in a way that suggested she didn't believe a word of it. 'But one of the other girls can do it. What is the name, please?'

'Dr Perry. Bayswater.'

'Ah, yes. You were here on the twenty-first. I'm afraid we're rather behind with orders, as you might expect, so this will be very much a first fitting. However' – she studied Margaret's figure, then the order book – 'I daresay there won't be a great deal to alter. Shall I—'

'Don't trouble,' said Margaret. 'I'd like to have Miss Balodis do the fitting. I'll return on Friday.'

'As you wish, madam.' Miss Price made a note in the ledger and smiled. 'At what time?'

'Three o'clock.'

'Very well.'

Margaret paused. 'This may sound like an odd request, but might I see the sewing room? I'd like to see how your garments are made.'

Miss Price lifted a section of the counter and the little gate below. 'Of course. There's nothing to hide, though I thought you were a doctor, not a reporter.'

'I am. I won't take up too much of your time.' Margaret stepped through. 'How long have you worked for Helene?'

'Four years,' said Miss Price. 'I learned cutting at the technical college, then applied here. I like to see a woman in charge of a business, though we have men doing the deliveries. I'm keen to have a place of my own one day. I'll take you through, but if the bell rings, we'll have to leave.'

'I won't take long. I'm not doing an inspection.'

'Thank heaven. We're sick of those.' Miss Price led Margaret through a double door into a workroom at the rear of the building with glass doors from floor to ceiling, open to let fresh air in. Light flooded the room, which was filled with an aroma combining lavender, cloth, sewing-machine oil and hot people.

The rattle of treadles and the whirr of drive-wheels and needles slowed as eight women looked up from their work. Nine workstations were evenly spaced, with plenty of room for a person to walk between them. Near the glass doors, at a large table, one woman was cutting fabric while another basted sections of a garment together and a third hand-stitched a lining into place.

As in Margaret's usual dressmaker's workshop, one seamstress read aloud from a book as the others worked, resting her hands, if not her eyes, and hopefully relieving some of the tedium. Two teenage girls moved between workstations: one sweeping, the other collecting finished items. Garments in various stages of completion dangled from hangers or adorned mannequins. It seemed calm and orderly. The few women who looked thin and haggard were perhaps those who had just stopped striking.

'Thank you,' said Margaret. She turned to go, then spotted, on a table near the exit, boxes lined with that familiar cream tissue, patterned sparsely with a plume of ostrich feathers. Another box was closed and sealed, the cardboard decorated with one larger plume. 'Will my outfit be in a box like that?'

'Similar,' said Miss Price, ushering her back into the shop. 'Those are the ready-mades which go to shops and abroad. Things have changed – off-the-peg does well among all classes nowadays. The snobbery is fading fast.' Her voice was enthusiastic. It was clear what she intended to do with a business of her own.

'Indeed,' said Margaret. 'By the way, was I wrong to call Helene Mrs Gascoigne?'

'Oh no, not at all. It's just that I've never known of anyone use it other than in correspondence. Gascoigne's her business name. She doesn't use her married one.'

'Which is?'

'I don't know,' admitted Miss Price. 'I only know her as Helene. I think she moves in different circles as a wife.'

'Oh, I see. Thanks again. I'll see you on Thursday.' Miss Price opened the door for Margaret to leave just as the postman approached. He touched his cap to both Margaret and Miss Price handing the latter a pile of papers and a small parcel.

Margaret was relieved to find the taxi still there. The cabbie ambled across the street to meet her. 'She your pal?' he said, as he let her into the car.

'The woman from the shop?' said Margaret. 'No. Why?'

'Married?'

'I've no idea.'

'They was talking about her when the postman stopped. Sounds like they're playing some sorta prank. Perhaps you should let her know.'

'Who were talking?'

'Two geezers came in the cafe and they was watching the door of the shop when you came out and the postman walked up. One of them said, "A lady won't read her husband's mail" and the other one laughed and said "Her old man will get his luvverly surprise without being forewarned".'

'Oh,' said Margaret, airily. 'That sounds like something nice. Maybe a birthday present.'

'Hope so,' said the cabbie. 'I don't like surprises, me. Now, let's get you to Whitechapel. Can you have my fare ready? I don't fancy hanging about in Ravel Street. Someone will have the chassis out from under me before you've finished straightening your hat.'

'Have it now,' said Margaret. 'Is that enough, plus a tip?'

'More than. Thanks, missus.'

As the cab moved off Margaret glanced at the café, but it was impossible to see beyond the glass. She had seen no one follow her, but clearly they had. The letter began to whisper again.

'Forgive me, Fox,' she said, taking it from her bag and opening it. Inside was the missing page of the soldier's book, numbered page ninety-seven on the top right of one side and ninety-eight on the top left of its reverse.

A typed letter was enclosed within:

Foxcroft-McSionnach

The birds are coming home to roost. This time, it will be the fox who's trapped.

Unless you stop seeking us, we will publish the whole of this book to prove you are a cold-blooded murderer. This is the page removed from the copy you have. You were so busy chasing dead ends you didn't notice we'd followed you to that library and saw what your wife saw. I doubt the librarian will ever realise the page is missing, or realise we have the only other copy from the printer. If you live long enough to stand trial, you will hang. Whether you live to hang or not, your family will be ruined as Norris Gastrell's family was ruined by you. If <u>they</u> live, that is.

Mrs Foxcroft-McSionnach, if you're reading this, perhaps you should heed the same advice. And perhaps you should read on and see what kind of man you married before going home to your cubs.

Her hands shook. She wasn't sure if she could face reading the page, but she had to. She had to know what it said. Fox had told her what happened. Whatever the old soldier said, she'd believe Fox first.

we saw Lieut. Foxcroft-McSionnach take out his revolver and aim. He shot Lieut. Gastrell without warning, shot him as he might a wild beast rather than a man, shot him three times in the back.

This was no better than what he'd accused Lieut. Gastrell of, and Lieut. Foxcroft-McSionnach was supposed to stand for the law. We were shocked.

Lieut. Gastrell faltered, then staggered on towards the trees by the river. It was hard to see where he'd been wounded, but he had surely been. When he neared the trees, he faltered once more, nearly overcome.

Lieut. Foxcroft-McSionnach continued his pursuit, revolver in hand.

We were so shocked that we didn't move for a while, then rose as one man to follow after. I feared then for others, in case the heat or fury had curdled Lieut. Foxcroft-McSionnach's brain and he shot others without conscience. He had, after all, tried to secure a charge against Lieut. Gastrell on the flimsiest of evidence. He seemed focused on one outcome alone – the destruction of Lieut. Gastrell - a man who had not had time to defend himself.

We closed in and I said, 'One of you go and get the captain. The rest of us must reason with him before he loses his mind. Get a doctor for Lieut. Gastrell too', and Moore said, 'Indeed we must.' Then he said 'Look out! Sir! Look out – the river bank is dry!'

Before anyone could do anything, we saw that Lieut. Gastrell had reached the edge. The ground crumbled under him and he fell into the river. It was not full, by any means, for it was summer. But it ran swiftly, nonetheless, and Lieut. Gastrell was in uniform and wounded. He struggled in the water and then sank from view.

Lieut. Foxcroft-McSionnach then surprised us by removing his belt and his boots and jumping in after Lieut. Gastrell. We watched them struggle in the water for a while, and I could not swear whether Lieut. Foxcroft-McSionnach aimed to save or drown the other. It was some minutes before he dragged Lieut. Gastrell out, apparently lifeless. By this time the captain had arrived, and seeing him, Lieut. Foxcroft-McSionnach turned Lieut. Gastrell this way and that as if to get the water from him. Afterwards

Margaret swallowed, heart thudding, fury rising. Whatever Fox said, if anyone saw the book with these two pages…

Her shaking hands perspired inside their gloves. She touched the cut edges of the page and closed her eyes, trying to visualise the preceding and following pages and recall what had gone before and after.

It's fake, she whispered. *It's completely fake. It's a hollow threat. This extract suggests that the writer felt sympathy for Gastrell. The rest of the book suggests the opposite. And the next bit says the soldiers were asked what they'd seen and it 'wasn't much', which completely contradicts this.*

She looked at the paper again. Was it the same size, colour and quality? She didn't know without comparing them directly. It wouldn't stand up in court, would it? If a jury read the book Margaret had been sent, together with what had allegedly been removed from it, they'd see they didn't match.

Then she remembered the article which had damned her and St J's. It wouldn't matter what a jury believed. If the press published it, the general public would believe there was no smoke without fire.

The point was to threaten, and scare. Now Margaret was in Whitechapel with someone following her, and presumably someone else was following Fox. And all the time, their children were so far away in Bayswater and neither of them could do anything to protect them.

Thirty-One

The building in Ravel Street seemed to lean more than ever. 'You sure it's safe to go in?' said the cabbie, opening the door for Margaret, despite his earlier threat to drive off as fast as possible. 'Looks like it'll crumble the minute someone sneezes.'

'I hope not,' said Margaret. 'A good many people work inside.'

'Sweatshop?'

'More than one.'

'What's wrong with the dressmaker in Islington? In fact, why can't you find one down Bayswater way? My missus'd make you a frock if you asked nicely. You won't get rooked by her.'

'I'm not buying,' said Margaret. 'I'm, er, inspecting.'

'Oh, I see.' The cabbie pulled a face as he closed the car door and looked around. Women pegged washing onto a line which would be winched high above the street paused to watch them, while small children with babies on their laps peered from doorways and a toothless old woman in black, slumped against a lamp-post, gummed soundlessly at them. A rag and bone man's horse and cart waited outside one of the houses while its owner haggled with a girl over an armful of battered saucepans.

There were few men about but two teenage boys loitered, smoking cigarette ends so small they could barely be held. A scrawny young woman with a black eye and a split lip trudged past with a grubby baby on her hip. A string bag with green potatoes swung from her hand and a barefoot toddler trailed alongside. Only the baby displayed curiosity, the mother and child concentrating on the pavement leading to whatever bit of shelter they called home.

'I don't feel comfortable leaving you,' said the cabbie. 'A sweatshop owner in Whitechapel ain't likely to be as nice as that girl in Islington, especially now he's got to pay more wages and can't cram as many people into the space.'

'I know.'

'Drive round a bit, shall I? If I don't pick up a fare, and I doubt I will, I could pick you up in ten minutes. That's all you'll need to see what they'll let you see.'

'That's really kind of you, but don't worry. A colleague is meeting me here. He'll make sure I get safely home.'

'Sure?' The cabbie hesitated, then climbed into his cab. 'Take care. And don't sneeze.'

He waited till she'd climbed the steps to the front door and then drove off, shaking his head.

As soon as he'd gone, Margaret hurried to the soup kitchen. The queue was longer now that the dockers' children had joined it, but they parted to let Margaret through. Anna looked up from the counter and her smile vanished as Margaret beckoned her.

Outside, on the pavement, she said, 'Is it Kavanagh? Is he … has he…'

'He's still alive and still a free man, Anna, but things are changing fast. If I tell you all the truth I know, will you tell me all the truth you know?'

Scrutiny, then a short, sharp nod.

'This is what I know,' said Margaret. 'Mr Kavanagh is really Mr Mallowan. He used to be in the army and fought in South Africa. He tried to give evidence about a thoroughly despicable man called Gastrell —''

'Gastrell?'

'You know him?'

'No. But I've heard the name. Who is he?'

'Was,' said Margaret. 'Among other things, he was a traitor who died before the investigation was complete. Mr Mallowan's daughter was called Dervla—'

'Oh gawd, is she dead?' Anna's face became paler.

'I'm afraid so,' Margaret touched the other woman's shoulder. 'Did you know her?'

'No. Just her father. Poor bloke. Go on about this Gastrell.'

'The people she was working for knew him before he died. They may want revenge on her father for offering evidence against him ten years ago and they're trying to have Fox accused of her murder.'

'Does Kavanagh know she's dead?'

'Yes. I'd have told him and you earlier if I'd realised there was a connection. The trouble is that there was another man who tried to give evidence against Gastrell: an old quartermaster called Moore,' said Margaret. 'He died a few weeks ago, in a very similar way to Abram Cohen. Not the same, but very similar. I stand by my belief that Mr Cohen's death was natural. However, Inspector Silvermann thinks that maybe he was murdered because of his connection with Mr Kavanagh, or murdered *by* Mr Kavanagh. I don't, but Inspector Silvermann isn't listening. Is there anything you haven't told me that can help? Then I can try and convince him without involving you.'

Anna ran a hand over her face. She looked exhausted. 'Don't tell Silvermann, tell Fox,' she said. 'I met Kavanagh in New York, like I said. We made friends because we want the same thing: not to be under the control of people who don't understand or care about us. Everything I told you was true, up to the bit about coming back. When Andris died, I wasn't sure what to do. I'd kept writing to Abram and he … he wanted me to come back and set something up with him. He said Sullivan's would end up in queer street. There were extra exports going out from Sullivan's which his people weren't actually making. Garments, things decorated with feathers, hatpins, reticules, brooches. Fob watches, even. Abram thought he'd be out on his ear and agreed with me that there must be a fairer way to run a business.'

'Was Abram your—'

'He might have been. His mother wouldn't have liked it, but ... he might have been. Anyway, I was trying to get him to come out to America so we could start a business together.' Anna's shoulders drooped. She looked round the narrow, grubby streets that she and Abram had grown up in as if looking for something to comfort her. 'I told Kavanagh about it. I didn't have no one else to tell. He thought I'd be better getting Abram to go to New York than coming to London. Then Kavanagh heard from his daughter in Dublin.'

Margaret's skin prickled. 'What did she say?'

'That someone was recruiting her because they knew she was involved with the Daughters of Ireland. They were offering funds for the cause in exchange for help and she didn't know what to do. She didn't exactly explain what the "help" entailed in the letter, just that it involved taking innocent-looking exports to and from London and ports. She got picked because she was skilled at getting things across borders. The code word was Gastrell.'

'Are you sure?'

'Yes. Kavanagh wrote back telling her not to get involved, but she replied that like him, she wasn't a traitor and didn't want to sell Britain to its enemies. She just wanted an independent Ireland. She thought that maybe if she joined them she could uncover what they were doing and give them up to the authorities. He wrote again to tell her not to get involved, but heard nothing by return. So he asked me to come back, help find her, and see if there was any connection to what Abram had said about Sullivan's.'

'And so you did.'

'Yes. Dervla had given Kavanagh some hints about contacts. I got a job with one of the seamstresses supplying goods for export who might be being used—'

'Helene Gascoigne?'

'Yes, though it took a while, because Dervla had said to look for someone called Rainer.'

'Rainer?' Margaret cursed herself for never thinking to mention the name to Anna before.

'It's the name of the person who organises everything.'

'His real name, or could he really be called Webber?'

Anna frowned. 'Webber? Dervla said there was a dogsbody called Webber.'

'Does the name Knox mean anything?'

'No. Should it? It's not Helene. Her business name is Gascoigne, like the woman who ordered the jacket. It seemed a bit strange, but maybe it's just one of them odd things. But her married name is - dunno how you pronounce it - but it's spelled -' Anna screwed up her eyes as she remembered, 'P-U-R-E-F-O-Y.'

'Purefoy?' Margaret stared at her. 'Are you sure?'

'Weird, ain't it? She's nice enough when she's getting what she wants, but she's not happy now the dockers are on strike. The longer things lie around in the wrong place, the bigger the risk of someone working out what's in them. They look all right to me, but there's something up. And I saw her going to Sullivan's this morning with two blokes. One is the one who comes about the exports all the time. He looks a bit like her only fatter and balder. I'm not sure who the other is, but he's tall, good-looking, tanned.'

'I see.' Margaret tried to focus. Lena had been at Gastrell's memorial under the name Gascoigne, albeit spelled wrong. Someone reported to be called Punifoy had been there, too. She mustn't get sidetracked. 'What did Abram find out?'

'He worked at Sullivan's as much as he could, more hours than he should. We couldn't find Dervla, but we were getting somewhere. Then the strike was called and we'd have no way of getting inside again. Abram decided to look for evidence once more before the strike started in earnest. We didn't want him to: he wasn't well. He was having terrible headaches.' Anna blinked. 'And then... then we had word that Dervla had been arrested and brought to London.'

'Fox arrested her, but he thought she had something to tell him and he'd have made sure she had a fair trial if she hadn't. You have to believe me about that.'

'I know, and I do.'

'Was it Kavanagh who helped her escape?'

Anna shook her head violently. 'No! If he had, she'd be safe. The people who recruited her must have done it and then...' She sniffed. 'And without Kavanagh or Abram, I can't even get into Sullivan's to see what's there.'

'No,' said Margaret. 'But I can.'

***

Margaret stood inside the old building and listened. Unlike the last time she'd visited, it was noisy, though the noise was muffled by the doors on each floor. She wondered which of Fox's men would meet her, and where. She'd seen no one she recognised in the street. Or would it be Fox himself?

She made her way to the first floor and paused outside the sewing room where Abram Cohen had been found three weeks ago. The rhythmic thud of the sewing-machine treadles rippled through her feet. There was no response to her knock on the heavy oak door and she entered.

When she'd seen it before, on a gloomy day, the room had been empty of workers and dark. It was still dark now, though the sun shone outside and gas lamps burned on the walls. Natural light fell only on the cutting table near the large window.

The women nearest the door slowed their sewing for only a moment to stare, but it was enough to make Mr Sullivan, sitting at his desk at the back of the room, look up. He left his cigarette smouldering in an ash tray, stood up and walked towards her. Margaret tried to work out what, if anything, had changed in the room. The same mannequin faced the sewing tables. She wore a different dress but the same hat, resplendent with ostrich feathers, only this time better secured. Previously, the mannequin had commanded twenty-five tables in a space only marginally bigger than Helene's. Now it stared down its nose at twenty, all occupied.

The room was stuffy, the smell of perspiration strong. Only the upper part of the window was open. Dust, lint and bits of thread lay in drifts between the tables, kicked up as a little girl walked between the lines collecting completed items. There was no one reading, no one talking, just the steady clatter-clatter of treadles and whirr of machinery. The girl paused as she reached Margaret and said 'I'm fourteen. I'm part time. I'll be in school this afternoon'. She stalked off with her basket towards the hand-stitchers by the window, even her back looking no older than ten.

'Good morning, Dr Demree,' said Mr Sullivan as he reached her. 'You still working for the police?' He didn't offer to shake hands, but touched the rim of his hat. His eyes were wary. 'Or are you a factory inspector now?'

'I don't work for the police,' said Margaret. 'And I'm not any kind of inspector. Though things look different from the last time I was here.'

'Yeah, well.' Mr Sullivan rolled his eyes. 'Better twenty working machines than twenty-five idle ones. If it ain't an inspection, what can I do you for? If you want to talk about – you know – I'll thank you to come to the office.' He jerked his head towards his desk.

'I just wanted to look round,' said Margaret. 'We're still trying to get to the bottom of things, and the day I came when – you know – had happened, I was concentrating on that, not the surroundings.'

'They've changed, like you said. What's the point?'

'Mr Sullivan, you've removed five tables and doubtless squeezed them in somewhere else, but that's not my concern, whatever my views may be. I would say that the floor needs sweeping, particularly as you smoke in here. That lint is like tinder and there's a lot of wood in this place. I might mention *that* to the owner of the building next door.'

Mr Sullivan licked his lips. 'Here, Bessy! Why ain't you keeping the floor clear?'

The ten year old dumped her basket, collected a broom and sullenly shoved it around the tables, earning curses from the seamstresses as she bumped their ankles.

'Garn, then,' Mr Sullivan jerked his head at Margaret. 'Do your worst. Ain't nothing to see. I just told Inspector Silvermann that.'

'He's here?'

'Was. And as it happens, he was looking for you.'

Thirty-Two

'For me?'

'Yeah. I said I hadn't seen you since – you know. Anyway, hurry up, will you? You're distracting the girls. We've got clients in the office arguing with the ole man and trying to knock off some of what they owe, cos the stuff's got to be exported from Dover instead of London this week. I need to go and add some muscle. It ain't our fault every bloody loafer goes on strike every other bleeding week. We can't afford to lose any more boodle.' He raised his voice. 'Or there won't be nothing to pay those higher wages with.'

'Exports?' She said the word as if it was a surprise, even though Mr Sullivan must remember she'd been there when the man he'd called Mr W popped his head round the door, saw the body, and made a retreat. She wished she'd been able to make him out properly. She was now certain in herself that he must be John Webber, but she could not swear to it. She started to walk around, not certain what she was looking for, wondering how she could stay long enough to see the clients come out of the back office.

'Yeah, our off-the-peg stuff goes all over the Empire. What's that got to do with the price of beer? The inspector wanted to know if that haberdasher Kavanagh had been here. You know, the one he said was rowing with Abram before he snuffed it. He was only a bit more interested in whether he'd been here than whether you had.' Mr Sullivan scrutinised her, eyes narrowed. 'What it is to be popular, hey? What have *you* done?'

Good question, thought Margaret. *Why would the inspector want me? Surely he doesn't think I had anything to do with Kavanagh's escape.* Keeping her face neutral, she neared the front row of tables. Bessy swept her toes with the broom, leaving a layer of dust and bits of thread. 'That child should be in school.'

'She's small for her age,' said Mr Sullivan. 'She'll be in school this afternoon, like she told you. Next week it'll be the other way round – mornings in school, afternoons here.'

'Let me guess. If I come back this afternoon or on a morning next week, her identical twin sister will be working here, also named Bessy?'

'What's a mother to do?' said Mr Sullivan, with a shrug. 'There are only so many names. Listen, I got a business to run. Are you gonna be long? The inspector was poking round too and we ain't got time for any of you.'

'Just a few photographs.'

'What of?' He glared at her. 'Not my workers.'

'Only as part of the whole room,' said Margaret. 'I don't want them to stop working.'

'*Then* will you slope off?'

'Yes.'

'Then get on with it. I've got to deal with this other bloke who asked about you.'

'Other bloke?' Margaret's bag slipped in her hands and the camera and Fox's letter made a bid for freedom. She caught them both, put the letter back and removed the camera from its case, hoping her trembling hands would be put down to the care needed for delicate machinery. 'What other bloke? Does he have a name?' If it wasn't Fox, Hare, Bert or Pigeon, it might be one of their colleagues. But she had only seen two others briefly the previous year and would struggle to recognise them.

'Mr W called him Knox. He's annoyed with Mr W about the exports, like it's Mr W's fault there's a strike. Can't see Mr W rousing anyone up.'

'Knox?'

'Know him?'

'What does he look like?'

'English. I told him to go to St J's later. Perhaps I should tell him you're here now.'

'That's quite all right. I'll catch up with him later.'

Mr Sullivan narrowed his eyes then shrugged again before peering into her hand. 'Is that your camera? Whitechapel mice are bigger than that. I'll stop worrying: you ain't going to get a photo worth looking at with a camera that size. Close the door when you leave, will you?' He went back to his desk and retrieved his cigarette, tapping the excess ash into the tray and watching her as he smoked.

Abram Cohen's body had lain between the first and second tables on the left. Now the space was larger. She crouched down and made sure her skirt couldn't get caught by the nearby treadle.

She stood up again then walked down the middle aisle, aware of brief, curious glances from the machinists. She raised the camera to take a photograph of the whole room, then turned to look at the handstitcher sitting cross-legged on the table by the window to fit a lining, and a cutter shearing a piece of gabardine with swift confidence.

In one corner were piles of boxes. One lay open on a cupboard, next to boxes of buttons and trimmings, revealing ostrich feathers dyed in pastel colours. It also held long, ornate cases for hatpins, decorated opera glasses, fancy combs and headbands.

'What do you use the feathers for?' she asked the cutter.

'Collars, scarves and shawls,' he said, without looking up from slicing a perfect curve in the cloth. 'And hat trimming, when asked. They come in from

South Africa, go out to the piece workers, poor schmucks, then come back and we send them out again.'

'What are feathers like to sew?'

'One wrong stitch and everything looks terrible. They make you sneeze and bits get down your throat. If the fashionable woman had to sew her own vanities once, she'd never demand them again.' He paused, then nodded at the mannequin. 'Besides, they look better on the ostrich.' Margaret thought of her feather-covered hats at home and winced.

A bigger pile of boxes, most tied with string and labelled, awaited collection, maybe for the export that was being haggled over in the office. Margaret approached them. The cream boxes were in various sizes. A few which had not yet been sealed, were packed with that familiar tissue, the small items wrapped and lined up neatly. On the outside of the closed boxes was printed the same plume of feathers as on Helene's. But a name label was also affixed: *Gascoigne St L'Argel*. The top box was addressed to Windhoek.

'People think French sounds fancy,' said the tailor, without looking up. 'But I always think if you rearrange the letters on that last bit, it says "Gascoigne T Gargles". Bet now I've told you, you won't be able to see it different.' He chuckled.

Margaret took a photograph, then walked towards the mannequin. The hat had been aslant under its own weight until it had been skewered in place. The hatpin was ornate, with a sparkling barrel top two inches long. Margaret had one or two that were similar. Sometimes you could keep things inside: an aspirin, a photograph of a loved one rolled up tight, a message for another suffragette that the police wouldn't realise was there, because they wouldn't think to look. The hat had been rearranged now, and placed properly.

Rearranged. Margaret frowned and went back to the boxes. St L'Argle. It wasn't a place, a person, or even a word that she knew. As an anagram, T Gargles was wrong: there was only one G and two Ls. She poked at one of the wrapped packages. It felt like a pair of opera glasses, smaller than usual. Dervla had had a case of hatpins in her bag. Were they hers? Was the fob watch one that her assailant had dropped in the grave, or one she'd been carrying? If you prised open a watch case, couldn't you hide something tiny? A photograph, a negative? Couldn't you get novelty opera glasses with tiny Stanhope photographs attached to the lens inside to look at. Scenery, a message, a building, or … plans?

Mr Webber had been a photographer, but now he was a civil servant with access to patents, sitting on a board which reviewed aeronautical designs.

A hatpin had been a few inches from Abram's hand, not far from a thimble. Had he been holding both when he collapsed?

Over the sound of machines, she heard voices. The door behind Mr Sullivan was partly open. Mr Sullivan himself was getting up, his gaze veering between the office, Margaret, and the main door. She started back towards him to say goodbye, hoping that at least she'd hear the names of the people behind the door, but then he slipped into the back office and closed the door.

She became aware of someone marching towards her. She turned, hoping to see one of Fox's colleagues, but it was Inspector Silvermann.

'Finally,' he said, very low, putting his arm through hers and drawing her aside. 'Now, without making a fuss, can you come with me?'

'Not yet,' she whispered back. 'I think there's something important here. If you cover me, I can get it for you. And we need to—'

'We don't need to do anything except go back to the station,' he said. 'If you don't come quietly, I'll arrest you for obstruction. I've enough evidence, and I don't need a warrant.'

'What are you talking about? The reason why Abram Cohen was here that night may not simply be work. I think it's in this room. They won't have realised. And I swear the people who have to do with Gastrell are in the office.'

'Tell me about it at the station, Dr Demeray. Do you want me to make a scene?'

'What precisely have I done?'

'Concealed the whereabouts of your husband.'

'What?'

'There's a warrant out for him and Sergeant Ainscough. If you want either of them to have any hope of a fair trial, you'll come with me.'

'A warrant? What for?'

'Assault on Mr Webber—'

'But—'

'And more importantly: murder.'

***

At the station, Margaret and Inspector Silvermann sat facing each other. Any vestige of friendliness was gone.

'What do you mean, my husband and Sergeant Ainscough are wanted for murder?' she said. 'They haven't murdered anyone. And they didn't assault Mr Webber either.'

'Can you prove that? Are they tied to your apron strings twenty-four hours a day?'

'If they were,' Margaret retorted, 'you'd be able to track them down. Since you can't, they're clearly not tied to me and you can't accuse me of obstruction. In addition, I know them.'

'You can never know anyone in Special Branch. Have a cup of tea, Dr Demeray. Sit back. This will take a while.'

'May I contact someone to join me while I'm interrogated?' said Margaret, ignoring the offer of tea.

'It's not an interrogation,' said the inspector. 'Let me tell you a few facts first, then you can decide who or what you need. I haven't arrested you: I just want some help.'

'I was offering to help you in Sullivan's. I think Abram Cohen wanted to examine the hatpin that was on the floor in Ravel Street. It's now in the mannequin's head, which is probably stuffed with as much sawdust as yours.'

'A hatpin! You mean he grabbed it to defend himself in case Kavanagh came for him? That's a woman's weapon, a suffragette trick. A real man wouldn't stoop so low.'

'It's an object,' Margaret said, through gritted teeth. 'They're generally used to pin hats. They may occasionally, by suffragettes or others, be used to protect against assault. As far as I know, no suffragette has murdered anyone with a hatpin. Anyway—'

'They've injured, people, though.'

'Probably. I haven't. Won't you—'

'You've injured men in your time.'

Margaret glared. Why wouldn't he listen? 'If you mean Black Friday in 1910, that was because a policeman was about to throw a girl of eighteen into the crowd. When I pulled him off her, he lifted me by grabbing my breast and groin as hard as he could. I had bruises for weeks afterwards. If someone did that to you, how would you react?'

'Want to see the scar a wildcat like you left on Dibbs?'

'No. Does Dibbs want to see photographs of injuries to women who'd never had a man touch more than their gloved hand until that day? Are you proud of your men for tipping a suffragette who couldn't walk out of her wheeled chair? For throwing girls into crowds of ruffians, to do as they pleased? It's just as well the ruffians were more decent than the police.'

'It was City police who did that. My men were just trying to keep order.'

'Do you dislike me simply because I want the vote? That's rid—'

The inspector slammed his fist on the table. 'It's the attitude I hate. You educated, nice women with your roomy houses, servants and plenty of food on the table, talking to men like me as if we're fools. Attacking men who are just doing their jobs. Being prepared to do anything – *anything* – for what you want. Why should I view a suffragette as any different to a Fenian, or an anarchist who'd put a bomb on the Tube?'

'Fenians haven't done that for years. Ask Kavanagh, now you've got him in custody.' It was a dirty move, but she had no choice. She couldn't let slip that she knew Kavanagh had escaped from St Julia's.

The inspector sat back and steepled his fingers. 'Why aren't you at work today?'

'I'm working tomorrow instead.'

'So you haven't been in contact with St Julia's?'

'No. Why should I be? More importantly, why are you accusing my husband of murder?'

'Why were you in Ravel Street?'

'Why are you accusing my husband of murder?'

'Why were you in Ravel Street?'

Margaret swallowed. 'Because I think the place is connected with a man called Norris Gastrell whom my husband investigated ten years ago, and Abram discovered the connection. If you'd listen to me about the hatpin—'

'What the blazes has a hatpin to do with anything? No one's been stabbed. If it was made of gold, Sullivan would have snaffled it long ago. Kavanagh probably sells that sort of—'

Margaret glared. 'I'd explain, but you won't listen. I'll ask the question again. Who are Fox and Bert supposed to have murdered?'

Thirty-Three

Inspector Silvermann contemplated her in silence and took a long sip of tea. It must be cold by now. Margaret's remained untouched.

'You know a Sir Broderick and Lady Selkirk socially, don't you?' he said.

Margaret's heart beat faster as the sensations of their last visit – the unspoken words, the invisible threat – came back to her. 'We're acquainted. They aren't close friends.'

'You visited them on Friday.'

'We had dinner there. They'll confirm that. Then the car broke down and we had the devil's own job getting home. We had to hire a motor taxi because I didn't want to leave the children.' Her voice broke a little and she looked at the clock. It was lunchtime, but anxiety had stoppered any hunger. She had to calm down, or she might make things worse. Fox, or one of his colleagues, might be at Sullivan's wondering where she was. 'The police in the local station can confirm what I've said.'

'They do. But after the car broke down, Sergeant Ainscough went off in a different direction, while you and your husband continued alone.'

'I wanted to see if there was a late train. Bert was trying to find somewhere to fix the car.'

'Why didn't you just go back to the Selkirks' place? They could have driven you to the station, or home, or put you up for the night.'

'We were much closer to the railway station than Archers Steading by then.' Saturday was a dreamlike blur. 'I thought…' If the inspector knew they'd been at the police station, he knew the rest. Was he just checking whether she told the same story?

'Why didn't Sergeant Ainscough go on, then?'

'He didn't think the car would get there: he needed to look at the engine. The station was definitely only two and a bit miles from where my husband and I were. We borrowed bicycles from a farmer called Mr Ivory.'

'So I hear. If Sergeant Ainscough had been with you, he could have fixed the car at Ivory's and there would have been no need for bicycles. But, oddly he left you to walk in the dark and when you finally got to the police station, lo and behold, Sergeant Ainscough was already there and you all took a taxi back to Bayswater.'

'Someone was following us. It seemed wise to split up, so at least someone could raise the alarm.'

'Oh yes, the mystery followers you told the local police about.'

'That's exactly right. I still don't understand what you're driving at.'

'Sir Broderick is dead.'

'What?' Margaret felt bile rise in her throat and her voice trembled. It couldn't be true. It felt like they'd only been playing cards the day before. 'When?'

'Last night. He'd been shot through the temple and he had his own revolver in his hand.'

'Suicide?'

'It looked that way. Lady Selkirk said that he'd been very agitated recently. A memory had stirred up things he had wanted to forget. He felt as if someone was asking him to take the blame for something. She thought he'd had a brain storm – a moment of madness. However, the police surgeon said the angle of the wound was wrong for it to be self-inflicted. It's a murder.'

'But none of us were there last night!'

'Can anyone swear to that?'

'My maids know where I was.'

'Can they testify for your husband and Sergeant Ainscough?'

'No, they... They're away on business.'

'Are they, now? Where?'

'How should I know? He can't tell me.' *I need to think. I need to get hold of Hare.*

'Lady Selkirk is distraught,' said the inspector.

'Well, of course she is. But why would Fox or Bert —'

'She said that everything was fine until her husband rekindled an acquaintanceship with yours. That your husband's man, who we eventually realised was Sergeant Ainscough, masquerading as your chauffeur, returned after your last visit and demanded to speak to Sir Broderick, after which his distress was worse. That Sergeant Ainscough was seen in their orchard yesterday evening.'

'No! I don't believe it!'

'And she thought Sergeant Ainscough was acting under orders.'

'Fox would never—'

'We mustn't forget Mr Wallace Moore, struck down in his own home before he could tell anyone what he'd seen and heard. Where were your husband and his men *that* night?'

'I can't even recall when—'

'And Dervla Mallowan was executed, like the traitor she may have been, by the method taught to men who are trained to deal with spies and traitors. A clean, efficient kill, just like Sir Broderick. Very little pain, but a problem solved. No time wasted on a trial. Funny how Dervla was arrested by your husband, helped to escape, and then found dead. Funny how her employer was attacked the same way. Funny how Dervla's father escaped just as he was about to be arrested. I hope he's feeling lucky.'

'Kavanagh?' Margaret was so horrified by the inspector's reasoning that her voice was a startled squeak. She hoped he'd take it as surprise at the escape.

'Yes, Kavanagh. Or rather, Mallowan.'

'Who knew and loathed Gastrell, They were in the same regiment in that war. Did you know? Gastrell, Mallowan, Sir Broderick and Webber.'

'Webber?'

'Yes.' *Put the pieces together, man.* 'It's no secret: Lady Selkirk showed me photographs herself. Fox has done nothing wrong, but someone is trying to stop him from uncovering whatever the people linked by Gastrell are doing now. They can only do that by having Fox falsely accused. This is the unfinished business Kavanagh – I mean Mallowan – spoke of.' The letter felt heavy in her bag. If she showed the inspector now, how would he read it? 'What if someone was blackmailing Sir Broderick about an occurrence in South Africa, and he couldn't live with the pressure any longer?'

'I told you. It wasn't suicide,' said the inspector. 'And it's nothing to do with Gastrell. Kavanagh dropped his real name, Mallowan, and joined an expatriate British anti-monarchist circle in New York. What do you suppose that group is stirring up?'

'Quite possibly, nothing. They probably meet to complain about the backwardness of Britain and say that tea just doesn't taste the same in America.'

'Nothing's going to taste right after being dumped in the harbour.'

'I'm not in the mood for joking, Inspector.'

'Nor am I.'

'What has any of this to do with—'

'That group includes a good many undesirables. Anarchists, strike raisers, Fenians.'

'You have this completely wrong!' Margaret slammed her palm on the desk. 'This is *not* about Irish independence.'

'What are your husband's views on Irish independence?'

'On a personal level, Fox has no opposition to it. He's simply opposed to any potential violence, whether republican or unionist. As am I.' Margaret sat back, arms folded.

A small, satisfied smile played on the inspector's lips. 'But his job is to follow the government's orders, same as mine. And some of the people he's after are as slippery as slime on a quayside ladder. Anyhow, Kavanagh comes back, discovers his daughter's been arrested, gets her sprung, somehow gets Olive offered a job with a theatre troupe, and inveigles Dervla into the maid's job to lie low till he can get her out of the country.'

'You're wrong. John Webber organised all that.'

Inspector Silvermann shook his head. 'Webber couldn't organise his own cufflinks.'

'Someone called Knox, then.'

'Never heard of him. I hope he's not another one who's crossed your husband.'

'Inspector,' said Margaret, clenching her hands together to stop them shaking and trying to stop her voice doing the same, 'let me guess what you're trying to say. You believe that my husband engineered Dervla Mallowan's death because it was simpler than letting her stand trial as a traitor and perhaps be acquitted. I don't believe it, and I'm not convinced you do either.' She watched the inspector's face, which remained impassive. 'Even if it were true, why murder Sir

Broderick? The only connection between him and my husband is an investigation ten years ago into something Norris Gastrell did which was witnessed by Wallace Moore and Joseph Mallowan. What had that to do with Fenianism? The Selkirks are Scots. The impression I got was that they're staunchly Unionist and feel strongly that the British Empire is the best thing to happen in the history of mankind.'

'Isn't it?'

'Everything manmade eventually disintegrates to reveal the tin under the silver-plate.'

'Is that poetry or New Testament?' The inspector raised his eyebrows and tapped his cigarette on the edge of the ash tray. 'I don't know either.'

'Neither, and you haven't answered my question.'

'You haven't answered many of mine. While in the military police, your husband investigated Gastrell after a request by Sir Broderick, but the investigation failed. Gastrell was about to go free when he accidentally drowned. Or perhaps your husband took the law into his own hands and Sir Broderick knew, but decided to keep quiet. Old Mr Moore enters his second childhood and starts remembering things and talking about them. Perhaps, after all this time, Sir Broderick decided the truth should be told. But your husband couldn't let that happen.'

The whispering of the envelope in Margaret's bag ceased. She could read nothing from the inspector's expression. Maybe he didn't believe a word of what he was saying, maybe he was repeating what a superior officer had deduced, but she couldn't give him something that could hang Fox until she could prove its falsehood.

'All I can tell you is this,' she said. 'My husband is not a murderer. He believes in the process of law.'

Margaret paused, trying to read the inspector, and decided to turn the tables. 'Why were you looking for me in Ravel Street, of all places?'

Did his calm falter? 'Because you like nosing about in the name of social justice. Everyone knows that. It was as good a place as anywhere.'

Don't rise to it, Margaret told herself. 'Sullivan's nasty little sweatshop links to a nice little dressmaking business called Helene's, which also exports goods abroad.'

Inspector Silvermann snorted.

'It's in Islington, Inspector. Your division. They use very similar containers.'

'They could get them from the same manufacturer.'

'With the same design? The same tissue paper as Dervla had in her camera case? The same image on embossed notepaper?'

'Sullivan's doesn't have embossed notepaper.'

'I'm telling you, it's all connected with Gastrell. They're exporting through Sullivan's via a business called Gascoigne St L'Argle.'

'It's nothing to do with Gastrell,' said the inspector. 'Any way you mix it up, he's dead. Very dead.'

Margaret opened her mouth to retort then took in his words. *Any way you mix it up.* She snatched a piece of paper from the inspector's desk tidy and scribbled on it. 'St L'Argle is an anagram! Look! It spells Gastrell.'

'Hatpins? Parlour games? Do you have brain fever?'

'No. Abram Cohen died in the sweatshop because he realised it was to do with those exports. He died when my husband was a very long way away.'

'Arresting Dervla Mallowan. And you said Abram Cohen died of natural causes, possibly brought on by overwork.'

'He did. But he was still where he shouldn't have been.'

'After an argument with Kavanagh. Mallowan.'

'And do your highly reliable drinker witnesses know who was arguing about what with whom?'

The inspector scowled. 'Kavanagh was trying to get Cohen to do something and Cohen was saying no.'

'For all you know, Kavanagh was trying to stop him going to Sullivan's. All I want you to investigate is whether I'm right. Whether nice Helene's in Islington, nasty Sullivan's in Whitechapel, and Gascoigne St L'Argel are linked via the John Webber who served with Gastrell. Webber may be the man my husband and I saw in an orchard at one in the morning, talking with the Selkirks on the night we stayed there. And I want you to find out who Knox is. I can't find out the way a policeman could. If that policeman would only stop staring in the wrong direction.'

'Temper, temper, Dr Demeray,' said Inspector Silvermann. 'Perhaps, if you'd told me all that earlier, I might have.' He lit a cigarette and took a drag, watching Margaret through the smoke when he exhaled. 'There's a warrant out for your husband's arrest. I'm warning you that if you conceal him, you will be arrested too. He will contact you. When he does, you must urge him to hand himself in to, at the very least, his superior officer. If you think he's lying low, tell me where. I give you my word that I'll see he has a fair trial. I've no urge to see a fellow copper go down for something he hasn't done.'

'I have absolutely no idea where he'd go if he were lying low,' said Margaret.

'Will you promise to do your damnedest to get him to hand himself in?'

'Will you promise to look into everything I've said, including the hatpins?' Margaret extracted one of hers.

'I hope you're not threatening me.'

'No. Look—'

There was a rapid knocking at the door and Constable Dibbs burst in. 'The Super wants you, sir.'

'Not now, Dibbs.'

'It's urgent. Kavanagh's been spotted. I mean Mallowan. The Super says we can't have him making a fool of us.'

Inspector Silvermann stood up. He glared at Margaret, but said nothing before following Dibbs out of the room.

Margaret stayed in her seat until he'd gone, shoved her hatpin back in place, then rose and opened the door. She saw the inspector turn a corner and disappear into the bowels of the police station. Two constables were conferring in the corridor. Neither noticed her watching. Straightening her back and gripping her handbag hard enough to risk breaking its handle, she put on her most supercilious expression. After a moment's reflection to remember the route, she left, and soon reached the counter where the desk sergeant sat. 'Inspector Silvermann has been called away,' she said. 'He asked me to see myself out. The man has no manners. I shall be writing to the Chief Constable.'

The desk sergeant stifled a grin. 'You do that, ma'am,' he said, unlocking the side door in the counter. 'Mind how you go.'

Head held high, Margaret walked away as slowly as she could. Different, conflicting urges fought for precedence, shouting at her to pay attention: *Go home, lock the doors and wait for Fox to call. Telephone his office. Telegraph his office. Go to Somerset House and see if Elinor is still there. Go to the last place where Inspector Silvermann would look for me.* He hadn't arrested her. He hadn't said she needed to stay, but he hadn't said she could leave either.

And what she had told him was true. She had no idea where Fox might lie low, and for all she knew, he'd been intercepted. Though if Webber and sister were in Sullivan's, and two men were following Margaret around, that surely wasn't possible. They couldn't have that many people working for them.

She turned a corner and entered a park. Then she ran.

Thirty-Four

Margaret ran, disregarding the signs to keep off the grass, hoping that anyone seeing her would think she was pursuing an errant child doing the same.

On the other side of the park, she slowed to a walk and tried to get her bearings. It was nearly impossible in her current frame of mind.

The street signs, advertisements and shop names were blurred, but a small narrow church stood nearby with its door open. An old church, incongruous among new buildings, built when central London absorbed all the little parishes around it and replaced everything but the places of worship. The yearning for a cool, calm space to think was overwhelming, and Margaret entered. All she took in at first was spacious, light airiness as she dropped into a pew and put her face in her hands.

She felt clammy and hot, and her head pounded. She wasn't hungry, but if she didn't eat the headache might turn into a migraine. A piece of bread would do. A bowl of thin soup would do…

The thought of soup reminded her of Anna, helping strikers' children get at least one meal every day. Anna, who'd trusted her to save Kavanagh.

Anna wouldn't understand the desire to seek peace by tethering yourself to something intangible, but Margaret did. She lifted her face and leaned back to absorb her surroundings. It was a simple nonconformist church with few decorations, the walls white except for a few panels with texts painted on them. She blinked and looked at them again. They were in French.

She remembered where she was: in one of the few remaining Huguenot churches in London. Her grandparents had become low Anglicans early in their marriage, but their forefathers, who'd fled persecution and set up a new life in England, would have known this place, might even have worshipped here. Perhaps some of the comfort Margaret felt was a link to an echo of them. She imagined them patting her shoulder, saying 'Assez pleuré! Allons-y!' *Enough crying! Let's go!*

'May I help you, madame?' The minister stood at the end of the pew, smiling.

She rose to leave. 'Please pray for justice, Pasteur. And courage.'

'Of course. Will you tell me your name? Or would you prefer not?'

'De Mareis,' she said. 'Marguerite De Mareis and my husband, Reynard. It's not really, but most things sound better in French.'

'Oui, Madame. Most things do.'

***

'It's you again,' said the same cabbie as before when she flagged him down, to their mutual surprise. 'At least I know you got outta Whitechapel safe. Where to now? Nice or nasty? Buck House? The docks? I wouldn't recommend them: worse than Ravel Street. Carts, wagons, lorries and trucks queued from Rotherhithe to Timbuktu, and only the army getting through. Language not fit for a lady's ears and the road knee deep in sh— 'orse apples. So, where is it?'

'Somerset House.'

'Thank Gawd for that.'

'And stop at the first telegraph office we come to.'

'Want to go round the 'ouses again?'

'Yes, please. I like a scenic route.'

'Oh yes, dead picture-skew. You must be made o' money. What's your old feller going to say when he sees you've spent the housekeeping on cabs?'

'Thank you, I hope.'

She climbed into the back and closed her eyes as the taxi pulled off. She was doing everything she could, but it might not be enough, or quick enough. If they'd caught Fox on his way home, his might be one more assassination, one more missing body. He'd warned her that one day he might not return. If it had to happen, she didn't want it to be today, or for this reason.

Had Elinor found Lena's marriage to old Dr Purefoy?

Cyril must be Carl. Perhaps he had been renamed for his adoptive father. Margaret had thought him a little strange as a person, but straight as an arrow, incapable of deception. Or was he just an excellent actor? The distress over the newspaper article and his respect for her had seemed honest; his fear that his father – or rather, stepfather – would withdraw his funding, genuine. But was that integrity real if he'd never questioned what he'd been taught to believe? What lies had his mother fed him over the years?

And Sir Broderick had done everything to stop Fox from digging. Was that why was he dead?

Margaret sent a coded telegram to Hare, then continued to Somerset House.

It was as hushed and calm as a library. The clerk refused to divulge whether anyone of Elinor's description had been there. Nor would he retrieve a record without a fee and a delay of three days.

'Purefoy's an unusual name.'

'It could be Saxe-Coburg,' he said, taking her money and date-stamping the form with enough force to make an indentation. 'It won't get precedence. We do all the requests in order. Those are the rules.'

'Has anyone else asked for the same name?'

The clerk stared back in silence.

'Is there a higher fee for a quicker search, then?'

'Expedited will still take no less than three hours,' he said firmly. 'And we don't take bribes, if that's what you're thinking. We Are The British Government.' Margaret wondered how Elinor talked the clerks into working quicker. She must have an different technique.

Margaret paid the additional fee, went outside and looked at her watch. It was ten to four. She'd promised Nellie she'd be home by four thirty. Every minute she was away, she wasn't protecting the children. She could only hope that Fox's men were still protecting the house, that Hare had understood her message, that another group of Hare's men would find Fox and Bert before either the police or Knox's men did. She had no idea how many men worked with Fox, but it had to be more than worked with Knox, Webber and Lena.

She looked at her watch again. The traffic was building and another taxi, regardless of expense, could be caught up in it. Feeling as if every man was watching her, and every tall woman looked like Helene, or rather Lena, Margaret walked as briskly as she could without breaking into a run, and towards Holborn Underground station. Surely Inspector Silvermann would have applied his brain by now and it was safe to go home without fear of arrest. There was next to nothing she could do now but gather her thoughts and wait for Fox's colleagues to contact her.

'Vera was called away about half an hour ago, ma'am,' said Nellie, when Margaret entered the quiet house and found everything as it should be. 'There's just me and the children here.'

'Called away?' said Margaret, trying to keep her voice light and her hands calm. 'By whom?'

'Her mother's sick. It wasn't a man, if that's what you mean. Well, her brother came, and he's a man. Not

Vera's chap. Not that *he's* not nice. I mean, you needn't worry.'

'Oh. I see. I hope everything's all right.'

'I'm sure it is.' Nellie put her head on one side. 'You seem worried, ma'am. I'll get your tea. Vera made the sandwiches and scones just before she went. A nice cuppa sorts everything out, doesn't it?'

'I wish it would.'

'Will you be able to manage the twins' feed while I do it?'

'Yes, I'll take them to the upstairs sitting room.'

Nellie pursed her lips. 'That's not the proper routine.'

'Everyone benefits from a change in routine now and then. Besides, it'll be more comfortable for us to have tea.'

'I can't have it with you!' Nellie exclaimed.

'You can today. I'd rather we stayed together.'

'If you say so, ma'am,' said Nellie, disapproval written on every freckle.

On the way to collect the children, Margaret telephoned Fox's office to say that she was in her lair.

'Ah,' said the voice. 'Someone went hunting and you weren't where they expected. Thanks for calling.'

Was it Fox? thought Margaret. *Is he near?* 'Who—'

'One of the men. There's no word from F. Don't telephone again. Wait for us to call you. Goodbye.'

Oh God, she thought.

She called Maude just to hear her calming, nonchalant voice, but Maude sounded tearful. 'Have you heard about the Selkirks, too?'

'Oh, Maude. Yes, I have. I'm so sorry. I know you're good friends.'

'It's terrible. I don't know what to think. Lady Selkirk telephoned me all of a gabble this morning. I couldn't make head nor tail of what she said. Why would Sir Broderick kill himself? He always seemed a happy soul.'

So the news had only got so far. Margaret paused before speaking again. 'And with their children dead too, Lady Selkirk must feel terribly alone.'

'Yes. I don't know what to do. Sending flowers seems futile.'

'How long ago did their son die? Could that be a reason? Leonard, was it? Lady Selkirk called him Len.'

'Lennox,' said Maude. 'I didn't know them when it happened, so it must have been at least eight years ago. I understood he'd resigned his commission, gone to the tropics and died of fever. Or maybe stayed in South Africa. Or maybe gone to America... Actually, I don't know. It was a little woolly and one doesn't like to probe.'

'No, one doesn't.'

'Will you and Fox come to the funeral?'

'Of course we will. Take care, Maude.'

Lennox. Knox. The tall, slender man in the garden that night, familiar with the Selkirks, appearing from nowhere then disappearing to leave them hugging each other in the dark. K Rainer the incomer living next to Webber, with his sunburnt face and colonial arrogance. The familiarity in the drawing was not that colonial arrogance but features that were like his parents, like an older, dried up version of the young soldier in the sketch on the dining room wall. She couldn't call Fox's office again without knowing that the line was safe. She daren't go to the telegraph office or send Nellie. She'd just have to wait to be contacted.

The afternoon dragged. Margaret sat by the window, tensing every time a vehicle slowed or anyone looked as if they might open the gate. No one appeared to be watching from the park or pavement. On any other day it would have been pleasantly quiet; now it was ominous. There was no mail, and there were no telephone calls. Nellie played with the children, putting them in the baby cage when she had to leave the room. Eventually, with great disapproval, she agreed to bring blankets for the twins to nap. When she returned, Margaret went to her bedroom and looked out of the window.

Juniper was on her favourite sun trap, the low roof outside. But instead of sprawling, she had the posture of a guardian: whiskers alert, body tensed. Margaret had often sat on the roof with Juniper, sketching the view from the back of the house: the brick walls, the chimney pots, the drop into what she called a back garden and Fox called a yard. Once, she'd stood out there in the rain. *Could Nellie and I escape that way if we had to? Could we do it with the children?*

She found two sturdy shawls in her wardrobe, then asked Nellie to show her how to strap the children to their fronts the way East End mothers did.

'Poor women do that,' said Nellie, with barely disguised disgust. '*We* have a baby carriage.'

'What if we didn't and we needed to go out by the back way in a hurry?'

'What? I mean pardon, ma'am? I wouldn't let you be seen dead lugging the twins around like that, not even in the lane. I wouldn't be seen dead doing it myself.'

'For goodness sake, Nellie! Try something new for once!' Margaret snapped. She turned away and paced with Edie strapped to her front, picked up the work she should have done that day, put it down, and stroked Edie's downy curls as she dozed against Margaret's breast, half-hidden by folds of wool.

It was hot, and Edie was heavy. Margaret adjusted the shawl and it helped. *Someone should be finding out what's happening at Sullivans and Helene's. Someone should be in Webber's house, finding out what they've planned for Fox. I should be asking Cyril Purefoy about his mother, about what he recalls of his father, of what she told him about his death. I should be asking poor Lady Selkirk about her son. A year ago, I wouldn't have sat here in the flat doing nothing, I'd have—*

'Ummmammma,' murmured Edie.

'Mamama,' echoed Alec, from Nellie's shoulder. 'Dadad?'

I could leave them with Nellie... Margaret watched Nellie gently rock her son, eyes downcast and lashes sparkling, refusing to use the shawl. She was just sixteen: little more than a child herself. She was Margaret's responsibility as much as the children were. *Oh God, Fox, how can I choose between all of you?*

'I'm sorry, Nellie,' she said. 'I shouldn't have snapped at you.'

'Very good, ma'am.' Nellie didn't meet her eyes. 'May I take them back to the nursery now?'

'No, I'd rather we all stayed here. Give me Alec, and get your book or your sewing if you like. What music shall I put on the gramophone?'

'Whatever you like, ma'am.' Without raising her eyes, Nellie put Alec into Margaret's arms and left the room.

At five thirty, Inspector Silvermann telephoned. His voice sounded cagey.

'Are you coming to collect me?' asked Margaret.

'No. I did a few parlour games of my own.'

'So you'll start looking the other way?'

'Yes, but I still need to speak with—'

'There's only me here.'

'No word?'

'None.'

'On your honour, as a gentlewoman and a doctor?'
'On my honour. I'm— I'm worried.'
'I'll see what I can find out. You all right there?'

I could send Nellie home, thought Margaret. *But what if someone grabbed her? What if she never got home? And what if I need to escape with the children, on my own? I could telephone Katherine or Maude and ask them to collect us, but wouldn't that just be taking the danger to a different place? And what if Fox comes back?*

'Bet you wish you had a Walrus watching you now,' said the inspector.

There was a long silence.

'Is the connection still required?' asked the operator.

'Yes,' said the inspector. 'Much as I don't want to condone such behaviour, doctor, remember what you did to my colleagues in November 1910 and repeat it if necessary. Be vigilant.'

'"Because your adversary the devil walketh about seeking whom he may devour."'

'Poetry or New Testament?'

'New Testament. It's been that kind of day.'

'Ain't it just,' muttered Inspector Silvermann. 'Farewell. And I mean it – fare well.'

Thirty-Five

Another two hours passed. With reluctance, Margaret let Nellie take the children to the nursery. Remembering the page in her bag, She found the book by the old soldier and compared the cut-marks inside with what had allegedly been cut from it. They didn't match, but there must be some other way of proving the point. Surely there couldn't be just two copies in existence. The family might have destroyed the old soldier's manuscript, but surely even a private printer would keep their copy of it for a few years. Something else nagged at her. Maybe there was a third copy at another library, or... Wasn't there a copy of every book that had ever been printed at the British Museum Library? There should be, at any rate. For the first time that day, something made her smile. Her father had a reader's ticket.

She wrote her reasoning down and put it on the top shelf of the bookcase with the book, the alleged missing page and the threatening note.

Another half hour passed.

At eight o'clock, Margaret made a simple meal which Nellie insisted they ate separately: Margaret in the cold dining room, Nellie in the kitchen. The last post rattled through the front door just as someone hammered on the kitchen door. Margaret pushed her uneaten food away and rushed to the hall, uncertain which way to turn. Two letters sat on the mat. She snatched them and ran to the kitchen, where Nellie was about to open the door. 'I'll do that.'

'But ma'am—'

Margaret opened the door a crack and peered out. Juniper was hissing from her perch on the roof above. In the passageway stood a dusty figure in motorcycle clothes, its head and face obscured by helmet and goggles. 'What do you want?' she asked.

'It's me, Mrs F.' The man lifted his goggles: Pigeon. 'I've come the back way. Let me in, quick.'

'Ooh, Mr Pigeon,' Nellie peered at him. 'You aren't half a mess.'

'Had a bit of a tumble, Miss Pinter,' said Pigeon. 'Don't suppose you could get me a flannel and basin?'

'Please do, Nellie,' said Margaret. 'And check the children, please. Don't wake them. Just check they're asleep, then come straight back.'

'Fox has been took,' said Pigeon, stepping into the kitchen and closing the door behind him as soon as Nellie had gone. 'We split up, and just as well. We lost track of Bert outside St Albans. It turns out the police arrested him – that's just being sorted now. Fox and I got away, he was behind me, and then he got ambushed. There was nothing I could do: I guessed what had happened too late. They'd bundled him in a black motor van and it overtook me. I thought it might have been the same one those "undertakers" used, only with different plates. I retraced my tracks and saw a couple of likely looking fellows, so I put my machine behind a hedge and went on foot. I saw them looking at Fox's motorcycle at the side of the road and laughing. They've got him, Mrs F, and I couldn't do a thing.'

'What were they saying?'

Pigeon bit his thumbnail.

'Tell me!'

'One said he felt sorry for you, because you'll find Fox in the last place you expect, and he'll die wondering what you'll do when you find him.'

'What does that mean?'

'I don't know.'

'What did the other one say?' Pigeon didn't speak. 'Tell me!'

'"She's one of those suffragette man-haters. She won't care." Then the other one said, "She doesn't strike me that way. I wouldn't fancy crossing her, but I'd rather do that than cross Mrs P or Knox."'

'Oh God, Pigeon. Did you come straight here? Is there a chance someone can track the van?'

Pigeon shook his head. 'I went straight to Hare. He was up in arms because the police had arrested Bert and wanted to arrest Fox, and he'd just sent men out to follow up something Miss Hedgehog had discovered. Lena Webber started a business under the name Helene Gascoigne, but now she's called Purefoy.'

'She found that out. Thank God. I found out that Knox is Sir Broderick and Lady Selkirk's son, but I didn't know how to get the message through.'

'Gawd.' Pigeon rubbed both hands down his cheeks, making the smears worse. 'That fits in with Miss Edwards finding out earlier today that Lady S's maiden name was Rainer. She thought it important. Hare thought it was just a coincidence but now …'

'Lennox Selkirk must have been working with Gastrell in 1902. Maybe he was the lead, and carried on afterwards. That's why Sir Broderick didn't want Fox digging then or now. He knew what his son had done and perhaps agreed to cover it up if Knox pretended he was dead and started afresh. But Knox must have just been running things from abroad instead. He's only come back because the information exchanges started going wrong due to the strike and because Dervla seemed likely to give evidence. It must have been him that Fox and I saw in the orchard the night we first visited. That's why Lady Selkirk didn't come to breakfast the following morning. That's why she was upset the next time when I hinted at officers being tried for their crimes. She knows what her son did, too.'

'What a mess.' Pigeon ran himself a glass of water and gulped it down. 'The police are getting a search warrant for the Webber house. I came here because we're worried about you and the kiddies. If anyone's watching the house, they're well hidden. Just in case, though, a car will be here soon to collect you, Nellie and the children and take you to your sister's. Every criminal in the neighbourhood knows what she does for a living and keeps away, because the police go in and out like rabbits.'

'These people aren't normal criminals.'

'They'll know, anyway. And your sister and brother-in-law have the house very secure. I'll stay to answer the door so I can be sure you're getting in the right car. Even then, you'll still be vulnerable.'

'I should stay here, in case Fox—'

'They have Fox. As soon as you've gone, I'll rejoin the hunt. It's getting harder.'

He just means that night's falling, Margaret told herself. *He doesn't mean the trail is fading. He doesn't mean they'll give up.*

Pigeon scratched his nose, then reached into his motorcycle jacket. 'I wish I could stay with you, Mrs F, but I can't.' He handed her a revolver. 'Fox says you know how to use one of these.'

'Yes, he trained me, but—'

'Put it in your pocket, quick. I can hear Nellie coming. Don't let her see it.'

'Where have they taken Fox? Webber's house? The Purefoys'?'

'We have all that covered. Ah, thank you, Miss Pinter, that's lovely. I'll just wipe the dust from my face and then go. Sorry to muck up your nice flannel.'

Pigeon smeared a clean space on his face and wiped his googles. 'Er, I think your missus has something to talk about with you. I'll wait in the hallway.'

Nellie frowned at the filthy flannel and the basin of brown water, then at Margaret. 'I don't know how to ask this, ma'am, but you've been funny since you got home. Is something wrong with the master? I know his work can be dangerous.'

'I'm sure he's all right.'

'You're shaking like a leaf, ma'am. You're going to drop those letters in a minute.'

'They can wait,' said Margaret, shoving them into her pocket. 'Are the twins fast asleep?'

'Dead to the world, ma'am. I reckon a bomb would go off and they wouldn't wake. Maybe you're right about doing things different. I'll have to ask my m—'

'Nellie, this will sound very peculiar, but we're going to go up and carry the children downstairs as careful as can be. Then we'll go to my sister's in a car the master's sending. We have to be very quick and quiet, and you mustn't ask questions.'

Nellie's mouth opened, then closed again. She was pale, but she nodded. 'I have a bag of baby things packed. Shall I—'

'Yes, there's no time to waste.'

'You're not going to make me carry them in a shawl, are you?'

'No.'

The children didn't stir as they were lifted, blankets and all, from their bassinets and carried down to the hall. Nellie snatched up a small bag and Margaret collected the items she'd put on the bookshelf earlier. Pigeon was listening at the front door. At a light, rhythmic tapping, he opened it, exchanged a few unheard words, then turned. 'Come along, ladies,' he murmured. 'I'll let myself out the back, Mrs F.'

'But our hats and coats!' whispered Nellie.

'No time.'

Margaret ushered Nellie out and followed her. A man she'd once seen in a bookshop and knew to be Fox's colleague led them to a waiting car. Alec was heavy with sleep, Edie stirring a little. When Margaret sat beside Nellie, she could feel her trembling. She wished she could take both the children and Nellie into her arms.

'What is it, ma'am?' Nellie said. 'What's wrong?'

'I can't explain,' said Margaret. 'You'll have to trust me. We needed to leave the house: there are burglars about. We'll be safe at my sister's. She's a detective, remember. She has a lot of police friends and her house is never bothered by criminals.'

The journey to Marylebone was as swift as it could be with the twists and turns the driver took. The light was fading when they arrived, the lamps on in the rooms at the front of the house. Katherine and James were waiting inside the door.

A maid took Nellie to the kitchen and Katherine took Edie from Margaret.

'What's happening?' asked Katherine. 'Please don't say it's nothing. Fox's colleague came and warned us you were on the way.'

'Someone Fox arrested is threatening us in the house,' said Margaret. 'They thought we'd be safer here. Your house is well known to be under the protection of the police.'

'They? Not he? Margaret, what do you mean?'

Margaret swallowed. Where was Fox? She tried to sense whether he was alive or dead, the way Kavanagh had known about Dervla, but only felt cold fear. She remembered the envelopes in her pocket. Might one of them be from the kidnapper?

The first was typed and addressed to her, the postmark Shepherd's Bush and timed at 2 pm.

Dear Mrs Foxcroft-McSionnach. I hope you had the chance to say goodbye properly to your husband. I hope your last words to him were full of love, not recrimination. Maybe it'll be speedy, maybe not. I shall tell him how much you and your children will suffer before he dies. When you see him again, he will be as empty of life as he was of compassion. And who knows? Perhaps you will be the one who gets the blame.

'Meg! What is it? Show me! Sit down, you look ready to faint.'

'I'm all right. Don't fuss, Kitty.'

The second letter was also addressed to her. It was scrawled, but she recognised the script.

Dear Dr Demeray

They do not know I am writing this. I am so sorry: I had no idea he was your husband. I am concerned that the justification with which I have been presented by Mama is incomplete because the evidence is so contradictory. If this were a hypothetical case then I am not sure I would diagnose what they tell me as the truth. I have not yet sworn to do nothing but good. However, I do not wish to do harm without justification. Please come back to St J's and stop this. I do not know how.

Cyril Gastrell Purefoy

Stop this… Stop what?

I do not know how. How to do what? Stop something happening?

Was Cyril at home in Shepherd's Bush with his mother? She looked at the postmark. It was Aldgate, stamped 6pm. He must have posted it as he left St J's.

Or ... or maybe he was still there. Pigeon had said that one of the assailants felt sorry for her, because she'd find Fox in the last place she expected, and he'd die wondering what she'd do when she found him. And now this letter from Shepherd's Bush said that perhaps she'd be the one who'd get the blame.

'Dear God. Dear God, no.'

'What is it, Meg?' said Katherine. 'You're as white as a ghost.'

'Don't say that. I have to go, Kitty.' Margaret kissed Alec's head and put him in James's arms, then hugged Katherine and Edie. 'I don't want to leave them, Kitty, but I can't take them. Please protect my children for me. Protect Nellie. I can't do it myself just now. Katherine, here's a telephone number. Please say "Mrs F has gone to Rose Cottage and hopes to have a friendly visitor join her very soon". James, will you lend me the car?'

'What if no one answers?' said Katherine. 'Should we come and help? Where should we send the police?'

'Someone will,' said Margaret. 'They'll know what to do. All I need you to do is take care of yourselves and my children. I need to find their father and bring him home.'

Thirty-Six

The mortuary wing's front doors were locked at night, making it pointless to try and enter that way. Margaret parked James's motor car as close to the main entrance of St Julia's as possible. Under the lamp-posts where the fruit and flower sellers normally stood, streetwalkers dressed to the nines watched Margaret covertly and formed a small huddle ready to see her off, then separated as she ran up the main steps and entered the foyer.

The desk clerk looked at her blankly. He knew her only vaguely, as she would normally go to any ward she wanted to without bothering him, and hadn't worked at night for over a year.

'Has anyone gone to the mortuary wing since they closed the main entrance this evening?' she said.

'Not while I've been here.' The clerk ran his finger down a piece of paper. 'Not while anyone else was here, either.'

'Has a body arrived?'

The clerk puffed out a breath and checked again. 'Mmm... Yes, before I came on duty. Someone got the keys and went to take a delivery for the cold room through the undertaker's entrance. I imagine the police or the workhouse were dropping something off for tomorrow. I'm glad they didn't trundle it through here.' He shivered. 'It's much nicer when they take them through the bay doors out back.'

'That's what I heard had happened. Who collected the keys?'

'Mmm ... either a consultant or a student. I can't quite read... Mr Pure-something. Student, isn't he?'

'Has he returned the keys?'

'No, but you know what students are like. He'll forget till tomorrow and then wonder what they're for.'

'Thank you. I'll go through.'

Margaret walked to the internal entrance of the mortuary wing. Its door was locked, but she had her own set of keys. As long as they hadn't left the key in the lock on the other side, hers would fit. If they had left the key in, she'd find tweezers and turn it even if she broke a wrist. She'd break the glass in the door if necessary. But her key turned without difficulty.

The doors were well-oiled. She slipped inside and waited at the top of the stairs, listening.

Nothing.

Then just the tiniest hint of whispering.

She slipped off her shoes and crept down the stairs, keeping close to the wall. The corridor felt strange: empty, resting, abandoned. The usual sound of footsteps, chatter and trolleys was replaced by near-silence. Darnell's desk was tidy, his chair empty. No light came from any side rooms or laboratories. She padded along and listened. The sounds were coming from the cold room. They were soft, staccato. She came closer.

Cyril's voice: 'Not here. It's the wrong place, Mama.'

Helene... no, Lena: 'Does that matter?'

'They'd know she wouldn't do it here.'

Lena: 'They'll think she went mad.'

A man's voice: 'We're wasting time: he's coming round. Get on with it.'

'I'm not a killer and I like his wife.'

Lena: 'You lost your inheritance through this man.'

Cyril: 'Norris Gastrell had had years to make sure I was legitimate and didn't. There would have been no inheritance.'

'He was going to marry me after the war,' snapped Lena.

'Is that the absolute truth, Knox?' Cyril's voice became clearer. 'You knew Father.'

'Do you doubt me?' Lena's voice rose, then became softer. 'Aren't you angry, Cyril? Don't you want revenge?'

'Norris Gastrell was cruel.' Cyril's voice cracked. 'He taunted you. He struck me.'

'He was misunderstood.'

'Was he? I saw a page from a book on your desk, Mama. It was about him, and the writer didn't like him. And I saw a page you'd written about what happened that was quite different. Why?'

'The book was lies. This man murdered your father.'

'Then tell the police to investigate. If you make me kill him, how are you any better than him? How would I be? And what do you think will happen when this man's body is found? I've read the doctor's notes. Darnell has listened at doors. I know she suspects Uncle John of killing the maid.'

'As if he could!' snorted Knox.

'She won't just let you blacken her husband's name,' persisted Cyril. 'There's nothing meek about her. And his colleagues – they're police, aren't they?'

Silence.

'If he's dead, do you think they'll let it go? You've got your business abroad. Let me put him under heavier sedation, to give you time, and you two and Uncle John can leave the country.'

'We need to be here.'

'Why? I'll stay with Papa and—'

'He's not your real father.'

'I wish he was. Being a father is about more than blood. All I want is to finish my medical degree. I don't care about revenge for a man whom no one but you liked, Mama. I'm not killing this man.'

Knox: 'For God's sake! We should never have involved you. I'll do it myself. Give me that scalpel.'

'No. And if you do, they'll know it wasn't Dr Demeray. She knows her job.'

Margaret stepped silently into the room. Before her, the woman she knew as Helene stood at the head of a stretcher, looking down on Fox, fury marring her features. There was a long trail of dried blood on Fox's head, leading from a large cut on his temple. His eyes were half open, moving under the lids as he struggled to come round. Cyril was on the other side, staring at a tall man with his back to her. Cyril's eyes flickered very briefly towards Margaret, then back to Knox.

Margaret raised the revolver and trained it on Knox's back, her finger steady on the trigger.

I could kill him, then I could wound Lena, and it would all happen before either of them could react. If I warn him, he could turn and overpower me. They might kill Fox and then me. Alec and Edie will be orphans… I could shoot him in the back without warning. It would be justifiable.

Wouldn't it?

'Lennox Selkirk, I will warn you only once,' she said. 'Step away from my husband or I will shoot you.'

Lena gasped and Knox turned. 'You wouldn't.' He sneered. 'You're a doctor. You've promised to do harm to no one.'

'I would,' said Margaret. 'And being a doctor means I know where to aim. Step away from my husband.'

Knox took a step towards her. 'Now what will you do? Arrest me, and expect me to hand myself in? There are three of us and only one of you.'

'Don't include me in this,' said Cyril. 'Doctor, I didn't know what they wanted to do – I swear it. Mama, stop this!'

'Give me that scalpel. I'll do it myself.'

'Mama! No! Dr Demeray has a gun!'

'Mrs Purefoy, your son is right,' said Margaret. 'I have a gun. I am prepared to shoot Mr Selkirk if he comes any closer to me. And I am quite prepared to shoot you if necessary.' The calmness in her voice was no reflection of how she felt.

Knox's lips narrowed. Margaret watched him size her up. He was working out the best way to unbalance and unarm her without being shot, calculating which direction to tip her in, how to distract her for long enough to get the better of her. *If he takes one more step in any direction, I'll shoot. I won't warn him again.*

Behind him, Lena had moved so that Margaret couldn't see her. She was obscured by Knox. If Margaret shot him at this range, was it possible that the bullet would go through him and hit someone else? The cold room was bare but for the trolley and the heavy vase of sickly lilies. Her hands were growing chilly, stiffening on the gun, but sweat was trickling down the back of her neck.

Knox smiled: he'd worked out what to do. Lena was back in view with something in her hands, but Margaret didn't dare change focus. She kept the gun trained on Knox.

He began to move forward and she fired into his right clavicle.

With a cry, Knox staggered backwards towards the trolley, then regained his balance. She aimed at his left shin then glimpsed Lena lifting something above Fox's head.

'Mama, no!'

'You can't win, doctor,' gasped Knox, taking a decisive step forwards.

'Let's see, shall we?' Margaret changed her aim and fired at the vase.

It exploded in Lena's hands, raining shards and water on her, Cyril and Fox. Lena screamed, then picked up a large piece of the broken vase and lunged, but Fox's eyes had opened. He reached up as the sharp edge came down, pulled Lena's arm so that she overbalanced onto him, then clamped her across his chest.

Knox, biting his lip and pale with pain, was frowning at Margaret. Was he planning another attack? Without hesitation, she shot his left shin and he collapsed with a short, sharp scream.

Could I kill him? She echoed what he was surely thinking. *Now? While he's just sitting there, bleeding?* Her grip loosened as her hands became clammy. She kept her eyes fixed on his and heard a deep, echoing cough. She couldn't gauge its direction but didn't dare look.

'Knox, deal with her,' Lena snapped. 'Then help me with— Ow! Let me go!'

'You touch a hair on her head, Selkirk,' Fox said hoarsely, 'and I'll kill you. But not before I tell Mrs Purefoy who was really responsible for Norris Gastrell's death, God rot his soul.'

'*You* shot Norris,' wailed Lena.

'I caught the top of his shoulder,' said Fox. 'The wound that made him fall was from a gun at much closer quarters. Wasn't it Selkirk? You were hidden by trees and you didn't trust him to keep his mouth shut if the army pushed for a dishonourable discharge. I've obtained Gastrell's medical records. I know the distance he was shot from the second time, and how badly he was injured before he went in the river. It wasn't my fault, and I did everything I could to save him.'

'Knox?' Lena's voice was plaintive. Out of the corner of her eye, Margaret saw her move as Fox let her go while struggling to sit up. 'You said Norris would have made an honest woman of me after the war, but this man killed him first. All I had to do was help carry on the business you two had started, and one day we'd track him down.'

'If you and Webber had managed the business better, I could have stayed abroad. Then Moore wouldn't have seen me.' Knox spoke through gritted teeth, his voice distorted by pain. 'And the intelligence services wouldn't have come looking for us. If you and Webber had kept your emotions out of things, I wouldn't have had to take charge.'

'How are *your* emotions?' said Fox. 'Your father knew, didn't he? You visited him and threatened him, but he wasn't willing to keep quiet any longer. Not when he realised you were still selling military secrets. So he had to die, and you made your mother lie about it.'

Sweat was pouring down Knox's grey face. Blood trickled through the fingers he'd pressed to his wounds. He moved his head to look towards Fox and Lena. Margaret was tempted to follow his gaze, but she didn't trust him. Despite the pain he must be in, it was another feint. Knox's left hand reached into his jacket. He must have a gun. Maybe he wouldn't be able to reach it, or fire – but maybe he would. And she wasn't sure who he'd aim at.

'I don't think so, Knox.' The door behind Margaret opened fully and she heard another deep, unpleasant cough. 'I'll have your left arm in pieces if you reach any further and I might hit your heart doing it. I wouldn't risk that if I were you.'

'Mallowan?' What little colour there was in Knox's face faded completely. 'I thought... I thought you were under arrest.'

Margaret risked turning her head.

Mallowan's gaze and gun were trained on Knox. 'This lady holds implausibly romantic memories of Gastrell,' he said, jerking his head towards Lena. 'It's amazing what time will do. I take it you never told her what he did to those innocent women and children in South Africa?'

'Whatever you're talking about, it's not true.' Lena was sobbing. Fox had sat up, and was gripping her arm.

'You weren't there,' snarled Knox. 'Nor was I.'

'But we knew. Every man who witnessed it was so disgusted that the whispers got out. Most men who heard about it were disgusted, too. Except you, Knox. Gastrell was a murderer, but he was hot-blooded. He was probably afraid and acted without thought. Whereas you... You'd have done the same thing for fun. I bet when you killed my girl you wished you didn't have to make it so quick. But do I feel the same about you?'

'Let him stand trial, Mallowan,' said Fox. 'Let the world hear what happened.'

The door behind Margaret opened again. Hare and Pigeon walked in, their revolvers trained on Lena and Cyril.

'Give me the gun, Dr Demeray,' said Hare. 'It doesn't suit you. And stop lazing about and embracing traitors, Fox. You shouldn't be letting a woman do all the work. I don't know what the world is coming to.'

Thirty-Seven

A week later, a few hours before she'd arranged to say goodbye to Anna at Waterloo, Margaret met Fox to view a four-storey house in Bayswater.

She'd spent the early part of the afternoon addressing the hospital board, and Fox had been cooped up with Inspector Silvermann, their respective senior officers and a pile of paperwork, most of which wouldn't be public information for at least fifty years.

Since the first part of the viewing was led by the house agent, Margaret hadn't been able to talk to Fox and hear how his meeting had gone. For herself, even after the agent had retired to the hall to let them go round the house alone, she still felt a little battered by hers.

'They're nice trees,' said Margaret, peering into the garden from a first-floor back bedroom. 'It doesn't matter that they're young. They'll grow. When the children are big enough to climb, the trees will still be small enough for them to do it easily.'

'The point of tree climbing is being too high for your mother to reach, looking at the world around you. Not that there's much to see but roofs around here.'

'But Bayswater's nice.'

'It's not the countryside.'

Margaret waved her hand in what she hoped was a westerly direction. She'd lost her bearings. 'Everywhere ten miles that way is being built on. It's countryside now, but it won't be for long.'

'Hmph,' said Fox. He put his arms around her. The bruise had faded on his forehead, and the cuts on his hands and face from the shattered vase had started to heal, but a nasty gash above his temple would become a permanent scar. 'How did the board meeting go?'

'They didn't fire me.'

'Even though you'd redecorated the cold room with Knox's blood?'

Margaret grimaced. 'One of the governors asked if I was trying to drum up work, which was quite funny, but only he and I thought so. Even Dr Jordan was less than impressed.'

'You shot a man at point-blank range.'

'He was in my way. How did *your* meeting go?'

'Inspector Silvermann isn't happy.'

'Why? He obtained enough evidence from Webber's house and Lena's to prove that they were sending photographs of designs for aircraft parts and weapons inside items addressed to Windhoek which would be intercepted and sent to Germany instead.'

'He's unhappy because we, um, lost Kavanagh while arresting the others.'

'Never mind,' said Margaret. 'Maybe he'll blame it on Special Branch rather than you.'

'Kavanagh, or rather Mallowan just wanted to find his daughter and untangle her from Lennox Selkirk's nasty little game. I told Inspector Silvermann the same as I told you: since Home Rule seems certain, Mallowan thinks the need for conflict is over. I fear he's wrong, but he won't live long enough to find out, will he?'

'No,' said Margaret. 'And I remain glad you lost him. Do you know if he's gone back to Ireland yet?'

'I believe so, with a handful of earth from Dervla's grave in St Patrick's Cemetery to mix with Irish soil in his family plot.'

Margaret sighed. She had no doubt that Joseph Mallowan would be buried there himself within months.

Fox rubbed at the scar on his forehead. 'This house is still some distance from St Js. Does that make a difference?'

Margaret didn't answer immediately. She turned from Fox to look out over the garden and rooftops, seeing herself leaving a different house to make that familiar journey. Or perhaps it would a different journey… 'Dr Naylor wants to discuss the job at Dorcas Free Hospital in Marylebone. I'm still not sure I want it, but it's closer. And even though Darnell's been dismissed for writing that article, the board may let Cyril stay. It would be rather hard to see him with a scalpel in his hand again.'

Fox pulled her into his arms and kissed her. 'You have some time to think. As you have some special leave from Dr Jordan, I've hired that New Forest cottage where you went as a child. It's nice and sprawling, so we can have a holiday without us and the children and the maids all being on top of one another. And when we're back… Shall we buy this house? It has a proper study where you can finish that essay.'

'Don't remind me. I expect Dr Naylor will want to see a draft when I visit Dorcas's to discuss the job. When I tell her that the whole book should be more digestible, it's possible she won't want me after all. She'll accuse me of sentiment.'

'Get scribbling anyway,' said Fox. 'If I can't get you employed by a circus as a sharp-shooter, I'd like to see your name in print. I'm so proud of you.' He took her hand and led her into the next room. 'So, do you like it?'

'I love it. Are the trees good enough?'

'Not bad.' Fox hugged her tight. 'When was the last time you climbed one?'

'About thirty years ago.'

'Want to try again now?'

'Whatever will the neighbours think?'

'Do you care?'

'No,' said Margaret. 'We might as well start as we mean to go on. Let's climb a tree.'

***

Anna stood at Waterloo railway station with a large portmanteau, watching Margaret approach with a mixture of derision and curiosity. 'Is that a baby carriage? I've never seen anything like it.'

'Pigeon made it for me,' said Margaret. 'He thought I'd like something I could fold up and get in and out of a tube train. It's certainly a head-turner.' Edie and Alec sat at either end, fighting each other with their feet. 'He hasn't any children, so I'm not sure he realises they won't just sit still. Nor that they'll grow. But it'll do for now.'

'Can I pick Edie up?'

'Of course.'

'Cor, she's heavier than she looks. Are you going to make them doctors, too? Or something else?'

'They can be whatever they like,' said Margaret. 'I'm sorry you're leaving again. What's New York got that London hasn't? I thought you might take on Helene's.'

'Miss Price is welcome to it. She's turning out ready-made stuff. I don't want to do that. And I don't want to be in charge of people neither.'

'You were in charge of people when you helped organise relief during the strikes in Whitechapel.'

'I wasn't profiting from that. But you're right. Perhaps I could have stayed to do more of that. It brought people together. People who'd never have spoken to each other a few years ago were helping to feed each other's kids. The Jews, the Irish, the English, the tailors and dockers, who knows who else, all pulling together for a while. Maybe it'll stand them in good stead one day.'

'I hope so,' said Margaret. 'Whitechapel's loss is New York's gain.'

'Who says I'm going to America?' said Anna.

'Well…'

'I'm getting the boat train. Then… Well, that would be telling. One thing about growing up in Whitechapel is learning a lot of languages. I might need to brush up on some, but the one thing everyone still wants is a dressmaker.'

Margaret's mouth dropped open. 'You're not going to Germany? Be careful, Anna. Be really careful. They're arresting people like there's no tomorrow at the moment.'

Anna shrugged. 'Don't be silly.' She put Edie back in the pram and picked up her portmanteau. 'Did you ever find out why Helene ordered a jacket to be delivered to herself?'

'Of all the mundane things, it was a tax dodge. But the police have a witness who saw her wearing it while talking to Dervla, after Dervla had escaped. She was talking her round, no doubt, encouraging her to lie low as a servant for a few days.'

'Because no one notices a servant.'

'Exactly. So Dervla thought she was safe when in fact she was anything but.'

'Poor Dervla,' said Anna.

'She was playing a dangerous game.'

'It's not a game, Margaret,' said Anna, putting out her hand. 'It's a calling. Goodbye.'

'Goodbye Anna. Like I said – wherever you're going and whatever you do next, be very careful.'

'Will you?'

'I'm not going anywhere,' said Margaret. 'Except perhaps to work at a different hospital.'

'You don't need to leave the country to get into trouble,' said Anna. She looked round at the busy station and Margaret followed her gaze. All the little moments of so many lives acting out in front of them - greetings and farewells, rushing people, ambling people, all going about their business as if nothing more important than a late train threatened them. 'Things are changing fast, ain't they? But the unrest - strikers, the suffragettes, the anarchists, the revolutionaries, the traitors - it's all leading somewhere, even if most people can't see it. And you'll get caught up in it. You're not the sort to sit still and not act. I doubt there's nothing you won't do to protect what's important to you.'

Margaret looked down at the children and wondered if she'd ever tell them what she'd done to save their father and if they'd understand. And if, with all the comforts she and Fox could give them, they'd grow up to be as brave as the young woman in front of her.

'All the same, Anna,' she said, looking back up. 'Please be careful. I'd hate to hear that something awful had happened to you.'

Anna took Margaret's hand, that rare smile transforming her face again. 'I *might* be careful,' she said. 'But life would be very dull wouldn't it? *Do svidaniya.*'

'What? Is - is that Russian?'

'Maybe I mean *Auf Wiedersehn*,' said Anna. 'Either way, it means see you again, Margaret. One day. And let's neither of us gets boring in the meantime.'

Margaret clasped her hand, then pulled her into a hug. 'I'll promise that if you will.'

'I promise. I've got a world to put right.' Anna briefly returned the hug, then extracted herself. 'Don't wave me off, Margaret. Go home to Fox. I'll be all right.' Then with one last smile, she turned and strode briskly towards the waiting train.

The Missing Page

It was at that moment that we saw Lieut. Foxcroft-McSionnach take out his revolver and call out a warning. 'Lieut. Gastrell! Stop where you are.'

Lieut. Gastrell ignored him and Lieut. Foxcroft-McSionnach called out again 'I will shoot.'

Lieut. Gastrell continued to run to the trees. Perhaps he could not hear, but we could. Then Lieut. Foxcroft-McSionnach fired. I would say that he was aiming a little to the right to avoid the heart but I could not swear to it. At that distance it was unlikely to have killed, merely injured and that not greatly.

Lieut. Gastrell faltered, then staggered on towards the trees by the river. It was hard to see where he had been wounded. When he neared the trees he swayed, struggling to remove his own revolver from its holster.

Lieut. Foxcroft-McSionnach continued his pursuit, revolver in hand.

We did not move for a while, then rose as one man to follow after. I feared Lieut. Gastrell might turn to shoot others without conscience as he'd done before, and in particular, Lieut. Foxcroft-McSionnah who had, after all, tried to secure a charge against him. But he seemed determined on one outcome alone – to get away, even though there was nowhere to run.

I said 'One of you go and get the captain and a doctor!' and Moore said 'Look out! I can't see them any more – they're hidden by the trees.' He called out: ' Don't go too close to the river's edge! The bank is too dry!'

Then we heard a cry and ran on. The ground on the river bank had crumbled. Lieut. Gastrell was in the river, floundering. It was not full, by any means, but it ran swiftly, nonetheless, and Lieut. Gastrell was in uniform and wounded. He sank from view.

Lieut. Foxcroft-McSionnach threw his revolver to the ground and jumped in after Lieut. Gastrell. We watched them struggle in the water for a while, and at some moments, as Lieut. Foxcroft-McSionnach pulled Lieut. Gastrell's head above water, it seemed Lieut. Gastrell was determined to pull them both below again.

It was some minutes before Lieut. Foxcroft-McSionnach dragged Gastrell out downstream, apparently lifeless, by which time the captain arrived. Lieut. Foxcroft-McSionnach turned Lieut. Gastrell this way and that to get the water from him.

Afterwards, we were asked what we had seen of his final moments, which of course was not a great deal, other than Lieut. Foxcroft-McSionnach's frantic attempts to revive Lieut. Gastrell to no avail, until he was quite exhausted, himself nearly drowned too. There is little else to be said on the matter, and we did say among ourselves that it had saved the army a good deal of disagreeable shame, aught else being but rumour. I strongly believe, however, that in the end, justice will somehow prevail.

FOR ADVANCED NEWS ABOUT THE NEXT BOOK IN THE SERIES, WHY NOT SUBSCRIBE TO MY NEWSLETTER?

You'll get news about my books and other writers', as well as the first chance to read Advanced Reader Copies of any new releases, please sign up at
https://paulaharmon.com/newsletter/

ACKNOWLEDGEMENTS

Thanks to Sam Thorne and my long suffering editor, Liz Hedgecock (any remaining errors are ones I've put back in) for alpha reading and my lovely beta readers: Christine Downes, Sim Sansford, Gosia Thornton and Val Portelli. And last but not least, my husband Mark for all his support.

HISTORICAL NOTE

This a work of fiction set within a real period of time.

During the years often called The Gilded Age there were a series of strikes and demonstrations in Britain as working people decided that they wanted a fair share of the wealth enjoyed by the extremely wealthy.

Fictional Anna Balodis's hope that people supporting each other in might stand the East End in good stead in future, is based on a real view that regardless of long-standing traditional and cultural differences, the mutual support in 1912 of striking tailors (who were mainly Jewish) and striking dockers (who were mainly gentile) to ensure that their respective children didn't starve, may have led to the solidarity of East End spirit which saw off Oswald Moseley's Black Shirts in the Battle of Cable Street twenty years later.

The suffragette movement, after Black Friday in 1910, had moved away from largely peaceful protest and firmly towards direct and increasingly violent action, including the smashing of windows in Oxford Street in March 1912 (for which fictional Maude had received a prison sentence and went on hunger strike). Emmeline Pankhurst is not going to back down easily.

In the meantime, the Home Rule bill has been passed which ought to be a move towards a self governing Ireland. But the opposing loyalist cause is gaining strength and it's yet to be seen what will happen next.

The Second Boer War of 1899-1902 was a campaign dogged with incompetence and mismanagement, which led to the unnecessary deaths of both soldiers and civilians, the latter in notorious concentration camps. While the final result was hailed as a victory in the British Empire, the way in which the war had been conducted was roundly condemned by other nations. Emily Hobhouse, a vicar's daughter from England tried to draw attention to what was happening in the concentration camps largely through incompetence and argue for better conditions, food and hygiene. Lieutenant Harry 'The Breaker' Morant and Lieutenant Peter Handcock were a real officers who were convicted and executed for what would now be called war crimes around the time that the fictional Fox is gathering evidence on the fictional Gastrell. The sentence of a third officer, Lieutenant George Witton, had his sentence commuted to life imprisonment and was eventually released from prison though not pardoned. All three men said that they had acted under orders and should not therefore have been tried.

ABOUT PAULA HARMON

Paula Harmon was born in North London to parents of English, Scottish and Irish descent. Perhaps feeling the need to add a Welsh connection, her father relocated the family every two years from country town to country town moving slowly westwards until they settled in South Wales when Paula was eight. She later graduated from Chichester University before making her home in Gloucestershire and then Dorset where she has lived since 2005. She is a civil servant, married with two adult children. Paula has several writing projects underway and wonders where the housework fairies are, because the house is a mess and she can't think why.

https://paulaharmon.com
viewauthor.at/PHAuthorpage
https://www.facebook.com/pg/paulaharmonwrites
https://www.goodreads.com/paula_harmon
https://twitter.com/Paula_S_Harmon

THE MURDER BRITANNICA SERIES
Murder Britannica
Murder Durnovaria
Murder Saturnalia

THE MARGARET DEMERAY SERIES
The Wrong Sort To Die
Death In The Last Reel
The Treacherous Dead

VICTORIAN DORSET MYSTERIES
The Good Wife (novella)

THE CASTER AND FLEET SERIES
(with Liz Hedgecock)
The Case of the Black Tulips
The Case of the Runaway Client

The Case of the Deceased Clerk
The Case of the Masquerade Mob
The Case of the Fateful Legacy
The Case of the Crystal Kisses
The Case of the Peculiar Pantomime

THE BOOKER AND FITCH SERIES
(with Liz Hedgecock)
Murder For Beginners
Death on Opening Night
Murder At Midnight

OTHER BOOKS
The Cluttering Discombobulator
Kindling (short stories)
The Advent Calendar (short stories)
An Invitation for Christmas (short stories)
Night Navigation (short stories)
The Quest (novella)
The Seaside Dragon (for children)
Weird and Peculiar Tales (with Val Portelli)

PLUS STORIES IN THE FOLLOWING ANTHOLOGIES
Wartime Christmas Tales
Dorset Shorts

SOME OF MY BOOKS ARE AVAILABLE IN AUDIO

Via Audible
https://www.audible.co.uk/author/Paula-Harmon/B01MV7DG7N

Via iTunes
https://books.apple.com/gb/author/paula-harmon/id929626974